THE CINEMA OF Errol Morris

David Resha

THE CINEMA OF ERROL MORRIS

WESLEYAN UNIVERSITY PRESS □ MIDDLETOWN, CONNECTICUT

Wesleyan University Press
Middletown CT 06459
www.wesleyan.edu/wespress

Manufactured in the United States of America
Designed by Eric M. Brooks
Typeset in Quadraat by Passumpsic Publishing

Wesleyan University Press is a member of the Green Press Initiative. The paper used in this book meets their minimum requirement for recycled paper.

Library of Congress Cataloging-in-Publication Data
Resha, David.
The cinema of Errol Morris / David Resha.
pages cm
Includes bibliographical references and index.
ISBN 978–0–8195–7533–3 (cloth : alk. paper)—
ISBN 978–0–8195–7534–0 (pbk. : alk. paper)—
ISBN 978–0–8195–7535–7 (ebook)
1. Morris, Errol—Criticism and interpretation. I. Title.
PN1998.3.M684R47 2015
791.4302′33092—dc23 2014037174

5 4 3 2 1

CONTENTS

PREFACE

When I first watched a dusty VHS copy of *The Thin Blue Line*, it was unlike any documentary I had seen before, and I was deeply moved by the experience. The film was funny, sad, and enigmatic. Sequences such as the slow-motion flying milkshake and Emily Miller's *Boston Blackie* fantasies stuck with me. I frequently invited friends to watch it with me, and I enjoyed it more with every viewing. But I could not get to the bottom of it. It was not a movie that merely taught or preached. It felt as if it was trying to get at something difficult, something deep—and was struggling with that investigation.

It was not easy to see Errol Morris's documentaries at the time. I once took a train down to a small, backroom screening of *Gates of Heaven* in a New York City bar. Weeks later, I bought a beat-up, dubbed VHS copy of *Vernon, Florida* on eBay. As I watched more of Morris's films, I started to notice continuities in his approach to his subjects. Morris's interviews did not always "stick to the issue." The films gave people the freedom to talk—about their past, their fears, and their dreams. And this seemed to interest Morris more than anything else, as the films would follow these tangents to see where they led.

Errol Morris's films were willing to tackle difficult philosophical problems without relying on ambiguity or obfuscation as an empty posture. Morris himself seemed to be both fascinated and terrified by the world, and the complexities of film style and structure in his films raised more questions than they answered. His films, as with all great films, reward multiple, careful viewings. If nothing else, I hope this book encourages people to not just watch Errol Morris's movies but also watch them closely.

ACKNOWLEDGMENTS

I owe a great deal to my professors, colleagues, friends, and family who helped me complete this book. I would like to thank Vance Kepley for his invaluable encouragement and guidance. Jeff Smith, JJ Murphy, Kelley Conway, and Julie D'acci provided perceptive feedback. I am grateful for all of the superb thinkers and teachers in the Communication Arts department at the University of Wisconsin–Madison, including Ben Singer, Bill Brown, and Lea Jacobs. I am also indebted to David Bordwell, whose scholarship, generosity, and kindness will always be an inspiration for me.

Thanks to my colleagues and friends from my cherished days in Madison. Brad Schauer, Pearl Latteier, Mark Minett, Heather Heckman, John Powers, Casey Coleman, Ethan de Seife, Kaitlin Fyfe, and Maureen Larkin all politely tolerated my love for documentary films and enthusiastically enabled my love for beer. Happy hour with Colin Burnett was consistently enlightening and whiskey tastings with Jake Smith helped clear my mind. I am particularly grateful for Jessica Newman's intelligence, humor, and compassion. This book would not have been possible without her. My parents and my brother Joe have always been loving and supportive, and I owe them a great deal.

Birmingham-Southern College has generously supported the process of writing this book. Mary-Kate Lizotte, Mark Schantz, and many others have generously assisted me throughout this time. Wesleyan University Press and Parker Smathers were very helpful with this process as well. In addition, many of Errol Morris's collaborators, including Jed Alger, Robert Fernandez, and Brad Fuller, kindly answered my questions.

Finally, I would like to thank Errol Morris. It has been a pleasure to watch and write about Mr. Morris's intelligent, challenging, and poignant films.

THE CINEMA OF Errol Morris

Introduction

THE EMERGENCE OF DIRECT CINEMA in the sixties marked an exciting new development in nonfiction filmmaking. At the time, large, heavy filmmaking equipment made it difficult for filmmakers to capture the unpredictable events. Conventional documentaries, typified by newsreels and educational films, would often use devices such as voice-over narration, interviews, and staged sequences to help communicate information about the world that was difficult or impossible to film.

Robert Drew formed Drew Associates in 1960 to produce observational films that would be markedly different from this standard approach to nonfiction filmmaking. In particular, Drew wanted to move away from what he called "lecture films": "My theoretical view developed that we . . . could capture real people, real stories, in real life, [and] edit them in such a way that the stories would tell themselves without the aid of a lot of narration."[1] Drew Associates films such as *Primary* (1960), *The Chair* (1962), and *Salesman* (1968) brought together new technological advances like lightweight, portable 16 mm cameras and synchronized sound with rigid limitations on the filmmaker's intervention in the filmed events, such as avoiding reenactments and formal interviews.

While some critics were enthusiastic about these observational films, others argued that these filmmakers were naive to connect their less intrusive style to a more objective representation of reality.[2] If Direct Cinema's claims to objectivity seemed problematic, then a more self-conscious or reflexive style appeared to some to be a more theoretically sound filmmaking approach. These reflexive works would not attempt to capture the unmediated reality of the world around us. They would instead turn their attention toward the form of documentary itself and engage the spectator with the problems of nonfiction representation. According to Bill Nichols, "Instead of seeing *through* documentaries to the world beyond them, reflexive documentaries ask us to *see documentary* for what it is: a construct or representation."[3] Reflexive documentaries often challenge the conventions of realism, inviting the viewer to question the idea that certain documentary techniques provide unproblematic access to the world.

Filmmakers produced reflexive documentaries decades before the emergence of Direct Cinema, for example, Dziga Vertov's *Man with a Movie Camera* (1929). There were increasing calls for a deliberate movement of reflexive nonfiction work by the 1970s. In a 1977 article, Jay Ruby argues, "I am convinced that filmmakers along with anthropologists have the ethical, political, aesthetic, and scientific obligations to be reflexive and self-critical about their work."[4] Reflexive documentaries did attain some degree of prominence in the 1970s and 80s. Films such as *No Lies* (1973), *Daughter Rite* (1978), and *Far from Poland* (1984) questioned the status and limitations of the documentary form.

By the late 1980s, when Errol Morris emerged to prominence, reflexivity was a prevalent critical framework for understanding innovative and challenging documentaries. Critics and theorists who championed the idea of reflexive documentaries embraced Morris's films and, in particular, his 1988 documentary *The Thin Blue Line*. Morris's use of highly stylized visuals and complex narratives, as well as his interest in exploring epistemological problems in his films, seemed to fit the emerging definition of the reflexive documentary.

There are central features in Errol Morris's work, however, that are lost in the reflexive characterizations of his films. Morris's films are not merely occasions to reflect on the problems of documentary representation. This characterization of his documentaries oversimplifies what are complex, emotionally engaging, and dynamic examinations of the world, examinations that are primarily interested in exploring the inner lives of its subjects.

As Morris's films engage the subjectivity of his interview subject, they also offer historical clarity by making clear and unquestioned claims about reality. This investment in making truth claims frequently offers perspective on the interview testimony, cueing the viewer to the interview subject's insights and errors. The convergence of the subjective and the real also reveals Morris's sustained, thematic interest in the nature and limits of human knowledge.

■ *The Thin Blue Line* and Reflexive Documentary Practice

Errol Morris began his filmmaking career in the 1970s. He became interested in the relocation of a Californian pet cemetery and released the resulting documentary *Gates of Heaven* in 1978. The subject matter for Morris's second documentary *Vernon, Florida* (1981) was just as peculiar. Morris interviews the eccentric residents of a small town in Florida, including a turkey hunter, a worm farmer, and a couple that believes their jar of sand grows by the day. Both *Gates of Heaven* and *Vernon, Florida* suffered from poor distribution and mixed reviews.

Morris's filmmaking career experienced a dramatic change with the 1988 release of *The Thin Blue Line*. Morris's third documentary investigates the murder of police officer Robert W. Wood in Dallas, Texas. Morris interviews an assortment of people involved with the trial of Randall Dale Adams, who was charged and convicted of the crime. Morris eventually reveals that David Harris, a sixteen-year-old at the time, was responsible for Officer Wood's death. *The Thin Blue Line* was a turning point for Morris's filmmaking career. The film was a major commercial and critical success, and established Morris as a highly innovative and thought-provoking documentary filmmaker.

Errol Morris's subsequent documentaries were well funded and widely distributed, due in part to the success of *The Thin Blue Line*. Many of these films have become among the most financially successful documentaries of all time. After *The Thin Blue Line*, Morris directed a documentary on Stephen Hawking's life and cosmological theories entitled *A Brief History of Time* (1991). Morris's next film, *Fast, Cheap and Out of Control* (1997), continues the profile element in *A Brief History of Time*, but Morris multiplies his focus to four men with different professions and personal interests.

Morris's next three documentaries represent a move to more political topics. *Mr. Death: The Rise and Fall of Fred A. Leuchter, Jr.* (1999) profiles Fred Leuchter, an execution equipment designer who becomes involved in Holocaust denial. *The Fog of War: Eleven Lessons from the Life of Robert S. McNamara* (2003) examines former secretary of defense Robert McNamara's life and, in particular, his involvement in the Second World War and the Vietnam War. Five years later, Morris released *Standard Operating Procedure* (2008), an investigation into the Abu Ghraib detainee abuses in Iraq. Morris returns to a more eccentric topic in *Tabloid* (2010). The film focuses on former Miss Wyoming Joyce McKinney, who became a tabloid headline in the 1970s for kidnapping and raping her Mormon love interest.

Since *Gates of Heaven*, critics and scholars had identified Morris as a reflexive filmmaker, and this reputation was firmly cemented by the release of *The Thin Blue Line*. The film's subject matter and reception are important in understanding why commentators identify *The Thin Blue Line* as a landmark of reflexive documentary practice. The film was a commercial success and widely seen throughout the United States, making it a shared reference for critics and scholars. The political nature of the film and its real-world effects seemed to show how the film's reflexivity is intimately connected to "the individual plight" of Randall Adams, which "causes the viewer to reflect upon the machinery of the social justice system operating outside the frame of the film."[5]

The Thin Blue Line is often viewed as a convention-shattering film that calls into question the claims to reality and truth at the heart of the documentary tradition, using the film's unconventional narrative and stylistic elements as examples of how it stands outside of the traditional documentary framework, while at the same time cueing the audience to critically question it. Morris rejects a strict chronological account by rearranging the events of the murder and Adams's trial. The film's narrative jumps back and forth in time and returns to the same event, namely, the murder, over and over again. In addition, Morris does not identify the killer at the beginning of the film, and viewers must navigate through a barrage of details and testimonies, some more reliable than others, to discover the identity of Officer Wood's murderer.

A related argument is that *The Thin Blue Line*'s repetitive, unreliable narrative elements represent a loss of faith in the coherence of narratives, and Morris is consequently foregrounding the indeterminacy of stories and storytelling.[6] Instead of providing the impression of direct and unproblematic access to the world, the reflexive mode of address changes the focus from the historical world to the properties of the text and the process of representation.

Morris's handling of the interview testimony is particularly important in understanding this reflexive reading of *The Thin Blue Line*. Morris frequently highlights the conflicting and contradictory testimonies of those involved in the trial, from the accused to the witnesses and the officers in charge of the investigation. While interview testimony is conventionally presented as trustworthy, the film ultimately undermines this reliability, and "'what really happened' becomes thoroughly enmeshed in the testimony's function within a liturgy of mutually contradictory statements of self-vindication."[7] Thus, Morris's use of the interview testimony does not provide insight into Officer Wood's murder but rather offers a commentary on the problems with the reliability of the documentary interview.

There is also the widely held view that traditional documentary filmmaking utilizes a relatively stable set of stylistic options, whose effect is to provide the impression that the images are accurate and objective reproductions of reality. This is what is conventionally understood as documentary realism. As Brian Winston explains, "The pretension to a superior representation of the real is deeply encoded. . . . Handheld, available light, available sound, long take, jump-cut, direct gaze, minimal graphs—all these signify 'evidence.'"[8]

Instead of adopting this traditional realist style, Errol Morris incorporates practices more typical of fiction filmmaking, such as the use of studios, scripts, and actors, thus blurring the distinction between fiction and reality, and challenging documentary's close adherence to a clearly defined film style.[9] Dagmar Barnouw cites Morris's "sophisticated camera work, the expensive camera, the artful lighting" that "flaunt the fictional mode" so that "the film focuses not on the question of Adams' guilt or innocence but on the question of documentary knowledge—on the conventional distinction between truth and deception."[10] And Richard Sherwin argues that the film's use of reenactments and fiction film footage constitutes "counter-images that make up (that perhaps even make fun of) the way we allow film images to capture our belief in the first place. It's all being framed, the film tells us. There is no place to go for objective, mediated truth."[11]

Errol Morris and Postmodernism

For some viewers, *The Thin Blue Line*'s reflexive approach is a paradigmatic example of postmodern documentary practice. There are many similarities between reflexive artistic practices and postmodernism, and the arguments about the film's reflexivity and postmodern characteristics are often quite similar. For instance, the unreliable testimony in *The Thin Blue Line* can be either a reflexive move away from traditional documentary narratives or a postmodern approach to storytelling, or both. John D. Dorst refers to Morris's "vernacular storytelling," characterized by "all the uncertainties, false starts, qualifications, self-fictionalizations, and incoherencies," which he views as a byproduct of our postmodern age, "marked by a loss of faith in the master narratives of western civilization."[12] In addition, due to the film's highly expressive visual style, *The Thin Blue Line* can be read as an intertextual work that defies the observational documentary's desire for "pure" filmic material. Shawn Rosenheim, for example, focuses on Morris's use of extremely stylized reenactments as constituting a "play of referential levels, frequent quotation and allusion, and lack of originating authority," which make the films "thoroughly postmodern."[13]

When viewed as a postmodern filmmaker, Morris's rejection of traditional style and story brings along with it a rejection of the ontological claims at the heart of the documentary tradition. More specifically, his films challenge the idea that there exists a reality to which documentary has privileged access. This issue is clearly articulated by Brian Winston: "If documentaries in general were not to claim a privileged relation to the real then their films or tapes could start to look, for instance, more like Errol Morris's *The Thin Blue Line*."[14]

These kinds of characterizations of *The Thin Blue Line*—is it reflexive or postmodern?—have created a scholarly paradigm through which *all* of Morris's films have since come to be analyzed and understood. According to this reflexive/postmodernist view, Morris's approach to style and structure contributes to his career-long examination, critique, and ultimate rejection of documentary style, traditional story structure, and documentary positivism.[15]

Reexamining these assumptions is the purpose of this book.

■ Investigating Human Subjectivity

The reflexive/postmodern characterization of Morris's documentaries does address unique characteristics in his films, in particular, how his documentaries diverge from some of the stylistic conventions of Direct Cinema. Morris handles this departure from the observational style in an explicit manner, making clear to the viewer that some of the footage has been staged for the film. This prompts viewers to reflect on important issues, such as the relationship between fact and fiction in documentary, the conventional authority given to the documentary interviewee, and the relationship between documentary images and the real world.[16] Such analyses tend to selectively focus on the more transgressive aspects of Morris's work, while ignoring many of the conventional stylistic and structural elements that make his films so compelling and provocative.[17] This book argues that Morris's films *do not* primarily function to problematize the relationship between documentaries and the world they depict. Rather, they often make resolute claims about reality and truth, including *The Thin Blue Line*'s central claim about Randall Dale Adams's innocence for Officer Wood's murder.

But if Morris's films are not primarily reflexive or postmodern critiques of the documentary tradition, how do we understand their form and function? As noted, Morris's documentaries look very different from earlier observational films as well as some contemporaneous documentaries. What is the purpose of this distinctive approach to the visuals in his films? In addition, why does Morris foreground mistakes and contradictions in the interview testimony if not to cue the audience to the indeterminacy of documentary storytelling? If Morris is not rejecting the documentary tradition, how does he fit in?

The Cinema of Errol Morris examines the form and function of Morris's films as the intersection between storytelling, aesthetics, and the thematic interest in human subjectivity. In all of his films, Morris allows his interview subjects to articulate their thoughts, beliefs, and dreams. But his films are not merely an uncritical venue for people to express themselves. Instead, they are investigations into and critical evaluations of this subjective engagement with the world. In the interview testimony, Morris uses mistakes to examine the troubled subjectivity of his interviewees. Specifically, he reveals the ways the interview subjects struggle to understand the world and themselves. Sometimes these people uncover a valuable insight, and other times their experience radically distorts reality. Morris sifts through these breakthroughs and errors, prompting the viewer to raise larger questions about the workings and limits of human knowledge.

Morris often provides a clear sense of what is real and true. For the viewer, it is important to understand the truth of the situation in order to determine whether someone's views are flawed or accurate. Morris's documentaries are particularly complex in part because there is not an authoritative voice to make clear distinctions between the imperfect subjectivity of his interviewees and the real world. The viewer must make subtle observations and connections throughout the film to determine, for instance, whether Randall Dale Adams is telling the truth when he proclaims his innocence in *The Thin Blue Line*.

Errol Morris's thematic interest in human subjectivity allows us to better understand his adventurous, highly stylized visuals. Instead of undermining the connection between documentary realism and reality, Morris relies on this association to cue the audience to the subjective elements in the film. Morris often uses stylized devices such as staged sequences, expressive lighting, and slow motion to illustrate the beliefs and assumptions in the interview testimony.

Morris's documentaries are not merely esoteric meditations about epistemology or documentary aesthetics. Morris has had commercial success throughout his career in part because he is an eloquent and sophisticated storyteller. As with most narrative films, Morris's documentaries raise questions and delay resolutions. The mistakes and confusions in the interview testimony help to engage the viewer's curiosity and emotions.

The Cinema of Errol Morris seeks to provide an accurate understanding of the variations in and evolution of Morris's approach. There are considerable changes in the visual style, structural organization, and subject matter across the course of his thirty-year career. One of the primary goals of this book is to track the continuities and changes in the films, in part by examining the production context of each film, including variables such as funding sources, technological changes, and conventions of documentary practice. At the same time that Morris's documentaries are changing, there are substantive continuities that unify his work.[18]

■ Book Organization

This book is designed to track the continuities and changes throughout Errol Morris's career, beginning with *Gates of Heaven* and ending with his most recent film *Tabloid*. Each chapter examines a single film with the exception of the first chapter, which combines *Gates of Heaven* and *Vernon, Florida* because of their strong stylistic and organizational similarities. Chapter 4 discusses

Morris's television series *Errol Morris' First Person* (2000–2001) and his prolific career in television commercial production.

Each chapter describes Morris's approach to style and structure as well as analyzes the function of these formal decisions. An overview of the film's production and reception precedes individual sections devoted to the film's style, structure, voice, reception, and ethical concerns.

Analysis of the film's style shows how Morris assembles both the interview and the cutaway footage in relation to the conventions of other documentaries at the time. We then examine how Morris structures these stylistic elements over the course of the documentary.[19] Morris often establishes a broad narrative framework, as in the progression of Randall Dale Adams's murder trial in *The Thin Blue Line*. Morris's documentaries are restrained and sometimes misleading in communicating information to the viewer. They ask the spectator to sift through incomplete and unreliable details. These documentaries are not wholly imprecise or open ended, however, as Morris leads the viewer to certain conclusions.

Carl Plantinga's distinction between the formal and open voice in documentary films helps explain the degree to which Morris's films assume an authoritative narrative voice.[20] Morris's documentaries make clear, reliable claims about the world, explaining historical events, biographical details, and theoretical concepts. This authority intersects with Plantinga's category of the formal voice, which "together with other textual elements constitutes an *explanation* of some element of the actual world."[21] For instance, a formal-voice documentary on Walmart might use a mix of voice-over narration and expert interviews to explain the origins of the company, the history of its incorporation, and its international expansion.

Formal voice documentaries also possess affinities with the classical fiction film narratives. In particular, they pose a clear question or set of questions and, at some point in the film, answer these questions. This process of raising and answering questions overlaps with Noël Carroll's "erotetic narrative," which "tells you, literally, everything you want to know about the action depicted, i.e., it answers every question, or virtually every question, that it has chosen to pose saliently."[22] In the Walmart documentary, the film might begin with the current status of Walmart and ask how it became the world's largest public corporation. The film's examination of Walmart's history and expansion would help answer this larger question.

Errol Morris's films, at their core, use this backdrop of clear, reliable information to help explore, rather than explain, human subjectivity. For this reason, Morris's documentaries predominantly employ an open voice, which "*observes* and *explores* rather than explains. Narration in such films is sometimes implicit rather than explicit, avoiding the overt narrational marks and knowledge claims of the formal nonfiction film."[23] Plantinga describes these open-voice films as "epistemically hesitant," as they often do not formulate a clear question that the film is designed to answer. If the open-voice film does present a question or a set of questions, "it offers no answer, or a tentative and ambiguous answer. It is reluctant to give explanations or to make high-level, abstract claims about the world."[24]

An open-voice documentary about our Walmart subject might take the form of an observational documentary following a female Walmart employee throughout a day in her life, including her morning routine, work experiences, and return home. We might ask questions about the employee's internal life, including her satisfaction with her job, her thoughts about the past and the future, and her feelings about her employer. The audience might make inferences about the employee based on facial expressions and interactions with others, but without the direction of a formal voice, these questions ultimately remain open.

Errol Morris's documentaries are largely open-voice films, as they prompt the audience to make associational, implicit connections without the explicit guidance of the film. They are designed to foreground the interview subjects' view of the world, but they do not determine our understanding of this subjective space. There are elements of the formal voice in many of Morris's documentaries, however, and the discussion of the films' structure will examine this relationship between the formal and open voice.

It is important to take into account the ethical implications of Errol Morris's approach. The documentary form's close relationship to the real world brings along with it certain expectations about accurately and respectfully representing reality. Morris's films frequently illuminate the boundaries of these expectations. Morris's willingness to critique his subjects' understanding of the world prompted some to characterize his documentaries as condescending and cruel. In addition, Morris's use of the open voice provoked complaints that he is neglecting his responsibility to accurately represent the world. The final section of each chapter will return to and investigate the reception of Morris's films and related ethical issues.[25]

This examination of Errol Morris's career attributes a wide range of decisions to "Errol Morris." The primary reason for this is that Morris is intimately involved in and has the final say for all of the creative decision in his films. Using Morris as a primary decision maker is also a convenience and not intended to diminish the contributions of his collaborators. Errol Morris has had the privilege of working with some of the most respected artists in the film industry. Although we will occasionally note how a collaborator's prior work influenced Morris's film, this does not properly acknowledge all of the different ways in which these artists participate in the creation of these important, inventive films.

A careful examination of the form and function of Morris's films provides a more nuanced understanding of his approach and contribution to the documentary form. *The Cinema of Errol Morris* proposes a shift in the way in which scholars have traditionally understood Morris's documentaries, as well as documentary film more broadly. Scholars often classify and analyze nonfiction films according to a split between documentaries that are both stylistically conservative and invested in claims to reality, and those that want to experiment with style and are generally cynical about the relationship between documentary representation and truth. A close analysis of Morris's films helps us rethink this division. Morris's documentaries are among the most formally inventive but also have much invested in notions of reality and truth.

The broader implication of this argument is that Errol Morris's films demonstrate the power and not the problem of documentary representation. Morris does not reject the documentary tradition. He experiments with many of its conventions to investigate reality and truth. By firmly placing his work within the documentary tradition, Morris's films demonstrate in compelling fashion that the documentary is a fluid, flexible form that often has a complex relationship to the real world. Morris's interest in exploring human subjectivity also reveals the capacity of documentaries to engage something subtle, delicate, and concealed: the ways in which people view the world and themselves.

1 *Gates of Heaven* and *Vernon, Florida*

ERROL MORRIS WAS PREPARING TO SHOOT *Gates of Heaven* in 1977. He needed a cinematographer but was short on money. Tom Luddy, programmer at the Pacific Film Archive, convinced cinematographer Ed Lachman to shoot for a day at no cost.[1] Luddy later discovered that Morris fired Lachman before the end of the day because Morris did not like the way the cinematographer was shooting, a disagreement that ended in a physical struggle for the Éclair camera.[2] The film's second cinematographer was equally problematic for Morris, as she insisted on engaging in a dialogue with the interviewees, at times even disagreeing with some of their statements. Morris fired her immediately and hired another cameraman, who lasted only a few days. Morris then hired his fourth and final cinematographer, Ned Burgess. Burgess had experience as an assistant cameraman on *Koko, A Talking Gorilla* (1978) and was able to adapt to the visual style Morris wanted for *Gates*. Satisfied with Burgess's work, Morris hired him back to be the cinematographer for his second film, *Vernon, Florida*.

Morris's early troubles with his cinematographers are informative because they suggest that his approach to filming was not only novel from the start but also somewhat defiant. Morris remembers that there was "such a strong, prevailing view of what nonfiction film should look like, it was difficult to convince them that it could be put together in a different way."[3] Morris's distinction between his films and the documentary tradition raises a few questions: What were the dominant approaches to nonfiction film in the late 1970s and early 1980s? How do *Gates of Heaven* and *Vernon, Florida* relate to this context of documentary production? What function do Morris's stylistic deviations serve in his films?

Errol Morris is interested in examining the world. In particular, *Gates of Heaven* and *Vernon, Florida* investigate the ways in which his subjects understand the world. Morris combines formal documentary interviews with carefully staged mise-en-scène, a nondirective interview approach, and an associational structure to foreground and explore the subjective elements of the interview testimony.

■ Background

Errol Morris's entry into the world of documentary filmmaking is intimately linked to his academic career. He graduated from the University of Wisconsin–Madison in 1969 with a degree in history and later applied for Harvard's history of science program. Morris was not accepted and eventually enrolled in the history of science graduate program at Princeton University.[4]

Morris remembers graduate school at Princeton as frequently combative and unpleasant: "I had imagined graduate school as a shining city on a hill, but it turned out to be more like an extended visit with a bear in a cave."[5] Morris's frustration was in part due to his tense relationships with the Princeton professors. Morris vividly remembers a class he took with Thomas Kuhn, who did not appreciate Morris's contentious disposition and, at one point, threw an ashtray at Morris (it missed).[6]

Kuhn eventually asked Morris to leave Princeton, and in 1972, Morris was accepted into the philosophy program at the University of California–Berkeley. Morris shifted his attention from the philosophy of science to serial killers and the insanity plea, leading him back to Wisconsin to conduct interviews with infamous serial killer Ed Gein. Berkeley did not encourage Morris's interest in the philosophical problems of mass murder, and after a few years, Morris was asked to leave the program.[7]

Morris became a regular at the Pacific Film Archive in Berkeley, which was an ideal setting to nurture his love for film noir. Tom Luddy was the director of the archive at the time and remembered Morris as unusual and occasionally confrontational: "There were a bunch of regulars and a bunch of eccentric regulars, and Errol was one of the eccentrics. I often had to defend him to my staff, . . . which was often difficult, because he would attack me for the programming."[8]

Despite their disagreements, Luddy introduced Morris to Werner Herzog, and they quickly established a friendship. Herzog was intrigued by Morris's stories about Wisconsin and, in particular, Morris's curiosity about whether or not Ed Gein dug up his own mother's grave. Morris and Herzog set a date in 1975 to find out for sure. Herzog arrived in Plainfield, Wisconsin, with a shovel, but Morris backed out of the plan. While in Plainfield, Herzog discovered a car-repair shop that he later used to film parts of *Stroszek* (1977). Morris was outraged and accused Herzog of "stealing a landscape." They eventually reconciled, and Morris stayed in Plainfield to observe Herzog finish the film.[9]

Herzog gave Morris two thousand dollars to compensate for his geographical intrusion, which was enough to fund Morris's plan to visit Vernon, Florida. Morris had previously read an article about the residents of this Florida town and their reputation for collecting insurance money after suspiciously losing limbs. The frequency of these "accidents" had caused some insurance insiders to dub the town "Nub City." Morris traveled to Vernon using the funds from Herzog and spent the good part of a year living with and talking to the residents. After encountering some hostility in Vernon, including a death threat, he returned to Berkeley and starting work on a script for a fiction feature entitled *Nub City*.[10]

Morris read an article in the *San Francisco Chronicle* entitled "450 Dead Pets Going to Napa Valley." The article detailed the exhumation of pets from one California pet cemetery and their relocation to another, a story that ultimately became the subject for his first documentary. Morris shot *Gates of Heaven* in the spring and summer of 1977 for around $125,000, most of which came from Morris's family and a wealthy former classmate.[11]

Gates of Heaven focuses on these two pet cemeteries in California. The first is in Los Altos, Foothill Pet Cemetery, which is forced to close after encountering financial difficulties. In the first half of the film, we hear from a variety of people affected by the closing, including the business investors and pet owners. The animals are eventually exhumed from the cemetery and relocated in refrigerated trucks to the Bubbling Well Pet Memorial Park in Napa Valley; this cemetery is the focus of the film's remaining scenes. We hear mostly from the Harberts family, who own Bubbling Well. For instance, Danny Harberts reflects on lost loves and playing guitar, and Phillip Harberts talks about his devotion to the principles of W. Clement Stone.

Gates of Heaven premiered in 1978 at the New York Film Festival, but a newspaper strike at the time limited the film's exposure. It also screened at festivals in London and Berlin but was not picked up by a distributor. *Gates of Heaven* did garner some attention, some of which was the result of Werner

Herzog's promise to eat one of his shoes if Morris completed the film. Commemorated by Les Blank's documentary *Werner Herzog Eats His Shoe* (1980), Herzog consumed his artfully prepared boot at the Berkeley premiere of the film. *Gates of Heaven* was later rereleased in limited national distribution by New Yorker Films in spring 1981.

In the interim, Morris revisited his original idea of making a film about Vernon, Florida. He drove down to Vernon in 1980 with a van full of equipment and a group of recent New York University (NYU) film-school graduates. Some of the residents were still unhappy about Morris making a film in Vernon and even attempted to run down cinematographer Ned Burgess with a truck. Morris had received funding for the film from New York public television affiliate WNET and ZDF, a German television production company. Feeling pressure to have something to show for their investment but also concerned about his safety in Vernon, Morris dropped the "Nubbies" angle and started shooting interviews with various citizens of Vernon.[12]

Vernon, Florida premiered at the 1981 New York Film Festival and aired on public television a year later.[13] As with *Gates of Heaven*, *Vernon, Florida* did not enjoy any significant distribution. Without the self-mutilation angle, the most significant feature that unites *Vernon, Florida* is the place itself. Morris interviews a variety of individuals, including a minister, a policeman, and a turkey hunter. Throughout the film, they talk about an even wider variety of subjects ranging from the meaning of the word "therefore" to the inexplicable growing of sand in a jar.

The production context for these films is quite different, but there are important similarities that influenced Morris's stylistic and structural choices. Morris produced both films with a relatively small budget, and the films are, in certain ways, products of a modest budget. *Gates of Heaven* and *Vernon, Florida* were filmed in a limited number of locations, avoiding costly travel expenses. The films also do not have sophisticated graphics or celebrity narrators found in larger budget documentaries, such as Carl Sagan's *Cosmos* (1980). Most significantly, Morris was not obligated to produce a commercially successful film and had a considerable degree of autonomy when making the films. This facilitated Morris's experimentation with style, structure, and voice throughout both films.

■ Morris's Style and Documentary Convention

When Morris positions *Gates of Heaven* against the "strong, prevailing view of what nonfiction film should look like," he is referring to the stylistic conventions of observational documentaries, characterized by handheld camerawork, synchronous sound, and the rejection of artificial lighting, staged sequences, and voice-over narration.[14] The question of control over the filmed events is central to this observational approach. Stephen Mamber writes that "the essential element in cinema verité is the act of filming real people in uncontrolled situations. . . . The filmmaker acts as an observer, attempting not to alter the situations he witnesses any more than he must simply by being there."[15]

In both *Gates of Heaven* and *Vernon, Florida*, the divergence from observational style is clear as Morris actively retains control of many aspects of the filmmaking process. Morris's camera is always on a tripod, often locked down preventing even the slightest adjustment or reframing. Morris also uses artificial light to illuminate his interior scenes. Instead of the occasionally shaking or shifting of handheld camerawork, Morris arranges highly symmetrical compositions throughout *Gates of Heaven* and *Vernon, Florida*. The compositional strategy is emblematic of what David Bordwell identifies as planimetric staging, in which "the background is resolutely perpendicular to the lens axis, and the figures stand fully frontal, in profile, or with their backs directly toward us."[16]

In perhaps the most overt rejection of observational cinema's dictates, Morris stages certain sequences, such as a burial ceremony in *Gates of Heaven*. The scene begins with an establishing shot of Calvin Harberts talking to a couple about their deceased dog Caesar. After Calvin asks the couple to say a few words about Caesar, we cut to a shot over Calvin's shoulder as the couple discusses Caesar's pedigree. An insert shot of Calvin's hand holding a picture of Caesar follows as Calvin remarks about the unique appearance of the animal (see figure 1.1). The adherence to analytic editing conventions, including carefully matching action across cuts, indicates that Morris arranged at least some scenes for the camera.

Scholars such as Paul Arthur and Linda Williams highlight Morris's deliberate intervention in filmed events. They conclude that his films represent

FIGURE 1.1. □ *Gates of Heaven*

a conscious, reflexive rejection of observational filmmaking and the corresponding claims to truth and objectivity. Michael Covino's 1980 review of *Gates of Heaven* illustrates this view: "The camera doesn't seem intent on capturing special 'moments,' or on recording people in action. In fact, there is little or no dramatic action (the most dramatic shot is of a young man mowing a lawn), no shaky, blurred or grainy images, no abrupt zooms, nothing is clumsily framed—the film has none of the usual signature shots of the documentary."[17] Covino continues that the film displays "a deep and unabiding contempt for the usual methods of documentary realism, a contempt for the quasi-aleatory methods of *cinema verité*, certainly the dominant tendency of the sixties and seventies."[18]

Covino's characterization of documentary at the time is typical among theorists and also problematic. While the observational documentary had become common in the seventies, it is misleading to characterize it as dominant, as documentaries at the time employed a variety of different approaches. Documentaries often relied on voice-over narration in everything from nature films to historical documentaries. Interview-based documentaries were also common, especially in films that focused on past events. For instance, *The Wobblies* (1979) uses interview testimony to recount the rise of the Industrial Workers of the World, a labor movement in the early twentieth century that rallied for workers rights.

Most nonfiction films during this time also combined a variety of different documentary elements. For example, Barbara Kopple's *Harlan County, USA* (1976) follows the struggles of a miner strike in Kentucky and uses observational footage of the strike along with more formal interviews, found footage, and historical photographs. *Image Before My Eyes* (1980) uses voice-over and interviews to tell the story of Jewish life in Poland between the two world wars. Journalistic television programming such as *60 Minutes* frequently mixes interviews, observational footage, and voice-over commentary as well.

Previous accounts correctly characterize Morris's first two films as innovative, but this originality is not primarily located in his embrace of reflexive film practice. Instead of stepping outside the documentary tradition in order to subject it to a critical examination, *Gates of Heaven* and *Vernon, Florida* intimately engage documentary norms, in particular those of both the interview and observational tradition.

■ *Gates of Heaven, Vernon, Florida,* and the Interview Documentary

Of all the prevalent documentary approaches in the late 1970s and early 1980s, the interview documentary is the most relevant to the visual style in *Gates of Heaven* and *Vernon, Florida*. Many of the stylistic features that differentiate Morris's first two films from observational documentaries connect them with the conventions of the interview. The interview film is useful in understanding Morris's stylistic approach, although neither *Gates of Heaven* nor *Vernon, Florida* are typical interview documentaries. By looking closely at the visual style of both films, we can better understand the extent to which *Gates of Heaven* and *Vernon, Florida* engage with these conventions and, more broadly, the documentary tradition as a whole.

The stable images that characterize Morris's films are common in interview films, primarily because the camera is often placed on a tripod during an interview. In addition, most interview documentaries use artificial lighting in interiors to illuminate the interview subject. Although Morris does rely on natural light in most exterior shots in *Vernon, Florida* and *Gates of Heaven*, he carefully arranges the lighting in interior scenes.

The relationship between the interviewer, the camera, and the direction of the interview subject's look has an influence on the visuals of the interview. Traditionally, when a subject is looking offscreen, the framing will place the head of the interviewee on one side of the frame to allow for appropriate looking space. When the look of the subject is on line with the axis of the camera lens, the subject's body will be more centered in the frame.

From the start, Morris wanted to create the impression of direct eye contact between the interview subject and the viewer: "I interviewed people by putting my head right up against the lens of the camera. It seemed as though they were looking directly into the lens of the camera, but not really. . . . My cameraman would grab the back of my head and pull me back because you could see the side of my head in the lens. When he yanked me back, it often hurt."[19] The centered, often symmetrical compositions in Morris's films are partially the result of this desire for eye contact with the audience, a common framing when the subject is looking toward the camera.

Morris's insistence on the impression of eye contact with the audience influences the shot scale of his compositions. In his article "Interrotroning History," Shawn Rosenheim argues that Morris infrequently uses close framings in his early films because it would have highlighted the fact that his subjects were not looking directly into the camera.[20] Documentaries at the time would often use close-ups and medium close-ups to frame the interview subjects, whereas Morris's films more frequently employ medium and medium-long shots during the interviews.

Maintaining continuity throughout an interview is a significant problem for documentaries. In practically every interview, parts of the testimony are cut out and rearranged, producing unwanted jump cuts as the position of the subject's body changes across edits. Interview documentaries developed a number of strategies to hide these jumps, including the use of a zoom lens and cutaway images.

Changing focal length when filming creates various shot scales throughout the interview. When an editor cuts together two parts of an interview with different shot scales, this will conceal some disruptions in continuity. Camera operators often change shot scale during a question or a pause in the interview so the editor will not have to wait until the zoom is completed to cut to the next shot. These changes in shot scale also provide visual variety in a scenario that offers little for interesting modifications in the image, especially if the interview subject is sitting.

In addition to varying shot scale, zooming during an interview serves expressive aims as well. Alan Rosenthal writes that "the experienced cameraperson . . . will know that you can afford to take a camera movement in or out on a change of topic, that you probably want to vary the size of the subject in the frame with different questions, and that you probably want to zoom in slowly on an intense answer."[21] Rosenthal's last point about zooming during an "intense answer" is a significant feature of the interview documentary. Cinematographers will often zoom in on a subject when they are responding in an emotional manner or discussing something of special significance to the film, cueing the audience to the importance of the testimony and to identify with the subject. In *The Life and Times of Rosie the Riveter* (1979), Lyn Childs explains how she had to leave behind her child during World War II in order make money working in the shipyards. Lyn begins to tear up as she says that her child still hurts from the experience, and when she clears her throat to hold back her emotions, the camera begins to zoom in on her face.

Errol Morris refrains from zooming during his interviews, often shooting with a prime lens that prohibits any changes in focal length. There are a number of reasons for this. Zooming during an interview would alter Morris's carefully organized, symmetrical compositions. In addition, these static, planimetric images serve a narrative function. Bordwell notes, "The perpendicular schema suits a dedramatized narrative. [By] resisting camera movement and scaling down figure action, such shots can create a sense of stillness, even serenity."[22] Although there is a more detailed discussion of the narrative elements of these films below, Morris is less concerned with establishing a strong emotional identification between the viewer and the interview subject. This detachment from the interview testimony is reinforced by Morris's avoidance of zooming, as well as the use of wider shot scales.

Much like the change of shot scale or camera position, cutaway images help cover breaks in continuity. In his 1963 book on documentary film production, W. Hugh Baddeley stresses the importance of these images and provides the following example: "A man makes a speech. We want the first sentence and last. We cut them out and join them. . . . We cover the splice with a *cutaway* shot of his audience listening. Cutaways must always be germane and they must always appear to be germane."[23] In accord with the norms of the interview, Morris does use cutaway images throughout both films, although far less frequently than most interview documentaries at the time. In *Rosie the Riveter*, *The War at Home*, *With Babies and Banners*, and *The Wobblies*, cutaway images constitute between 82 and 87 percent of the total shots. Morris's first two films use cutaways about half as often, comprising 44 percent of the total shots in *Gates of Heaven* and 49 percent in *Vernon, Florida*.

Morris is able to avoid breaks in continuity throughout both films, although he does not change focal length during the interview and infrequently uses cutaway images. Morris often includes the pauses, digressions, and mistakes in the testimony, elements that most directors would cut. For instance, Morris uses a five-and-a-half-minute interview with Florence Rasmussen in *Gates of Heaven* as a transition between the Foothill Pet Cemetery and Bubbling Well, in which only one cutaway of a newspaper headline interrupts the interview footage. Instead of editing the testimony to identify the relevant pet cemetery elements, Morris allows the interview to play. Mark Singer describes the result: "Rasmussen manages to contradict most of what she has to say. It seems that she knows certain things, but then, in the next moment, she trots out contrary information: I have roots with the earth; I'm lost in this world. People have been very good to me; I'm all alone, surrounded by strangers, my own flesh and blood treats me badly."[24] In *Vernon, Florida*, a pastor provides a meticulous account of his examination into the meaning of the word "therefore," and Morris allows his sermon to play uncut for close to three minutes.

■ Observational Filmmaking and Art Cinema

The stylistic conventions of the interview documentary are central in understanding Morris's approach, but there are connections with other nonfiction traditions as well, including observational documentaries. Although we earlier examined the ways in which Morris's intrusive style diverges from the norms of observational documentaries, there are ways in which it also reproduces some of these observational conventions. For instance, his early films avoid voice-over narration, nondiegetic music, and titles identifying interviewees, which were common features in many documentaries of the time but were often eliminated from observational films.[25]

Morris's approach to the interviewing process, in which he says as little as possible, also has a close relationship with some of the basic principles of observational filmmaking. Morris discusses how his nondirective interview technique began even before he started making films: "I started interviewing people long before I had a camera. And the goal in my interviews was to say nothing. I would play this game—I would come in for an interview, I would put my tape recorder on the table, and hopefully the other person would start talking. The game was to keep them talking, no matter what; to not interrupt, no matter what."[26] This unobtrusive interview method has clear affinities with observational cinema's principles of nonintervention.

It is also important to note the connections between Morris's approach and art cinema. For instance, Morris's static framings, planimetric compositions, and long takes all overlap with stylistic practices in art cinema. Morris's friendship with Werner Herzog may also inform this connection. Some of Herzog's early documentaries, such as *Fata Morgana* (1971), and fiction films, like *The Enigma of Kaspar Hauser* (1974), exhibit these art cinema conventions. Morris's use of an associational structure and an open voice, which we will examine later in the chapter, also connect with art cinema narratives.

In sum, Morris had developed a distinctive visual style in *Gates of Heaven* and *Vernon, Florida*. Many of the stylistic markers of his films are a result of the deliberate control over elements such as lighting, camera movement, and composition, which stands in opposition to some principles of observational filmmaking. This distinctive style is not one that represents a blanket rejection of particular documentary traditions but rather a unique blend of different documentary and fiction styles, including aspects of interview and observational filmmaking.

Structure

Many scholars underscore Morris's visual style in *Gates of Heaven* and *Vernon, Florida*. They generally neglect the structure of the films, however, which is arguably more innovative than his visual style. Reflecting back on the editing process for *Gates of Heaven*, Morris remarks about how the film's structure deviated from the conventions of the interview documentary: "I had tremendous difficulty editing the movie, because there was no principle for editing that kind of thing. I don't think that it's even clear now how radically different that movie is from other movies. It involved these very strange dioramas, edited against each other. You can say it's talking heads, but it's not talking heads in a context where they've been stitched together by voiceover and various kinds of visual detritus."[27]

Carl Plantinga's categories for documentary structure allow for a better understanding of how Morris organized his first two films. Plantinga identifies four different structures common in documentary: narrative, rhetorical, categorical, and associational. Most interview-based documentaries make use of the first three structural forms. For instance, *The Wobblies* provides a narrative account of the Industrial Workers of the World, and Peter Davis's *Hearts and Minds* (1974) employs a rhetorical structure to illuminate the absurdities and horrors of war. Les Blank's *Garlic Is as Good as Ten Mothers* (1980) is a categorical documentary, as it examines different ways people use and celebrate garlic.

Gates of Heaven and *Vernon, Florida* use an associational structure. In his analysis of nonnarrative formal systems, David Bordwell describes the associational form as juxtaposing "loosely connected images to suggest an emotion or concept to the spectator. Perhaps we find grocery stores cramped and oppressive. We could film the store's contents to look bleak, and we could insert metaphorical material to cue the audience to respond negatively to what they see."[28] While Bordwell's description primarily deals with images, Morris uses both images and testimony in an associative manner, cueing the audience to make these connections as the film progresses. This structure is quite uncommon in interview documentaries and more common in observational films such as Frederick Wiseman's *Titicut Follies* (1967).[29]

The associational form in *Gates of Heaven* is complicated by suggestions of a narrative account of the Foothill Pet Cemetery and its deceased residents, who are eventually moved to the Bubbling Well Pet Memorial Park. The film begins with Floyd McClure remembering how his childhood in North Dakota inspired the idea of a pet cemetery business. Now in California, Floyd says that he needed financing to get the project off the ground. Morris cuts to interviews with several investors, who discuss their involvement in the business. Floyd returns and describes the business as a "kismet idea" designed for animal lovers who do not want to use the garbage can as a resting place for their departed pets.

Plantinga notes that the beginning of a formal narrative film suggests frames of reference for the viewer in understanding the film, "posing questions and answers, or problems and solutions, by the end of the film having answered most of the salient questions posed, and having offered solutions to problems it identifies."[30] The beginning of *Gates of Heaven* sets up the foundation for a possible narrative structure, introducing us to the subject matter and the people involved in the project, and raising questions about the status of Floyd's pet cemetery. The beginning also establishes the expectation that the narrative will continue to trace the development of the Foothill Pet Cemetery.

After Floyd's second appearance in the film, Morris breaks with this development. We are introduced to Mike Koewler who works at a rendering plant and discusses the origins and benefits of the rendering industry. This begins a lengthy digression in which interviews about the work involved in the pet cemetery are intercut with testimony about the rendering business and anecdotes about the death of animals, clearly breaking from the Foothill Pet Cemetery narrative. For instance, Floyd tells a story about how a girl accidentally puts her pet cat in the dryer, killing the animal. A few minutes later, Mike talks about a "gal" that worked at the plant and quit her job because the idea of rendering animals "bothered her mind."

Instead of advancing the narrative of the Foothill Pet Cemetery, this section represents a disruptive deviation from this story, while also establishing associational links between the contrasting views on the treatment of animals after death. In one way or another, all of the testimony in this section relates to the death of animals and how humans respond to them. We are not following the chronology of the Foothill Pet Cemetery business; instead, we are making associational connections between, for instance, what Floyd says about tragedy of the dead cat in the dryer and Mike's amused confusion about his former coworker.

This disruption of narrative threads continues throughout *Gates of Heaven*. We learn from a newspaper caption that the Foothill Pet Cemetery pets are being reburied in Napa Valley, which marks the transition to the second half of the film that focuses on the Bubbling Well Pet Memorial Park. There is then a five-and-a-half-minute interview with Florence Rasmussen, an older woman who lives in the Los Altos area. Rasmussen's interview is at first relevant to the transfer of the pets: "Now, they've taking them all away from here up to the—What's the name of that place up above here a little ways? That town? Begins with a *b*. It's Blue Hills Cemetery, I think the name of it is. Not too far, I guess about maybe twenty miles from here."[31]

Rasmussen's testimony might set up an expectation that she will provide information about the move or the new cemetery, perhaps reestablishing a narrative thread. It does not take long before Rasmussen wanders into a monologue about her unfortunate medical condition, the problems with her grandson who owes her money, and her belief that she will never grow old. Rasmussen jumps from one topic to another, eventually contradicting most of her previous testimony. For instance, Rasmussen says about her grandson, "He has not married. Never get married, he says. He was married once—they're divorced." Despite the circularity of Rasmussen's testimony, she never returns to the issue of the pet cemetery or what is happening to the exhumed pets, again disrupting any narrative progression in the film.

Rasmussen never reappears in the film, and Morris shifts focus to the Bubbling Well Pet Memorial Park. The film repeats the pattern of reestablishing a narrative at the beginning of the section and then disrupting it with digressive mini-narratives that do not fully reconnect with the initial story. Calvin Harberts, the owner of Bubbling Well, begins the section discussing the reburial of the Foothill pets: "The thought of trying to bury four hundred pets was pretty hard to accept at the outset. However, we felt like we had an obligation to pet owners, because if we were not to take on this endeavor, it would leave many pet owners with a sour taste and could set our industry back for a very long time." Calvin's testimony raises a number of questions: How is Calvin going to bury so many pets? Where is he going to bury them? How are the pet owners going to react to the new cemetery?

The film never answers any of these questions, and this is the last time in the movie where the pets from Foothill are mentioned. We instead listen to a variety of interviews from the Harberts family, including Calvin's two sons, Phillip and Danny, as well as couples who have pets in the cemetery. Topics of discussion include how the birth control pill touched off an explosion in pet ownership, Phillip Harberts's theoretical musings about business and life, Danny Harberts's memories of lost love, and one couple's urgent plea to have dogs neutered. Instead of resolving any of the narrative questions raised throughout the film, the ending of *Gates of Heaven* consists of Calvin's assurance to pet owners that they will eventually be reunited with their pets. We then see a series of shots of artificial animals around the cemetery, followed by a final shot of an altar in the cemetery.

The rejection of a clear narrative thread in *Gates of Heaven* does not imply a random or unmotivated structure. Morris develops a network of associational connections that link various subjects and different pieces of testimony. Florence Rasmussen's disjointed interview, for example, connects in a number of different ways to other testimony throughout the film. Her troubles with her grandson are relevant to the family dynamics in the Harbertses' business, and her concerns about growing old resonate with the central theme of how humans understand their own mortality. In addition, Phillip Harberts's reflections on effective business strategies relate to the financial troubles of Floyd's cemetery. Most significantly, everyone's testimony in the film to some extent illustrates their beliefs, feelings, and memories about animals, love, and death. These concepts are what help tie together the interviews and provide an underlying structure that unifies the images and testimony throughout *Gates of Heaven*.

These associational links are also central to the form in *Vernon, Florida*. At the start of the film, we see three shots of a car driving through the deserted streets of Vernon. This car releases what one might assume is a cloud of pesticides into the air that eventually drifts toward and over the camera. Albert

Bitterling then discusses his move from Chicago to Vernon, where he now has paid off his mortgage and does not have to pay taxes. An interview with Henry Shipes follows Bitterling, and Shipes talks about his love of turkey hunting. We then return to Bitterling who describes his purchase of a jewel but is uncertain if the jewel is real: "I don't know if the jewel is genuine or not. Take a look. I don't know what I'm looking for."

Much like the structure in *Gates of Heaven*, we can locate associational connections between Bitterling's and Shipes's testimony. For instance, at the end of his description of the turkey hunt, Shipes says, "We spend time like this, day in and day out, day in and day out, not hearing nothing. But you know they're here." This connects to what we see next: Bitterling talking about his inability to see if his jewel is legitimate. Although the topics are quite different, both men are describing their frustrated attempts to find something—either a turkey or an indication of authenticity.

Such associational links are present throughout *Vernon, Florida* and allow us to make connections between the interviews. About ten minutes into the film, Vernon police officer Roscoe Collins sits in his patrol car and waits for speeding vehicles on a main road in Vernon: "'Bout the only thing you can do around this time of day—sit around and wait."[32] Morris then cuts to Henry Shipes, who talks about getting up early to hunt for turkeys because "they gobble better in the earlier part of the morning, and the later in the morning they get, the less they gobble." Although their desired object is different, both men are in pursuit of something elusive, and both indicate the importance of the time of day in their task. Morris's juxtaposition of the interviews foregrounds the associational link between the two, uniting the thoughts and experiences of Collins and Shipes.

Morris's use of an associational structure in *Gates of Heaven* and *Vernon, Florida* ties together these interviews in a variety of ways. Sometimes the topic of conversation links them, such as when Floyd McClure and Mike Koewler both discuss their views on the rendering business. In other sequences, indirect elements of the testimony function as uniting devices, as when Bitterling and Shipes discuss the elusive nature of the turkey and the indications of jewel authenticity. In all of these cases, we are asked to discover the connections between pieces of testimony that do not have an overriding narrative, rhetorical, or categorical thread.

Voice

Interview documentaries contemporaneous with *Gates of Heaven* and *Vernon, Florida* make use of a variety of documentary structures, including the rhetorical, narrative, and categorical form. Within these different structures, they all generally employ a formal voice, where explanation is a central objective and the primary questions posed throughout the film are at some point answered.[33] For instance, *Rosie the Riveter* uses interviews from five different women to instruct us about the experiences of women who entered the workplace after a shortage of manpower during World War II. Questions such as "What will happen to the women's jobs when the men come back from the war?" are raised in the course of the film and then at some point are clearly answered.

Implicit in the explanatory function of the formal voice is the openness and reliability of such explanations. Bill Nichols observes that most interview documentaries uncritically present the interview testimony: "The film says, in effect, 'Interviewees never lie.' Interviewees say, 'What I am telling you is the truth.'"[34] In *Rosie the Riveter*, the perspective provided by the women becomes the perspective of the film, as we accept their testimony as the correct version of the historical events. There can be conflicts in testimony, but formal-voice documentaries eventually and clearly resolve these conflicts. For instance, the women in *Rosie the Riveter* discuss the obstacles and hardships that went along with their jobs during the war, and these accounts conflict with newsreel footage that condescendingly portray women as joyfully taking over the factory jobs. The conflict is resolved through the film's presentation of the newsreel footage as old fashioned, sexist, and silly, while the women's testimony is more detailed, emotional, and ultimately more grounded in historical reality.

Together with an associational structure, *Gates of Heaven* and *Vernon, Florida* make use of an open voice. Unlike the highly communicative and reliable formal voice, Morris employs an open voice that presents limited epistemic authority. *Gates of Heaven* and *Vernon, Florida* are not presented as completely transparent and trustworthy. They lack an authoritative voice to properly guide viewer's understanding of the events and testimony in the film. For instance, there is occasionally incompatible testimony in the films, as in *Gates of Heaven* when Floyd McClure and Mike Koewler provide conflicting accounts about the necessity and humanity of the rendering industry. The film never sides with one perspective over the other, and if anything, both views are overstated and suspect. In *Vernon, Florida*, three men disagree about the physical possibility of shooting oneself in the head with a shotgun. Again, such disagreements are never settled by privileging one perspective over another.

We sometimes question the reliability of the testimony without the presence of a conflicting viewpoint. For example, Mr. and Mrs. Martin describe their trip to the White Sands Proving Ground in *Vernon, Florida*. After returning home with a bottle of sand from the missile base, the Martins explain how the sand has grown and will soon completely fill the jar.[35] In *Gates of Heaven*, Calvin Harberts attributes a recent rise in pet ownership to the birth control pill: "Most people don't know it, but we are in the middle of a pet explosion, throughout not only the United States but throughout the world. . . . I would say that the pill is probably largely more responsible for the pet explosion than any other single factor." Despite the unlikely nature of these claims, Morris does not actively undercut the testimony. He instead allows the Martins and Calvin Harberts to tell their story, and we then move on to the next scene in the film.

The open voice is also common among observational films. Stephen Mamber writes of the observational documentary film, "Whatever the filmmaker's initial interest in the subject, the final film does not try to make the material seem as if it was included for the purpose of proving one specific point. The lack of 'mood' music and guiding narration are part of a general outlook that does not try to push the viewer in one direction and one direction only. Room is left for responses as individual and complex as the situation itself."[36] Allowing the viewer more freedom to determine connections and meaning is important to the voice of the observational film, and it is something that Morris also relies upon in both *Gates of Heaven* and *Vernon, Florida*.

Morris's use of an open voice does not mean that these films do not shape the viewer's engagement with the interview testimony. In both *Gates of Heaven* and *Vernon, Florida*, Morris complicates the traditional function of interview testimony by raising doubts about its reliability and consistency. Both films consequently prompt the viewer to consider different readings of and judgments about the interview testimony.

■ Subjectivity

At this point in our examination, we have noted a number of important features concerning Morris's approach. First, the visual style of his first two films, characterized by carefully organized mise-en-scène, minimal camerawork, and explicit acknowledgment of the camera, does not constitute a rejection of documentary conventions. Rather, it is a unique synthesis of a number of different approaches to nonfiction filmmaking, including interview and observational conventions. Morris also uses an open voice and an associational structure in these films, both of which are common in observational filmmaking. If these stylistic and narrative choices are not intended to make us question the documentary tradition, then what is the function of Morris's design?

As with most interview documentaries, the foundation of both *Gates of Heaven* and *Vernon, Florida* is provided by the interview testimony. The testimony in these films does not primarily advance a narrative, make an argument, or provide information about a particular topic. The associational structure and open voice instead allow Morris to interrogate people's use of language and what it reveals about their view of the world: "From my first film, *Gates of Heaven*, I believe I've been involved in . . . revealing an interior world, a *mental landscape*, how people see themselves as revealed through how they use language. If you listen to what people say, that gives you a route into how they see themselves."[37] Morris's use of a meticulously controlled visual style, an open voice, and an associational structure functions to explore this "interior world" of his interview subjects.

The interview format is by nature engaged with subjectivity, as specific individuals provide personal testimony that is, in some sense, inherently subjective. Even when an interviewee is supplying expert testimony, it is from one of many possible perspectives on the subject. Morris's expressed interest in the subjective elements of his interview subjects goes beyond the naturally personal features of any individual's testimony. Morris instead wants to interrogate the thoughts, memories, and beliefs of his subjects. This particular interest in subjectivity is quite uncommon for interview documentaries, in which, as Bill Nichols notes, "the individual identity, autobiographical background, or idiosyncratic qualities of those interviewed become secondary to an external referent: some aspect of the historical world to which they can contribute special knowledge."[38] For Morris, these subjective features of his interviews become fundamental, often at the expense of the testimony contributing to our knowledge of the world beyond these individuals.

Errol Morris also engages higher-level, philosophical implications of these particular views of the world. Common among these themes are epistemological questions about the nature and limitations of knowledge, and the relationship between language, meaning, and reality. Carl Plantinga provides a useful distinction between first-level states of affairs, such as features of the observable world, and second-level states, which "consist of more abstract propositions, having to do, for example, with standards of morality, religion, the origins of the universe, political systems, and the extent and effects of racism."[39] Using this distinction, we can characterize Morris's thematic interests as falling into the second-level tier, explicitly connecting them with his subjects' individual perspectives.

Drawing out these second-level states of affairs is a difficult, nuanced enterprise, especially considering Morris's use of an open voice. Plantinga notes that "discourse in the open voice confines itself for the most part to representing first-level states of affairs and usually refrains from explanations; this is why the term 'observation' fits the open voice well. Discourse in the formative voice, on the other hand, *explains*, and thus routinely asserts second-level propositions about the project world. It is thus more likely to use voice-over narration."[40] Morris's challenge is to bridge the gap between an open voice and second-level states of affairs in order to foreground the subjective features of his interviews and their philosophical implications.

Returning to the organization of *Gates of Heaven* and *Vernon, Florida*, the associational structure helps to reveal and explore this subjectivity. First, it challenges the expectation that the film will organize the interviews in a conventional manner, to develop a narrative, a rhetorical position, or a categorical overview of a topic. Because the testimony is not being subsumed under one of these purposes, we must try to find alternative connections among the testimonies.

While some of these connections fall into topical associations, Morris occasionally disrupts these loose groupings. For instance, in the second half of *Gates of Heaven* there is a substantial section devoted to the business approach and duties involved in the Bubbling Well Pet Memorial Park. Morris interrupts this section, first with an insert of a Dorothy Gurney poem that has been inscribed on a plaque in the cemetery: "Kiss of the sun for pardon; The song of the birds for mirth; One is nearer to God's heart in a garden; Than anywhere on earth." Following this, a married couple explains how their deceased dog Trooper "was the type of dog that didn't have other dogs to relate to. He lived with adult human beings and having the inability to communicate like human beings do through conversation, he did it with his mannerisms and his eyes and reception." The film then resumes with the Harberts family discussing the many different aspects of the pet cemetery business, including combing dead animals' matted hair and making sure the holes in the ground are the proper size for the coffins.

These kinds of interruptions not only pull both *Gates of Heaven* and *Vernon, Florida* away from what might develop into a categorical structure but also create new associations and connections, often stressing the subjective elements of the testimony. In the above example, there is little topical connection between the information about Trooper the dog and the various duties at the pet cemetery. When they are cut together, however, two very different views of animals are highlighted. The couple has such a personal attachment to their dog that they endow him with human qualities such as the ability to understand human conversations. Animals are lifeless work chores for Danny and Phillip Harberts, who must prepare their dead bodies for burial.

Morris's use of the associational structure also creates a gap between the intention of the testimony and its function in the film. For example, the couple's testimony is about their dog Trooper and how he interacted with people. The associational structure of *Gates of Heaven* abstracts this testimony from Trooper the dog to the ways in which humans understand and relate to animals.

Establishing such distance from the voice of the interview subject allows contradictions, ironies, and mistakes, as well as new questions and truths, to emerge in the testimony. For instance, Morris includes the insert of the Gurney poem in the context of testimony about Bubbling Well's theological positions. Although the poem is about a garden, the placement of the plaque in the Bubbling Well cemetery gives the poem a new, ironic meaning that could read, "One is nearer to God's heart in a cemetery; Than anywhere else on earth." The relationship between God, death, and a troubled hopefulness for life after death is a central theme that runs throughout *Gates of Heaven*. As the associational structure pulls out similar themes in the testimony about

Trooper and the work at the cemetery, the film opens up different readings and implications by disconnecting it with the interview subjects' intentions.

Morris uses beginnings and endings to help cue the audience to this subjectivity and the deeper philosophical questions that follow. Plantinga notes that the beginning of a documentary film often "initiates the cognitive processes of the spectator, encouraging hypothesis- and inference-making about the narrative and the knowledge it (ostensibly) imparts. The beginning of the film suggests frames of reference that the viewer may employ in comprehending the text."[41] The frames of reference suggested by the opening of *Vernon, Florida* include a question about the relationship between the place of the documentary and "reality." We first observe three shots of a truck driving through the streets of Vernon, spraying an unidentified cloud of material throughout the town, eventually overtaking the camera. Albert Bitterling then asks, "Reality? You mean this is the real world? [*laughs*] I never thought of that." From the beginning of the film, we are prompted to think about the testimony in relation to questions such as, What is the nature of the filmed world? How does this world relate to reality? And what are the film subjects' thoughts and beliefs about reality? All of these questions continue to play a central thematic role throughout *Vernon, Florida* and all of Morris's films.

Endings in documentaries also cue the viewer to important elements in the film: "The *overarching* function of the ending is epistemological rather than dramatic. Formal endings guide the backward-directed activity of the spectator in comprehending the film. The ending may fill in gaps, sum up main points, or suggest a 'correct' frame by which the previous data can be interpreted."[42] As a result of the associative structure and open voice, the endings in *Gates of Heaven* and *Vernon, Florida* do not fill in story gaps or resolve narrative threads. Much like the beginnings of Morris's films, they do help reinforce frameworks with which the audience can understand what might appear to be a disjointed assortment of interviews. For instance, at the end of *Gates of Heaven*, a couple discusses their rationale for believing that they will be reunited with their dead pet: "There's your dog. Your dog's dead. Where's the thing that made it move? It had to be something, didn't it? There's your spirit." When the husband responds, "I hope she's right," the wife asserts, "I think I'm right. In fact, I almost know I'm right."

"Almost knowing" again raises the epistemological questions that are at the heart of the film, which is reinforced by the last piece of testimony in

Gates of Heaven. Calvin Harberts says, "My assurance to the pet owner [is] that they will be reunited with their pet at some time in the future—maybe under different circumstances and in a different form. As remote as this might be, and it's hard for them to visualize, it still gives them a degree of hope." The idea of having this kind of blind hope in the face of such uncertainty or, even worse, despair is underscored by a series of shots of decorative animals that populate the cemetery, pleasant to the eye but unmistakably fake. This forceful juxtaposition of human subjectivity against a somewhat bleak reality again suggests a thematic framework from which to understand the film.

Morris's visual design is also important in understanding how his documentaries function. The reflexive reading of Morris's films correctly observes that Morris maintains intimate control over the visual elements in his films. It is also important that this break from the conventions of observational filmmaking, which have strong connections to documentary realism, is clear to the viewer. This divergence helps to cue the viewer that Morris is primarily interested not in realism but rather in the dreamlike world of human subjectivity. Instead of undermining or calling into question the conventional connection between observational style and realistic representation, Morris relies on this association, breaking with observational norms to highlight the subjective elements of the testimony.

Let us now return to some of the distinguishing stylistic features of *Gates of Heaven* and *Vernon, Florida* and examine how they function in relation to the interview testimony. First, the impression of eye contact with the interview subjects, together with the absence of Morris's voice in the films, gives a heightened sense of direct communication from the interview subject to the viewer. Bill Nichols describes the effect on the viewer: "The presence of the social actor and the visual/aural absence of the filmmaker gives the appearance of a kind of 'pseudomonologue,' which appears to deliver the thoughts, impressions, feelings, and memories of the individual witness directly to the viewer. It violates the dictum 'don't look at the camera' in order to achieve a more immediate sense of being addressed by the subject."[43] The impression of direct contact between the witness and the viewer amplifies the subjective qualities brought out by the associational structure.

The eye contact with the camera in *Gates of Heaven* and *Vernon, Florida* intensifies a confessional relationship between the interview subject and the viewer. Morris's stylistic handling of these interviews, however, does not actively encourage a sympathetic response to the testimony. Morris avoids close framings and zooming during the interviews, even during particularly affecting moments in the testimony. For instance, Floyd McClure provides one of the most emotional moments in *Gates of Heaven* as he talks about the demise of the Foothill Pet Cemetery and how the closing of the business left him "not only broke but broken hearted." Instead of zooming into Floyd's face, Morris frames Floyd in a static medium shot and then cuts to a shot of Floyd sitting in his wheelchair, facing away from the camera. This refusal to engage Floyd's face, made explicit by the shot of him with his back to the camera, does not mean that we cannot empathize with him. In fact, this is the first time that we see Floyd in his wheelchair, which may amplify our empathy for his situation. We might also see Floyd's heartbreak as an inevitable, or maybe even a deserved, consequence of his naive view of the world. The detached style leaves open a number of different possible responses to the testimony, reinforcing the open voice of the film.

Morris's use of cutaway images also constitutes a significant divergence from the norms of interview films. In W. Hugh Baddeley's quote cited above, he asserts that cutaways not only are used to hide cuts but also "must always be germane and they must always appear to be germane." The extent to which the cutaway is germane is of central importance to the interview documentary. When a cutaway appears over a subject's testimony, the viewer will attempt to determine the connection between the two.

By and large, most interview documentaries use images of illustration, in which the images function to illustrate the verbal testimony. For instance, in *The War at Home* (1979), Paul Soglin discusses a demonstration against the Vietnam War at the University of Wisconsin–Madison: "The whole place was like a war zone. . . . The critical moment was [when] the crowd began to gather because classes were just over when the cops moved in. And so suddenly, with the crowd getting larger and the crowd getting meaner, they start using the tear gas."[44] On the image track, we see actual footage of the demonstration, including the tear-gas canisters being deployed into the crowd. This cutaway serves to ground the testimony in reality, acting as visual evidence for Soglin's claims.

Morris frequently challenges and undermines our expectations for illustrative images. For instance, Floyd McClure describes the plot of land right across the street from his home in Los Altos that he wanted to use for the pet

FIGURE 1.2. □ *Gates of Heaven*

cemetery, which was "the most beautiful piece of land as far as I was concerned in the whole valley." Morris cuts to a high-angle panning shot of the landscape that, despite the highways that run through it, is surrounded by lush trees and an appealing landscape (see figure 1.2). This cutaway appears to illustrate the testimony that the piece of land is attractive.

An investor later talks about the same land: "I was made aware of this property that is in Los Alles on Foothill on Highway 280, and we felt that that would make a great place for a pet cemetery because it had tremendous visual ability and the thousands of the cars that went past 280 and the property leaned in other directions as well. It was a marvelous location for a restaurant or motel or various sundry things." Morris again cuts to a pan of the property, but the camera is placed at a lower angle that eliminates many of the green trees and highlights the passing traffic (see figure 1.3). Although we might have initially understood the first pan as functioning in an illustrative manner, both now take on a subjective function. Floyd admires the land for its natural beauty, while the investor sees its business potential, and the corresponding cutaways foreground each particular perspective. Instead of

FIGURE 1.3. ▫ *Gates of Heaven*

images of illustration that ground the testimony in reality, we instead have two significantly different images that highlight the subjective perspective of each interview subject.

Throughout *Vernon, Florida*, Morris cuts to images that lack the object of the testimony, again frustrating our expectation for illustrative cutaways. For instance, turkey hunter Henry Shipes talks about turkeys and what to expect on a typical hunt: "They are a smart bird. The smartest we've got in this country. Seeing that we spend time like this day in and day out, day in and day out, not hearing nothing, but you know that they're here." Instead of cutting to a turkey, perhaps hiding in the woods, Morris cuts to a pan across dense woods, devoid of any turkeys. The cutaway shows the world from a certain limited perspective, in this case someone who cannot see any turkeys. It also puts into question Shipes's knowledge about the turkey's presence, as we do not have an image that reinforces his claim that he knows they are in the woods.

Many of the images throughout *Vernon, Florida* function in a similar manner, highlighting the subjective limitations of the interviews. Later in the

FIGURE 1.4. ▫ *Vernon, Florida*

film, Albert Bitterling describes how he had taken some pictures of the night sky: "I don't know if this is a star or what. Well, no it couldn't be that. Well, that's a picture of the star . . . I just took the camera and pointed it up there. I didn't even sight it and then took the picture that way. Of course, you can see that the picture ain't too good." Morris cuts into the picture that Albert is holding, which is a dark, torn photograph that has a blurry light in the middle (see figure 1.4). Again, the image does not clarify or ground the testimony but instead foregrounds the limitations of the testimony and perhaps the interview subject.

There are other moments in the films where Morris refuses a cut-in or cutaway when we would expect one. At the beginning of *Vernon, Florida*, Albert Bitterling discusses a jewel he purchased for fifteen dollars: "I don't know if the jewel is genuine or not. Take a look." Albert then holds the jewel up to the camera, takes out a jeweler's loupe, and holds the jewel up to his eye: "I don't know what I'm looking for. I don't know. What does a jeweler look for?" (see figure 1.5). Morris refuses to clarify Albert's confusion by providing a close-up of the jewel or some kind of verification of its authenticity, even when Albert holds it up to the camera. By not answering Albert's question about the authenticity of his jewel, Morris is able to shift our attention from the story of the jewel to Albert's uncertainty about it.

FIGURE 1.5. ◻ *Vernon, Florida*

In the above examples, we can see a pattern of emphasis on subjective views, limited knowledge, and imperfect beliefs: Floyd McClure and the investor have very different views of the same piece of land; Henry Shipes cannot see the turkeys he is hunting but somehow knows they exist; and Albert Bitterling cannot discover the identity of either the object he photographed or the item he purchased. Thematically, these issues all center on epistemological problems and are central to all of Morris's films throughout his filmmaking career. Morris's use of cutaway images in *Gates of Heaven* and *Vernon, Florida* help to highlight these thematic concerns.

The mise-en-scène in *Gates of Heaven*'s interview compositions also plays an important role in foregrounding subjectivity. Many documentary filmmakers arrange the interview mise-en-scène. In his book on documentary production, Alan Rosenthal advises that "if the story is about research, then you probably want to go for the laboratory background. If you are talking about the development of the modern university, then a dynamic campus backdrop is probably better than a dull home location."[45] We can see such an attempt to match the backdrop to the content of the interview in *Rosie the Riveter*. As Lyn Childs discusses her job as a burner in a shipyard during World War II, she is framed against a background of a shipyard.

Rosenthal offers additional advice for the documentary filmmaker who is

FIGURE 1.6. □ *Gates of Heaven*

planning the background of the interview image: "At this stage, you must ask yourself three things: Will the background add to the mood and drama of the story? Will the interviewee feel at ease in the location, with the possibility of numbers of people around to interfere and distract? And is there any danger of the background being so strong that it distracts from the interview?"[46] In the above example from *Rosie the Riveter*, the background is relevant to the testimony and does not pose a risk of interrupting the interview. In addition, the background is not distracting for the viewer, in part because it is slightly out of focus.

Morris's manipulation of the interview mise-en-scène is distinct from this traditional approach. First, *Gates of Heaven* and *Vernon, Florida* are much less reliant on cutaways than are other interview documentaries at the time. This allows the interview subjects to speak for longer periods of time without interruption from b-roll images. Morris also provides rich visual detail in the background of these interviews. For example, in figure 1.6, Morris composes the mise-en-scène around Floyd, placing items such as a balance scale, what

FIGURE 1.7. ▫ *Gates of Heaven*

appears to be his bronzed infant shoes, and a sketch of two horses in clear view. Morris carefully lights these objects, further highlighting the items.

The objects placed around Floyd's body are more pronounced than is the background in Lyn Childs's interview, for instance. They are clearly lit, in crisp focus, and are given their own space in the frame. Other examples of this foregrounding of mise-en-scène elements can be found throughout *Gates of Heaven*. For example, Lucille Billingsley is framed with a picture of her dog above her and a clock prominently displayed next to her (see figure 1.7). Perhaps the most overt mise-en-scène is in Phillip Harberts's interview in his office (see figure 1.8). The trophies and photographs around Phillip almost overwhelm the frame, surrounding him in the background as well as on the desk in the foreground. In all of these examples, we are aware of these objects, and it is clear that Morris wants us to notice and reflect on them.

So the question becomes, What function do these objects serve in relation to the interview? One answer again brings us back to Morris's interest in subjectivity, as the objects in the frame underscore the beliefs, attitudes, and

FIGURE 1.8. □ *Gates of Heaven*

memories of the interviewee. Much like the cutaways, when we are presented with features in the frame that are highlighted in some way, we attempt to connect them to relevant elements of the interview. Returning to Floyd's interview, the objects around him are not mere reflections of the topic at hand; rather, they have a more metaphoric significance to the interview. On the left of the frame there is an uneven balance scale, which we may connect to Floyd's sense of injustice after he loses his pet cemetery. Or the bronzed baby shoes to his right have an informative relationship to Floyd's simplicity and innocence, also reinforced by the childlike sketch of the horses behind his head. As Lucille Billingsley reminisces about her dog, the clock placed next to her adopts a metaphoric significance to her testimony about memory and loss.

Morris could establish these more abstract connections with the testimony by cutting away to these objects. Morris instead distances himself from the illustrative use of b-roll, which grounds the testimony in reality with images that provide some kind of visual proof for the interview. The deliberate manipulation of the elements in the frame refuses a naturalistic environment in favor of an expressive mise-en-scène. The trophies stacked around Phillip Harberts provide a somewhat comical presentation of Phillip's mindset that "everything is possible; you just have to look at it with the right frame of mind. And that's important—your mind." Phillip explains how he would organize his office for job interviews to display the maximum number of trophies so that job candidates would be "taken away." The world packed with trophies and motivational messages is not *the* world but Phillip's world, and the mise-en-scène of the interviews in *Gates of Heaven* helps to create that subjective space.

A significant difference between Morris's first two films is that *Vernon, Florida* does not exhibit the same kind of mise-en-scène construction as does *Gates of Heaven*. There are times when Morris pans to relevant objects in the frame. During his interview with Henry Shipes, Morris pans to a number of mounted turkey beards as Shipes describes his various hunting triumphs. *Vernon, Florida* is not any less interested in the subjective qualities of the testimony, but it is less reliant on mise-en-scène elements to express them.

Although the primary thematic concern of the films is this interest in the problems of human subjectivity and some philosophical questions attached to them, this does not mean that every aspect of Morris's visual style needs to be completely explained in terms of the films' thematics. Morris's careful control over the visuals also contributes to the aesthetic beauty of the films. Morris's use of color in both *Gates of Heaven* and *Vernon, Florida* is striking as he matches and contrasts different hues and tones throughout the frame. In *Gates of Heaven*, the yellows, browns, and beiges of the investor's clothes closely match the colors of the couch and on the wall behind him. In Scottie Harberts's interview, her brown patterned shirt match the shades of brown throughout the room, while a blazing red flower in the left foreground adds a shock of color. In *Vernon, Florida*, the various shades of gray and brown in Joe Payne's clothing echo the colors of the house and ground behind him, and a bright purple tree in the background adds a bubble of visual energy to the frame. By closely controlling the visual elements, Morris is able to develop a dynamic color palette as well as cue the audience to the subjective elements of the testimony.

Reception and Ethics

Film critics were divided in response to Morris's first two films. Some critics charged that Morris was belittling his subjects in *Gates of Heaven*. A 1978 review from *Variety* accused *Gates of Heaven* of being "unsparing in letting its people reveal their stupidity. It allows them to ramble on, disgorging their impossibly warped theology which meets the Little Goodie Two Shoes and Adolph Eichmann spectrum test for the banality of evil. While Morris undoubtedly showed them the camera, it's clear that his subjects are his victims."[47] A review of the 1978 New York Film Festival noted, "There were charges that Errol Morris had cruelly exploited his pet-owning subjects."[48] The charges against *Vernon, Florida* were much in the same vain; during the 1981 New York Film Festival, Morris was again accused of making fun of his subjects, and *Variety* called the film "tasteless."[49]

There are a number of possible explanations for why viewers think that Morris is treating his subjects unfairly. Michael Covino's review of *Gates of Heaven* provides insight into one option: "Morris is a naïf who has made an impolite movie: he doesn't seem to realize that it's an unspoken rule that one's not supposed to show real people, ordinary people, looking so sad, so silly, so depressing. . . . It's permissible to catch powerful people in lies, in contradictions, to show them for the megalomaniacs that they might be, or to elicit sympathy for the poor, the incarcerated, the deranged. There's a grammar for documentary filmmaking which Morris has ignored."[50] Covino's characterization of Morris's transgression, which is applicable to both *Gates of Heaven* and *Vernon, Florida*, is indeed a significant difference from other documentaries at the time. Undermining a subject or putting a piece of testimony into question in a documentary is reserved for someone who *deserves* such treatment. In *Hearts and Minds*, for instance, General William Westmoreland testifies, "The Oriental doesn't put the same high price on life as does a Westerner. Life is plentiful. Life is cheap in the Orient."[51] The statement is obviously absurd, and the film actively undermines Westmoreland by contrasting his testimony with images of "Orientals" grieving over family members killed in bombings. We consent to the film's rejection of Westmoreland's testimony because he is on the wrong side of the Vietnam War. Westmoreland represents power, corruption, and oppression. We accept the film's ridicule of Westmoreland because he has inappropriately victimized others.

Scared Straight (1980) uses actual convicts to frighten a group of juvenile delinquents about life in the penitentiary. Throughout the film, the children are shouted at, insulted, and intimidated, often to tears. Although the children's arrogance at the beginning of the film may justify such harsh treatment, most people understand that this is not a punishment as much as a process to help these young people better their lives. Unlike the Westmoreland example, we empathize with the children and want them to succeed. By exposing their weaknesses, their faults, and their fears, the film makes the case that the children will benefit in the future.

Gates of Heaven and *Vernon, Florida* are different. None of the subjects have committed the offenses of a Westmoreland or the crimes of the children in *Scared Straight*. Everyone in *Gates of Heaven* seems to be simple, honest, and well intentioned. We do not feel that the characters in either film deserve to be ridiculed, despite their quirks, inconsistencies, or missteps. Unlike most interview documentaries, we are not prompted to empathize with Morris's subjects, and the gap between the testimony and the voice of the film can be understood as condescending. For instance, Floyd McClure describes the wretched smell of the rendering plant: "We'd even sit down in the evening time to our meal and the only thing that hit your nostrils wasn't that good piece of meat you bought to eat, or the vegetable, or the nice dessert that's put on your table, but you first had to grab the wine glass off the table and take a whiff of that to get the smell of the rendering company out of your nostrils before you could eat." The irony here, apparent to the audience but seemingly unknown to Floyd, is that his personal objections to the process of rendering dead animals are comically undermined by the "good piece of meat" that he has cooked for dinner.

In *Vernon, Florida*, Joe Payne removes an opossum from a large box in his backyard. Holding the animal by the tail as it tries to scamper away, Payne explains that a friend brought him the animal after it was eating his chickens because "he said I was the only fella that knew what to do with an opossum." We then watch as Payne continues to hold the animal's tail as it again attempts to run away. "Knowing what to do with an opossum" seems to mean keeping it in a box in the backyard and holding it by its tail. Payne later explains that he plans on selling it for "twelve to fifteen hundred dollars," but the irony of the above moment has already carried the scene.

Gates of Heaven and *Vernon, Florida* are populated with scenes such as this, where it might appear as though everyone, including Morris, is laughing except for the subjects themselves. It might seem not only "impolite," as Covino explains, but also unethical for a filmmaker to take advantage of his subjects. We might connect this kind of mistreatment to some of the exploitive, quasi-ethnographic films in the 1960s and 1970s.

This connection with ethnographic filmmaking is informative, as Morris assembles different kinds of subcultures in his first two films. While ethnographic films usually focus on a more foreign or exotic culture, Morris is engaging in something resembling a "domestic ethnography." In *Gates of Heaven*, we have groups of people who are both geographically close and involved in pet cemeteries in one way or another. *Vernon, Florida* is perhaps even closer to a traditional ethnographic film, as all of the participants live in a clearly defined part of the world.

The use of the associational structure reinforces this connection with ethnographic filmmaking. As we noted earlier, the associational structure asks us to locate the connections among the interview subjects, uniting their various thoughts and beliefs into a sense of a shared community. In this way, we start to see the participants as taking part in a shared way of life, an aim that is at the heart of many ethnographic films.

This ethnographic element of *Gates of Heaven* and *Vernon, Florida* also serves to amplify the ethical concerns with Morris's approach. When ethnographic filmmakers enter another culture, there is an expectation that they will suspend judgment on the peculiarities of that culture. David MacDougall notes, "The film-maker becomes a potential threat to the culturally unbiased vision of the camera, likely to impose distortions on the film-making process."[52] As we have already seen, Morris often calls into question the beliefs of his interview subjects, actualizing this imposition.

In addition to the detractors, *Gates of Heaven* and *Vernon, Florida* have high-profile admirers as well. Michael Covino praised the film's unique style that "has none of the usual signature shots of the documentary."[53] Gene Siskel named *Gates of Heaven* the best documentary of 1978, and Roger Ebert wrote enthusiastic reviews for both films.[54] Ebert wrote about *Gates of Heaven* that is was "surrounded by layer upon layer of comedy, pathos, irony, and human nature. I have seen this film perhaps thirty times and am still not anywhere near the bottom of it. All I know is, it's about a lot more than pet cemeteries." Ebert also named the *Gates of Heaven* "one of the ten greatest films of all time."[55]

The following anecdote from Ebert illustrates the widely divergent responses to Morris's films. When Ebert was asked to lecture and show a movie, he often brought *Gates of Heaven*: "Every time I show this, it plays differently. . . . Some people think it's about animals. Some people think it's about life and death. I've shown it to a group of bankers, who believe it raises all kinds of questions about success, about starting a small business. People think it's funny or sad or deadpan or satirical. They think that Errol Morris loved the people in the film, or that he was being very cruel to them."[56]

Instead of taking sides concerning what is the most reasonable, justified reaction, let us instead examine *why* there are such very different responses to the films. First, the open voice is significant, as it avoids determined meanings of the formal voice and leaves room for different readings and responses to the films. Plantinga explains: "The open voice may withhold high-level generalizations about its subject not in the name of imitation, but in an unwillingness to offer neat explanations and contextualizations. Withholding such high-level explanations also may facilitate a democracy of interpretation, allowing the spectator to come to her own conclusions."[57] In both *Gates of Heaven* and *Vernon, Florida*, we have characters saying and doing things that might seem silly, ironic, and puzzling, or they might seem honest, endearing, and inescapably human. Refusing devices such as voice-over narration and a more formal structure, Morris does not determine the viewer's responses to the interview testimony.

Morris's stylized visuals further complicates these ethical issues brought about by the open voice, again prompting concerns about Morris's manipulation of his subjects. Covino's review of *Gates of Heaven* is instructive: "People sit in these spotless, carefully arranged living rooms that might well be show rooms in furniture-store display windows. . . . It's as though Norman Rockwell, whistling on the way to work, has bicycled with his easel and palette into *The Twilight Zone*. Has the film-maker cheated? Has he arranged things, perhaps even suggested to people what to wear?"[58] The carefully controlled compositions and mise-en-scène may amplify the impression that Morris is manipulating and victimizing his subjects. This kind of influence over the visuals, working with the structure of the films, highlight the subjective features of the testimony, raising questions related to the nature and limitations of human knowledge. This function of highlighting subjectivity does not bring with it a clear judgment about the validity or scope of these issues, however; that remains open.

2 The Thin Blue Line

ERROL MORRIS'S FILMMAKING CAREER was filled with frustrations and disappointments after *Gates of Heaven* and *Vernon, Florida*. Although both films did receive some critical attention, neither achieved significant distribution or box office success. Still eager to continue making films, Morris embarked on a number of different projects, including a story about two bank robbers in Missouri financed by Edward Pressman and an adaptation of a Stephen King short story for Dino De Laurentiis. Both of these projects and many others folded. Morris's career stalled as he continued to struggle financially.[1]

Morris's brother Noel died of a heart attack in October 1983, after which Morris made a temporary change in occupation: "Shortly after my brother's death, I became so disgruntled with Hollywood and disheartened with the failure to get financing for my next film that I took a job as a private detective, investigating fraud on Wall Street. After more than a year of that, the money for 'Dr. Death' came through, and I said, 'Thank God, I don't have to be a private detective anymore.' I was wrong."[2] Morris originally conceived "Dr. Death" as a documentary about the infamous state psychiatrist Dr. James Grigson. This idea developed into *The Thin Blue Line*, in which Morris investigates the murder of police officer Robert Wood and the conviction of Randall Dale Adams for the crime.

Many scholars argue that Morris's investigation of Officer Wood's murder in *The Thin Blue Line* functions as an investigation into the conventions of documentary filmmaking. Other scholars make the overlapping claim that the film is an investigation into the possibility of objectivity and truth. In addition, many analyses position such theoretical investigations as an exclusive interest of the film, evident in Morris's handling of the interview testimony, the overarching structure, and the visual style of *The Thin Blue Line*.

As an alternative, we can better analyze and understand *The Thin Blue Line* as an examination of Randall Dale Adams's murder trial. Morris structures the film as an investigation into Officer Wood's murder, prompting the audience to ask questions about the identity of the murderer, the reliability of the witnesses involved in the trial, and ultimately the reasons for Adams's wrongful conviction. Morris develops a compelling narrative by delaying and frustrating answers to these questions. The case against Adams is also filled with inconsistencies, contradictions, and untruths, and Morris uses these aspects of the trial to explore the workings and frailties of human subjectivity. Morris again designs a sophisticated, stylized aesthetic and uses associational connections to cue the audience to the subjective elements throughout *The Thin Blue Line.*

The subject matter in *The Thin Blue Line* presents new challenges for Morris's approach to the documentary. Morris continues his open exploration of human subjectivity but, unlike *Gates of Heaven* and *Vernon, Florida*, Morris is dealing with a serious situation in which a man was murdered and another man's life is at stake. *The Thin Blue Line* is unique and powerful in part because Morris combines an open voice with definitive conclusions about past events.

■ Background

As we noted above, Morris was frustrated with the film industry and found steady work as a freelance private detective investigating securities and commodities fraud on Wall Street. Morris continued to refine the interviewing technique that he had developed while interviewing murderers in graduate school. Much like his interviews with film subjects, Morris found that the less he spoke, the more people were inclined to talk. Morris used his detective work to support himself and his wife Julia Sheehan, an art historian whom he married in 1984.

Morris continued to pursue support for his film projects. In 1985, he conducted preliminary research on Dr. James Grigson, a Dallas psychiatrist who had testified for the prosecution in death-row cases for well over a decade. After the death penalty was reinstated in the mid-1970s, Grigson received some attention in the national press, including a 1981 article in *Time* magazine that gave insight into Grigson's nickname "Dr. Death": "In each of more than 70 proceedings since 1967, Grigson has testified that the defendant was a 'sociopath' who was dangerous to society, and every time, with a single exception, the jury has unanimously voted for the ultimate penalty:

in Texas, death by injection. Says Peter Lesser, president-elect of the Dallas County Criminal Bar Association: 'He is a witch doctor. They call him Dr. Death for a reason.'"[3] Grigson would offer predictions about whether defendants would commit violent crimes in the future, often after examining the defendant for only an hour. Grigson sometimes provided such opinions without ever interviewing the defendant. For Morris, Grigson embodied many of the themes he had explored in his first two films, including questions of knowledge, certainty, and death.

Morris obtained a grant to begin his research on Grigson with the help of Suzanne Weil, who was the head of programming at PBS at the time.[4] Morris, as with most documentary filmmakers, turned to a variety of funding to finance the film beyond the initial research grant. WNET New York, a flagship station of PBS, gave Morris funding for *Vernon, Florida*, and this relationship continued with *The Thin Blue Line*. Morris also obtained some of the largest grants available for nonfiction filmmakers, including National Endowment for the Arts and the Corporation for Public Broadcasting grants, and received additional funding from the Chubb Group of Insurance Companies. American Playhouse, an anthology television series broadcast on PBS, and Channel 4 coproduced *The Thin Blue Line*. In the end, the film cost about a million dollars, significantly more than most documentaries at the time.

Morris traveled to Texas with his initial grant money from PBS. Grigson suggested that Morris interview inmates about their cases and experiences with Grigson. Morris's initial intention was not to prove the innocence of these inmates but rather to investigate Grigson's involvement in their cases. While conducting the approximately twenty-five interviews with inmates, Morris met Randall Dale Adams, an Ohio native who had been convicted of killing Dallas police officer Robert Wood in 1976. Morris became particularly troubled by Adams's case after reading the transcripts from his trial.[5]

David Harris, a sixteen-year-old boy who had picked up Adams on the day of the murder, became a central figure in the trial. Adams had run out of gas that day, and Harris was joyriding around Dallas in a stolen car. Harris testified that, after spending the day with Adams drinking, watching a movie, and smoking marijuana, Adams shot Officer Wood during a routine traffic stop.

Randall Dale Adams was convicted in 1977 and sentenced to death. Three days before his execution, the U.S. Supreme Court ordered a stay after ruling that Dallas district attorney Henry Wade violated proper jury-selection procedure. Texas governor Bill Clements later commuted Adams's sentence to life in prison.[6]

Randall Dale Adams complained to Morris that David Harris framed him and that it was Harris who killed Robert Wood. Morris scheduled a meeting with Harris in a bar outside of Beaumont, Texas, in April 1985, during which Morris became increasingly troubled about the conviction of Randall Dale Adams.[7]

Morris eventually decided to shift the focus of the film from "Dr. Death" to the Adams case. He spent over a year and a half investigating the details of the murder and interviewing the various participants in the case. Adams was concerned about Morris's intentions and the danger of being exploited by a "New York filmmaker." Adams refused to sign release forms for over a year and a half, at one point pulling out of an interview with Morris at the last minute. Randy Schaffer, Adams's attorney, felt as though Morris was attempting to take over the case.[8]

Despite the problems, Morris and the finished film played a significant role in the eventual release of Randall Dale Adams. Morris obtained a copy of the district attorney's files that revealed information about Adams's innocence.[9] During their final interview, Morris recorded David Harris making a series of incriminating statements about his involvement in the murder. Morris's camera was not working during the interview, but he was able to record Harris on a tape recorder, parts of which were included in *The Thin Blue Line*'s final scene. Morris testified in court in 1986 on behalf of Randall Dale Adams and offered unedited interview footage of the prosecution's witnesses undermining their own credibility.[10]

Some credit *The Thin Blue Line* for setting Adams free from prison, but it was not the sole reason for Adams's release. Morris's film did help organize and clarify the facts of the case, however, as well as reveal new information that established Adams's innocence. It also brought national attention to Adams's ongoing appeals and prompted press outlets throughout the country to pick up the story. The charges against Adams were officially dropped on March 23, 1989.

The Thin Blue Line premiered a year earlier in March 1988 at the San Francisco Film Festival. The film was originally planned to run as a PBS special, but Morris wanted *The Thin Blue Line* to be distributed theatrically first. Both

Orion and Miramax were interested in the film, with Miramax winning the distribution rights.[11] *The Thin Blue Line* played in theaters across the country, mostly in small art cinemas, and later aired on PBS on May 24, 1989. Morris produced *The Thin Blue Line* for one million dollars, and the film grossed about 1.5 million dollars, becoming one of the most financially successful documentaries of its time.[12]

The release of *The Thin Blue Line* catapulted Morris into the spotlight of the documentary film world. The critical responses to *The Thin Blue Line* were overwhelmingly positive. Many critics pointed to the film's innovative features, including the unique handling of the story and the use of reenactments. The National Board of Review, the New York Film Critics Circle, and the National Society of Film Critics all awarded the film "Best Documentary" honors.

Despite the critical attention, *The Thin Blue Line* was not nominated for an Academy Award. This exclusion fueled existing discontent with what many thought was the Academy's overly conservative approach to documentaries. The film's focus on a social injustice was in line with previous Oscar winners, such as *Down and Out in America* (1986), about the effect of the recession in the 1980s on Middle America, and *The Times of Harvey Milk* (1984), which examines the life and assassination of the important gay politician. This led some to claim that Morris's irreverence toward documentary narrative and style disqualified him from proper consideration by the Academy.[13]

■ Style

Errol Morris uses interview testimony in *The Thin Blue Line* to guide us through the story without the presence of a voice-over narrator. There are a number of documentaries in the late 1980s that also rely exclusively on interview testimony, including *Comic Book Confidential* (1988), *Cane Toads: An Unnatural History* (1988), and *Common Threads: Stories from the Quilt* (1989). These films are a useful cross-section of films to contextualize the stylistic features in *The Thin Blue Line*. While they are similar in format and release date, they also represent the diversity of interview documentaries in the late 1980s. In terms of subject matter, *Common Threads* investigates the lives of those who died of AIDS, *Comic Book Confidential* examines the history of the comic book, and *Cane Toads* details the spread of the sugar cane toad across

Australia. The tone of the films is also quite different. *Common Threads* is a serious, emotional examination of those affected by AIDS, while *Comic Book Confidential* and *Cane Toads* both approach their topics with humor that occasionally approaches parody.

Morris again directs the look of the interview subjects close to the camera lens in *The Thin Blue Line* and places their bodies in the center of the frame. This practice is common in documentary interviews, although it is unusual that Morris composes every interview this way. Morris also uses artificial lighting and planimetric compositions for the interviews in *The Thin Blue Line*. Again, you can find these features in other documentaries during this time, but it is unusual for a documentary to *insist* on such visual elements.

Nonfiction films in the late 1980s tend to zoom in and out during interviews, although not as frequently as documentaries a decade earlier. This practice provides different framings for editing, helps add visual variety, and can intensify poignant moments in the interview. Morris's static framing in *Gates of Heaven* and *Vernon, Florida* allows the viewer to notice and reflect upon the intricate mise-en-scène of the interview.

The Thin Blue Line also refrains from zooming or any camerawork in the interviews, but Morris handles some elements of the interview mise-en-scène differently. Morris's first two films use wider framings to provide space for a more complex mise-en-scène, but the framing in *The Thin Blue Line* is tighter on the interview subject. All of the interviews are framed in medium close-up, which is significantly closer than the predominant medium and medium-long shots in *Gates of Heaven* and *Vernon, Florida*. Although it is unusual to have a documentary shoot all its subjects with the same framing, the medium close-up is common in other documentaries at the time.

The interview backgrounds in *The Thin Blue Line* are somewhat conventional in their simplicity. There is not the purposeful object placement we see in Floyd's interviews or the depth and color coordination we see in Scottie Harberts's interview in *Gates of Heaven*. The backgrounds in *The Thin Blue Line* are often quite basic, as we can see in Internal Affairs investigator Dale Holt's interview, where he is in front of a white wall and door with the door's window framing Holt's head (see figure 2.1).

In the previous chapter, we observed that Morris's complex interview mise-en-scène serves a narrative function. Morris's move away from this in *The Thin Blue Line* is compensated by a move toward a greater reliance on

FIGURE 2.1. ▫ *The Thin Blue Line*

cutaway images. Cutaways constitute 67 percent of the total shots in *The Thin Blue Line*, significantly greater than *Gates of Heaven* and *Vernon, Florida*, in which cutaways constitute only 44 and 49 percent of the total shots respectively.

The cutaway images in *The Thin Blue Line* consist of a variety of visual materials, including newspaper headlines, maps, pictures, reenactments, and found footage from old movies and television shows such as *Dillinger* (1945), *Boston Blackie* (1952), and *Swinging Cheerleaders* (1974). Morris's reenactments of events such as the murder of Officer Wood and Randall Adams's interrogation have garnered the most attention, in part because of Morris's stylized approach. The reenactments are carefully lit and deliberately framed without the camera movement or zooming characteristic of observational documentary footage.

Morris also employs a wide variety of distinctive aural material throughout *The Thin Blue Line*. For instance, Morris amplifies the sounds in the reenactment scenes. In the Adams interrogation sequence, the clicking of the interrogator's shoes as he walks in the room, the snap of the pen hitting the desk, and the typing of the typewriter are all forceful elements in the scene. In addition, Philip Glass composed the score for *The Thin Blue Line*. The score is typical of Glass's minimalist music, as it consists of musical phrases that repeat again and again throughout the film. Within these larger phrases, there is often repetition of smaller musical units; for instance, Glass frequently uses arpeggios as a foundation for these musical phrases.

Many scholars argue that this diversity of visual and aural material constitutes a definitive break from documentary tradition. When we look at other documentaries during this time, however, we can see a similar variety of material. For instance, *Common Threads* includes newspaper clippings and found footage (including a clip from the 1952 Columbia Pictures film *A Member of the Wedding*); *Comic Book Confidential* uses found footage, pictures, and animated sequences; and *Cane Toads* incorporates animated maps. In addition, all of these films use original music scored for the film, with *Common Threads* incorporating music from well-known composer Bobby McFerrin.

Reenactments are also quite common in documentaries during this time. There are reenactments in both *Comic Book Confidential* and *Cane Toads*, with *Cane Toads* using these staged sequences even more frequently than does *The Thin Blue Line*. These reenactments also do not display the realism or seriousness of "traditional documentaries." *Cane Toads* incorporates stylized and playful reenactments of the spread of cane toads throughout Australia, including a sequence that parodies the shower sequence in Hitchcock's *Psycho*. There are animated and live-action retellings of comic book scenes in *Comic Book Confidential*, including Bill Griffith's *Zippy the Pinhead* comic series, where we see animated "Zippy" sequences as well as scenes where Griffith himself is dressed as "Zippy."

This use of reenactments or staged sequences was increasingly common in the late 1980s, with documentaries such as *The Indomitable Teddy Roosevelt* (1986), *The Beer Drinker's Guide to Fitness and Filmmaking* (1987), *Eddie Murphy Raw* (1987), and *The Confessions of Robert Crumb* (1987) all employing reenactments. The Academy of Motion Picture Arts and Sciences has also acknowledged some of these films. For example, *The Ten Year Lunch* incorporates animated reenactments of the Algonquin Round Table meetings in the 1920s and won the Oscar for Best Documentary in 1987. The Academy's openness to fictional sequences was not merely a product of the late 1980s. Sixteen years earlier, *The Hellstrom Chronicle* (1971), in which Lawrence Pressman plays fictitious on-screen narrator and mad scientist Dr. Nils Hellstrom as he guides us through the possibilities of an apocalyptic future, also won the Best Documentary Oscar.

We can trace the use of reenactments further back in the history of documentary. Staging fictional scenes in newsreels, for instance, was regularly practiced, including the highly regarded *March of Time* series. In his book *The American Newsreel*, Raymond Fielding notes, "For every genuine news film photographed under difficult and sometimes dangerous conditions, an equal amount of energy was spent by the same producers to fake outstanding news events of the day."[14] The *March of Time* reenactments did not try to hide their status as fictional, acknowledging and even publicizing their use of reenacted scenes. The use of staged footage can be used to question traditional documentary representation, as it is in Jill Godmilow's *Far from Poland* (1984), but its presence does not necessarily signify a reflexive commentary on documentary conventions. What is needed is not merely a description of the kinds of visual material used but also a specific account of how this footage functions in each particular film.

Although *The Thin Blue Line* incorporates a number of stylistic approaches found in other nonfiction films, such as reenactments, this does not mean that it is merely a conventional documentary. Morris's close attention to stylistic detail in both the interview and cutaway footage makes his film among the most visually sophisticated documentaries of its time. For instance, while other documentaries might use reenactments, very few look as polished or aesthetically mature as those in *The Thin Blue Line*. In addition, the reenactments play an important role in structuring Morris's investigation into the Adams murder trial and cueing the audience to significant details and problems in the interview testimony.

Structure

The structure of *The Thin Blue Line* is significantly different from *Gates of Heaven* and *Vernon, Florida*. Morris's first two films employ an associative structure that requires the viewer to locate topical and thematic connections between different sequences. *The Thin Blue Line* is more reliant on a narrative structure, focusing on Randall Dale Adams's trial and conviction for the murder of Officer Wood. Morris's use of a narrative structure does not mean that the spectator is effortlessly guided through the story, however. The viewer must reassemble the chronology of events, fill in gaps in the story, and sift through a flood of information about the case, some of which is more reliable than others.

The Thin Blue Line starts with Adams's arrival into Dallas. After the opening credits, we see a series of buildings in downtown Dallas. Adams remembers, "We got into Dallas on a Thursday night. Friday morning, while I'm eating eggs and drinking coffee, I get a good job."[15] Morris also introduces David Harris, who describes how he ran away from home with a couple of firearms and a stolen car. Adams's and Harris's stories then converge as they describe their first meeting. Adams recalls getting picked up by Harris after running out of gas and Harris describes buying beer and going to a movie with Adams. The film continues with a dramatic re-creation of Officer Wood's murder and then the arrest and interrogation of Adams, who remembers intense police intimidation. A reenactment of the interrogation illustrates Adams's testimony, which is then contradicted by the detectives running the interrogation. One of these detectives remembers, "I had what I'd call a casual, friendly conversation with him to start with to try to size him up."

We can see a chronological account here, beginning with Adams's arrival in Dallas and continuing through his arrest and interrogation by police. The overall shape of the film follows this model, as we hear testimony about the continuing investigation into the murder and then Adams's trial, his eventual conviction, and the subsequent appeals. Morris often highlights this chronology through the use of cues in the interview testimony. For example, appellate attorney Melvyn Carson Bruder describes Adams's appeal: "When the Court of Criminal Appeals of Texas voted nine-zero against us, I was a little upset about that. I felt we: A, should have won; and B, certainly shouldn't have been slapped so hard with the unanimous decision against us." Don Metcalfe, the judge in the original trial, reiterates the Texas appeals court decision and also reports the subsequent Supreme Court decision: "Our highest state appellate court, the Court of Criminal Appeals in Austin, affirmed the case nine to nothing, and then it was reversed by the United States Supreme Court eight to one." In this sequence, both interview subjects provide a clear account of the progression in Adams's appeal process, as their agreement on the appellate court decision reinforces the chronological link between the testimonies.

Within the larger chronological structure in *The Thin Blue Line*, Morris shuffles the events in the story and returns to the same event a number of times. Table 2.1 shows a sequence from the beginning of the film, starting with the first account of Officer Wood's murder. Looking at the "events in

TABLE 2.1. □ Event Repetition in *The Thin Blue Line*

Plot	Description	Event in Reality
1. Murder of Officer Wood	A reenactment of the murder, followed by images of Wood before and after he died.	1
2. Adams's interrogation	Adams and the police provide conflicting accounts of the interrogation, which includes reenactments of the interrogation.	5
3. Murder of Officer Wood	Police describe the murder, adding that there was a good chance Wood was going to let the driver go with a warning.	1
4. Search for the murderer	Police describe the search for the culprit; they look for the criminal's car.	2
5. David Harris found in Vidor, TX	Harris brags to friends about killing Officer Wood but later changes his story when confronted by police.	3
6. Harris accuses Adams of murder	Harris recounts what he told the police the night of the murder, and there is another reenactment of the murder.	4, 1
7. Adams describes what happened	Adams recounts what happened the night Officer Wood was shot, and we have another reenactment, this time of Adams and Harris watching a movie at a drive-in.	1
8. Adams's interrogation	Adams describes the interrogation after they bring in a stenographer, who types up a statement that Adams eventually signs.	5

reality," we can see that there is some chronological progression here (see plot 3–6), but Morris also complicates this by rearranging the events. For instance, Morris inserts an account of Adams's interrogation early in the sequence (see plot 2) and returns to it at the end of sequence as well. In addition, we return to the scene of the murder three different times, again preventing a strict chronology in the film.

We can find similar ruptures in this chronological account throughout

The Thin Blue Line. There are a total of three reenactments of the interrogation scene and eight reenactments of the shooting scene in the film, returning us again and again to the same moments in the story. We also flash back to Harris's childhood, very much outside the chronological time line of the murder and trial, as he remembers the death of his brother and reflects on the psychological impact of that event.

Despite the reflexive readings of such diversions from chronology, this kind of structure is not unusual for documentaries. For example, Chip Selby's *Reasonable Doubt* (1988) is a documentary about the assassination of John F. Kennedy. After describing the events leading up to and after the assassination, the film returns again and again to the details of the murder, consulting different experts who complicate the "single bullet theory" proposed by the Warren Commission. Even Ken Burns's conventional *Huey Long* (1985), which chronicles the life of the famous Louisiana politician, rearranges the chronology of Long's life (e.g., the film begins with a reflection on the end of Long's life).

There are several reasons for Morris's deviation from a strict chronological account in *The Thin Blue Line*. First, there is a dramatic function to the structure of *The Thin Blue Line*, as it is a movie intended to stimulate interest and entertain. Second, *The Thin Blue Line* is not merely a *report* of Adams's trial but also an *investigation* into the details of the case. As with *Reasonable Doubt*, pausing, reflecting, and evaluating claims is central to the narrative. Finally, this approach to structure helps highlight the subjective elements of the testimony, which we will examine later in the chapter.

The beginning of the film establishes some of the dramatic functions of the narrative. The first few minutes of *The Thin Blue Line* fulfills the formal function of the traditional narrative beginning, in which "an initial 'steady' state . . . is violated and must be set right."[16] Adams establishes this steady state in the first lines of the film, describing how he arrived in Dallas, got a good job, and things were generally going well. The introduction of David Harris acts as the violation of this state that leads us into the first reenactment of the murder. The beginning thus sets the dramatic core of the film into motion and cues the viewer to some of the important questions raised in the film, such as, Who killed Officer Wood?

Morris positions the viewer as a detective in *The Thin Blue Line*. The audience must scrutinize the evidence presented to answer the questions surrounding the death of Officer Wood. As the visual style of the film evokes a film noir aesthetic, the narrative structure of the film drives home the connection with the crime film. David Bordwell provides a useful account of the detective narrative in his *Narration in the Fiction Film*, and many features overlap with *The Thin Blue Line*.[17] For instance, Bordwell argues, "The fundamental narrational characteristic of the detective tale is that the syuzhet [plot] withholds crucial events occurring in the 'crime' portion of the fabula [story]. The syuzhet may conceal the motive, or the planning, or the commission of the crime (an act which includes the identity of the criminal), or aspects of several of these."[18]

The Thin Blue Line withholds not only the facts of the murder, including the identity of the murderer, but also some of the details surrounding the crime. For instance, the film does not reveal why Adams signed a statement saying that he did not remember anything while driving on Inwood Road, where the murder took place. Highlighted by a reenactment of the statement being typed, this is an important piece of evidence that puts Adam's credibility into question. In his own account of the trial in his book *Adams v. Texas*, Adams explains that he did not understand the importance of this intersection and decided to sign the statement because he was incredibly tired.[19] Morris withholds any explanation of Adams's decision in the film.

We can begin to understand the purpose of such gaps by looking at their dramatic function in the film. Bordwell writes that the detective film "justifies its gaps and retardations by controlling knowledge, self-consciousness, and communicativeness. The genre aims to create curiosity about past story events (e.g., who killed whom), suspense about upcoming events, and surprise with respect to unexpected disclosures about either story or syuzhet. To promote all three emotional states, the narration must limit the viewer's knowledge."[20] *The Thin Blue Line* employs restricted narration to tap into these emotions. We are, for instance, curious about who killed Officer Wood and shocked when the prosecution introduces three surprise witnesses.

Let us look at the scene in *The Thin Blue Line* in which the prosecution reveals the three new witnesses to better understand specifically how this works. At this point in the film, there are indications that Adams is innocent but still lingering uncertainty about whether he was actually convicted of the crime. No interviewee up to this point has explicitly mentioned the conviction, and both Adams and Harris appear to be speaking from a prison location. Adams finishes discussing Officer Teresa Turko's testimony, in which he convincingly points out the inconsistencies in her statements. Edith James then expresses her optimism about the case: "Friday afternoon—I think it was Good Friday—we came back into the courtroom that afternoon and we were sort of elated because we thought, well, he's gonna walk. And there's nothing really in that evidence, there's just a little David Harris, and nobody believes him." Adams's and James's testimonies set up a hopeful outlook on Adams's chances of beating the charge.

James then quickly undermines this expectation as she describes the sudden appearance of the new witnesses: "Mrs. Miller got on the stand that last afternoon. And she said, 'that's the man—I saw that man! I saw Randall Adams's face just right after . . .' She said, 'I saw the gun sticking out of the car when he shot that police officer, and that's the man.' And she waved her finger right toward Randall Adams. She's the one that got him convicted." This moment would not have the same dramatic punch if there were not gaps in the narrative. That is, the dramatic value of this moment would have been lost if we had already known that Adams had been convicted, if it was already clear that the introduction of three witnesses were responsible for Adams's conviction, or if the film had not raised expectations about Adams's exoneration.

The stylized reenactments in *The Thin Blue Line* also have an important dramatic function. First, it is important to note that they are not completely removed from reality. There are certain elements of the reenactments that are true to reality: a patrol car pulls over a blue car; Officer Wood steps out of the patrol car and approaches the blue car; Wood is shot several times; and a blue car speeds away. These are all historical facts and are depicted without variation in the reenactments.

In addition, the third reenactment in the film is completely reliable, as Investigator Dale Holt describes the scenario of Officer Wood's murder: "[Officer Wood] got out of the car and walked up. And before he got to the window where the driver was, he was in the right position: this man just turned around and just pop, pop, pop, with a little small-caliber pistol. The first shot hit him in the arm. He had his flashlight. It hit the flashlight, as I recall, and went into his arm. And the next one hit him right in the chest." In the accompanying images, we see a reenactment of these events without revealing the identity of the shooter. This sequence of events is never put into question. Our understanding of the rest of the film is dependent on our trust that these events happened the way that Holt describes them.

Occasionally the reenactments are *more* reliable than the testimony in the film. For instance, Dale Holt describes what Officer Turko remembered from the night of the murder after being hypnotized: "She couldn't remember anything particularly about the car. She remembered getting a malt, and they'd stopped in the fast food. It was a 'Whataburger.'" In the reenactments of the murder, however, we see a reflection of a Burger King sign in the windshield of the patrol car. Here, the reenactments correct what is a mistake in the testimony, as Wood and Turko did indeed stop at a Burger King before the incident.[21] Morris decided to reenact the truth instead of what Holt believed was the truth, in part because "in a documentary film, where an implicit claim is made about the relationship between the movie and reality, faithfulness to the facts is a central issue."[22]

Morris also employs the reenactments to illustrate frequently problematic memories of past events. Michael Randell, one of the surprise witnesses in the Adams case, describes what he saw the night of the murder. Randell boasts that he has developed "something like total recall. I don't forget places, things, or streets." However, he struggles to remember the details of the night: "The officer, he walked up to the vehicle. He had walked up. His car was, let me see, I don't know if it was behind or in front, but I knew he had him pulled over, and he was up to the car. I think he was up to the car. Let me think. Yeah he was up to the car, and I was going by, he had to have been up to the car." During his testimony, Morris cuts away to another reenactment of the murder scene. In accord with Randell's statements, we see two men in the car, although we know (or soon find out) that this was not the case on the night of the murder. David Harris was in the car by himself when he shot Officer Wood. So here the reenactment is illustrating a falsehood. Whether it was an honest mistake or a deliberate lie, we see a reenactment of an account that never happened.

The discordant relationship between the reenactment and reality again has a dramatic function. After Randall's interview, Dallas homicide detective Jackie Johnson says, "We have three people that testified and identified [Adams] as positively being the driver at the time that Wood was walking up right beside the car. So we know that he was the driver, from the witnesses, and we also know that it was the driver that shot Officer Wood, coming from his partner." A central concern in the film is how Adams was convicted of a crime he did not commit. The Randell sequence helps answer that question by highlighting one of the most important elements of his flawed testimony: there were two men in the car when Officer Wood was shot.

Morris also repeats reenactments to highlight important elements in the murder investigation and raise questions about reliability of the interview testimony. In the film's iconic milkshake sequence, Morris provides two different reenactments of the same event. The first accompanies Dale Holt's testimony about proper police protocol when they pull over another vehicle: "Procedure, when there's a two person unit, when either one approached the car, the other positions himself to the right rear, to where they can watch all the activity in the car. And then if the man on the left to the driver gets into trouble, the partner's in a position to help." On the image track, we see a reenactment of Officer Turko getting out of the patrol car and positioning herself at the back of the car.

Holt then continues with another scenario: "Speculation at the time was that his partner was sitting in the car. That's where the discrepancies were: just a matter of time, and whether or not she was out of the car, completely out of the car, or partially out of the car, or just sitting in there with the door closed." We again see a reenactment, but this time Turko is inside the patrol car sipping a fast-food milkshake. After gunshots on the audio track, Turko throws the milkshake out of the window and it splatters on the ground. The sequence highlights the image of the milkshake as we see, in separate shots, the milkshake thrown out the window, flying through the air, and landing on the ground, and later a diagram of its place next to the patrol car (see figure 2.2).

The reenactments illustrate two possible scenarios of what happened the night of the murder. The visual emphasis on the milkshake is helpful in understanding these reenactments beyond mere "illustration," and it has an important dramatic function in the film. The spilled milkshake is an indication that Turko was in the patrol car when Officer Wood was murdered. If she was in the car, then her description of the occupants in Harris's stolen car, which helped get Adams convicted, would be untrustworthy. The milkshake thus functions as a symbol of Turko's unreliability and, more broadly, the mistakes, deceptions, and confusions surrounding Adams's conviction.

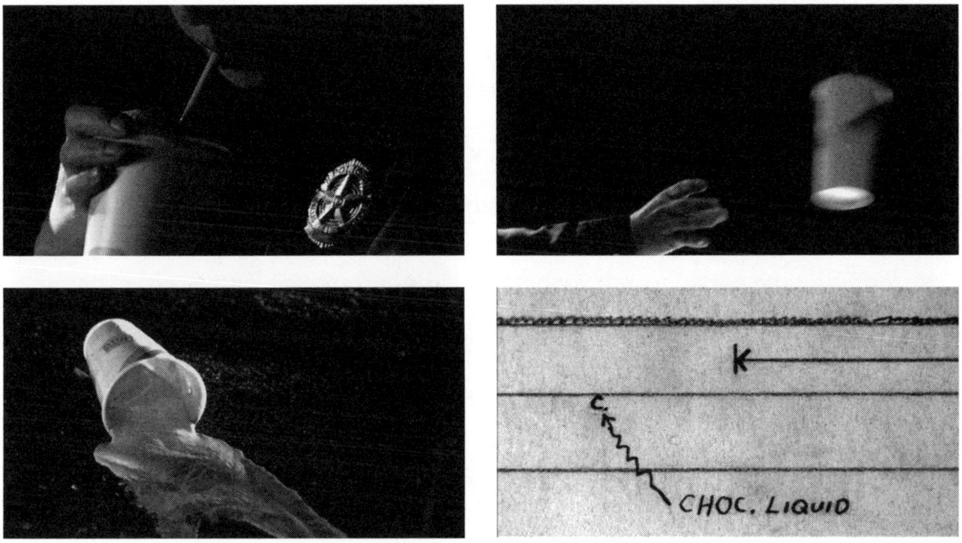

FIGURE 2.2. □ *The Thin Blue Line*

Adams describes Turko's change in testimony later in the film: "She went through weeks in internal affairs; when she comes out, her testimony changes. She goes in saying one thing, she comes out saying another. Something happened. What? 'Oh well, we refreshed her memory.'" After this, we see a repetition of the shot in the reenactment where Turko's hand throws the milkshake, reinforcing the connection between the milkshake image and Turko's unreliability.

The stylistic features of these reenactments also help foreground their narrative function in the film. For instance, the use of close framings, slow motion, and the black background in the milkshake sequence aid in directing the viewer's attention to the importance of the milkshake. Morris uses these kinds of techniques throughout the film to highlight significant elements of the story.

Many scholars analyzing *The Thin Blue Line* focus exclusively on abstract issues related to truth and objectivity. These analyses often lose sight of the fact that the film's structure and style are organized to communicate narrative information in an engaging manner.[23] The degree to which the film assumes narrational authority in communicating this information also relates to the film's voice.

Voice

Our engagement with *The Thin Blue Line* is, to some extent, dependent on the ways in which it asks and answers questions throughout the course of the film. If the beginning of the film revealed all of the details about the murder, it would not be nearly as engaging a story. We can imagine a film that begins with stating Adams's innocence for the crime and then spends the rest of running time pursuing and condemning those responsible (the prosecutor, the judge, the three witnesses, etc.). This is in fact a common approach for documentaries in which an injustice has occurred. For instance, Michael Moore adopts a similar structure in *Roger and Me* (1989).

The Thin Blue Line instead pursues questions about Officer Wood's murder throughout the course of the film. A central "what" question in the film is, What happened the night Officer Wood was killed? There are hints of David Harris's involvement in the killing throughout the film. Much of the physical evidence points to his guilt, for instance, and his behavior after the murder suggests that he is a person inclined toward criminal activity. At the end of the film, this central question is answered. When Morris asks him about Adams's innocence, Harris replies, "I'm sure he is . . . 'cause I'm the one who knows."

The settling of this central "what" question consequently fixes the truth of a number of other "what" questions that the film raises. Once we know that Adams's testimony about what happened the night of the murder is more reliable than Harris's, we then generally trust the time line of events described by Adams. By the end of the film, for example, we understand that the events described by both Adams and Harris took place two hours earlier than in the police's time line.

The ways in which *The Thin Blue Line* clearly answers these narrative questions raised throughout the film marks the presence of a formal voice in the film. Morris's intention is to ultimately explain to the audience who is responsible for the murder of Officer Wood, as Morris himself explains: "To me in *The Thin Blue Line*, there's a truth of who shot the cop. The Dallas cop stops a car without headlights, walks up to the driver's window, and the driver pulls a gun from underneath the seat and shoots him five times. There are lots of recherché possibilities, but it was either Randall Adams or David Harris."[24] The film leaves no doubt as to Harris's guilt, which is further supported by the film's role in facilitating Adams's release from jail.

Despite these elements of a formal voice, *The Thin Blue Line* is ultimately an open-voice documentary. For many of the questions raised, the film does not provide a definitive, reliable answer. Morris instead presents a complex network of answers that are not neatly contextualized or have a strong sense of closure. This is true of some of the "what" questions in the film, such as if Officer Turko was inside or outside of the patrol car when the murder took place. The film introduces both possibilities and represents them a number of times through reenactments. Although this is an important detail in determining the identity of Officer Wood's murderer, Morris does not provide a clear answer. He instead leaves the question open.

The Thin Blue Line is interested in not only *what* happened the night of the murder but also *why* it happened, a concern that Morris establishes early in the film. After describing his meeting with David Harris, Adams asks, "Why did I meet this kid? I don't know. Why did I run out of gas at that time? I don't know. But it happened. It happened." While these specific questions are not primary to the film's narrative, the question of *why* is of central importance. We are asked to think about not just *what happened the night of the murder* but also *why did the police choose to arrest Adams and not Harris*; *why did Mrs. Miller testify against Adams*; and *why did Harris accuse Adams of murder?*

The *why* questions are in some ways more complicated than the *what* questions in the film. For example, why did Emily Miller testify against Adams? This, as with most questions posed in the film, has a complex answer. Edith James, Adams's attorney, describes how Emily Miller and her husband expressed interest in the reward money offered by the police. In addition, the Miller's daughter was in jail at the time, and Dennis White suggests that her testimony was given in exchange for her eventual release. The film also presents a psychological answer. Shortly after her introduction, Miller discusses her desire to be a detective: "When I was a kid, I always wanted to be a detective all the time because I watched all the detective shows on TV." Morris cuts to scenes from the *Boston Blackie* series in which a woman helps Blackie apprehend a criminal. Miller's personal desire to be involved in murder mysteries helps answer the question of why she became involved in the Adams case.

The description of this approach to these questions as "open" does not imply that their answers are less important to the film than the formal voice answers, or that the above-described possibilities are untrustworthy. The difference is that, instead of clearly establishing one definite answer as with the formal voice, "the open voice *shows*, *provokes*, and *explores*."[25] In the case of Miller's motives for testifying, we are not given the same kind of answer as "David Harris murdered Officer Wood." The film provides options to examine, contemplate, and connect Miller's motivations with other elements in the film.

Morris uses the open voice throughout *The Thin Blue Line*. The film provides multiple answers, perspectives, and possibilities for a number of important questions such as, Why did David Harris shoot Officer Wood and commit all of the other crimes throughout his life? Randall Adams and Dennis White both suggest that Harris has troubling mental problems. Morris gives Harris himself a chance to answer this question toward the end of the film. Reflecting on his childhood, Harris tells the story of his brother's death when he was young. He describes his brother as "daddy's favorite" while Harris did not receive the same kind of acceptance. Harris concludes, "Maybe a lot of the things I did when I was younger was an attempt to get back at him for the way he treated me. But I wasn't doing nothing but hurting myself."

At first blush, this might seem like a plausible explanation for Harris's behavior. It is the only attempt in the film to seriously look at Harris's personal history and to trace the origins of his criminal behavior. The explanation is laced with problems, however. Not only has Harris been proven to be an unreliable witness throughout the film, but also his statement "I wasn't doing nothing but hurting myself" is clearly untrue. Harris has hurt many people throughout his life, including Officer Wood and Randall Dale Adams. In what might have become a moment of self-discovery instead turns into an illustration of Harris's self-delusion, leaving open the *why* question regarding Harris's crimes. This does not necessarily mean that Harris's insight into his past is to be rejected outright, but it strips Harris of the ability to act as a formal voice in answering this particular question. Morris's own characterization of Harris echoes this open approach to his testimony: "Harris has always for me remained an enigma. I wish I could say I had some easy explanation for his behavior."[26]

Morris avoids many of the formal-voice features we would expect in a film about a murder. For instance, we do not have an omniscient narrator informing us of Adams's innocence, nor do we have interview subjects who are completely reliable in their account of Officer Wood's murder. It is the responsibility of the viewer to sift through a barrage of differing accounts and problematic claims in order to piece together the facts of the case. In this way, the viewer is put in the position of a detective and must reach conclusions about the questions raised in the film without any explicit instruction. While the film eventually answers some questions, such as the identity of Officer Wood's murderer, it leaves many others open.

The Thin Blue Line is not just a film about a murdered police officer but also a story about a wrongful conviction. At the same time as the film establishes Adams's innocence, it also asks the viewer to contemplate the reasons Adams was charged and eventually found guilty of murder. Understanding Adams's unjust conviction is in large part a process of discovering errors and inaccuracies from the very beginning of the story. Part of what makes *The Thin Blue Line* a unique documentary investigation is that it does not suggest Adams's conviction was the result of a conspiracy on the part of the police, along the line of the conspiracy orchestrated by the Warren Commission in *Reasonable Doubt*. Morris instead suggests that Adams's conviction is the product of convenience, miscalculation, and self-deception.

Raising questions about the reliability of the interviews aids in Morris's examination of what is a central thematic interest in *The Thin Blue Line*: the particular ways in which the interview subjects understand the world around them. As with *Gates of Heaven* and *Vernon, Florida*, Morris wants to explore questions about subjectivity and the limits of human knowledge. *The Thin Blue Line* is different because such questions are focused on the specifics of the Adams case, but the larger thematic interest is similar.

Morris relies on different strategies to foreground the subjective elements in the testimony throughout *The Thin Blue Line*. As Morris establishes a narrative framework in the film, departures from the narrative help to signal moments of subjective reflection. Elements of the film's visual style are also important in underscoring the individual perspectives of the interviews, including the use of found footage and reenactments. Again, there are other functions of these narrative and stylistic features of the film, but their relationship to the subjective taps into one of the film's main thematic concerns.

Throughout *The Thin Blue Line*, narrative digressions temporarily stray from the Adams case, and these digressions help cue us to the moments when the more personal is on display. Edith James and Dennis White discuss their frustrations with the Adams trial, for example, and Morris cuts to the first interview with Judge Don Metcalfe. Instead of talking about the case, Metcalfe reflects on the relationship between law enforcement and his family history. Metcalfe's discussion of his family provides some insight into his personal life and, more importantly, shifts our attention to his particular view of the world: "I grew up in a family where I was taught a great respect for law enforcement." This "respect" for the police later returns as Metcalfe later admits to welling up when District Attorney Doug Metcalfe gives his final argument about "the thin blue line of police that separates the public from anarchy." We can read this emotional bond with the police as having an effect on the Adams case, as James and White earlier complain about Metcalfe refusing to admit important pieces of evidence.

Metcalfe then describes how his father, an FBI agent, was at the Biograph Theater the night John Dillinger was killed: "He told me that the 'Woman in Red,' she had on an orange dress. This is trivia. Okay? It looked red under the lights. He said it was really orange. So the Lady in Red—she got to be known as the Lady in Red that fingered Dillinger—he said, 'It was really the Lady in Orange.'" Again, this is clearly a digression from the Adams case, as even Metcalfe himself describes the Dillinger story as "trivia."

Within the context of the trial, however, the Dillinger tale carries a thematic significance. It is a story about an error of identification, and one that people perpetuated for decades. The arrest and eventual conviction of Randall Adams is similar, although clearly not as trivial as the "Lady in Red" story. To drive home this connection, Morris cuts to a newspaper headline that reads, "Witness tells of seeing officer killed" at the end of Metcalfe's story.

Part of the scene's irony is that Metcalfe does not recognize the possible connections between the Dillinger case and the Adams trial. For instance, the police have misidentified David Harris, the boy who "fingered" Adams, as innocent. In addition, as with the "Lady in Red," the police sent Harris back home after they got what they needed.[27] The danger of misidentification, which Metcalfe himself introduces, is apparently trumped by his emotional connection to law enforcement.

Morris uses this digression from the Adams case to highlight some of Metcalfe's underlying beliefs and attitudes. There is also an implicit criticism here, as Morris uses irony to underscore an inconsistency in Metcalfe's point of view. Similar to *Gates of Heaven* and *Vernon, Florida*, there is a move to not only foreground the subjectivity of the interviews but also contextualize, and even criticize, it.

Disruptions in narrative development are not the only way in which Morris foregrounds the subjective. Beyond providing interesting visual material, fictional footage also cues us to the subjective elements of the testimony. Perhaps the most notable instance is during Emily Miller's interview, in which Morris uses clips from the 1952 television series *Boston Blackie*. After Edith James attributes Adams's conviction to Miller's testimony, we see Miller for the first time: "When I was a kid I used to want to be a detective all the time because I used to watch all the detective shows on TV. When I was a kid they used to show these movies with *Boston Blackie*, and he always had a woman with him. And I wanted to be a wife of a detective or be a detective, so I always was watching detective stories." In the accompanying *Boston Blackie* clip, a detective pursues a criminal with the help of a female. Miller is actively fantasizing about being a part of this fictional world. Clearly this has to do less with historical facts than with the personal desires of the interview subject.

Much like the Metcalfe example, the film illustrates and critically evaluates these subjective elements. Not only is Miller's testimony eventually revealed to be faulty, but also even her fantasy is subjected to scrutiny. Morris presents Miller's desire to become a detective and solve crimes ironically, and comically. Instead of solving the murder, she instead commits an offense by falsely accusing Adams. Miller is blissfully unaware of her own participation in the crimes, however: "It's always happening to me, everywhere I go, you know, lot of times there's killing or anything, even around my house. Wherever. And I'm always looking or getting involved, you know, find out who did it, or what's going on." Miller is so captivated by the idea of solving crimes that she mistakes her fantasies for reality, and the use of the fictional film footage helps cue us to this confusion.

Morris's fictional found footage in *The Thin Blue Line* does not constitute a dramatic break from the documentary tradition. Other documentaries at the time not only include fictional footage but also use it to critically examine subjective attitudes. For instance, *Heaven* (1987), a documentary directed by Diane Keaton, employs a flood of fictional footage, including clips from *Metropolis* (1927), *The Green Pastures* (1936), *The Horn Blows at Midnight* (1945), and *A Matter of Life and Death* (1946), to illustrate and critique different ideas about heaven, religion, and the afterlife.[28] We can also locate this practice in earlier documentaries. For instance, Academy Award–winning *Hearts and Minds* (1974) uses a musical number from the 1943 film *This Is the Army* to characterize the excessively patriotic, naive, and somewhat arrogant mindset of Americans after World War II.

In the above examples, the fictional status of the footage helps to cue us to the subjective elements in the interview testimony. The fictional status of the reenactments in *The Thin Blue Line* works in the same way. That is, it is important that we recognize the reenactments as "fictional," because, as Morris himself attests, "they're illustrations of what people claimed had happened."[29] The highly stylized visuals in the reenactments are not designed to blur the distinction between fact and fiction but in fact rely on the distinction to cue the audience to the subjective elements of the sequences.

About eighty minutes into the film, David Harris describes how he was a scared sixteen-year-old kid when the police directed his testimony to help convict Randall Adams of the murder. Another stylized reenactment, this time of a movie theater concession stand, plays on the image track. We see a series of images from the concession stand, including close shots of the popcorn and a few close-ups of the clock behind the counter.

At this point in the film, we understand that the identity of the murderer is connected to the time at which Harris and Adams were at the movie theater. If they were there earlier in the evening, this would corroborate Adams's version of the events. If they watched the movies at around midnight, this would support the police's theory that Adams shot Officer Wood. Harris discusses the importance of the time in his testimony: "Police give you the time of this and the time this happened, whatever, and you just correlate from those events, you know. You just estimate from that event what time it was. You don't know. You're taking a guess." On the image track, a popcorn popper is in the foreground, through which a clock shows twelve o'clock, although it is difficult to see because the glass is smudged. The film then cuts to a shot in front of the stand, and the clock again clearly indicates twelve o'clock; then there is a close-up of the popcorn, and it's back again to the same shot in front of the counter (see figure 2.3). Harris continues, "Police tell you, 'Well, it was 12:30 when this crime happened. What time did you leave the movie?' I know it was sometime around midnight." Morris cuts to three shots of the clock, with successively closer framings on the clock's

FIGURE 2.3. □ *The Thin Blue Line*

FIGURE 2.4. □ *The Thin Blue Line*

hands placed on the twelve, and then another close-up of the popcorn (see figure 2.4).

There is a narrative function to the reenactment images in this sequence. Morris's close framings of the clock help to cue us to the importance of the time in the murder case. In addition, the clock is visible in six out of the eight shots and is the exclusive object in three of them. This redundancy is critical as there is not an authoritative voice stressing the importance of the time line to the investigation.

The reenactment images also function to highlight David Harris's testimony about the night of the murder. The clock in the reenactment is initially at twelve o'clock, which is the time to which Harris testified but not the actual time they were at the theater. We should not understand this as strictly subjective. Harris did not *believe* that he was at the theater at midnight but rather suggested this in order to evade responsibility for the murder. This element is an enactment of Harris's testimony, instead of his subjective belief.

There is a subjective element in the sequence, however, that is set up by the first shot. Instead of merely presenting the clock at twelve o'clock, Morris first shows it through the smudged glass of the popcorn machine. Morris later returns to this popcorn imagery as he cuts to very close shots of the popped kernels, highlighting the tactile texture of the popcorn. Why does he emphasize the popcorn? It in part gives us insight into Harris's own perspective at the time, which Harris characterizes as "just a young, dumb kid." A sixteen-year-old boy at a movie theater would be more focused on the popcorn in the concession stand than on the time of day.

This subjective priority is manifest in Morris's reenactment compositions. The emphasis on the popcorn helps cue us that the sequence is illustrating not merely "what happened" but also to some extent Harris's frame of mind the night of the murder. The stylistic elements of the sequence, including the tight close-ups, the obstructed faces of the people, and the pulsating music, all contribute to a dreamlike quality of the reenactment.

There is also a subtle shift in the time on the clock as the sequence progresses. After describing how he told the police that they left the movie "around midnight," Harris then qualifies the statement: "It might have been before then. I don't know. I didn't have a watch on." Morris cuts to a television schedule that lists *The Carol Burnett Show* starting at nine o'clock and then cuts back to the first shot of the popcorn machine, but this time the clock is clearly visible through the glass, and the time is 9:10 p.m. (see figure 2.5).

The instability of the time on the clock distances the sequence from any notion of objective reporting about the night in question, but it does not remove it from reality all together. At this point in the film, we trust Adams's version of the night's events, which places them at the movie theater much earlier in the night. The switch back to 9:10 p.m. is thus a change that brings us closer to reality, which is reinforced by the clarity with which we can now see the new image clock.

FIGURE 2.5. □ *The Thin Blue Line*

The complex relationship between the error in Harris's testimony and the film's handling of that flaw provides insight into the larger thematics of the film. In a traditional social issues documentary, you often have a variety of trustworthy interview subjects who provide authoritative testimony on a particular topic, as well as a select number of dissenting voices who are clearly positioned as incorrect. In this context, *The Thin Blue Line* adopts a unique approach. No interview subject speaks as an authority, as the film raises questions about the reliability of most of the testimony. Returning to the above "popcorn scene," Harris eventually reflects on the ways in which

Doug Metcalfe coached his in-court testimony: "I didn't really ponder on it, but he was deceiving the jury, see. He wanted to deceive justice." Harris does not seem to realize that he himself was also deceiving the jury, deceiving justice. At the same time as Harris provides an important clue to how the police and prosecution altered the evidence against Adams, he also exposes his own troubling self-deception about his role in Adams's conviction.

Morris highlights these thematic threads in the film through the interplay of the interview testimony and the cutaway images in *The Thin Blue Line*. After establishing these thematic connections to the images, such as that of the popcorn, the milkshake, and the clock, Morris sometimes repeats these visuals and they develop into a series of motifs interwoven in the design of the film. After a series of repetitions, the image of the popcorn acquires significance beyond the specific disagreement about when Harris and Adams were at the movie theater. The popcorn becomes a symbol of self-deception as well as innocence. The milkshake not only is a clue to whether Officer Turko was inside the police cruiser at the time of the murder but also develops into a visualization of confusion, dishonesty, and absurdity. These visual motifs are thus not merely at the service of the testimony but also gestures that highlight the undercurrent of absurdities, mistakes, and deceptions throughout *The Thin Blue Line*.

In concert with the visual motifs, the repetitive nature of Philip Glass's music establishes and develops certain narrative and thematic relationships. For instance, Morris uses the same musical motif with both "milkshake" sequences. As noted earlier, we first see the reenacted milkshake when the police describe how Officer Turko was either inside or outside of the patrol car when Officer Wood was murdered. The second occurrence is after Adams identifies the mistakes and inconsistencies in Turko's testimony and, instead of an entire reenactment of the murder scene, Morris repeats a short shot of the milkshake throw. Because of the fragmentary nature of the second milkshake shot, the repetition of the musical motif helps identify the two sequences as the same event. More significantly, the same musical motif underscores the importance of this action. If Turko was in the patrol car at the time of the murder, which the milkshake indicates, then her testimony identifying Adams at the scene of the murder is not reliable. The milkshake is consequently connected to the unreliable, and the foregrounding of both the milkshake image and the accompanying musical motif highlight the subjective elements, in particular the errors and deceptions, in the story.

Morris's interest in subjectivity is not completely new to documentary filmmaking. Michael Renov argues that as early as the late 1950s, Jean Rouch "had begun to explore the power of the camera to induce the display of subjectivity," an exploration that is in opposition to the traditional use of documentary as "scientific instrument."[30] Continuing through contemporary documentaries, this interest in subjectivity often manifests itself as a kind of filmic confessional, in which reality is grounded by the personal and experiential.

Within the context of other documentaries in the late 1980s, *The Thin Blue Line* stands out as groundbreaking in the ways in which it handles these subjective elements of the testimony. As we have discussed here and in the previous chapter, Morris seeks to not merely illustrate or express such subjective elements but also evaluate them. This is an important point at which Morris's films do break with tradition. Morris is interested in critically examining the very personal ways in which people view and understand the world and finding different ways of extracting themes about the nature and limits of human knowledge.

■ Reception and Ethics

Documentary filmmaking is fraught with ethical dilemmas, and any approach to documentary film will likely bring with it certain ethical questions. The same elements that set Morris's films apart from others also provoke objections about the ethics of his approach. We have already examined some of the problems Morris encountered with his first two films, and several of these problems persist. *The Thin Blue Line* also faces a set of ethical issues that Morris did not encounter in either *Gates of Heaven* or *Vernon, Florida*, in part because it is dealing with the murder of one man and the imprisonment of another.

Fixing the identity of Officer Wood's murderer is an important element in the overall narrative structure of *The Thin Blue Line*, and the resolution of this question also has an ethical dimension. While Morris's first two films dealt with issues such as the relocation of dead animals, *The Thin Blue Line* is engaged with a much more serious question, in which a man's freedom is at stake. There is consequently an ethical responsibility to take seriously, if not definitely establish, the identity of Wood's murderer. Although Morris withholds this information at the beginning of *The Thin Blue Line*, he does eventually make it clear to the viewer that Davis Harris killed Officer Wood.

Morris acknowledges the significance of the factual claims in *The Thin Blue Line*: "I actually think of myself as an odd activist. I was very much an activist in *The Thin Blue Line*. I was in no way indifferent to Randall Adams's situation, his mistaken conviction in the murder of Dallas police officer Robert Wood. I believe there was a terrible miscarriage of justice. People get confused about this sort of thing. I remember one Dallas reporter saying to me, 'If you had just made this "straight" documentary, Randall Adams would have gotten out a lot sooner, instead of delaying everything by shooting these re-enactments, using a score by Philip Glass, et cetera, et cetera.' Yeah, maybe. I made the movie I wanted to make, and at the same time, I did what I believe was a really, really scrupulous investigation into that murder."[31]

The presence of this "activist" dimension in *The Thin Blue Line* does not mean that the film is immune from ethical objections. Dave Kehr of the *Chicago Tribune* writes, "At the same time that Morris is driven to dramatize the material—to turn it into a parable of cruel destiny—he also seems to be condescending to it, finding a smug, hipster's comedy in the perceived gaucheries of the Southwestern characters."[32] This criticism about Morris's patronizing attitude toward his subjects is similar to the reviews of *Gates of Heaven* and *Vernon, Florida*.

The previous chapter argued that the connection with ethnographic filmmaking is informative in understanding some of the ethical concerns with Morris's first two films. The relationship between ethnography and *The Thin Blue Line* may appear to be weaker than these earlier films, in which a common interest or profession (*Gates of Heaven*) and shared environment (*Vernon, Florida*) creates a sense of community. Some of these more biographical elements are missing in *The Thin Blue Line*. For instance, Dennis White explains how the people in Vidor characterized him as an "Eastern-educated, civil liberties attorney," but the film never communicates the specifics of White's personal history.

Morris does connect the people in *The Thin Blue Line* as participants in a society of convenience. Emily Miller understands the world through her delusional detective fantasy, Michael Randell brags about his skill of "total recall" despite failing to remember most of the details about the murder, and David Harris criticizes but fails to take proper responsibility for the false conviction of Randall Dale Adams. Throughout the film, Morris is able to create a subculture of limited perspective that ties together the various participants in the film.

Morris actively foregrounds unreliable and mistaken testimony within this subculture of convenience and develops it into a central thematic concern of the film. It is Morris's "active" role that can be especially troubling, as he is exploiting his power as the filmmaker to highlight the flaws of the people who have willingly participated in the film. One could argue that the interview subjects have placed an implicit trust in Morris to present them fairly, if not favorably. When *The Thin Blue Line*, *Roger and Me*, or even *Hearts and Minds* present these people in a critical manner, especially those who are perceived as less knowledgeable or sophisticated, the filmmakers are open to the criticism of being condescending to their subjects and neglecting their ethical responsibilities. In addition, many of the errors in *The Thin Blue Line* are not merely misstatements or understandable lapses of memory. Morris turns a critical eye toward the fundamental ways in which these people view the world, ways that are much more personal and perhaps more sensitive than superficial errors in judgment.

Morris's use of irony and humor in *The Thin Blue Line* further intensifies the ethical concerns with the film. Kehr's characterization of the film as a "smug, hipster's comedy" touches on a larger concern that many critics have had with filmmakers such as Morris, Michael Moore, and others that incorporate a humorous tone into the critique of their subjects. It is one thing to recognize documentary subjects as misguided, but a line is conceivably crossed when they become a punch line in a documentary.

There is also a way in which one can defend Morris's approach as a more nuanced and perhaps even a more sympathetic approach to the interviews compared to a traditional "activist" documentary. *Roger and Me*, for instance, presents General Motors CEO Roger Smith as elitist, uncaring, and perhaps even cruel. Morris presents the faults of the wrongdoers in *The Thin Blue Line* in a more sympathetic manner. While most of the testimony in *The Thin Blue Line* is problematic or unreliable to some extent, no one appears consciously malicious. As with Morris's first two films, we understand the interview subjects as falling victim to a number of errors that are quite "human," from

Jackie Johnson's ironic gaffe confusing "Comet" and "Vega," to Emily Miller's deeply rooted self-deception.

Morris could have portrayed David Harris as a selfish, heartless liar who, in collusion with the police, helped send an innocent man to prison. The film is instead somewhat sympathetic toward Harris, as it reveals him to be more preoccupied or confused but not knowingly deceitful. Emily Miller, Don Metcalfe, and the others are not essentially bad people but are rather engaged in misunderstandings and self-deceptions. Importantly, no one in the film is immune from such flaws, connecting even the most troubling "wrongdoers" with the rest of the people in the film.

However, even this sympathetic reading of *The Thin Blue Line* does not resolve the ethical concerns about the film, as many of them are inherent in the nonfiction tradition as a whole. Documentary filmmakers and critics have always been concerned about the problematic power relationship between the filmmaker and the film subject. We continue to see such ethical concerns throughout the next two decades of Morris's career. For *The Thin Blue Line*, many of the possible criticisms have been tempered by the real-world effect of the film: the release of Randall Adams from prison.

3 A Brief History of Time

IN A 1992 INTERVIEW WITH David Beers of *Mother Jones* magazine, Errol Morris describes *The Thin Blue Line* as "an essay on self-deception. Not on the unknowability of truth, but on people's vested interest in avoiding the truth."[1] Throughout the film, Morris explores the ways in which his subjects' memories, fantasies, and delusions clouded the investigation into the murder of a Dallas police officer. The theme of people's troubled relationship with truth also runs throughout Morris's first two films. *Gates of Heaven* and *Vernon, Florida* feature interview subjects that struggle with the complexities of life, love, and death.

It may be surprising that Morris's fourth documentary, *A Brief History of Time*, is about Stephen Hawking. Hawking is an English physicist and cosmologist whose theoretical work has been credited with getting us closer to the truths about the universe. Hawking has made major contributions to our understanding of general relativity, the behavior of black holes, and the origin of the universe. Hawking has also become a public intellectual, writing several popular science books introducing the general public to complex cosmological theories. *A Brief History of Time* (1988) is his most popular book, selling over ten million copies.

The *Brief History of Time* project presented Morris with a number of new filmmaking conditions and problems. *A Brief History of Time* is an adaptation of a popular book, which generates expectations about the film being faithful and comprehensive. The book is also primarily about scientific concepts, whose visual representation presents different challenges than, for instance, a murder on the side of the highway.

A critical challenge for Morris involved combining Hawking's theoretical work in *A Brief History of Time* with Morris's continuing interest in investigating the limits of human knowledge. Morris locates a solution in Hawking's own biography, and for the first time uses a single human psyche as the centerpiece of this investigation. The film cues the viewer to make subtle and complex connections between Hawking's life and his theoretical work. *A Brief History of Time* ultimately uses Hawking's biography as a way to understand his scientific work, saturating Hawking's cosmological theories with his subjective engagement with the world.

■ Background

Errol Morris's career underwent a number of significant changes after the release of *The Thin Blue Line*. The critical and financial success of the film established Morris as a premier, innovative filmmaker. Morris became a member of the Academy of Motion Picture Arts and Sciences and signed with Creative Artist's Agency, a powerful Hollywood talent agency.[2] In 1989, Morris was awarded the MacArthur Fellowship "Genius Award" for "changing and expanding the notion of documentary films."[3]

Morris's newfound reputation in the film industry generated more interest in his projects. After *The Thin Blue Line*, Morris considered a number of different subjects for his next film, including a documentary about the disappearance of Einstein's brain. Morris pitched some of the ideas to Amblin Entertainment, a production company founded by Steven Spielberg, Kathleen Kennedy, and Franklin Marshall. Amblin was responsible for producing some of the most successful films in the 1980s, including E.T. (1982), *Gremlins* (1984), and *Back to the Future* (1985).

Around the same time, producer Gordon Freedman contacted Amblin about adapting Stephen Hawking's *Brief History of Time*.[4] Spielberg and Kennedy expressed interest in the *Brief History* project and thought that Errol Morris would be a good choice to direct the film. Morris agreed to the proposal and put his other projects on hold.[5]

The budget for the film was set at three million dollars. This was a large amount considering that only four documentaries prior to 1992 grossed over three million: *Imagine: John Lennon* (1988), *Roger and Me* (1989), *Madonna: Truth or Dare* (1991), and *Paris Is Burning* (1991). Out of these four, only *Truth or Dare* had a budget over three million, with *Roger and Me* costing a mere one hundred and sixty thousand dollars.[6] *The Thin Blue Line*, widely considered a breakaway hit, grossed under two million dollars.

The overwhelming success of Hawking's book was an important factor in the budget for the film. Hawking wrote *A Brief History of Time* as a popular science book designed to explain some of the most important concepts in cosmology, including the origin of the universe, string theory, and black holes. The book was published in 1988 and quickly became a huge commercial success. It spent a record-breaking 237 weeks on the *Sunday London Times* best-seller list. The popularity of the book ensured an audience who had either read or were interested in the book.

Part of the rationale for making the documentary was to clarify some of the concepts for those who had read the book. Hawking originally planned for the book to be accessible to a general audience. In the acknowledgments, Hawking writes, "The basic ideas about the origin and fate of the universe can be stated without mathematics in a form that people without a scientific education can understand. This is what I have attempted to do in this book."[7]

Despite the aspiration, many publisher watchers characterized the book as an "unread bestseller," in part because of the book's complexity.[8] For instance, Hawking provides an account of the rise of string theory in the mid-1980s. Much of string theory is difficult to grasp, such as the idea that there are objects that are not particles and have a length but no other dimension.[9] Four years after the publication of *A Brief History of Time*, Hawking admitted that everyone who bought the book "may not have understood everything they have read. If they had, they would be ready to start a Ph.D. in theoretical physics."[10] A documentary on the book may be able to simplify and clarify some of its complicated cosmological concept. Hawking himself also acknowledges that the film was "the only way to reach a larger audience."[11]

In addition to the appeal of the book, there was also a general interest in both cosmology and Stephen Hawking at the time. Popular movies like *The Adventures of Buckaroo Banzai across the 8th Dimension* (1984) and television shows such as *Star Trek: The Next Generation* (1987–1994) often featured black holes. Popular culture frequently referenced Hawking, as in the science fiction novel *The Coming of the Quantum Cats* (1986) and the comic *Bloom County* (1980–1989). Hawking even made a personal appearance in *Star Trek: The Next Generation*.

But why would this project appeal to Morris? The success of *The Thin Blue Line* ensured that Morris would have easier access to financial support for his next film, so the funding commitment from Amblin and others would not be a necessity. Also, the proposed film itself was, in many ways, a dramatic shift from Morris's previous films. It was an adaptation of a well-known book by an international celebrity, as opposed to the "ordinary" people in Morris's first three documentaries. The film would also be participating in the well-established science documentary genre, whereas Morris's previous films had not closely fit into any such category.

Although it is difficult to account for all of the factors involved in Morris's decision to direct the film, there are some informative connections between the *Brief History* project and Morris's established interests. Morris's graduate study in the History of Science program at Princeton University is a clear personal connection to the subject matter. Hawking's book also contains some of the themes we have seen in Morris's previous films. The book is about scientific findings and theories, but it also touches on some larger philosophical issues addressed in all of Morris's documentaries, such as the limits of human knowledge. For instance, chapter 4 is entitled "The Uncertainty Principle," in which Hawking examines our ability to measure the present state of the universe and precisely predict future events. In addition, while the book does not often address his personal life, Hawking's biography is so unusual and compelling that it provides fertile ground for Morris to incorporate the subjective into the film.

After agreeing to the project, Morris traveled to England in 1990 to shoot the film. He brought a number of previous collaborators with him, including cinematographer Stefan Czapsky and production designer Ted Bafaloukos. Shortly after starting work on *A Brief History of Time*, Robert Redford invited Morris to direct his first dramatic feature entitled *The Dark Wind*, an adaptation of Tony Hillerman's 1982 novel. The story follows Jim Chee, a Navajo tribal policeman, as he investigates a number of different crimes in Arizona. Morris enthusiastically accepted and suspended the production of *A Brief History of Time*.

The Dark Wind was plagued with difficulties, many of which arose from the decision to shoot on location on Hopi and Navajo reservations. Morris compared making *The Dark Wind* to "a film about the Palestinians and the Israelis and shooting it on the West Bank."[12] There were also reported conflicts between Morris and the producers. Morris was let go after shooting wrapped and prevented from providing input in the editing of the film. The problems with *The Dark Wind* continued as the distributor of the film, Seven Arts, closed its doors before the film was released.[13]

Morris returned to the *Brief History* project and ended up shooting two hundred hours of footage.[14] He edited the film in 1991 with the help of Hawking, who spent weeks in the editing room with Morris reworking his narration for the film.[15] *A Brief History of Time* premiered at the Sundance Film Festival on January 20, 1992. The film had already secured rights to be shown on NBC but was still on the market for a theatrical distributor.[16] Three months later, Triton Pictures acquired the domestic theatrical rights, and Anglia Television/Gordon Freedman Productions agreed to distribute the film internationally. *A Brief History of Time* played in more than one hundred theaters in the United States and grossed over two million dollars, making it the fifth-highest-grossing documentary at the time.[17] After its theatrical run, a group of international networks, including NBC, Channel Four, and Tokyo Broadcasting, broadcast the film on television.[18]

A Brief History of Time was a considerable critical success as well. *Time*, the *Los Angeles Times*, and the *San Francisco Chronicle* placed the film on their "Top Ten Films of the Year" list. *A Brief History of Time* also won the Grand Jury Prize at the Sundance Film Festival and the "Filmmaker's Award" from the National Society of Film Critics. While Morris was once more overlooked for an Oscar nomination, he again established himself as one of the most highly respected documentary filmmakers.

■ The Science Documentary and Reflexivity

As with Morris's previous films, scholars connect *A Brief History of Time* with a reflexive mode of representation, as it shares many of the reflexive markers as his other documentaries. For instance, as in *The Thin Blue Line*, Morris uses a variety of cutaway materials, including archival photographs, fictional found footage, computer-generated graphics, and staged sequences. Sybil DelGaudio argues that this visual material firmly aligns *A Brief History of Time* with Bill Nichols's category of the reflexive documentary: "Morris consistently interrupts the presentation of scientific theory with images (often computer-generated, animated images) that highlight its epistemological nature while they simultaneously question cinema's ability to represent the world of scientific theory."[19]

The previous two chapters demonstrated that this reading of Morris's films fails to properly position Morris's films within documentary film history and account for how the films function on a more local level. This argument again applies to *A Brief History of Time*. Morris's film is intimately connected to the documentary tradition and has an investment in representing and making claims about the world. Throughout this and subsequent chapters, we will continue to examine the ways in which Morris's documentaries engage facts, truth, and subjectivity, as well as documentary conventions at the time. We will spend less time addressing these particular reflexive/postmodern readings.

Our earlier examinations also placed Morris's first three films in a context of broad trends in documentary style, structure, and voice. This chapter focuses on the ways in which *A Brief History of Time* relates specifically to the history and conventions of the science documentary. To help provide this context of the science documentary, we will refer to a number of films including *The Birth and Death of a Star* (1974), *Starlife* (1983), and the science series *Cosmos* (1980) and *The Astronomers* (1991).

In this context, the phrase "science documentary" is specifically referring to documentary films whose purpose is to explain scientific observations and theories. The science film has a distinct challenge of representing and explaining these abstract ideas and processes. Even a science film more concerned with observable reality will also generalize these observations into a more conceptual principle or theory. For instance, the 1992 PBS series *Earth Revealed: Introductory Geology* investigates specific rock formations and geological events such as earthquakes, but it also examines what these observable phenomena reveal about plate tectonics theory.[20]

The science documentary tradition is an instructive framework in which to understand Morris's approach to style in *A Brief History of Time*. When placed in the context of other science documentaries, we can better understand how Morris participates in the documentary tradition as well as experiments with documentary style. This context also illuminates the ways in which Morris connects Hawking's scientific theories with his personal life.

■ Style

Amblin's decision to ask Morris to direct *A Brief History of Time* might seem puzzling at first. Morris's first three films are distinct from one another in a number of ways, but none of them seem to overlap with a documentary on cosmology. In addition, the *Brief History* project participates in the well-established science documentary subgenre, while Morris's previous films do not neatly fit into a similar documentary category. There were certainly other filmmakers who would be a clear fit for the project, such as Adrian Malone, director of a number of science-oriented television series including *The Ascent of Man* (1973), *Cosmos*, and *Spacecraft* (1987).

Morris was an attractive candidate to direct *A Brief History of Time* in part because of the success of *The Thin Blue Line*. Morris demonstrated that he could make a critically and, perhaps more importantly, commercially successful documentary. Morris also showed that he could tackle difficult conceptual issues in a thoughtful, nuanced manner. This would prove useful in a documentary that deals with complicated theoretical issues. In addition, *The Thin Blue Line* established Morris's skill at creating striking, imaginative visuals.

Science documentaries are traditionally dependent on inventive visuals, in part to illustrate complex, abstract theories. Over the years, these documentaries have used different combinations of devices to aid in such illustration, including voice-over narration, interviews, observational footage, nondiegetic music, staged sequences, reenactments, as well as hand-drawn and computer-animated graphics. For instance, *The Astronomers* series uses a combination of Richard Chamberlain's voice-over narration, observational footage, formal interviews, reenactments, and animated graphics.

Animated graphics have been particularly important to science documentaries in visualizing events in the world that are difficult or impossible to capture on film. Science documentaries were increasingly reliant on computer graphics as they became more sophisticated and less expensive throughout the 1970s and 80s. Carl Sagan's *Cosmos* series used cutting-edge computer graphics to great effect, aided by its eight-million-dollar budget. For instance, Sagan guides us through the different parts of the universe on a "Spaceship of the Imagination," which integrates an elaborate set with digital effects.

Morris's ability to combine stylistic variety and narrative clarity makes him an appealing choice to adapt Hawking's book. In *The Thin Blue Line*, Morris demonstrates an interest in drawing upon a wide variety of visual material, including photographs, found footage, and staged reenactments. In addition, he employs these elements to help disentangle the confusions in the Adams case and clearly establish David Harris as Officer Wood's murderer.

Because of the flexibility of the science documentary format as well as the difficulty of the concepts involved, *A Brief History of Time* would allow Morris to continue to experiment with the visuals and how they engage the subject matter. We can locate such experimentation in both the interview and cutaway visuals in the film. As with all of his films, Morris uses the formal interview as the narrative backbone of the film, while the cutaway visuals illustrate, expand, and contextualize this testimony.

Unlike the location shooting in his previous three films, Morris conducted the *Brief History* interviews on over thirty sets at Elstree Studios in London.[21] Many of the sets were detailed reconstructions of different spaces, including rooms in Hawking's home and his office. There were a few pragmatic reasons for using studio sets for the interviews. They allowed Morris to carefully control the lighting and the sound without the unpredictable conditions of location shooting. In addition, Morris interviewed family members dispersed across England and scholars from all over the world. By bringing the subjects to a central location, the production was able to reduce travel expenses as well as create distinct backgrounds for each interview subject.[22]

There is some uniformity to these interview visuals. Along with frequent collaborator Ted Bafaloukos, Morris creates environments flush with "realistic" detail and lighting. For example, physicist Dennis Sciama sits in front of a desk cluttered with items such as books, a desk organizer, and a stapler. In the background, a window reveals nighttime lighting, as a single light softly falls through the glass. Stephen Hawking's office, which Morris replicated down to the Marilyn Monroe poster on his wall, is another useful illustration of this emphasis on realism (see figure 3.1). Such attention to detail is reminiscent of the interview mise-en-scène of *Gates of Heaven*, although the environments in *A Brief History of Time* are almost hyper-realistic in their use of depth, light, and detail.

Morris frames his subjects in a fairly consistent and stable shot scale. All of the subjects in *A Brief History of Time* appear in either medium shot or medium close-up without any zooming or camera movement.[23] The subjects all look toward the lens of the camera, again giving the impression of eye contact with the viewer. Morris's placement of the subjects in the frame is more varied than in his previous films. Although Morris places some interview subjects in the middle of the frame, others are positioned on one side of the frame, as in the interview with Hawking family friend Basil King (see

FIGURE 3.1. □ *A Brief History of Time*

figure 3.2). This asymmetrical composition suits Morris's use of deep space in the interview mise-en-scène. Morris places the interview subjects well into the foreground and often extends the sets deep into the background. For instance, King sits on a cushioned chair in a living room setting. A doorway in the background reveals another room, brightly lit and somewhat out of focus. By placing the subject on one side of the frame, Morris has a larger, uninterrupted space in which to reveal the background while maintaining a balanced composition.

Morris's handling of Hawking's body is different than the other interviews, as he is not a conventional interview subject. Hawking's inability to speak prevents him from being a "talking head." Without the constraint of showing Hawking's face during his testimony, Morris is free to explore the 360-degree space around Hawking. Wheelchair-bound Hawking frequently appears together with his computer system, the apparatus that allows him to communicate (see figure 3.3). Morris also fragments Hawking's body into dynamic, occasionally abstract compositions.

Morris's handling of Hawking's body functions in part as a visual investigation into his physical condition. Morris is very much interested in Hawking's amyotrophic lateral sclerosis (ALS) and how it relates to his theoretical work. The close, static shots of Hawking's eyes, wheelchair, and computer

FIGURE 3.2. □ *A Brief History of Time*

system foreground his immobility. Morris pays particular attention to Hawking's hands, one of the few mobile parts of Hawking's body and the means through which he operates his computer. Hawking's almost imperceptible hand movements illustrate the fragility of his condition.

The static quality of both the formal interviews and the images of Hawking stand in stark contrast to the cutaway images. When we leave the interview images, we enter an active, vibrant world of spinning dice, smashing teacups, and flying wristwatches. Morris also draws upon a diverse assortment of visual material, including archival photographs, fictional found footage, and computer-animated graphics. Many of the cutaways are close, fragmentary framings of objects such as a roulette wheel and medical equipment (see figure 3.4). Morris develops some of these visual elements into repeated visual motifs, such as images of staircases and teacups, throughout *A Brief History of Time*.

Morris again uses a Philip Glass score for *A Brief History of Time*. The music is characteristic of Glass's minimalist style and, in a number of ways, similar to the music in *The Thin Blue Line*. Glass uses melodic themes that repeat in an individual sequence, and these music sequences occur throughout the film. While a two-note alternation played throughout much of the music in *The Thin Blue Line*, the music in *A Brief History of Time* is more reliant on a

FIGURE 3.3. ◻ *A Brief History of Time*

staccato pulsing over which the individual melodies play. In addition, horn and woodwind instruments are the most prominent instruments in the *Brief History* score, often lending the music a fanfare-like quality.

While Morris continues some elements from previous films such as the use of visual motifs and the Glass score, he also introduces a visual device that becomes more prominent in later films. We occasionally see a "blink" to a black screen in the middle of a sequence. For example, toward the end of the film, astrophysicist Christopher Isham discusses the possibility of sharing consciousness with other people. In the middle of this sequence, Morris cuts to black for a fraction of second and then cuts back to Isham's interview. Many documentaries use this black screen, or "slug," to transition between different interviews and often apply fades to integrate the black into the visuals. Morris's approach is different in that he often uses a hard cut to black in the middle of an interview subject's testimony.

It may be tempting to read these cuts thematically. For instance, one could point to the black slugs as a reflexive gesture, highlighting the constructed nature of the film. Or perhaps the black screens connect with the topic of black holes, which are a frequent topic of discussion. The reason for this blinking is perhaps more pragmatic, however. Interviews are often edited and rearranged, and this process frequently creates jump cuts in the

FIGURE 3.4. □ *A Brief History of Time*

image. While cutaways are often used to hide these jumps, a black screen can also achieve the same effect. These cuts also add a rhythmic quality to the sequence, breaking up the interview image with a percussive flash of black. Finally, there are earlier documentaries that also use these bold cuts to black. For instance, Emile de Antonio intercuts images of war with extended black slugs at the beginning of *In the Year of the Pig* (1968).

Morris's experimentation with the visuals in *A Brief History of Time*, including the use of black screen during the interview testimony, are not merely stylistic impositions on the conservative conventions of the science documentary. Nor are they reflexive affronts to the documentary tradition. Documentaries and science films often experiment with visual material. *A Brief History of Time* was an opportunity for Morris to continue his exploration of documentary style. Morris's use of depth, compositional lines, color, and light all contribute to a dynamic visual design. They also allow the viewer to better understanding the story and the film's thematic interests.

■ Structure

Much of Hawking's book is devoted to an explanation of the history of cosmological ideas as well as Hawking's own contributions to the field. The chapters in the book are often focused on a particular subject in cosmology. For instance, the first chapter presents a history of different models humans have used to understand the universe, and the sixth chapter deals with the development of theories about black holes.

Morris's documentary, on the other hand, is structured by the chronology of Hawking's life. Morris uses a series of twelve intertitles to indicate the year of the events addressed in that section. The first of these intertitles is "1942," the year of Hawking's birth. Hawking's mother discusses life during World War II, and Hawking's sisters reflect on life in the Hawking home. We then continue to follow the major events in Hawking's life, including his early academic career, the onset of ALS, and his major cosmological findings up through 1991.

While Hawking's personal life is a central focus in the film, it is only occasionally addressed in the book and is usually put in the context of a specific cosmological question or finding. For instance, in the chapter entitled "The Origin and Fate of the Universe," Hawking provides an anecdote about a 1981 conference in Moscow. Hawking uses this personal story to illustrate the developments in the inflationary model of the universe, however, and not to provide insight into his character or this particular time in his life.

Hawking initially responded negatively to the shift toward the more personal in Morris's film: "When they began to make the film, it seemed it was going to be almost exclusively about my life, with very little about science. When I protested, I was told that the kind of film I had in mind would have appeal to only a fairly small number of people. To reach a mass audience, it was necessary to combine the science with material about my life."[24] After working with Morris, whom Hawking describes as "a man of integrity," Hawking gained confidence in the project because he felt that it did not lose sight of the book's purpose.[25]

In addition to Hawking's biography, the film also focuses on the scientific theories with which Hawking grappled throughout his life. For instance, a quarter of the film's total running time of eighty minutes is devoted to black holes. This section of the film features an examination of the origin of the term "black hole," a description of a black hole, a hypothetical account of what it would be like to fall into a black hole, and a discussion of how black holes are not truly black because they radiate particles. The beginning of the film establishes this interest in cosmological issues, as we hear Hawking ask a series of questions about the origin and nature of the universe: "Did the universe have a beginning, and if so, what happened before then? Where did the universe come from, and where is it going?"[26]

This combination of the individual and scientific is unique in science documentaries. Some science documentaries are devoid of anything inflected with a particular individual's personality or voice. For instance, *Starlife* uses an offscreen, omniscient voice-over to guide the viewer through the different stages of a star's life, and we never see or learn about any person in particular. The television series *The Astronomers* includes more personal elements, such as segments in which astronomers offer individual reflections on their professional work. For instance, in the second episode entitled "Searching for Black Holes," John E. Conway discusses the difficulties of having to frequently move to different jobs, during which we see Conway riding his bike as expressive music plays on the audio track. In the *Cosmos* series, subtitled "A Personal Journey," Carl Sagan is often on-screen, leading us through the episode and occasionally providing some personal reflections on the topic at hand.

One element that sets *A Brief History of Time* apart from all of these films is that Morris *infuses* Hawking's cosmological theories with his personal life. It is not just that Hawking's personal life sometimes impacts or informs his work but rather that we can read the scientific work through the his individual perspective, and vice versa. *A Brief History of Time* continues Morris's exploration of human subjectivity, while also introducing theoretical science as another way we can gain access and insight into the complexity of the human experience.

Morris structures the film to connect Hawking's personal life and his scientific theories. In the first half hour of the film, which is mostly dedicated to Hawking's life prior to his professional career, Hawking's voice-over helps establish the relationship between the personal and the theoretical. For instance, we hear Hawking say, "In the 20th century, it was thought that the universe existed forever, or had been created sometime in the past more or less like it is today. People found comfort in the fact that, although they may grow old and die, the universe was eternal and unchanging."

Hawking's sister Mary then describes how Hawking invented his own board game called "Dynasty." His mother Isobel remembers, "The game was almost a substitute for living as far as I can make out. It took hours and hours. I thought it was a perfectly terrible game. I couldn't imagine anyone getting taken up with that. But Stephen always had a very complicated mind, and I felt as much as anything it was the complication of it that appealed to him."

In one sense, the two sequences are quite different. Hawking references the history of scientific thought, while the subsequent scene is about Hawking's childhood. The juxtaposition of the two encourages a search for connections beyond these apparent differences. One common element between the voice-over and Hawking's mother's testimony is this idea of the eternal and how people, including Hawking, find it appealing.

The connection between Hawking and the comforting appeal of the eternal reverberates throughout the rest of the film. For example, the film devotes a significant amount of time to black holes, one of Hawking's areas of expertise. The idea of the eternal returns as a number of theorists address the hypothetical of an astronaut falling into a black hole. Hawking explains that, by entering the black hole, an astronaut could ensure that her or his "image lasted forever, but the image would fade rapidly and grow so dim that no one could see it."

In this same sequence, we also see a clip from the Disney film *The Black Hole* in which Dr. Hans Reinhardt describes what will happen when he enters the black hole. Dr. Alex Durant asks "And life?" to which Reinhardt responds, "Life, forever." While Hawking's testimony provides a matter-of-fact account of the journey, *The Black Hole* clip, with its silly dialogue, stilted acting, and outdated graphics, pushes the entire sequence away from a straightforward illustration of a scientific theory. When placed together, the sequence takes on a more metaphoric exploration of the *idea* of a black hole and what it tells us about Hawking's subjective engagement with the notion of the eternal.

The broad trajectory of *A Brief History of Time*'s structure is chronological in nature. We can also see how various connections, some being more explicit than others, infuse the form of the film with an associational structure we have seen in Morris's previous films. The structure prompts us to locate associational links between these personal events and Hawking's cosmological theories. These connections also help foreground the subjective, as we are given insight into the ways in which Hawking views the world and himself.

The film continues to explore this relationship between abstract concepts, such as that of the eternal, and Hawking's personal life. We are consequently primed to make this association whenever one or the other is addressed in the film. For example, a "1963" title introduces us to a sequence about the onset of Hawking's ALS. Hawking's Oxford classmate Derek Powney describes what the doctors told Hawking about the disease: "[Hawking] was gradually going to lose the use of his body. And [they] told him eventually he would essentially have the body of a cabbage but his mind would still be in perfect working order." After this sequence, a "1965" title begins a segment on the origin of the universe. We learn about Roger Penrose's theory about the death of stars and how they collapse into an infinitely dense singularity. Hawking explains, "Penrose proved that a dying star shrinks to a singularity. I realized that if I reverse the direction of time, I could prove that the universe had a beginning."

The juxtaposition of the ALS and "death of a star" sequence foregrounds the relationship between the collapse of a star and Hawking's degenerative disorder. Without being too literal, Hawking's diminishing control of his body, down to the mere functioning of his mind, is like a star's collapse to a singularity. The parallel between the life of a star and Hawking's own life again connects Hawking's scientific work and his personal views and experiences. The sequence also has a close relationship to Hawking's interest in the eternal and how it might be clarified or complicated with an explanation of how the universe began. This web of relationships continues to expand throughout the film, connecting different elements of Hawking's life and his theoretical work.

Philip Glass's music, and in particular the repetition of musical motifs, also helps connect different sequences and foregrounds the role of Hawking's subjective experience in the film. For instance, Hawking discusses how he had a preference for studying cosmology, "the study of the very large," instead of elementary particles, "the study of the very small." Accompanying this sequence, we hear a playful bassoon theme in triple meter. Morris repeats this music later in the film as Hawking describes what happens when one enters a black hole. This repetition connects to the topic of cosmology in both scenes. It also establishes an associational connection between Hawking's subjective preference for studying the "very large" and the previous associations with black holes and Hawking's ALS. This musical connection does not demand a particular reading of either scene, but it is another stylistic and structural element that encourages understanding Hawking's cosmological ideas as inflected with or driven by his subjective desires.

Returning to the broad narrative structure in *A Brief History of Time*, we can see that the film does provide a clear chronological account of Hawking's life. This chronology is made clear by elements such as the intertitles and the testimony, in which the interview subjects speak about the progression of Hawking's life and cosmological theories. The film's structure also establishes associational connections between Hawking's personal life and the scientific theories introduced in the film.

■ Style and Subjectivity

The stylistic elements in *A Brief History of Time* reinforce the associational connections between scientific theory and subjective experience. A number of the stylistic features in Morris's previous films continue to foreground the subjective in *A Brief History of Time*. For instance, the impression of eye contact with the film's subjects again contributes to the confessional quality of the interviews, and the highly stylized images pull the film away from a realist aesthetic.

The interview footage in *A Brief History of Time* is relatively static, particularly in relation to the wide variety of stylized cutaway visuals. Morris's treatment of Hawking's body represents a synthesis of the dynamism of the cutaways and the stasis of the interviews. On the one hand, the shots of Hawking do not have any camera movement or changes in shot scale. These

FIGURE 3.5. ◻ *A Brief History of Time*

fixed shots match Hawking's own immobility, as the most movement we see is his hand softly pressing the computer device. On the other hand, Morris's camera actively explores Hawking and the space around him. The last shot of the film is perhaps the best illustration of exploration, as we see Hawking's wheelchair drift into outer space (see figure 3.5). Morris makes the most immobile of his interview subjects the most visually dynamic. Building upon the associational connections discussed above, we can see this visual treatment of Hawking's body as a convergence of Hawking's physical immobility and the vast capacities of his mind.

Morris's use of visual motifs also reinforces the connections between the scientific and the personal. For instance, in a section exploring the possibility that the universe did not have a moment of creation, Hawking asks, "Where does the difference between the past and the future come from? The laws of science do not distinguish between the past and the future. Yet, there is a big difference between the past and the future in ordinary life. You may see a cup of tea fall off a table and break into pieces, but you will never see it gather together and jump back on the table. The increase in entropy, or disorder, is what distinguishes the past from the future, giving a direction to time." On the image track, we see a teacup falling and breaking on a black-and-white checkered floor as Glass's score pulses and repeats (see

FIGURE 3.6. □ *A Brief History of Time*

figure 3.6). A "1985" intertitle transitions into a discussion of how it became increasingly difficult for Hawking to communicate with others because of ALS, which led to the development of Hawking's speech computer system.

The juxtaposition of these two sequences establishes a relationship between Hawking's fragile, failing body and the shattered teacup. This connection is reinforced later in the "1985" sequence as we see the image of the teacup repeated twice more. The smashed teacup first reassembles itself in slow motion as Hawking discusses how he "felt the universe had to return to a smooth and ordered state when it recollapsed. If this were so, people would live their lives backwards. They would die before they were born and get younger as the universe got small again—eventually returning to the womb." Hawking then admits he had made a mistake in this calculation: "I was using too simple a model of the universe. Time will not reverse direction when the universe begins to contract. People will continue to get older." As with the first teacup sequence, we again see the cup breaking on the floor.

In both sequences, Hawking makes the connection between a scientific theory of time and lived experience. The first sequence of the teacup then broadens this connection directly to Hawking. The final realization that time will not reverse direction is not merely a scientific insight but also a personal one. Hawking's condition is not reversible or curable. The visual motif of the teacup, earlier associated with Hawking's degenerative disease, now takes on a metaphoric role. It repeats along with Glass's cyclical score to continue to link the scientific and the personal.

It is important to note that the structure and the style in *A Brief History of Time* are not serving one narrow function here. The patterning in the film does prompt us to make associations between the theoretical and the subjective, but the possible meanings and relationships in the film are not closed down to a single reading or explanation. The viewer is instead asked to explore different connections without the determining control of a formal voice.

Voice

A Brief History of Time's particular fusion of the personal and the scientific is unusual for science documentaries. While scientists sometimes guide us through a scientific finding or theory, the focus rarely shifts to the personal life of these theorists. *A Brief History of Time* takes this incorporation of the personal a step further. The film asks us to understand the cosmological theories as metaphors for and manifestations of Stephen Hawking's life and his view of the world.

This linking of the subjective and theoretical does not constitute a subversion or rejection of scientific truth. Much like *The Thin Blue Line*, *A Brief History of Time* does take seriously certain factual claims, devoting a significant amount of time to the explanation of cosmological findings. For instance, as with *A Brief History of Time*, many documentaries about the cosmos address the nature and effects of black holes. These films often use the hypothetical situation of a person taking a trip to or falling through the black hole to illustrate this distant and illusive phenomenon. In *The Birth and Death of a Star*, for example, a physicist explains to the camera what a black hole would look like from a nearby space capsule. The film uses rudimentary graphics to illustrate this hypothetical voyage. The graphics in *Starlife* and *The Astronomers* series are more sophisticated, and their voice-over narration extends the scenario to an observer actually falling through the black hole.

Morris incorporates this "falling into a black hole" scenario in *A Brief History of Time*, as it also appears in Hawking's book. In the film sequence, Hawking describes an astronaut entering a black hole. As the astronaut

FIGURE 3.7. ▫ *A Brief History of Time*

approaches the singularity and is slowly "crushed into spaghetti," his companions from a nearby spaceship see the astronaut's image, represented on the image track by a wristwatch, slowing down and eventually freezing: "You could ensure your image lasted forever, but the image would fade rapidly and grow so dim that no one could see it" (see figure 3.7). Although any cosmological theory is open to debate and refutation, such claims about black holes are never put into question in the film.

Sequences such as this are able to stand by themselves as explanatory in nature. The film takes these theories seriously, and we are not given an explicit reason to doubt them. Perhaps more than any of Morris's other films, *A Brief History of Time* incorporates smart, articulate interview subjects who are among the most knowledgeable in the world about physics and cosmology. Throughout the film, we do *learn* from their testimony.

A Brief History of Time is not a formal-voice documentary, however. As with Morris's earlier documentaries, the structure of the film is not principally driven by a traditional notion of clarity and coherence. That is, the primary purpose of *A Brief History of Time*'s structure is not a transparent explanation of Hawking's theories of the universe. Although there are sequences that do provide explanation, such as the black hole sequence discussed above, this is not the dominant role of the film's organization or style. Instead, the film employs an open voice in its *exploration* of the connections between Hawking's life, his scientific theories, and his personal view of the world.

As noted above, the structure and style of *A Brief History of Time* establishes certain connections between Hawking's personal life and his scientific theories. Although the film forms these connections through juxtapositions, repetitions, and motifs, they are not explicitly articulated or explained to the viewer. The film instead establishes a series of frameworks through which the viewer can connect and extend the relationships between the different aspects of the film.

Returning to the black hole sequence, there are a number of ways in which we can expand on the connection between Hawking's life and black holes. Initially, we may discover that, as with a black hole, Hawking's ALS is inescapable. We can also continue to develop this connection. We might notice that the groundbreaking finding that tiny particles can escape a black hole also links to the state of Hawking's ALS. He is completely paralyzed but can communicate through the very limited movement of his hand on the computer device (the "escape" from the black hole). There is no formal voice to either firmly establish this connection or demarcate its limits. In this way, the film's open voice encourages exploration.

While the formal voice at some point clearly answers the questions raised in the film, *A Brief History of Time* leaves some questions open. At the beginning of the film, Hawking asks, "Which came first, the chicken or the egg? Did the universe have a beginning, and if so, what happened before then? Where did the universe come from, and where is it going?" Although these questions are addressed throughout the film, there is never the equivalent of a discovery or final answer. Rather, they are questions that Hawking struggles with throughout *A Brief History of Time*, and it is the exploration of this struggle that becomes a central interest of the film.

Morris also takes conventional formal-voice features and tempers their explanatory function. For instance, *A Brief History of Time* both satisfies and challenges the expectation for illustrative cutaways. There are some sequences where the images do illustrate the testimony. At the beginning of the film, Isobel Hawking describes the firebombing during World War II and we see corresponding found footage of the bombings on the image track.

There are other times when the cutaway images are more closely related to a particular point of view instead of a general establishment of fact. For

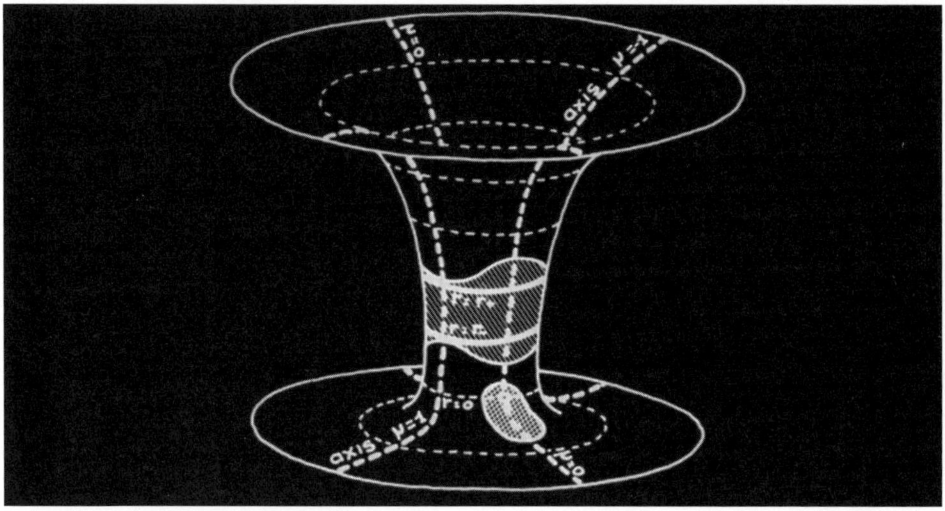

FIGURE 3.8. □ *A Brief History of Time*

instance, Stephen Hawking describes how he "tended to think in pictures and diagrams" because his illness made it difficult for him to write things down. On the image track, we see a quick succession of figures and charts without any explanation of what they represent (see figure 3.8). The cutaway images are more of an illustration of a particular subjective experience, in this instance Hawking's ability to think in complex images, rather than a straight illustration of the testimony. Throughout the film, there is this movement away from a formal voice that explains or clarifies and toward an open voice that expands and explores particular points of view.

Morris's handling of Hawking's voice-over also challenges the expectation for reliable and comprehensive guidance through the film. Hawking's computer-generated voice does not have the same authoritative, omniscient function as the voice-over in most science documentaries. For example, Hawking admits to making a mistake with his theory that the universe would eventually stop expanding and begin to contract. He previously theorized that, during this contraction, people would live their lives backward and eventually return to the womb. Hawking recognizes, "I had made a mistake. I was using too simple a model of the universe. Time will not reverse direction when the universe begins to contract. People will continue to get older." At the end of the film, Hawking's mother Isobel explicitly acknowledges that her son is not infallible: "Not all things Stephen says should be taken as gospel. He's a searcher; he is looking for things. And if sometimes he may talk nonsense, well, don't we all. The point is, people must think, they must go on thinking, they must try to extend the boundaries of knowledge; yet they don't sometimes even know where to start."

Sequences such as this not only pull Hawking's narration away from omniscience but also stress the subjective elements in the voice-over. Stephen Hawking ends the film with the following reflection: "If we do discover a complete theory, it should be understandable by everyone. Everyone can take part in the discussion of why we and the universe exist. If we find the answer to that, it would be the ultimate triumph of human reason. For then, we would know the mind of God." By the end of the film, we understand that these claims are not factual findings about the world. Instead, they are the product of one man's attempt to grapple with deep, difficult problems, such as the essence of the universe.

Such acknowledgments in the film do not fundamentally undermine Hawking's authority. He remains a reliable expert in these matters. Rather, through the strategies discussed above, the film positions his narration as less pure explanation and more an investigation into the ways in which he understands the world. The fact that they are Hawking's thoughts gives them more credibility and weight, but again they are not elevated to the status of omniscience. This shift in focus to the more subjective also helps to reinforce the exploratory nature of the open voice. The audience is not asked to merely comprehend the lessons of the film. Instead, we must discover the many possible connections between Hawking's theories and his personal life.

How do we reconcile the open voice in the film with the explanatory components discussed above? There is no reason that the two need to be reconciled. They can both be present at the same time. In the black hole sequence, for instance, it is not surprising that the film establishes how a black hole behaves in order to make informative connections to Hawking's personal life. Without establishing some explanation of the phenomenon, there would not be much to explore. As was the case in *The Thin Blue Line*, there can be a predominant open voice in the film, but there can also be a firm establishment of truth or facts at the same time. Instead of making a superficial choice between "pure" objectivity and subjectivity, Morris again provides a sophisticated example of the versatility of the documentary form to explore the many different facets of humanity and the world around us.

Morris's use of an open voice in *A Brief History of Time* is an innovative approach to the science documentary form. The vast majority of science films use a formal voice to explain observations, facts, and theories. Morris introduces these scientific theories but also adds another layer to the film, in which we see science as a manifestation or expression of the personal. Morris's choice to fuse the personal with the scientific adds depth to our understanding of Hawking's subjective view of the world around him. This approach also diverts attention from a straightforward explanation of these theories.

■ Reception and Ethics

Morris's first three documentaries all received the objection that they were exploiting and degrading the interview subjects. Critics argued that Floyd McClure in *Gates of Heaven*, Joe Payne in *Vernon, Florida*, and Emily Miller in *The Thin Blue Line* appeared silly, simple, and naive. As the filmmaker, Morris is in a position of power. By foregrounding the unflattering features of his subjects, Morris provoked ethical objections about his approach.

A Brief History of Time avoids this problem to some extent. As with those involved in pet cemeteries, the residents of Vernon, and the people in the Adams murder case, Morris is again dealing with a particular subculture in *A Brief History of Time*. In contrast to his previous films, Morris's interview subjects participate in a highly educated and well-respected cultural community. David Beers's review of the film puts it plainly: "Up until now, Morris has made documentaries about society's bottom feeders, and let the camera run and run and run while they rambled their crackpotisms and confessions. Here, he's chosen to profile one of the planet's highest minds."[27]

Hawking and others do acknowledge some mistakes in their theories, and the film does not adopt Hawking's voice-over narration as omniscient commentary. We respond to these mistakes or limitations differently, partly because they are tackling particularly complex theoretical issues. For instance, Hawking's flawed model of the universe is fundamentally different from Emily Miller's mistaken view of herself as a crime-solving detective.

The fact that critics do not claim that Morris ridicules his subjects in *A*

Brief History of Time does not mean that the film avoids all objections about the depiction of its subjects. The inclusion of prominent scientists carries along with it certain representational expectations. For instance, Morris does not provide identifying titles for his interview subjects. Many of the reviews of *A Brief History* criticize this decision. Henry Sheehan complains that the lack of "usual explanatory undertitles" sometimes makes the identity of the speaker unclear, and Kenneth Turan calls this omission "irritating."[28] Glyn Jones, writing for *New Scientist*, issues the most explicit objection: "The most infuriating device of all was not to give name captions to the speakers, so we cannot know in each case who is doing the talking."[29]

It should be noted that, throughout the course of the film, we often do learn the names and occupations of the participants. For example, about thirty minutes into the film, Hawking says, "In my third year at Cambridge, Roger Penrose published his discovery about the death of stars." The film cuts to an unidentified interview subject who describes the day when he came up with an important discovery. We correctly infer that the interviewee is Penrose.

At the heart of these objections is not just a desire for clarity. Morris had never included identifying titles in any of his previous films, and yet there were no objections. The interview subjects' notoriety and importance in *A Brief History of Time* adds an expectation that Morris will provide proper respect to these people. This includes some account of why they are important. The idea of "*proper* respect" is significant here, as the expectation that the film will identify Roger Penrose as a professor at Cambridge is higher than identifying Emily Miller as a former convenience-store worker.

Beyond the frustration expressed by the film reviews, Morris's decision not to include identifying titles has additional effects. Identifying the name and title of the interviewee often imbues the testimony with authority and reliability. Morris's films are ultimately less interested in explanation than exploration, and this kind of authority can either be unnecessary or, even worse, counterproductive. Morris wants us to actively evaluate the claims made in the film. Identifying Penrose as a professor at Cambridge, for instance, may stifle this kind of critical engagement with the testimony.

The omission of identifying titles also conforms to Morris's general approach to the documentary form. Morris frequently avoids stylistic conventions that are used to make narrative or thematic elements explicit.

For instance, he does not use voice-over narration to guide us through the narrative, or zooms during interviews to cue us to important or emotional moments in the testimony. The lack of identifying titles is part of a broader approach that contributes to the open voice.

The criticism of Morris's decision not to identify the interview subjects is also symptomatic of a deeper expectation that we have when watching documentary films. Viewers anticipate that documentaries should provide a proper explanation of the topic at hand. This is necessarily vague because each documentary plays a significant role in establishing the specifics of these expectations, especially at the beginning of the film. For instance, Ken Burns's *Huey Long* (1985) begins with found footage of Huey Long, followed by a title card with the following quote by Robert Penn Warren: "If you were living in Louisiana you knew you were living in history defining itself before your eyes and you knew that you were not seeing a half-drunk hick buffoon performing an old routine, but witnessing a drama which was a version of the world's drama and the drama of history, too: the old drama of power and ethics."[30] After this sequence, there is an expectation that the film will chronicle the drama of Long's tumultuous life and place it within the context of Louisiana and world politics. Throughout the course of the film, *Huey Long* fulfills these expectations by providing a clear account of the events in and significance of Long's life.

A Brief History of Time is different in this respect. Morris establishes an interest in both Hawking's personal and his professional life, creating an expectation that he will give appropriate attention to both. By dividing our attention between Hawking's complex theoretical ideas and equally rich personal life, some will complain that Morris does not properly account for one or the other, or both. The expectations are particularly high in terms of the film's handling of science, partly because it is the primary focus of Hawking's book. Some reviewers such as Gary Panetta and Todd McCarthy complain that the science in the film is "difficult to follow" and "not entirely understandable."[31] Others, such as Daniel Neman and Michael MacCambridge, argue that, while the film should be accessible to viewers, Morris oversimplifies Hawking's theories.[32]

The expectations about the handling of Hawking's personal life seem to be lower, perhaps because the book does not provide a detailed account of Hawking's life. Some reviewers do criticize Morris for not addressing Hawking's widely publicized divorce from his first wife Jane and his subsequent relationship with his nurse Elaine Mason. Morris's explanation for the omission is simple: "It was clear [Hawking] didn't wish to have that included."[33] If the film had only focused on Hawking's scientific research, the breakup of Hawking's marriage would not be an issue. Morris's interest in the personal opens up this expectation.

These complaints about *A Brief History of Time* are perhaps not as clear an ethical issue as the objection that Morris is belittling his interview subjects. There is an "ethics of explanation" in most documentaries, however, where the viewer expects the film to accurately and adequately represent the issues addressed in the film. These expectations differ depending on the film and the subject, but there is nonetheless a sense that a film's inability or refusal to do so can go beyond a mere failing and amount to an ethical violation.

This is not to say that these issues were raised in every, or even most, of the reviews of *A Brief History of Time*. In fact, the majority of reviews were complimentary. Richard Schickel's review praises the film's "metaphorical richness," and Vincent Canby characterizes the film as "a kind of adventure that seldom reaches the screen, and it's a tonic."[34] The film also won a number of prestigious awards, including the Grand Jury Prize at Sundance.

The criticisms of *A Brief History of Time* are informative, however. Morris's use of an open voice does allow for narrative and thematic complexity. It can also frustrate expectations for clarity and comprehensiveness. These frustrations are amplified by Morris's engagement with the science film, which brings along with it added expectations for explanation and transparency.

4 Television Commercials and *Errol Morris' First Person*

TELEVISION HAS BEEN THE MOST IMPORTANT SOURCE of funding and exhibition for documentaries throughout the last sixty years. Many key documentary movements and filmmakers, including Direct Cinema, Frederick Wiseman, and Barbara Kopple, have relied on television for financial support and distribution. Errol Morris's filmmaking career is no exception. *Vernon, Florida* was funded in part by New York public TV affiliate WNET and German television production company ZDF. All of Morris's subsequent films were also partially funded by public and network television, and aired on television after their festival and theatrical runs.

Errol Morris's career producing television commercials is another critical source of funding for his documentary films. Since the release of *The Thin Blue Line*, Morris has produced hundreds of commercials that help him finance his feature films. The relatively large budgets for commercial production also offer Morris opportunities to experiment with different technologies and visual techniques.

Morris's television series *Errol Morris' First Person* was another influential outlet for experimentation. The series budget was limited, but Morris used the opportunity to test technology such as his Megatron interviewing device and digital video. These experiments produced a television series that is stylistically innovative and adventurous.

Morris's television work is important in understanding his career as a whole. The changes in visual style after *The Thin Blue Line* are in part explained by Morris's ability to test different filmmaking technologies and techniques in television. For instance, Morris first experimented with an intervalometer in a commercial campaign for Robertson Stephens before using the device in *The Fog of War*. Throughout the chapter, we will track the influence Morris's experiences in television and commercial production has on his subsequent documentary films.

■ Television Advertising

During a trip to Los Angeles, Morris had a brief encounter with another filmmaker. Morris remembers him saying, "'I love your work.' I asked him which films he liked and he said, 'The ones you did for Miller High Life.' No one in the commercial world even knows I *make* documentaries and vice versa!"[1] Morris's anecdote might suggest that his television commercial work is a completely discreet, and perhaps surprising, element of his artistic career.

Morris's participation in commercial production is not usual for feature-film directors. Directors have been involved in television advertising since the 1960s, when filmmakers such as Richard Lester, director of *A Hard Day's Night* (1964), and Robert Downey Sr., director of *Putney Swope* (1969), also directed commercials. There was a stigma at the time attached to commercial work, however. Former head of the Association of Independent Commercial Producers Jerry Bernstein explains, "There was a time when even actors wouldn't do commercials. The feeling was it was not a great art form."[2]

This stigma has diminished over the last couple of decades. Production houses such as A Band Apart and Moxie Pictures have set up special divisions specifically designed to ease this transition from feature filmmaking to commercial production.[3] Commercial production houses have also expanded into talent management and feature-film production.[4] On the personnel side of the industry, some of the most successful contemporary feature filmmakers such as Ridley Scott, Alan Parker, and Tony Scott started directing commercials before producing major blockbusters. In addition, directors such as David Lynch, Martin Scorsese, and David Fincher went on to direct television commercials for companies such as Calvin Klein, American Express, and Nike after establishing successful careers in feature-film production. Errol Morris falls into the latter category, as he started directing commercials after the release of *The Thin Blue Line*.

Commercial production is not merely a discrete part of Morris's artistic career, as his commercial work frequently has a measurable impact on his documentary films and vice versa. Morris's documentaries, and in particular his approach to visuals, often provide an aesthetic model for his advertisements, while his commercials provide funding, opportunities for experimentation, and physical production resources for his feature films.

Before we trace out Morris's commercial career, it is important to first understand the structure of television commercial industry and the role of the commercial director in this system.[5] There are three primary parties in the development of a television commercial: the client, the advertising agency, and the production company. Each individual production can be different, but there are a few general roles each company plays in the process. The client, such as Nike or American Express, communicates information about the product to the advertising agency, sets the budget, and pays for the commercial. Once given the product and the basic parameters for the advertising campaign, the advertising agency develops the commercial's concept or message and provides any needed media research for the campaign.

After the client and advertising agency develop the specifics for the commercial campaign, they begin the search for a company to handle the production of the commercial. The commercial director, who is under contract with either a production company or a freelance artist, is often an important component in this search. Commercial directors' reputations can be based on their previous commercial accomplishments, their particular visual style, or their established relationships with clients and advertising agencies. Once the client and ad agency decide on a number of possible directors, these different production companies begin a bidding process to win the contract. In addition to the projected cost of the production, the director's ideas about the commercial are also included in each bid. The reputation and vision of the director are two of the most important factors in this hiring decision.

Morris's commercial career started with the production company American Pictures before moving on to Vanguard Films and then Chelsea Pictures. During this time, he produced a number of commercial campaigns for clients such as Liberty Mutual Insurance and the brokerage firm Quick and Reilly.[6] Morris joined Boston-based Picture Park in 1993, where he directed antismoking public service announcements for the Massachusetts Department of Health, as well as spots for Stop & Shop, American Express, 7-Eleven, and Ford.[7]

Errol Morris joined @radical.media in 1998 "to develop a larger presence on national television," directing spots for Adidas, Volkswagon, Dell, Levi's, Mastercard, Eastman Kodak, Nissan, Volkswagon, Hewlett Packard, United Airlines, and many others.[8] It was this first year with @radical.media that marked a turning point in Morris's commercial career. The Portland-based advertising firm Wieden + Kennedy approached Morris to direct a campaign for Miller High Life beer. The incredible success of the subsequent commercials made Morris a sought-after director in the industry. Morris changed production companies again in 2005, moving with producer Robert Fernandez from @radical.media to Moxie Pictures, where has continued to make commercials for clients such as Sharp, AOL, and UPS.

To best understand Errol Morris's entry and success in the advertising industry, it is important to note the value television advertising places on eye-catching visuals.[9] While a feature filmmaker may be more expensive and less experienced than directors that work exclusively in advertising, one of the benefits of a director such as Errol Morris is that he has developed a distinctive visual style that may be advantageous to a campaign. Dan Levinson, the president of Moxie Pictures, notes, "The Hollywood directors who have been most successful on Madison Avenue are those who are known for their signature points of view—companies tap them when their cinematic style is one they want for an ad campaign."[10]

The Thin Blue Line demonstrated that Morris could create unique, memorable images, particularly in the film's reenactment scenes. Morris remembers, "When I started working on ads people wanted me to do reenactments because of what they had seen in *The Thin Blue Line*."[11] This connection with *The Thin Blue Line* is evident in many of Morris's commercials, including his Miller High Life campaign.[12] During the reenactments of Officer Wood's murder, the events are often fragmented into a series of specific actions framed in close-up: a hand drops off a steering wheel, feet walk up to the car, a gun emerges from the dark, feet twist and spin, and so forth. Faces in the reenactment scenes are also fragmented into eyes, ears, and mouths. Morris's High Life commercials also use close framings that crop the filmed objects, including the working-class men that populate the commercials. For example, as a mosquito attempts to attach itself to one of the High Life men for the blood that is "teeming with man juice from Milwaukee," there are shots of the man's head. We see the side of his head, half of his face, the top of his head, but never the whole head or face (see figure 4.1).

Morris's visual style in *The Thin Blue Line* has been the most influential element in shaping Morris's reputation in the advertising industry, although clients and advertising agencies have also used Morris's other documentaries as inspiration for their campaigns. For example, the creative team at

FIGURE 4.1. □ *The Thin Blue Line* and "Mosquito" for Miller High Life

the Fallon Worldwide advertising agency contacted Morris about directing a campaign for Citibank after watching *Gates of Heaven*. The agency was struck by one scene in particular: a single, static, forty-six-second shot of Zella Graham and her dog singing "I love my mama" to each other. Morris shot twenty-four thirty-second ads for Fallon and Citibank working with the tagline, "There is more to life than money."

The well-financed Citibank campaign allowed Morris the flexibility to shoot with multiple cameras and a wide range of film gauges and stocks, a luxury Morris did not enjoy when shooting *Gates of Heaven*. These commercials nonetheless bear a strong resemblance to Morris's early films, in particular the Graham scene in *Gates of Heaven*. For instance, many of the Citibank commercials are comprised of a static, single take and sometimes have the same symmetrical framing as the *Gates of Heaven* scene. The topics and themes of the commercials also resemble the quirky nature of *Gates of Heaven*. In a spot entitled "Bunny Girl," for instance, a young girl makes "bunny lips" for thirty seconds in a stationary close-up. Morris also takes a portion of the Graham scene and uses it as one of the Citibank commercials.

Morris's feature films were an important reference for ad agencies at the beginning of his commercial career, as they provided models for what he could accomplish in his commercial work. After a number of successful campaigns, Morris developed distinct and identifiable stylistic continuities in his advertising work.[13] Surprisingly, Morris did not start using interviews in his commercials until after the September 11, 2001, attacks on the World Trade Center. Morris produced a series of commercials for United Airlines in which employees of the airline discuss topics such as their history with the company, their thoughts about flying, and what it means to be an American.

After seeing his United Airlines commercials, Laura Ziskin, a producer for the Seventy-fourth Annual Academy Awards, asked Morris to produce a short film for the introduction of the show.[14] Morris interviewed dozens of people, including artists, scholars, and politicians, for the four-minute short. Morris shot the interviews against a white backdrop.[15]

In both the United Airlines campaign and the Academy Awards film, Morris used his Interrotron interviewing machine. The Interrotron technology is adapted from the teleprompter, a device that uses a two-way mirror to project text on a screen placed directly in front of the camera lens. The teleprompter permits the speaker to read prepared remarks while also maintaining eye contact with the camera lens (and the viewer). Morris uses two teleprompters for his Interrotron, one to film his interview subject and the other to film himself in a separate space. Instead of projecting text on the teleprompter screen, Morris projects each interview image on the other teleprompter. This allows the interview subject to speak to an image of Morris and Morris to speak to an image of the interview subject. This also ensures the interview subject maintains eye contact with Morris during the interview, or more precisely a video image of Morris, as well as eye contact with the camera lens.[16] Morris first used the Interrotron in 1992 when interviewing Fred Leuchter, and continued to use it for all of his documentaries from *Fast, Cheap and Out of Control* up through *Tabloid*.

Interviewing subjects with his Interrotron against a white background developed into a signature style for Morris, as he repeated it in a number of subsequent advertising campaigns.[17] For instance, after seeing the Academy Awards film, Steve Jobs, CEO of Apple, hired Morris to direct Apple's "Switch" campaign using the same white background format.[18] Morris also employed this approach for a series of MoveOn.org political ads for the 2004 presidential campaign. Morris used the Apple "Switch" campaign as a model and interviewed over forty men and women from all over the country. They describe how they voted for George W. Bush in 2000 and why they will "switch" and vote for John Kerry in 2004.[19] Four years later, Morris directed a "People in the Middle for Obama" campaign where individuals discuss why they were voting for Barack Obama. For both the Kerry and Obama ads, Morris again shot the interviews against a white backdrop. Morris also uses this "single character against a white background" in his spots for UPS, Quaker Oats, Kentucky Fried Chicken, and Depend undergarments.

In addition to this use of a white backdrop, Morris often employs visual elements such as slow-motion photography, canted angles, and shallow depth of field in his commercials. Chris Lange, a creative director at advertising agency Fallon Worldwide, identifies Morris's approach to framing in particular as a defining feature of his PBS commercials: "He (and DP Peter Donahue) used a unique approach and way to frame close-up shots so they appear untraditional."[20] In his PBS commercial "Photobooth," for instance, Morris uses both the framing and the green curtain to crop the actor's upper body (see figure 4.2).

Many of these stylistic devices also help foreground the product in the

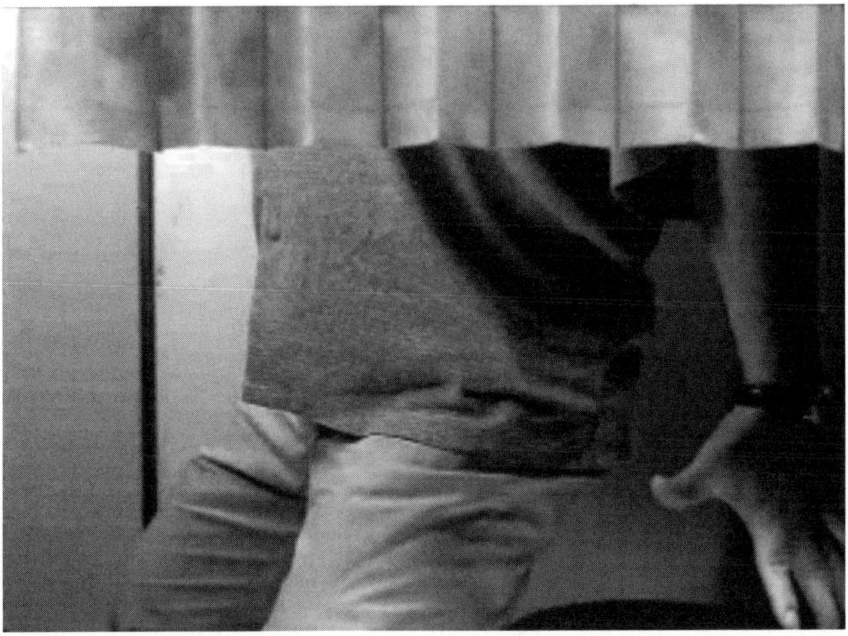

FIGURE 4.2. ▫ "Photobooth" for PBS

advertisements. For instance, in the commercial "Diane" for Quaker Oats, Morris arranges objects in multiple planes of the image and uses the shallow depth of field of a long lens to foreground the Quaker Oatmeal box. These devices can also serve exterior demands such as federal advertising regulations. For example, commercials for alcohol are not allowed to show the actual consumption of the beverage. Morris's cropped framings in his Miller High Life campaign occasionally obscure the actor's mouth while at the same time revealing the beer bottle and suggesting consumption.

The advertising world began recognizing Morris's contributions to the field after about a decade of directing commercials. The Association of Independent Commercial Producers asked Morris to give a presentation at the Museum of Modern Art in 2000. A year later he was the first director to be nominated for two Academy of Television Arts and Sciences prime-time Emmy nominations for his "Light" and "Phonebooth" PBS commercials.[21] He was also nominated for the year's best commercial director for 2003.[22] Errol Morris has become an established, well-respected commercial director, and his name is widely recognized throughout the advertising industry.

So if clients and advertising agencies were attracted to Errol Morris because of his distinctive visual style and eventually his reputation in the industry, what was Morris's attraction to being a commercial director? One obvious reason is that commercials allow Morris to fund his other projects. Morris's films are among the most financially successful documentaries ever made, but the relatively small profits are not enough to consistently and fully finance his subsequent films. Commercial directing is a lucrative business if one is successful, and Morris's television ads allow him to continue to make documentaries.

Morris's advertising work also provides production resources and opportunities for experimentation. Unlike the limited budgets for his documentaries, Morris explains that his commercial budgets allow for the incorporation of new technology and stylistic techniques: "I usually have an awful lot of money at my disposal. I like the opportunity to experiment with all this equipment and cinematic toys. I've gained a lot of experience this way."[23]

Morris also acknowledges that this experimentation sometimes makes its way into his subsequent films: "A lot of the techniques I've learned in commercials I've applied to my documentary filmmaking and vice versa."[24] In a 2000 campaign for Robertson Stephens, for instance, Morris locked down the camera and shot a series of single takes at different speeds using an intervalometer, which counts intervals of time and triggers exposures. Morris then layered the shots so that the moving, semi-opaque people in the foreground are set against the unchanging, solid buildings in the background. Morris was impressed with the resulting images, explaining, "The fixed element and the elements moving at different speeds ended up really quite beautiful. I've never seen anything quite like it."[25] Morris later used this technology for some of the cutaway footage in *The Fog of War*, creating the same kind of semi-transparent layering of humans in the foreground set against the solid background of the market (see figure 4.3).

Morris's commercials also supply filmmaking resources and personnel for his documentary films. Morris explains, "Often, I've been able to shoot segments of my features on the back end of commercials. In *The Fog of War* there are scenes we filmed in Shanghai and Tokyo. I didn't take a crew over to those places specifically to get those shots. We were there shooting a [Cisco] commercial and at the end of the working day spent a time collecting

FIGURE 4.3. □ "Different" for Robertson Stephens and *The Fog of War*

material for the McNamara film."[26] Morris also uses the same crew, as when director of photography Peter Donahue worked on both the Cisco commercials and *The Fog of War*.[27]

Morris's ability to develop distinctive visuals and experiment with different technology is in part allowed by the *kinds* of commercials he produces. All of Morris's commercials can be categorized as brand advertising, as opposed to retail advertising. Jed Alger, an advertising writer and collaborator on a number of Morris's commercial campaigns, describes the general distinction between retail and brand advertising: "Strictly speaking, you could say that a retail ad would require some kind of selling proposition—'High Life Lite, now only $8.00 a twelve pack.' Or a car ad that touts a rebate plan. Or zero percent financing or something. [Brand advertising includes] ads that promote the personality behind the company or the product in the hope that people will identify with the brand and, in the end, buy lots of stuff."[28] Brand advertising allows for greater flexibility in the form of the commercial, as it is not obligated to make a specific product pitch. It rather has to connect a general idea, attitude, or emotion to the client's brand.

Morris describes his commercial campaign for Citibank as being centered around a fairly broad concept: "The idea was to use these moments—I'm not exactly sure how you would describe them—quintessential moments, idiosyncratic moments, strange moments, whatever."[29] Although Morris is severely restricted in terms of the length of the spots, thirty seconds in the Citibank ads, these brand commercials permit an openness, in both concept and form, that would not be possible for a more retail-oriented campaign.[30]

In our examination of Errol Morris's filmmaking career, his television commercials may at first glance seem tangential to his more serious, personal, and creative nonfiction films. It is important to recognize that Morris's commercials allow experimentation that is sometimes incorporated into his feature documentaries. These commercials permit directors such as Morris to survive as artists and continue to make films.

■ *Errol Morris' First Person*

Errol Morris encountered a much different financial situation in his television series *Errol Morris' First Person*, which he describes as "being done for a budget of a couple commercials."[31] Despite the small budget, the *First Person* series also allowed Morris to test new approaches to visual style and filmmaking technology, and represents some of his most stylistically adventurous work.

In the mid-1990s, Morris began pitching a television series, at first titled *Errol Morris: Interrotron Stories*, to a number of different networks. The idea for the series was to profile individual people or events with odd, tabloid-like stories. Morris's first pilot, entitled "The Stalker," profiles Bill Kinsley and his conflicts with fellow postal worker Thomas McIlvane, who subsequently shot nine former colleagues at the post office. Morris screened a rough cut to ABC, and they expressed interest in airing the pilot episode but eventually put a hold on the production because of the case's pending litigation. Morris then submitted an idea for a new episode about an Alabamian man's involvement in the Ku Klux Klan. ABC decided not to pick up Morris's series, in part because they feared Morris's choices in subject matter would continue to produce legal problems.[32]

Britain's Channel Four and Fox Broadcasting Company also expressed interest in the series, with Fox paying for an additional pilot. In this second pilot, entitled "The Parrot," Morris investigates the murder of Jane Gill. There are no witnesses to the crime except for Jane's talking parrot Max, whose cryptic utterances may be the key to discovering Jane's killer. Fox planned on airing five hours of the series in the fall of 1995 but ultimately passed on the show.[33]

The American cable channel Bravo eventually picked up the series, whose name was changed to *Errol Morris' First Person*. The series began on March 1, 2000, with "Stairway to Heaven," a half-hour interview with diagnosed autistic and slaughterhouse designer Temple Grandin. The short film had originally premiered at the 1998 Telluride Film Festival.

Bravo aired a total of eleven half-hour episodes at the 10:30 p.m. time slot on Wednesday nights, part of what Bravo called "Counterculture Wednesday." *First Person* was paired with *Talelights*, a show that documents the travels of journalist Jay Schadler as he hitchhikes around the country.[34] The quirky, sometimes bizarre nature of Morris's interview subjects fit well into this "counterculture-programming" concept. For instance, "I Dismember Mama" examines Saul Kent's pioneering work in cryonics, as well as the criminal charges that he decapitated his mother and froze her head before she was actually dead. In "You're Soaking in It," Morris interviews Joan Dougherty, whose stepson killed himself with a shotgun and, after having to clean up the remains of the suicide, started her own crime-scene cleaning business.

A year later, Bravo's sister cable channel, Independent Film Channel (IFC), picked up the second and final season *First Person*. IFC aired six episodes of the series, two of which were an hour long.[35] Morris continued his examination of the surprising and strange in the second season, although the subjects were generally less tabloid oriented than in the first season. For instance, "Mr. Personality" is about forensic psychologist Michael Stone and his formula for determining a criminal's cruelty quotient, and "One in a Million Trillion" examines Rick Rosner and his fight with the TV game show *Who Wants to Be a Millionaire* over what he believes to be an unfair question. The second season also includes Morris's most serious episode of the series, entitled "Leaving the Earth," which explores Denny Fitch's heroic handling of a seriously damaged United Airlines plane in 1989.

First Person received some critical praise throughout its two seasons. *Time* magazine named the first season as one of the top ten television shows of 2000.[36] Despite the acclaim, Morris could not find a network to produce a third season. The reasons for this failure bring us back to Morris's initial difficulties with attracting a network. In addition to their concerns about potential legal issues, ABC had difficulty figuring out how the show would fit in its prime-time lineup.[37] Morris's interview-based stories were not straight news, such as the ABC series *20/20*, nor were they conventional dramas such as ABC's *The Practice*. Fox Broadcasting Company had a similar reaction to the show, and Morris remembers a Fox executive saying, "[Television viewers] want at most ten to fifteen percent new. Now what we have here, Errol, this looks to me like forty percent new. This might be even fifty percent new. There's just too much new here."[38]

The idea that *First Person* was "too new for broadcast television" is not merely a generous explanation of why ABC and Fox rejected the show but also an informative account of how the show compared to other television shows at the time. While a show like *20/20* would cover issues such as new research on schizophrenia and conduct interviews with celebrities like Barbra Streisand, Morris examined people and stories on the margin, such as Sondra London and her multiple relationships with mass murderers. Beyond the subject matter, Morris's handling of these subjects, both in terms of the visual style as well as Morris's particular interests in these stories, is quite different from the anchorperson-centered journalism at the time. Morris used the series as another avenue for experimentation that differentiated it from other television programs as well as his feature documentary films.

It is important to first note a number of basic similarities between Morris's documentaries and the *First Person* series, with perhaps the most evident being the basic interview format of the television show. Morris uses his Interrotron interviewing device and incorporates a variety of cutaway footage, including archival photographs, fictional found footage, and stylized reenactments. All of the episodes in both seasons have music as well, composed by either John Kusiak or Caleb Sampson, with the latter also scoring *Fast, Cheap and Out of Control* and *Mr. Death: The Rise and Fall of Fred A. Leuchter, Jr.* A number of Morris's feature-film collaborators also worked with him on the series, including cinematographer Peter Donahue, editor Karen Schmeer, and production designer Ted Bafaloukos.

There are also thematic intersections between Morris's television series and his documentary films. Human subjectivity and epistemological questions often become the central thematic elements in *First Person*. For instance, attorney Murray Richman discusses his career representing mobsters in "The Only Truth." Morris explores Richman's rationalizations for his defense of thieves, thugs, and murderers, including Richman's postmodern treatise on truth: "The only truth in life is that there is no truth." In "The Smartest Man in the World," Morris profiles Chris Langan, a nightclub bouncer who has the highest recorded IQ in history. Langan describes what it is like to have superior intelligence and proclaims that he is "closer to absolute truth than anyone before me." The tone of these episodes is also familiar. Morris brings a critical, ironic sensibility to these people and topics, and the episodes are often a mix of humor, eccentricity, and sentiment.

Much like his television advertising, the *First Person* series provided Morris with an opportunity to try new approaches to visual style. Morris occasionally experiments with devices he introduced in earlier films. For example, Morris employs jump cuts and black screen interruptions in earlier documentaries, but he includes these disruptions more frequently in the *First Person* series. It is not unusual to see a black screen every other cut or successive jump cuts four or five times in a sequence.

Morris also repeatedly uses computer-generated sequences in *First Person* episodes. In "Mr. Personality," forensic psychologist Michael Stone discusses

FIGURE 4.4. □ "Mr. Personality" and *The Fog of War*

the "descriptors" that help rank the seriousness of any particular psychopath. Morris cuts to a number of different computer-animated shots of these descriptors printed on pieces of paper falling through the air. Morris later uses this "falling objects" animation in *The Fog of War*, as computer-animated numbers fall from the sky onto Tokyo during Robert McNamara's testimony about the firebombing of the city (see figure 4.4).

Errol Morris also introduces new visual elements and filmmaking technology in his *First Person* series. He has frequently used artificial light to illuminate the interviewees. In a few of the *First Person* episodes, Morris for

FIGURE 4.5. □ "The Killer Inside Me"

the first time changes this lighting during the interview itself. In "The Killer Inside Me," Morris first darkens the key light on Sondra London's face as she talks about her romantic dreams about the Grim Reaper and then increases the intensity of the light, overexposing the left side of her face (see figure 4.5).

Morris's Interrotron images in his documentaries are completely stable

FIGURE 4.6. ◻ "The Parrot"

without any camera movement, as are all of Morris's interview images in every documentary up to this point. Throughout the *First Person* series, Morris breaks with this pattern as he pans, tracks, zooms, cants, and rocks the camera back and forth. Sometimes this movement is relatively subtle, whereas other times it is quite pronounced. For instance, in an interview with Evelyn Bruce in "The Parrot," Morris begins a shot with a canted close-up of Evelyn's face and continues to track and pan left until Evelyn's face is almost out of the frame (see figure 4.6).

Morris uses the Interrotron in four episodes of *First Person*, after which he begins experimenting with a modified version of the interview system called the Megatron. The Megatron uses the same teleprompter system but adds up to twenty digital cameras, a combination of prosumer and small lipstick cameras placed around the interview room. Unlike the mobile primary camera, these additional cameras are locked into place and cannot move. Morris could not afford to have all of the different cameras recording on their own deck, so the cameras are fed into an eight-channel video board. A technician uses a switcher during the interview to determine which of the cameras are recorded to tape.[39]

Morris decided to shoot on digital video in part because of the series' limited budget. It would have been expensive to shoot on film, especially using up to twenty different cameras. Digital video was not only less expensive but also allowed Morris to shoot for extended periods of time without interrupting the interview to change film rolls. As we noted in previous chapters, Morris's approach to interviewing involves letting his subjects talk without interruption, and he is better able to achieve this less obtrusive approach with digital video.[40]

Digital video also presented some challenges. Morris was not happy with the image quality of video.[41] At the time, digital video also had an inherently large depth of field, in which much of the image is in focus. The resulting image can look somewhat flat, as focus differences do not demarcate different planes of depth. In order to solve this problem, Morris sometimes positioned semi-opaque screens behind the interviewee. Together with the lighting, these screens contribute to a sense of depth behind the subject. Morris later used this interview mise-en-scène in *The Fog of War*, which he also shot on digital video (see figure 4.7).

While digital video's depth of field was a problem for Morris, the Megatron offered a number of new stylistic options. The most dramatic difference between the Megatron and all of Morris's previous work is that many of the camera angles do not provide the impression of eye contact with the viewer. Most of the cameras are not placed behind the teleprompter screen, and Morris often cuts to oblique angles, sometimes fragmenting the subject's face.

Morris also puts the Megatron device and himself on display throughout the *First Person* series, marking the first time he is visually present in his work. In "Mr. Debt," for instance, Morris cuts to a lipstick camera slightly above the lower mirror of the teleprompter system. Morris also has additional cameras directed back toward the main Interrotron camera itself and occasionally shows the viewer this distinctive setup (see figure 4.8).

We also frequently hear Morris's voice as he interacts with his subjects. Morris's voice is present in earlier films, but his audible interactions in *First Person* are of a different nature. For instance, at the end of *The Thin Blue Line*, Morris asks David Harris basic questions about the murder: "What do you think . . . about whether or not [Adams] is innocent?" Morris becomes a more distinct personality in the *First Person* episodes. About halfway through "Mr. Debt," for instance, Morris tells consumer advocate Andrew Cappocia about his own run in with a hounding creditor: "I used to have a guy call me

FIGURE 4.7. □ "Mr. Personality" and *The Fog of War*

every morning, Mr. Montori, from a credit agency. And he would leave these messages because I would never, of course, pick up the phone. 'Mr. Morris, have you no sense of shame?'"[42] This is the first time that we ever hear Morris as something other than a questioning voice, and it is not the only example in the series. In "The Killer Inside Me," Morris shows us how Sondra London's dissatisfaction with one of his questions makes him change the query. When Morris asks, "Why this attraction to serial killers?" London replies, "What a lame question. You can do better than that. That is lame."

FIGURE 4.8. ◻ "Mr. Debt" and "Smiling in a Jar"

Morris stumbles and then asks, "Why the attraction to Danny Rolling?" a question that London then answers.[43]

As an opportunity for experimentation, Morris tests certain techniques and approaches in the *First Person* series. Some of these evolve and Morris uses them in later films, and others he does not. For instance, Morris does not use the Megatron in any subsequent documentary, nor does he show this degree of personal involvement with the interview subject. But Morris does have more of a presence in his later work; he uses digital video for later films and continues to play with different framings and backgrounds for his interviews.

Beyond his experimentation with technology and visual style, the *First Person* series allowed Morris to develop his documentary narratives around single-person profiles. While all of Morris's films have a "profile" element to them, *First Person* is different from these earlier films because Morris focuses on one individual's perspective. With the exception of "The Parrot," all of the *First Person* episodes isolate a single interview subject, without anyone else's voice or viewpoint (excluding Morris). Morris's later films, in particular *The Fog of War*, embrace this focused, profile-oriented approach.

Errol Morris's television work is separated from his feature films in part to simplify the organization of this book. It is important to keep in mind how centrally important his commercials and television series are to his financial stability and aesthetic development after *The Thin Blue Line*. These television works can also stand by themselves as rich, innovative works of art.

5 *Fast, Cheap and Out of Control*

IN AN INTERVIEW WITH ERROL MORRIS, Megan Cunningham asks, "Why have you avoided traditional techniques?" Morris responds, "Doesn't interest me. It's not so complicated. One of the things that's interesting about documentary is that you have an opportunity to *create* something, not just in terms of content but that's also stylistically, very different. And not just different from feature films, but different from other documentaries as well. It's the opportunity of doing something that is innovative. And I have played around in different ways with what it *means* to make documentaries."[1] Morris's response points to two of my primary arguments in this book. First, Morris identifies his films as participating in the documentary tradition, breaking with the conventional argument that his work constitutes a reflexive rejection of the form. To support this idea, we have investigated the ways in which Morris's films draw on nonfiction practices and make definite claims about his subjects and the world around them. Second, Morris attributes the experimentation in his films in part to the flexibility of the documentary form. His interest in employing reenactments, nondiegetic sounds, and fictional found footage does not constitute a rejection of the nonfiction film but rather is part of a long tradition of creatively using style and structure to investigate the world.

Errol Morris's 1997 documentary *Fast, Cheap and Out of Control* represents his boldest experiment with visuals, sound, and structure. There are important continuities with Morris's earlier documentaries, such as a wide variety of visual material, an associational structure, an open voice, and a primary interest in the nature and limits of human subjectivity. *Fast, Cheap and Out of Control* also tests the limits of this approach to the documentary form. Morris's previous films ask the viewer to make subtle connections between interview testimony and visual elements to uncover the films' thematic concerns. *Fast, Cheap and Out of Control* pushes this further by focusing on four interview subjects with few if any apparent connections. The film also employs a frenetic visual style and a loose associational structure that challenges the audience to make meaningful connections between the people and ideas in the film.

Fast, Cheap and Out of Control is not merely an open challenge to locate similarities and differences in the lives of these men. As with all of his films, Morris actively highlights particular pieces of testimony to draw out themes related to human subjectivity. As the title of the film intimates, *Fast, Cheap and Out of Control* investigates the ways in which these four men understand and try to control the chaotic world around them. Morris locates this disorder in their personal histories and their professions, and each man uses his own specialized expertise to organize and make sense of their lives. *Fast, Cheap and Out of Control* also focuses on how these men deal with death, the one aspect of their lives that is very much out of their control.

Background

Morris began planning *Fast, Cheap and Out of Control* in 1993, shortly after the release of *A Brief History of Time*. He originally conceived the film as a profile of many different subjects who would not be directly related to one another. That is, they would not be connected by a particular place, as were the people in *Vernon, Florida*, nor would they be united by a specific event, as were those involved in Randall Dale Adams's murder trial in *The Thin Blue Line*. The concept remained the same, but Morris eventually settled on the modest number of four interview subjects before starting production.

Morris's choice of subjects was partially influenced by their proximity to his Cambridge, Massachusetts, home and office. Julia Sheehan, Morris's wife, read an article in *Connoisseur Magazine* about Rodney Brooks, a robotics researcher at nearby MIT. In addition, Morris always had an interest in topiary gardens and discovered there was a garden in Portsmouth, Rhode Island, where topiary gardener George Mendonça sculpted animals out of boxwood and privet.[2] Morris also developed a curiosity about mole rats and spoke to a number of scientists about them. He then read an article in the *New York Times* about Ray Mendez, an African mole rat enthusiast and Hollywood insect wrangler for films such as *Creepshow* (1982), *The Silence of the Lambs* (1991), and *Joe's Apartment* (1996). Mendez was living in New York City at the time, and after setting up a meeting, Morris decided to put him in the film. The fourth subject in *Fast, Cheap and Out of Control* is Dave Hoover, a retired lion tamer whom Morris began filming when he was planning *The Thin Blue Line*.[3] Morris borrowed the title for his four-person documentary from Rodney Brooks's 1989 article "Fast, Cheap and Out of Control: A Robot Invasion of the Solar System," which argues that chance and sheer volume are the best principles for using artificial intelligence in space exploration.[4]

Morris's decision to focus his film on four ostensibly unrelated men had certain production advantages and disadvantages. Morris did not have to do the same kind of extensive research and investigation as for *The Thin Blue Line*, and he was able to film *Fast, Cheap and Out of Control* in only ten days in a Boston studio.[5] On the other hand, Morris's subjects did not provide a clear structuring principle for film, such as that of a murder investigation in *The Thin Blue Line* or the preexisting material of a book adaptation in *A Brief History of Time*. As a result, Morris and his editors, Shondra Merrill and Karen Schmeer, spent three years editing the film.[6] Morris remembers, "Someone once asked me about the editorial strategy in that movie, and it took literally *years* to edit and, at one point I gave up on it, completely, because I could *not* edit it!"[7] In between the time when Morris wrapped shooting and finished editing the film, both his mother and stepfather passed away, and Morris includes a dedication title to both at the end of *Fast, Cheap and Out of Control*.

Morris extended his relationship with PBS American Playhouse, who sponsored *The Thin Blue Line*, and Channel 4 TV, sponsor of *The Thin Blue Line* and *A Brief History of Time*, as both companies produced *Fast, Cheap and Out of Control*. The film had its world premiere at the Sundance Film Festival in January of 1997 and was released theatrically by Sony Classics ten months later.[8] *Fast, Cheap and Out of Control* grossed over eight hundred thousand dollars, substantially less than both *The Thin Blue Line* and *A Brief History of Time*, but nonetheless making it among the top one hundred grossing documentaries of all time.[9] The film also received a number of critical awards in 1997, including being named "Best Documentary" by the National Board of Review, the National Society of Film Critics, the New York Film Critics Circle, and the Boston Society of Film Critics. In addition, *Fast, Cheap and Out of Control* won the Independent Spirit "Truer than Fiction" prize at the Independent Spirit Awards.

■ Style

Ever since his first film, Morris has wanted to provide the impression that his interview subjects were making eye contact with the audience. Morris's desire for eye contact is in part a response to what he understands as a larger problem in documentary filmmaking: "Almost all interviews are filmed verité style with a camera, an interviewer and subject. You have a triangle where the camera takes the role of an observer, even voyeur. The camera is the third person observing two people talking. It's off to the side, and even though I'm looking into your eyes and you're looking into mine, this eye contact is something that the camera, sitting some feet from us both, doesn't capture. This means that the audience isn't really part of the conversation. They are merely observing it."[10] Morris would often place his head close to the camera to achieve the effect of a more immediate connection between interview subject and audience, although the subject's line of sight was always slightly off-axis.

Morris developed the Interrotron as a solution to this problem. The Interrotron is an interviewing system that his wife facetiously named by combining the words "interview" and "terror." As noted in the previous chapter, Morris uses a rigged teleprompter system in which the interview subjects speak to a projected image of Morris's face and Morris speaks to a projected image of their face. This interview system allows Morris to make eye contact with his subjects while his subjects look directly into the lens of the camera. Morris boasts that the Interrotron marks "the difference between faux first person and the true first person. . . . The Interrotron inaugurates the birth of true first-person cinema."[11]

One disadvantage of the Interrotron is that Morris's interview subjects are looking at his projected image instead of his actual face. This physical disconnect with the interviewer has the potential of negatively affecting the interview subject's comfort as well as the reliability and depth of the testimony. Morris recognizes this problem: "Seeing myself on screen like that for the first time I remember thinking 'How could anybody talk looking at this person?' But thankfully they do. . . . My production designer, Ted Bafaloukos, said to me, 'The beauty of this thing is that it allows people to do what they do best: watch television.' But the people being interviewed aren't watching regular TV. They're watching a TV set that really cares and wants to know more."[12]

It is difficult to resolve this question about the influence of the Interrotron on the interview testimony, but it has had definite impact on Morris's visual design. As we observed in the first chapter, Morris's desire for eye contact influenced the shot scales in his earlier films. Closer framings would highlight the fact that his interview subjects were looking not into the lens but rather at Morris offscreen. This is one reason *Gates of Heaven*, *Vernon, Florida*, and *A Brief History of Time* most frequently use medium shots for the interviews.

The interview framing patterns in *Fast, Cheap and Out of Control* are significantly different than all of Morris's previous documentaries. While just over half of the interviews are framed in medium close-up, Morris uses close-ups 33 percent of the time. Some of the close-ups in *Fast, Cheap and Out of Control* even border on extreme close-ups, cropping the subject's forehead and chin.

This increase in close-ups is in part due to the Interrotron, which places certain limitations on filming the interviews. Morris's face is significantly smaller on the teleprompter screen than it would be in real life. As a result, the camera cannot be further than eight feet from the subject because they need to see a clear picture of Errol on the teleprompter. Morris is thus limited on how wide he can frame the interview subject.

Morris's interview framings also have an effect on the interview mise-en-scène. In earlier films, Morris would carefully organize the space around the interview subject to create complex compositions that often had an informative relationship to the interview testimony. While the closer framings in *Fast, Cheap and Out of Control* provide the impression of direct eye contact with the viewer and highlight the facial expressions of the interview subject, they also place much of the background offscreen. Morris employs minimal, flat backgrounds, using desaturated browns and grays for *Fast, Cheap and Out of Control*, in contrast to the rich detail, intricate color design, and deep space in many of Morris's earlier interview compositions (see figure 5.1).

As the interview mise-en-scène becomes less relevant to the interview testimony, Morris becomes more reliant on cutaway images in *Fast, Cheap and Out of Control*. Morris uses almost twice as many cutaways as *The Thin Blue Line*, more than three times as many as in *A Brief History of Time* and almost eighteen times as many as in *Vernon, Florida*.

The Interrotron is not the only catalyst for change in Morris's visual style. In addition to more frequently using cutaway images in *Fast, Cheap and Out of Control*, Morris also experiments with the quality of the images. Up until

FIGURE 5.1. ◻ *Fast, Cheap and Out of Control*

Fast, Cheap, Morris valued the look of 35 mm film stock and, even when he had to shoot on 16 mm because of financial constraints, "the idea was to shoot 16 mm so carefully that the 16 mm would look like 35 mm."[13] Morris's attitude changed when he hired Robert Richardson as the director of photography for *Fast, Cheap and Out of Control*. Richardson, a well-established Hollywood cinematographer, had experimented with different film gauges and stocks on movies such as *Natural Born Killers* (1994) and *JFK* (1991), the latter of which earned him an Academy Award.

While Richardson and Morris shot all of the interview footage on 35 mm film, they used different stocks and gauges in the cutaway images for *Fast, Cheap and Out of Control*, shooting with color, black and white, video, Super 8 mm, 16 mm, Super 16 mm, and 35 mm.[14] Morris and Richardson also took some of the 35 mm dailies, transferred them to video, and then filmed them off a low-resolution television set. Morris remarks that this process of degrading of the imagery "produced some of the most beautiful images that I've ever seen, images that are in some very real sense reprocessed, a kind of visual equivalent of Velveeta Cheese. But somehow, unlike Velveeta Cheese, simply great."[15] Figure 5.2 is an image of George Mendonça walking through his topiary garden, in which the reprocessing of the image removes much of the visual detail and produces a strikingly abstract representation of the space.

FIGURE 5.2. ▫ *Fast, Cheap and Out of Control*

Morris employs a variety of visuals in all of his films, although *Fast, Cheap and Out of Control* displays a far greater variety of different angles (high, low, and canted), speeds (fast and slow), exposures (over and under), and found footage (documentary and fictional). For example, *The Thin Blue Line* uses fictional found footage from *The Student Body*, *Swinging Cheerleaders*, *Boston Blackie*, and *Dillinger*. Not only does *Fast, Cheap and Out of Control* double the number of different fictional sources used in *The Thin Blue Line* with its integration of clips from *The Big Cage* (1933), *King of Jungleland* (1936), *Zombies of the Stratosphere* (1952), *The Deadly Mantis* (1957), *Gigantor* (1964), and *Gobots* (1986), but also these clips appear much more frequently than in Morris's earlier films.

In addition, Morris has previously explored different ways of cutting together interview footage beyond the standard interview/illustrative cutaway format, from the long takes in *Gates of Heaven* to the use of black screen in *A Brief History of Time*. Morris pushes the boundaries of this interview/cutaway relationship in *Fast, Cheap and Out of Control*. For instance, he continues to cut to black during the interviews but does so more frequently and holds these black screens for longer periods of time than in *A Brief History of Time*. About twenty-two minutes into the film, for example, Morris cuts to black as a transition between interviews with Dave Hoover and Ray Mendez. The black screen continues for five seconds over the first half of Mendez's first sentence, significantly longer than any sequence in *A Brief History of Time*. Morris also includes jump cuts in the interviews as well as "lip flap" or "lip-sync errors," during which we hear a character speaking but the movement of their mouth does not match the testimony on the audio track.

Morris uses nondiegetic music in *Fast, Cheap and Out of Control*, but for the first time does not use a Philip Glass score. Morris hired Caleb Sampson, who had earlier worked with Morris on his *First Person* series, to compose the music for the film. Sampson had extensive experience composing music for silent films, fiction features, and documentary television series such as *Nova*, *The American Experience*, and *Scientific American*. Sampson's score for *Fast, Cheap and Out of Control* displays some similarities with Glass's scores for *The Thin Blue Line* and *A Brief History of Time*, as it often repeats musical phrases and motifs. Sampson's melodies include playful, staccato themes, and he often uses synthesizers and percussion instruments such as mallets and xylophones. The instrumentation and lively melodies frequently resemble circus music that, as we will examine later, connects to a central theme throughout the film.

The remarkable diversity of the audio and visuals, together with the film's focus on four distinct interview subjects, created a problem for Morris. He had an enormous amount of varied material that required organization. His solution involved the introduction of another technological first in his career: an Avid nonlinear editing system. Avid systems were increasingly popular with filmmakers in the 1990s, as they allowed editors to more quickly and freely arrange and reorder the film. Morris remarks, "It's a movie that could not have been made without an Avid. I can tell you that much. . . . There was media all over the place."[16]

Fast, Cheap and Out of Control represents Morris's most visually adventurous documentary. It is also a transitional film in terms Morris's visual style, introducing new technology and visuals that Morris continues in later documentaries. The most significant of these continuities is Morris's Interrotron, which he uses in every subsequent film.

Structure and Voice

Fast, Cheap and Out of Control is not merely an outlet for Morris's visual and technological experimentation. The film is also one of Morris's most structurally complex films. The visuals, sound track, and organization all combine to form a network of intricate layers and connections among the interview subjects. *Fast, Cheap and Out of Control* asks the viewer to locate connections between the subjects' professions, their personal histories, and the particular ways in which they view and understand the world around them.

This process of discovering similarities and differences among the interview subjects is not completely open to the viewers' inclinations. As with all of Morris's films, *Fast, Cheap and Out of Control* uses elements of style and structure to actively foreground particular topics and themes. This process of highlighting ideas and connections does not determine the viewer's understanding of the film, but it does create a framework through which the audience makes associations. These associations often connect to the role of knowledge, control, and death in these four men's lives.

The associational connections in the film do not come easily, however, leading critics such as Stephen Hunter to call any underlying concept of the film a fabrication: "Really, what unites them is merely the fact that Morris filmed his interviews with them."[17] In his article entitled "Errol Morris's Forms of Control," Ira Jaffe agrees to some extent with Hunter, arguing that Morris's experimentation with sound and image results in a film that is "considerably liberated, in its choices and arrangements of images and sounds, from documentary norms of clarity, causality, and continuity, and from the usual adherence to the actual historical world. . . . Although the audience may expect the subsequent images to mirror or illustrate the character's voice-over words, Morris's images often skid away. If their whimsical course does not entirely abandon the words, the relationship at least becomes ambiguous, rippling with irony, play, and contradiction."[18]

While some connections and questions in *Fast, Cheap and Out of Control* are left open as Jaffe's claims, the film is also considerably invested in clarity, causality, and continuity in order to tell its story. The stakes for explanation are not as high as in *The Thin Blue Line*, in which Morris needed to establish the identity of a murderer, or as in *A Brief History of Time*, where Morris had to provide some explanation of Stephen Hawking's scientific theories. Morris does nonetheless establish a range of information about his interview subjects in *Fast, Cheap and Out of Control*. As in all of his films, Morris is directing our attention in order to communicate certain facts about his subjects and make particular connections between them.

In order to avoid an incomprehensible mixture of audio and visuals, Morris provides some basic information about the men in the film. Sound and image are most straightforwardly informative at beginning of the film, when the audience is in most need of this kind of guidance. Once we learn some background details about these men, such as what they do for a living and how they became interested in these professions, Morris can more openly explore different the sound-image relationships without confusing the audience.

At the start of the film, Morris introduces the four subjects in the film and their areas of expertise. The film begins with a montage that includes robots, scenes from a circus, mole rats, and a topiary garden. After a scene from the Clyde Beatty film *King of Jungleland*, *Fast, Cheap* shows Dave Hoover, who remembers, "When I was a kid, I did want to be a wild animal trainer. I wanted to be a Clyde Beatty. A lot of kids want to be firemen, they want to be cowboys, whatever, but I wanted to be a wild animal trainer. I was really interested in it. There was a Catholic priest friend of ours that was a circus fan. My mother told Father Berney to have a talk with me to try to change my mind. Instead, he encouraged me. . . . He told her that the world had to have lion trainers, too."[19] On the image track, we see Hoover speaking as well as cutaway images of the circus and lions. An identifying intertitle appears after this segment that reads, "wild animal trainer dave hoover." The introductions of the other three interview subjects follow the same format. The interview subject discusses how he became interested in his area of expertise, and we see illustrative images as well as an identifying intertitle.

These conventional introductions at the beginning of *Fast, Cheap and Out of Control* are not the only moments of clarity and illustration. After this introductory segment, Hoover continues to discuss his childhood fascination with Beatty: "He was a motion picture personality as well as a circus performer in those days. And we didn't have television, but we did go to the movies every Saturday morning. You know, the serials, thirteen exciting episodes. And even by the standards then, it was pretty corny, but kids loved it." On the image track, we see the title credits for the 1936 Beatty serial *Darkest Africa*. The accompanying images illustrate Hoover's testimony, and the choice of the title credits clearly identifies the man on-screen as Beatty. It is important for the audience to recognize Beatty, as Morris frequently uses found footage of his movies to establish parallels between Hoover and Beatty.

Morris again employs an associational structure to foreground the similarities and differences among these men. In *The Thin Blue Line* and *A Brief History of Time*, Morris established a quasi-narrative structure by using the chronologies of a court case and Hawking's life to organize the films. Although *Fast, Cheap and Out of Control* begins with the subjects talking about their childhood, Morris does not provide this kind of chronology. Morris instead organizes the film around general topics and establishes associational links between the different pieces of testimony. *Fast, Cheap and Out of Control* is, in this way, closer in structure to Morris's first two films, *Gates of Heaven* and *Vernon, Florida*, which both have a looser associational organization.

Fast, Cheap and Out of Control begins with one of these general topic segments, within which Morris builds associational connections among the interview subjects. The men discuss how they became involved in their area of expertise; then they describe the early trials and errors in their careers. For instance, Hoover talks about how he once made the mistake of training his lions while wearing a wristwatch, which one of the lions used to seriously injure him. Ray Mendez then discusses the problems with finding an appropriate building material and organization for his mole rat exhibits: "I'm always telling myself stories, while I'm designing things, about how things are going to function. I thought I had a really beautiful nest chamber at the end of this pattern, and we found out that [for] mole rats, the last chamber is used as the bathroom." In this sequence, we can make an associational connection between Hoover's and Mendez's struggles to learn about lions and mole rats.

Morris also uses images and sounds to generate meaningful connections among the interview subjects. After the opening credits of the film, Hoover talks about his long-held interest in being a wild animal trainer. After Hoover orders a lion through a burning hoop, Morris cuts to a circus procession that includes clowns, men on stilts, and elephants. With Caleb Sampson's playful, staccato music playing over the transition, Morris cuts to a shot of George Mendonça's topiary garden that includes a giraffe, a camel, an elephant, and George himself arranged in a circular pattern reminiscent of the previous shot (see figure 5.3). This continuity in the composition and content (e.g., elephants), as well as the music playing over the cut, suggests a connection between the two spaces and the two men.

These visual and auditory connections are relatively straightforward at

FIGURE 5.3. ▫ *Fast, Cheap and Out of Control*

the beginning of the film. Morris, for the most part, pairs the "appropriate" images with each interview subject. When we hear Rodney Brooks talk about robot technology, for instance, we usually see robot-related imagery.

The sound-image relationships become increasingly complex as the film progresses. Morris often takes images that are initially associated with one particular interview subject and begins overlapping them with the testimony from the other subjects. For example, about thirty-five minutes into the film, Dave Hoover talks about his favorite lion John-John. Hoover describes the lion as "good natured" as we see images of Hoover training the lion to stand upright. George Mendonça then discusses the benefits of hand shears over electric shears to properly carve his topiary animals, or else "your animal has that brown look." Morris uses illustrative footage of John-John the lion and George using his hand shears for both of these interview segments.

Rodney Brooks then speaks about the creation of robots: "Many people have said to me, 'This is something that men do because men can't have babies themselves, and this is a way of building your own baby.'" Over this first part of Brooks's testimony, Morris uses footage of Mendonça sharpening and inspecting his hand shears. While Brooks is referring to building robots, the image of Mendonça modifies the referent of "this" in Brooks's testimony. Brooks continues, "I think there is some deeper-seated thing which crosses the sex boundaries: of understanding life by building something that is lifelike." And we are prompted to retroactively apply these reflections back on Mendonça and his construction of topiary animals. We can also apply this reading back further, as Hoover is training a lion to stand like a human.

Caleb Sampson's music also helps connect these sequences. After Hoover's interview, a delicate waltz carried by woodwind instruments plays over Mendonça's testimony about the advantages of hand shears. The music then continues without interruption during Brooks's discussion about building robots. This continuity in the music may not by itself indicate that there are important similarities between the interview subjects. Together with the organization of the testimony and the visuals, the music strengthens the applicability of Brooks's claim about "understanding life by building something that is lifelike" to the other men in the film.

This retroactive reading reinforces the previous and subsequent testimony in the film, and Brooks's statement becomes a central thematic issue in *Fast, Cheap and Out of Control*: Hoover, Mendonça, Brooks, and Mendez are training/sculpting/building/studying as a route to knowledge about themselves and the world around them. Various aspects of the men's professions often replicate human life and behavior. When Morris combines testimony such as "understanding life by building something that is lifelike" with the overlapping of one subject's images over others' testimony, the viewer is prompted to generalize the claim and consider the implications for the other interviewees.

Morris expands the idea that each interview subject's profession is an avenue for knowledge. Immediately following an interview with Mendez about the concept of death, Mendonça discusses a heavy storm in 1954 that destroyed much of the garden and decapitated his topiary giraffe. He remembers Miss Brayton, the owner of the garden, complaining that she would not live long enough to see another head on the giraffe "because I'm only going to live one more year." Mendonça then observes, "She was in her sixties at the time, and she lived to be ninety-four. It's just cut and wait. Cut and wait." When he mentions "cutting" and "waiting," Mendonça is referring to the gardening and topiary process. The placement immediately after Mendonça's discussion of Brayton's death, and reinforced by Mendez's reflection the concept of death, gives the testimony a new meaning. In this new context, the audience can augment Mendonça's testimony to something such as "it's just cut and wait for death."

With the recurring idea that these men's professions are, in some ways, an instrument for understanding themselves and life, we can generalize Mendonça's insight about gardening to a rather gloomy view of existence. The interview subjects in *Fast, Cheap and Out of Control* are frequently confronting circumstances that are erratic and volatile. Hoover has to train wild and dangerous animals, Brooks is trying to animate metal and wires, and Mendez is attempting to understand a small, enigmatic animal. Mendonça is not only struggling to tame the natural growth of his plants but also battling the weather. After describing a devastating snow storm that damaged his garden animals, Mendonça discusses the difficulties of being a topiary gardener: "You're fighting the elements to try to get them to grow where you want them to grow, get them to do what you want them to do. If it's not one thing, it's the other. . . . It's a constant battle all the time."

These four men are not passive in the face of their capricious professions, and one of Morris's primary interests in the film is their reaction to what seems to be inevitable. The question of control is of central importance in the film, as the men try to control the unruly world around them. For instance, Hoover often discusses his strategies to direct his lions' behavior, not only to put on a good performance for his audience but also to avoid injury. At one point, Hoover reflects on his learning process as a lion tamer: "You have to experience an injury. You have to experience chaos." This connection between an injury and chaos brings along with it a link between safety and control. Control, and the surrender of control, thus becomes a way of understanding Hoover's behavior.

While these men's professional expertise enhances their ability to control their surroundings, Morris frequently introduces the issue of death in the film, a fact of life that is ultimately out of everyone's control. We examined the role of death in the above Mendonça and Miss Brayton example, and this issue becomes most present at the end of the film. Hoover reflects on the death of Clyde Beatty, and Brooks describes how some people think silicon-based machines will eventually replace human beings. A montage of apocalyptic clips from a Beatty film is intercut with images of the circus, mole rats, and robots, after which Mendonça offers the final testimony in the film: "She said, 'Don't let anything happen to Green Animals. Keep Green Animals going.' I said, 'Well, as long as I live, I'll take care of it.' I don't know what will happen after that.'" Sampson's melancholy string music enhances the sadness of the inevitable as well as the courage of these men, in their struggle against the unstable, dangerous, and absurd nature of the world.

Fast, Cheap and Out of Control is a particularly complex film because each interview subject engages these issues of life, death, and control slightly differently. For instance, the objects of study for Brooks and Mendez have the potential to outlive humans, while Mendonça's and Hoover's professions, or at least their approach to the profession, are quickly dying out. Instead of all of the interview testimony intersecting with a similar issue, such as a court case or cosmology, the audience has to make meaningful connections and distinctions among four different people.

Morris uses the visual motif of the circus to reinforce the connections and themes in the film, much like the repetitions of the murder scene in *The Thin Blue Line* and the falling teacup in *A Brief History of Time*. Morris first associates the circus with Hoover, as it illustrates his profession. As the film progresses, Morris increasingly uses this footage over the other interview subjects' testimony. About thirteen minutes into the film, Brooks discusses the relationship between programming robots and their behavior: "Sometimes I feel a little like Yoda. I have to say, sort of, 'Just feel the force. Don't try and control the robot but feel how the world is going to control the robot.'" Mendez then describes his fascination with the mole rat: "To me, it's this incredible mammal that breaks the rules. A mammal that has a queen, king, soldiers, workers, all playing roles that they will play out, as far as we know, [for all] their life." Over both of these interviews, Morris cuts to footage of humans performing in the circus (see figure 5.4).

FIGURE 5.4. □ *Fast, Cheap and Out of Control*

These juxtapositions open up a variety of possible associations in the film. For instance, we are prompted to reflect on Brooks's observation and ask how the world controls *human* behavior. These connections are then further developed as Mendez's testimony and the circus images create associations among humans, other mammals, rule following, and social roles.

The circus is a useful visual analogy because it connects with many of these major themes in the film. For instance, the circus involves humans trying to control animals in order to make them perform. This performance also involves a certain amount of danger and the possibility of death, as these animals are not completely predictable and capable of injuring those around them. The connection between the circus and death is established at the beginning of the film as we see a clown running with a skeleton on its back (see figure 5.5).

The connections between the four men in *Fast, Cheap and Out of Control* are extended to human experience as a whole as the film progresses. About an hour into the film, Hoover says about his lions, "Once they've established this is their cage wagon, this is their cage. This is where they eat, this is where they sleep, this is where they drink; all their creature comforts are connected with that cage. They particularly don't want to leave it. They don't really consider themselves caged. Outside is the cage; inside is their world."

FIGURE 5.5. ▫ *Fast, Cheap and Out of Control*

Instead of using illustrative footage of lions in their cages, Morris cuts to a shot inside the cage directed out toward the audience, making it appear as though the audience is inside the cage (see figure 5.6). The circus audience is not a distinct character in the film, and there is no reason to think that this connection would apply to this particular group of people alone. The film is thus prompting the viewer to generalize this observation to the human condition.

The idea that humans have their own "cage world" that is distinct or disconnected from the world outside connects to Morris's career-long interest in exploring human subjectivity. As we have seen in all of Morris's films, this subjectivity can produce both profound insights into and strange distortions of the world "outside the cage," and the men in *Fast, Cheap and Out of Control* are no exception. Rodney Brooks describes how his research is leading to a world where robots will be everywhere and "everything about us will become intelligent. . . . These much more intelligent systems are going to infiltrate our lives, and they'll just be there operating in the background." Morris plays a scene from the 1952 serial *Zombies of the Stratosphere* in which a ridiculous-looking robot steals from a giant bank safe and fends off the bullets from a police officer's gun. As with the Disney film *The Black Hole* in *A Brief History of Time*, this juxtaposition of silly science-fiction footage

FIGURE 5.6. ▫ *Fast, Cheap and Out of Control*

with Brooks's testimony does not necessarily undermine or contradict it but rather positions it as a subjective vision or desire rather than a completely reliable prediction.

The progression from the more conventionally biographical elements at the beginning of the film to these conceptual associations brings us back to the importance of clarity and coherence in *Fast, Cheap and Out of Control*. The first part of the film helps familiarize the audience with the interview subjects, their biography and interests, as well as the relatively fragmented, associational structure of the film. After this orientation phase of the film, the audience can more comfortably comprehend the structurally and conceptually difficult elements in the second half of the film.

My argument that the film has an open voice does not mean that the viewer constructs these associations out of whole cloth. Morris initiates the possibility for and also shapes these associations through the use of sounds, images, and organizational strategies in the film. Morris wants the audience to understand the role of elements such as knowledge, control, and death in each of the interview subjects' lives and also how the men's testimonies intersect and inform one another. Morris's stylistic and structural decisions open up these connections more than determine their meaning, and this contributes to the complexity and the beauty of the film.

Reception and Ethics

The intersection of Morris's intimate control over the style and structure and the open quality of the film's voice again introduces ethical issues. Owen Gleiberman's *Entertainment Weekly* review of *Fast, Cheap and Out of Control* provides the most potent objection to the film, in which Gleiberman calls Morris's documentary "smug and callow," explaining, "The underlying message—and it's a snide one—is that the men themselves are dehumanized, mere reflections of their anthropomorphic hobbyhorses. The trouble is, it's the film that insists on seeing them that way. Morris is a master of the condescending detail (we're invited to snicker at one man's nerdy bow tie), but apart from the fact that the subjects are framed as geeks, nothing about them is all that strange—or fascinating. (Someone has to study mole rats.) Their status as 'characters' hinges solely on our laughter."[20]

It is important to note that Gleiberman's review is not a typical response to the film. Many reviewers praise the film's innovative approach and Morris's treatment of his subjects. For instance, Larry Worth notes in his review for the *New York Post* that Morris assembles "an eclectic group of oddballs, to be sure. But while some directors might make fun of these eccentrics, Morris chooses to celebrate them."[21] There are these positive characterizations of Morris's ethics in *Fast, Cheap and Out of Control*, but Gleiberman's complaints about the film are still informative. They echo many ethical concerns about Morris's earlier films and suggest a possible continuity in Morris's treatment of his subjects.

Gleiberman makes a number of claims in his review of *Fast, Cheap and Out of Control*, so let us examine them one at a time. The first assertion is that the film's subjects are "mere reflections of their anthropomorphic hobbyhorses," making them appear "dehumanized." This, in part, is a claim about Morris's explanatory range in the film. Morris does include some degree of explanation in the film, and that explanation is necessary to create informative connections between the subjects. But most of this explanation is centered around these men's areas of expertise and not much else. We do not get to know about Rodney Brooks's family or Dave Hoover's favorite recreational sport.

The overarching themes of the film, such as control, change, and death, are subsequently filtered through each subject's particular career. Hoover's retirement from lion training, the death of his hero Clyde Beatty, and his dreams of lions chewing on his head all inform how he deals with "passing" in his life. This is not an objection to the depth of explanation in the film, as are the concerns about Morris's failure to adequately explain Stephen Hawking's theories of the universe in *A Brief History of Time*, but instead has to do with the narrow range of explanations in *Fast, Cheap and Out of Control*. Gleiberman presumably thinks that this restricted focus prevents an adequate examination of their lives and personalities, and the interview subjects appear shallow as a result.

Morris's somewhat narrow focus in *Fast, Cheap and Out of Control* is in part due to his choice to connect four unrelated men with different professions. There are not obvious links among the four men and, along with that, there is any number of possible relationships between them. For instance, they are all older men, they all have some connection to animals or animal-like objects, and they all have strong ideas about how to best approach their profession. Morris wants to direct our attention to particular connections and themes, and if he were to expand the focus of the film beyond their professions, it would only complicate that objective. In addition, Morris only has a feature-length running time to profile each of these four men and access how they view the world around them. These constraints do not excuse Morris from Gleiberman's objection, but they do provide some context to Morris's decisions in the film.

The second part of Gleiberman's objection relates to the first: Morris's choice of subjects, or at least what he shows us of them, are so unremarkable that it allows Morris to exploit the foolish details of their appearance and lives. *Gates of Heaven*, *Vernon, Florida*, and *The Thin Blue Line* all provoked similar responses, although *Fast, Cheap and Out of Control* is somewhat different. As with Stephen Hawking's testimony in *A Brief History of Time*, *Fast, Cheap and Out of Control* presents all four subjects as highly knowledgeable and articulate about their areas of expertise. This is in stark contrast to, for instance, Morris's humorous treatment of Phillip Harberts's claims to business-management expertise in *Gates of Heaven* and Michael Randell's claims about acute memory recall in *The Thin Blue Line*. Gleiberman's objection is not that the film's subjects are inherently misguided or foolish but rather that these men are so ordinary that we are prompted to laugh at the foolish details of their lives.

FIGURE 5.7. ▫ *Fast, Cheap and Out of Control*

In an interview with Peter Chattaway, Morris responds to Gleiberman's review, at first addressing the claim that he is making fun of Mendez's butterfly bowtie (see figure 5.7). Morris explains, "Ray Mendez showed up wearing that tie. So then the question becomes, am I supposed to tell him to take the tie off? . . . Ray Mendez is possessed of . . . a sense of irony and of the fact that he's funny, and he's a really, really funny guy, and intentionally so."[22] Morris continues to explain that Mendez would not sign a release until he saw the finished film because of a bad experience with a previous documentary. Mendez loved the movie and quickly signed the release.

Although Mendez's bowtie is a very small detail in the film, the claim that Morris is making fun of this article of clothing points to a larger ethical issue in the film. What makes Gleiberman think that Morris is making fun of this tie? No one in the film ever mentions the bowtie, and Morris never foregrounds it with something such as an insert shot.

The problem may lie with Morris's highly controlled style, as the audience is aware that they are not watching an unobtrusive, observational film. Morris makes clear his creative intrusion into the filmed scenes, as he describes in the following interview with D. W. Leitner: "There's a moment in the filming of *Fast, Cheap, and Out of Control* in the garden. . . . It's 2 a.m., and we're shooting 120 frames a second, so it's necessary to light this place up like a

Christmas tree. We have huge HMIs, three Condors, rain towers, fog machines, a crew of 40 people, and the gardener walking in the rain, and this friend of mine leans over and says, 'Well, you may be a fly on the wall, but it's a 500-ton fly on the wall.'"[23] One possible effect of these highly stylized scenes is that the whole film appears to be under Morris's tight control. That does not mean that Morris necessarily selected Mendez's tie, for instance but rather that its presence is the result of a deliberate decision by the filmmaker, much like the slow-motion photography and the artificial rain in the topiary garden. If Ray Mendez's tie seems unfortunate or silly, it is thus easy to attribute this to Morris's attitude about Mendez.

This issue is related to the tone of Morris's films. Humor has always been an element in Morris's documentaries, but they are never *just* funny. His films always have a mixture of the humorous and the serious, the whimsical and the morbid, even in his later political films. David Ansen's review of *Vernon, Florida* points to these divergent tones: "There's a taste of Samuel Beckett in the film's tone of droll forlorn hopefulness, and something of Buster Keaton in the spacious frames and the exquisitely deadpan comic timing with which Morris crosscuts between his subjects. *Vernon, Florida* isn't sociology at all, it's philosophical slapstick, a film as odd and mysterious as its subjects, and quite unforgettable."[24] Morris never provides clear guidance when one tonal element ends and the other begins, and there are many moments that seem to exhibit both humor and seriousness. This may contribute to Gleiberman's impression that the humor in *Fast, Cheap and Out of Control* is, at times, inappropriate and condescending.

Gleiberman's objections also connect to the documentary filmmaker's obligation to present her or his subjects in a particular light, and protect them from any potentially negative responses from the viewers. To this question, Morris responds, "You know, there's this idea somehow that documentary filmmakers are supposed to be making commercials for humanity. It's like you're hired by some exclusive advertising agency to sell humanity to itself, that you should provide some kind of life-affirming, valetudinarian portrait of the world, and people can say, 'Ah! How wonderful life is! What a finely wrought thing is man!' . . . To me, I guess my response to that idea would be, 'Why!?'"[25]

The different possible answers to Morris's "why" question cuts to the heart of several ethical concerns about Morris's documentaries. Many of these objections suggest that Morris is merely using his subjects to illustrate his deep-seated cynicism, and they subsequently become unsuspecting victims of his worldview. On the other hand, Morris is trying to address some fundamental questions about humanity and its relationship to the world. In *Fast, Cheap and Out of Control*, for instance, Morris is interested in the ways in which the four subjects cope with the erratic, volatile, and fleeting nature of the world. A proponent of Morris's approach might argue that it would be disingenuous to construct the documentary around the idea that these men have found the answers, or that there is no humor or error in this journey.

The different readings of *Fast, Cheap and Out of Control* as either condescending or celebratory speaks to the complexity of Morris's treatment of his subjects. This issue continues to emerge throughout Morris's career, although it takes a markedly different turn as Morris interviews a Holocaust denier in *Mr. Death*, the secretary of defense during the Vietnam War in *The Fog of War*, and those involved in the prisoner abuses at Abu Ghraib in *Standard Operating Procedure*.

6 Mr. Death: The Rise and Fall of Fred A. Leuchter, Jr.

IN A 2003 *NEW YORK TIMES* ARTICLE, Barry Gewen examines the prospect of "Holocaust fatigue" in documentary filmmaking, where the supply of Holocaust documentaries is outstripping demand.[1] Gewen cites Annette Insdorf's book *Indelible Shadows*, which records that since 1990 a Holocaust documentary has been released at the rate of one every two months.[2] The recent Holocaust documentaries have also dominated the Academy Awards Best Documentary category. In the six years between 1995 and 2000, four documentaries on the Holocaust won Oscars: *Anne Frank Remembered* (1995), *The Long Way Home* (1997), *The Last Days* (1998), and *Into the Arms of Strangers: Stories of the Kindertransport* (2000). Two earlier Holocaust-related films, *Genocide* (1981) and *Hotel Terminus: The Life and Times of Klaus Barbie* (1988), also won for Best Documentary.

Errol Morris's *Mr. Death: The Rise and Fall of Fred A. Leuchter, Jr.* participates in this Holocaust documentary subgenre, although it is not a traditional Holocaust film. Fred Leuchter is the film's principal interview subject as he discusses his early career building electrocution equipment, his involvement in the Ernst Zündel neo-Nazi trial in Canada, and the unfortunate effects that this participation had on his personal life. Morris also includes interviews with scholar Robert Jan van Pelt, Nazi sympathizers David Irving and Ernst Zündel, chemist James Roth, and Leuchter critics Shelly Shapiro and Suzanne Tabasky.

It might be surprising that Morris chose to make *Mr. Death*, considering the ubiquity of Holocaust documentaries. Morris developed a reputation for his distinctive approach to the documentary form as well his films' idiosyncratic subject matter, exemplified by his previous film *Fast, Cheap and Out of Control*. *The Thin Blue Line* most closely resembles a traditional political documentary, as it investigates the errors in a murder trial and has certain underlying criticisms of the criminal justice system. *The Thin Blue Line*'s focus on the peculiarities of the people in Randall Dale Adams's trial is quite different from a more traditional documentary such as *Who Killed Vincent Chin?* (1989), however, which uses the killing of Vincent Chin to examine civil rights and hate-crime issues.

Mr. Death constitutes a broader shift in Errol Morris's filmmaking career, as Morris continued his exploration of political documentaries. Four years after *Mr. Death*, Morris released *The Fog of War*, which profiles former U.S. secretary of defense Robert McNamara, including his involvement in the Vietnam War. Morris's next film, *Standard Operating Procedure*, investigates the Abu Ghraib prisoner abuse scandal during the Iraq War.

Other aspects of Morris's career were also increasingly intertwined with politics. Morris teamed up with the political action committee MoveOn.org to create a series of political ads for John Kerry's 2004 presidential campaign against George W. Bush. Based on his popular "Switch" campaign for Apple, Morris donated his time to interview people who had voted for Bush in 2000 but were now "switching" their vote to Kerry. Four years later, Morris directed another set of television campaign commercials for Barack Obama. As with the Kerry commercials, "People in the Middle for Obama" featured interviews with voters about why they were supporting Obama. Morris actively promoted the Kerry and Obama campaigns, including an appearance on Fox News in 2004, where the studio audience gave his John Kerry commercials a chilly reception.

Mr. Death is not merely a product of Morris's sudden interest in politics, however. Morris began interviewing Leuchter in 1992 and initially considered including him in *Fast, Cheap and Out of Control*. In addition, *Mr. Death* is not a traditional political film or Holocaust documentary, as it does not provide a historical overview of political events or make an argument about who was responsible for past wrongdoings. Morris is instead interested in exploring the way Leuchter views the world and the connections between his once-successful engineering business and his ill-fated involvement with Holocaust denial. As with the science documentary in Morris's *A Brief History of Time*, this political subgenre of documentary filmmaking placed certain expectations and constraints on Morris's approach to *Mr. Death*. This context also helps explain how *Mr. Death* communicates a story, represents reality, and explores subjectivity.

■ Background

Errol Morris first came across Fred Leuchter in a 1990 *New York Times* article entitled "Making Execution Humane (Or Can It Be?)."[3] The article examines the possibility of a humane execution and focuses on Leuchter's career constructing execution equipment. There were also concerns about the effectiveness of Leuchter's lethal-injection device as well as his testimony on behalf of a neo-Nazi group. The article ends with the following: "Nowadays, Mr. Leuchter says he does not get much work. Wardens nearly everywhere shun him."[4]

The Leuchter story taps into a number of primary thematic concerns evident throughout Morris's career. Leuchter's peculiar relationship to death and, in particular, his attempts to control it overlaps with all of Morris's films, especially *Fast, Cheap and Out of Control* and *Gates of Heaven*. In addition, the idea of a man trying to make execution "humane" contains the irony and dark humor characteristic of a Morris film.

Morris learned that Fred Leuchter was living in nearby Malden, Massachusetts, and began interviewing him. Morris also traveled to Nashville and filmed Leuchter with the execution system he built there, accumulating about seven hours of footage.[5] Morris considered including Leuchter as an interview subject in *Fast, Cheap and Out of Control*, but Morris's wife advised him that "Hitler is not a spice."[6] Morris agreed, expanding on the analogy: "By adding Hitler to the soup, it immediately becomes Hitler-flavored. It dominates everything. So I decided to leave it out."[7]

Morris eventually put the Leuchter project on hold, in part because he could not raise the funds to finish the interviews. The money arrived in 1998 when he received two million dollars from IFC and Britain's Channel 4 to complete the film. Morris continued interviewing Leuchter while also traveling to Poland to film reenactment footage of Leuchter's infamous trip to the Auschwitz concentration camp.[8]

Morris edited *Mr. Death* relatively quickly, as the film was shown as a work in progress at the 1999 Sundance Film Festival. The film received positive early press coverage, including an extended article by Mark Singer in the *New Yorker*. *Mr. Death* had its official premiere at the Toronto Film Festival on September 16, 1999, and was released in theaters three months later. The film was a box office disappointment, grossing only a half a million dollars through March 2000.[9] *Mr. Death* did receive some critical recognition, however, including being named best documentary at the Dallas–Fort Worth Film Critics Association Awards.

Style

Mr. Death employs many of the stylistic devices Morris has used throughout his career, such as highly stylized cutaway images, reenactments, fragmented framings, and slow-motion photography. *Mr. Death* also incorporates some, though not all, of the visual strategies Morris introduced in *Fast, Cheap and Out of Control*, such as a more neutral interview background, various film and video formats, and the Interrotron.

Morris used the Interrotron interviewing device for his initial interviews with Leuchter. Although Morris experiments with the Megatron in his *First Person* series, he abandons the multicamera system in favor of the single-camera Interrotron for *Mr. Death*. Morris again directs the interview subject's gaze into the lens of the camera, and there is not the cutting to more oblique angles that we often see in the *First Person* series.

Morris shot all of the interviews in a studio, which allowed him to carefully control the lighting, sound, framing, and camera movement. The interview footage in *Mr. Death* bears a strong resemblance to *Fast, Cheap and Out of Control* in part because Morris originally planned to include the Leuchter interviews in *Fast, Cheap and Out of Control*. Morris shot the interviews on 35 mm film and frequently uses close-ups, static framings, black slugs, and jump cuts.

In terms of cutaway footage, family photographs and home movies help illustrate Leuchter's past. For instance, as Leuchter discusses his father's work in the Massachusetts Correctional System, we see a home movie of Leuchter and his father at a prison. *Mr. Death* also uses found documentary footage, similar to all of Morris's films since *The Thin Blue Line*, including a sequence from Leni Riefenstahl's *Triumph of the Will* (1935) and Thomas Edison's *Electrocuting an Elephant* (1903).

Morris's handling of reenactment scenes also connects to his earlier films. Morris frequently uses stylized lighting, close framings, and shallow depth of field in these visuals. Much like his previous reenactment scenes, Morris repeats some of these reenactments, including Leuchter chiseling the

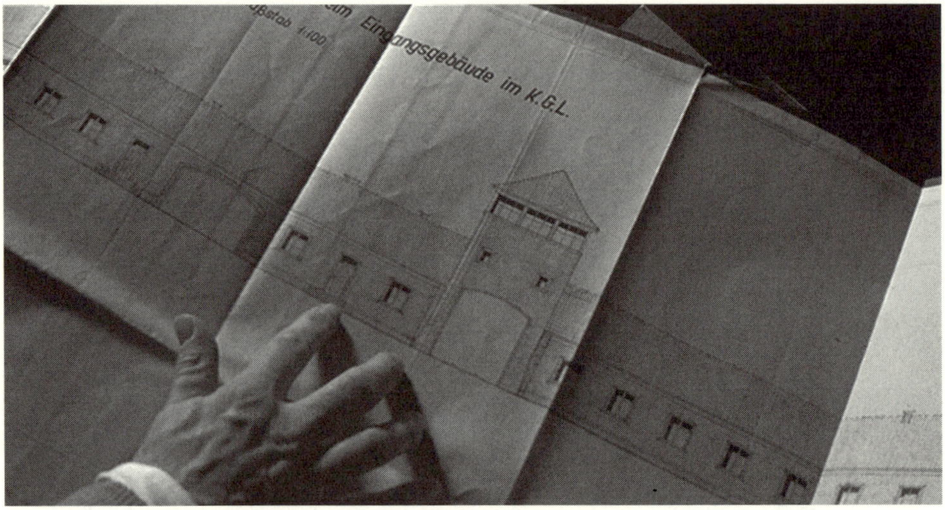

FIGURE 6.1. ◻ *Mr. Death: The Rise and Fall of Fred A. Leuchter, Jr.*

walls of the now-dormant gas chambers in Auschwitz. The repetitions of these visuals develop into visual motifs throughout *Mr. Death*.

Historical documents play a particularly important role in *Mr. Death*. Morris frequently employs them with van Pelt's testimony to investigate and critique Leuchter's claims about the past. For example, Morris uses blueprints from the Auschwitz Museum Archives to provide context for Leuchter's discussion of gas chambers in the concentration camps (see figure 6.1).

Caleb Sampson, who composed the music for *Fast, Cheap and Out of Control*, again worked with Morris in scoring *Mr. Death*. The Sampson score resembles *Fast, Cheap*'s minimalist music, with repetitious melodies and pulsing rhythms throughout *Mr. Death*. At the same time, the music is more expressive than in any of Morris's previous films. *Mr. Death* has quirky, playful melodies similar to those in *Fast, Cheap and Out of Control*, but Sampson also composes slow, melancholy waltzes to accompany Leuchter's pathetic fall into obscurity.

One particular scene in *Mr. Death* is worth noting, as it is stylistically quite different from all of Morris's previous films. In an interview with Leuchter early in the film, Morris uses a handheld camera as Leuchter explains his Tennessee State Prison electrocution system. This is the closest Morris ever comes to a conventional handheld vérité interview, although Morris's handling of the scene is unlike a traditional vérité sequence. Morris's camera constantly rocks back and forth, often shooting Leuchter at severely canted angles. When Leuchter pushes the operation button for the electric chair, Morris cuts to a close-up, black-and-white image of the action, which is punctuated by dark, foreboding music. This stylized treatment of the observational footage pulls it away from anything resembling a typical vérité sequence.

As we have seen in previous chapters, Morris's highly stylized visuals do not constitute a reflexive rejection of documentary practice. The nonfiction tradition has been an outlet for many filmmakers' experiments with visuals such as expressive lighting and staged sequences. If there are documentary subjects that might require a more subdued approach to style, however, one might think that the Holocaust would be a likely candidate. There may be an expectation that the films' style should match the particularly "sober" discourse of the film, to borrow the concept from Bill Nichols. Nichols argues that documentaries are "sobering because they regard their relation to the real as direct, immediate, transparent."[10] This could foster the view that the form of Morris's films should be suitably reverent considering the suffering and loss of life involved in the Holocaust.

Previous documentaries addressing the Holocaust often display the kind of visual variety found in Morris's *Mr. Death*, however. Arnold Schwartzman's 1982 *Genocide*, for instance, is just as visually adventurous. The film combines archival footage, fictional found footage, archival photographs, animated sequences, and audio reenactments of the horrors inflicted upon the Jewish people.

This open approach to style adds visual and aural variety and contributes to the aesthetic beauty of *Mr. Death*. Visual elements such as fictional found footage, reenactments, and animated sequences also help direct the audience's attention to the important elements in these stories. This is particularly important for documentaries examining past events whose visual record may be incomplete or nonexistent.

Structure

The subject matter in *Mr. Death* overlaps with the political documentary subgenre, as the Holocaust has traditionally been a popular topic for documentaries since the 1960s. Within the broad scope of the Holocaust, nonfiction filmmakers have focused on a wide variety of particular interests. For instance, *Genocide* addresses the history of the Jewish people in Europe and the rise of the Nazis; *Paragraph 175* (2000) examines the consequences of a German law that prohibited homosexuality; and *Hotel Terminus: The Life and Times of Klaus Barbie* (1988) investigates the life of a Nazi war criminal.

Within this diversity of topics, these films generally share a number of storytelling and structural conventions. Most significantly, the majority of these documentaries adopt narrative structures, in which the films provide a predominantly chronological account of the events in question. For example, *Into the Arms of Strangers: Stories of the Kindertransport* (2000) chronicles the secret transportation of thousands of Jewish children out of Nazi Germany to England for safety. Although the film weaves together about a dozen different stories of children fleeing to England, it nonetheless establishes a clear chronology as these children encounter a variety of challenges when the war begins and escalates.

Mr. Death also employs a narrative structure. Morris's profile of Leuchter's life becomes the focus on which Morris constructs the film's narrative structure. At the same time as *Mr. Death* chronicles significant events in Leuchter's life, the film also investigates how he engages with the past and both understands and misunderstands the world around him.

The narrative structure in *Mr. Death* is largely chronological, although there are a few diversions from this chronology. For example, the film begins with Leuchter's experiences building electrocution and lethal-injection equipment: "I became involved in the manufacture of execution equipment because I was concerned with the deplorable condition of the hardware that's in most state prisons, which generally results in torture prior to death."[11] We later turn to Leuchter's youth as he discusses his childhood visits to the prison where his father once worked and then return to his adult life.

Leuchter recounts the events in his life, and the temporal relationship between events is always clear. For example, the first part of *Mr. Death* is primarily focused on Leuchter's career building execution equipment. After about thirty minutes, Morris transitions into Leuchter's involvement in the defense of Ernst Zündel, which is the catalyst for his fateful trip to Poland. Morris makes this transition clear to the audience by using the intertitle "The Trial of Ernst Zündel." Leuchter's testimony then reinforces this temporal shift: "Because of my expertise in the construction of execution equipment,

I was asked to testify by the defense team of Mr. Ernst Zündel, a German national living in Canada, for some twenty odd years, who published a pamphlet, 'Did Six Million Really Die?'"

Mr. Death profiles Leuchter's life but also conducts an investigation into his work building electrocution and lethal-injection equipment, and his examination of gas chambers, among others. This combination of a chronology and an investigation is similar to *The Thin Blue Line*, which used the framing story of the Adams trial to investigate the facts of the case and the identity of Officer Robert Wood's murderer. *Mr. Death* is explicit about this investigative element, which is introduced after Leuchter describes his methodology for examining the gas chambers at Auschwitz. Historian and Holocaust scholar Robert Jan van Pelt expresses his disgust for the Holocaust denial and decides to map Leuchter's journey as a way to deal with this revulsion: "I have a job to do, and my job, my first job, is to try to understand where this guy was and at what time. To take that tape and to record every camera angle, where it was, what piece of wall they were looking at, where he took the samples. It was important to be able to follow that trail very, very precisely. I wanted to see how he had done it."

Mr. Death adopts van Pelt's mission. The film examines not just whether or not there were gas chambers in Auschwitz but also *how* Leuchter conducted his research and reached his conclusions. We listen to Leuchter's own account of his research as well as expert testimony that evaluates Leuchter's findings. For instance, Leuchter discusses how, when entering the gas chambers, he expected to see structural features such as explosion- and leak-proof areas, openings for exhaust fans and pipes, and devices for introducing the gas into the air. Leuchter confidently testifies: "These things didn't exist."

Morris immediately cuts to a lengthy reply by van Pelt, who provides three specifics that Leuchter neglected in his investigation. Van Pelt first describes Auschwitz as decaying space in which everything has changed three or four times since it operated as an extermination camp. Van Pelt then points to archival blueprints of gas chambers that provide "evidence about ventilation systems, evidence about ways to introduce Zyklon B into these buildings, evidence of gas chambers, undressing rooms. But then of course, I don't think [Leuchter] knows German, so it wouldn't have helped very much." During this testimony, Morris cuts to images of these archival documents, reinforcing their existence and relevance. Van Pelt also discusses the "coded language" in the archival documents in which the Nazis never used terms such as "gas chamber" or "extermination" but instead used euphemisms such as "special action" and "special treatment." Morris again uses the archival documents to illustrate van Pelt's testimony. Van Pelt's immediate and lengthy reply to Leuchter's process constitutes a central structuring component in *Mr. Death*'s narrative.

The conclusion of Morris's investigation in *Mr. Death* is quite unlike *The Thin Blue Line*, in which David Harris admits responsibility for Officer Wood's death. Leuchter instead offers a final avoidance of his own past mistakes. Morris asks Leuchter about his conclusions regarding the existence of gas chambers in Auschwitz: "Have you ever thought that you might be wrong, or do you think that you could make a mistake?" Leuchter responds, "No, I'm past that. When I attempted to turn those facilities into gas execution facilities and was unable to, I made a decision at that point that I wasn't wrong."

Leuchter's willful ignorance does not prevent Morris from clearly establishing Leuchter's errors. Rather than blocking Morris's investigation, the ways in which Leuchter recasts and avoids Morris's questions furthers Morris's interest in exploring Leuchter's particular way of understanding the world. This confluence of clear truth claims and a more open exploration of subjectivity in *Mr. Death* connect to the voice of the film.

■ Voice and Subjectivity

There is a clear formal voice in *Mr. Death*. Van Pelt provides the most reliable explanations in the film about the history of the gas chambers and the errors in Leuchter's investigation. For instance, Morris alternates Leuchter's description of his methods for investigating the existence of gas chambers with van Pelt's persuasive indictment of Leuchter: "Leuchter doesn't have the training. It was not that he brought any experience, the specific experience needed to look at ruined buildings. The only experience he had was design modifications for the Missouri gas chambers in Jacksonville."

Despite all of Leuchter's appalling and dangerous errors, he also, on occasion, reliably explains elements of the past and about his personal experiences. For instance, when Leuchter describes his initial involvement in the construction of execution equipment, this account is not challenged or undermined. Leuchter explains that, after building an electrocution system for Tennessee, New Jersey contacted him to build a lethal-injection system. Leuchter remembers that other states then began requesting that he update their execution equipment as well: "The reasoning here is that I built helmets for electric chairs, so now I could build lethal-injection machines. So I'm now competent to work on gas chambers because I've done all of the other three. And what really makes you competent is the fact that you have the necessary background, you do the investigation, you find out what the problem is, and you solve it."

Morris does not question or complicate Leuchter's account of his entry into the execution business, or the "reasoning here" that the different states assumed that Leuchter could build various kinds of execution equipment. Much of Leuchter's account of his life throughout *Mr. Death* is authoritative, including his recollection of his childhood visits to a Massachusetts state prison.

This does not mean the voice of *Mr. Death* is equivalent to the interview testimony. Morris's structures *Mr. Death* as an investigation into historical events as well as the interview testimony. We are prompted to question, and ultimately reject, Leuchter's conclusions about the existence of gas chambers at Auschwitz.

Mr. Death is ultimately not an advocacy film, however. Morris does not structure the film around explaining that the Holocaust is a historical fact, or to identify those guilty for the atrocities. Morris is more interested in how Leuchter struggles to understand these events and what this reveals about his, and our, subjective frailties.

Morris employs associational connections, together with the narrative structure in *Mr. Death*, to connect different aspects of Leuchter's life and explore the subjectivity of his testimony. As with the murder sequence in *The Thin Blue Line*, the breaking teacup in *A Brief History of Time*, and the circus in *Fast, Cheap and Out of Control*, Morris utilizes visual motifs to develop the associational links in *Mr. Death* and highlight these subjective views.

Mr. Death repeats and varies a number of distinctive visuals, the most prominent of which is that of Leuchter "chiseling." When Leuchter discusses his fact-finding trip to Poland, Morris incorporates the original grainy video documentary footage that Zündel commissioned to document the journey. We see Leuchter on a plane to Poland, arriving at the concentration camp,

FIGURE 6.2. ◻ *Mr. Death: The Rise and Fall of Fred A. Leuchter, Jr.*

entering the crematoria, making measurements, and most significantly, chiseling the walls of the gas chambers to collect his samples. During this found footage sequence, Leuchter provides a detailed, matter-of-fact account of his investigation: "We made paint scrapings and chiseled plaster from locations that are not immediately noticeable but still were proper locations for condensation of cyanide gas. We made detailed scale drawings of the rooms with arrows showing the location it was removed."

The legitimacy of Leuchter's investigation is immediately questioned after this sequence. Van Pelt describes his disgust for Holocaust denial: "Holocaust denial for me is so revolting, and the way for me to not immediately become sick with having to deal with Leuchter was by saying, 'Okay, I am going to map his journey.'" Morris cuts to a staged sequence that matches van Pelt's stated mission, as we enter the crematorium, view diagrams of the different camera positions in Leuchter's videotape, and see hands pointing to the damaged walls. At the end of the sequence, we see a closely framed shot of a chisel penetrating a concrete wall (see figure 6.2). Through this identification with van Pelt's mission, the film adopts the task of investigating, and ultimately refuting, Leuchter's claims about the absence of gas chambers in the concentration camps.

The chisel breaking the surface of the concrete wall takes on new mean-

FIGURE 6.3. □ *Mr. Death: The Rise and Fall of Fred A. Leuchter, Jr.*

ings as Morris repeats and varies the image throughout the film. After a lengthy sequence in which van Pelt provides archival evidence of the existence of gas chambers, Ernst Zündel describes how Leuchter was able to convince him to doubt the Holocaust: "Fred was able to purge his own mind within a matter of a week. That's amazing to me. So I said, 'Fred, what convinced you?' He said, 'Ernst, it wasn't what I found; it was what I didn't find.' That blew me away. It never, ever occurred to me that a man could be convinced by something that is not there." Morris cuts to reenactment footage of Leuchter in the rubble of the gas chamber, including eight different shots of him chiseling the walls (see figure 6.3).

In the context of van Pelt's expert testimony refuting Leuchter's findings, Zündel's testimony adopts a particular irony. Although Zündel sees Leuchter's mind purging as an indication of his objectivity, we now understand it as a symptom of Leuchter's colossal error. This error is again ironically illustrated by Zündel's testimony: "It never, ever occurred to me that a man could be convinced by something that is not there." Leuchter's inability to find evidence of gas chambers does not mean that evidence does not exist. Rather, it is an indication of Leuchter's self-deception (facilitated by Zündel) that he is qualified to do the proper research to find the truth.

The accompanying chiseling motif raises the question of how Leuchter's mistaken view of himself as an expert relates to his deeply flawed research. This question also brings us back to Leuchter's earlier explanation of why he was asked to build different kinds of execution equipment: "I built helmets for electric chairs, so now I could build lethal-injection machines. So I'm now competent to work on gas chambers because I've done all of the other three. And what really makes you competent is the fact that you have the necessary background, you do the investigation, you find out what the problem is, and you solve it." Leuchter's reasoning that his ability to construct an electric-chair helmet ultimately qualifies him to build a gas chamber is one of the primary catalysts for his downfall at the end of the film.

Leuchter's belief that competency means that you "have the necessary background, you do the investigation, you find out what the problem is, and you solve it" may be true in an abstract sense but does not hold true in Leuchter's investigation into the Auschwitz concentration camps. Leuchter did not have the necessary background, nor did he do the proper investigation (i.e., the chiseling) to answer his question. Morris's placement of Leuchter's competency proclamation early in the film suggests that the internalization of this rationale is a causal factor in Leuchter's self-deception later in *Mr. Death*. Morris uses this clear pronouncement of Leuchter's error to open up Leuchter's subjective view of the world and connect it with a long string of inconsistencies, confusions, and mistakes in Leuchter's life.

The connection between the chiseling imagery and Leuchter's self-deception is reinforced and expanded as the film progresses. For instance, we see the chiseling rock motif one last time at the end of the film, when Morris asks Leuchter about the possibility of being wrong. Leuchter answers, "No, I'm past that. When I attempted to turn those facilities into gas execution facilities and was unable to, I made a decision at that point that I wasn't wrong. And perhaps that's why I did it. At least it cleared my mind, so I know that I left no stone unturned. I did everything possible to substantiate and prove the existence of gas chambers, and I was unable to." Morris cuts to a staged sequence in which Leuchter hammers a pile of rocks that is overexposed by a strong key light (see figure 6.4).

At this point in the film, Morris, with the help of expert testimony, has completely undermined Leuchter's investigation and conclusions. Leuchter's answer to Morris is a final illustration of his self-deception, and the chiseling of the rocks does not represent his investigation, as it perhaps did

FIGURE 6.4. ▫ *Mr. Death: The Rise and Fall of Fred A. Leuchter, Jr.*

at first, but rather the futility and the danger of his venture into Holocaust denial. The "chiseling" motif thus helps the audience tie together a number of seemingly disparate features of Leuchter's life to access this element of Leuchter's view of the world.

The degree to which Morris explicitly undermines Leuchter's claims changed in different preliminary iterations of *Mr. Death*. The sensitive, volatile nature of the Holocaust and Holocaust denial did not comfortably fit with Morris's open approach to examining human subjectivity. Unlike Morris's earlier films, the ethical objections to his approach emerged during the editing process and dramatically changed the way Morris completed *Mr. Death*.

▪ Reception and Ethics

There has always been a tension in Morris's films between clearly establishing facts and exploring the peculiarities of human subjectivity. The tension erupted at a rough-cut screening of *Mr. Death* at Harvard University.[12] This preliminary edit of the film exclusively used Fred Leuchter's interviews without chemist James Roth, Robert Jan van Pelt, or any of the other interview subjects. After the screening, a number of students expressed sympathy with

Leuchter's sad story and his view that the Holocaust never occurred. Morris explains, "I guess it's a little bit like the Stockholm syndrome. You're trapped in a room with this one man—namely, Leuchter. He's talking and talking and talking and talking. There is no one in the movie to grab you by the shoulders and say, 'You know, this is, of course, nonsense.'"[13]

Morris understood that, with an issue as serious as the Holocaust, he needed to make certain concessions, especially after a number of students called him a Jewish Nazi: "I realized I had to go back and rethink the movie. Pretty soon I decided I'd have to open the story out beyond just Fred."[14] Morris subsequently interviewed a number of additional subjects, including Leuchter's then ex-wife Carolyn Devine and Ernst Zündel. Most importantly, Morris interviewed Roth and van Pelt, who both provide expert testimony that refutes Leuchter's argument about the existence of gas chambers at Auschwitz.

Many reviewers understood that Morris's active refutation of Leuchter's findings did not constitute the primary interest of the film. Stephen Holden's review observes, "Although *Mr. Death* offers overwhelming counterarguments to Mr. Leuchter's research, the movie finally is not about who is right or wrong. Any sensible person (including the filmmaker) accepts the reality of the Holocaust. The movie is really a study of hubris, the myth of objectivity and the fatal attraction of needy people to attention and flattery even if it comes from the wrong quarters."[15]

Morris returned to the idea of exclusively using a single interview subject in his next film, *The Fog of War*. Morris interviewed Robert McNamara about his life and, in particular, his involvement in World War II and the Vietnam War. Like Leuchter, McNamara is a controversial figure, but Morris decided not to interview others to clearly explain McNamara's errors. As a result, *The Fog of War* encountered similar objections as did the *Mr. Death* rough cut and provides some insight into Morris's original vision for *Mr. Death*.

7 The Fog of War: Eleven Lessons from the Life of Robert S. McNamara

IN *MR. DEATH*, ERROL MORRIS INVESTIGATES and clearly undermines Fred Leuchter's findings in *The Leuchter Report*, in part by using expert testimony that thoroughly debunks Leuchter's claims. Morris was not completely happy with the results, however: "I had to put in other voices, though even today I still feel I shouldn't have. The problem was that I don't want to be seen as being irresponsible, or, actually, also being irresponsible."[1]

Morris decided to eschew multiple interview subjects and isolate a single voice in his next film. *The Fog of War: Eleven Lessons from the Life of Robert S. McNamara* examines the life of Robert McNamara, a former secretary of defense who had an influential role in the bombings of the Vietnam War. McNamara is the only interview subject in the film, and as a result, much of the information about these past events is filtered through his individual perspective.

Morris organizes *The Fog of War* into eleven "lessons" from McNamara, including "maximize efficiency" and "get the data." As these particular lessons suggest, Morris is interested in the ways in which McNamara's highly calculated way of thinking led to such devastating decisions in World War II and the Vietnam War. *The Fog of War* also raises criticisms of McNamara's view of the world, indicated by other lessons that include "belief and seeing are often both wrong" and "you can't change human nature."

Morris's approach to *The Fog of War* provoked a number of objections. Morris is again interested in exploring the contradictions and complexities of the human psyche, but this concern also frustrates expectations for historical and moral clarity. Morris's choice to only interview McNamara provoked the same criticisms that were made against the initial cut of *Mr. Death*, in part because of the political nature of *The Fog of War*. In addition, Morris's treatment of McNamara is somewhat sympathetic, as he characterizes McNamara's errors as inherently human, instead of merely a product of his individual immorality or political affiliations.

■ Background

The Fog of War developed out of Morris's television series *Errol Morris' First Person*. Morris had wanted to interview McNamara for many years, and his television series provided an opportunity to meet with McNamara: "We were all set up shooting *First Person* and had the studio booked so I thought, 'What the hell. I'll just call him and see if he's willing to come up to Cambridge.' He'd just written a book and had been traveling around the country on a book tour. I think . . . that he saw me as part of his book tour."[2] McNamara agreed to talk with Morris for a single day in 2001, and after the first interview, Morris was able to convince him to stay for a second day. McNamara then returned months later for another two days of interviews.[3] In the interim, Morris conducted extensive background research on McNamara's role in the Second World War and the Vietnam War, including newly released government documents and transcripts.[4]

Morris's approach to *The Fog of War* bears some resemblance to its origins in the *First Person* series. Morris exclusively uses McNamara's interview in *The Fog of War*, a practice that he commonly used in the *First Person* series but never before in a feature film. Throughout *The Fog of War*, McNamara provides an account of his life from birth through his time as president of Ford Motor Company to his tenure as secretary of defense during the Cuban Missile Crisis and Vietnam War. There is no other interview subject that provides context or counterpoint to McNamara's testimony.

The Fog of War premiered at the Cannes Film Festival in May 2003 and was released theatrically in December of that year. The film grossed over four million dollars domestically, making it Morris's most profitable film.[5] *The Fog of War* is also one of Morris's most critically successful documentaries. Among the numerous distinctions, the film was named the best documentary of 2003 by the Toronto Film Critics Association, the National Board of Review, the Los Angeles Film Critics Association, the Chicago Film Critics Association, and the Independent Spirit Awards. Most significantly, Morris received his first Academy Award nomination and win for Best Documentary. Morris's acceptance speech expressed what many thought was an overdue award: "I'd like to thank the Academy for finally recognizing my films."

Morris continued his interest in engaging political topics outside of filmmaking as well. He began publishing editorials on current political issues in newspapers and in his online blog for the *New York Times*. For instance, in a 2003 *Los Angeles Times* article, Morris examined the idea of preventative war.[6] Morris looks back on a variety of military conflicts in the twentieth century, including the two world wars and the Cuban Missile Crisis. At the end of the article, Morris asks, "Shouldn't we have learned by now that war doesn't reduce hostility, anger and instability but instead creates more of the same? And we might ask ourselves: Do we want more of the same for this next century?"

Morris also wrote a number of editorials on the *New York Times Opinionator* blog. And Morris's "Where's the Rest of Him" editorial critiques the John Kerry presidential campaign for not properly highlighting Kerry's opposition to the Vietnam War.[7] "Not Every Picture Tells a Story" reveals new contextual information about the infamous photographs at Abu Ghraib, and "Photography as a Weapon" examines the political use of photographs, in particular manipulated photographs.[8]

■ Style

McNamara's interview visuals bear some resemblance to Morris's *First Person* series. Morris again used his Interrotron interviewing machine for the interviews with McNamara. McNamara looks directly into the lens as he discusses his life and ideas, and Morris continues to break up and vary these images with black slugs and jump cuts.

Morris shot McNamara's interview using 24 p hi-definition video, which was a significant improvement from the lower-resolution digital video in the *First Person* episodes. As with many video formats, this hi-definition video produces a wide depth of field in which both the interview subject and the background are in sharp focus. Cinematographer Robert Chappell explains that Morris placed four semi-transparent screens behind McNamara in order to "build something neutral behind him and keep it out of focus" (see figure 7.1).[9] The screens create an "out of focus" effect behind McNamara and are similar to the translucent colored screens Morris used in his *First Person* series.

Morris's approach to camera movement and framing in *The Fog of War* also has strong connections to his *First Person* series. As with many episodes in the television series, Morris tilts the camera on the z-axis, producing

FIGURE 7.1. □ *The Fog of War: Eleven Lessons from the Life of Robert S. McNamara*

canted angles of McNamara's face. Morris also tracks the camera in front of McNamara, frequently pushing his face to the end of the frame. This fluctuation in the interview image is again similar to his *First Person* series and in stark contrast to the static, often-symmetrical framings of his earlier films.

The cutaway images in *The Fog of War* are typical for an Errol Morris film. We again see stylized, slow-motion photography, staged reenactments, and asymmetrical, fragmented framings. Morris also includes a variety of film gauges and stocks, as well as different video formats. *The Fog of War* also draws from a wide assortment of government training films, television news, and war footage. The reenactments in *The Fog of War* incorporate canted angles, slow motion, and cropped framings.

Morris uses both publicly recorded events and privately recorded discussions that intersect with McNamara's claims about his life. For example, Morris includes audio recordings between Lyndon B. Johnson and McNamara about the handling of the Vietnam War. Many of the private conversations are audio recordings, so Morris often uses images of a tape recorder to accompany the audio, similar to the final scene in *The Thin Blue Line*.

Morris collaborated with Philip Glass, who had earlier written the music for *The Thin Blue Line*, for the score in *The Fog of War*. Glass again composes melodies that repeat over pulsating rhythms, but similar to *Mr. Death*, the music in *The Fog of War* is more expressive than Morris's early films. Glass's score employs a larger dynamic range, more melodic flourishes, and a greater sense of urgency than the music in *The Thin Blue Line*. For instance, as McNamara describes the firebombing of Tokyo during the Second World War, strings and synthesizers quickly pulse under woodwind embellishments.

The wide variety of visual and aural material in *The Fog of War* is not unusual for documentaries addressing the Vietnam War. For instance, *Hearts and Minds* mixes interviews, observational footage, and both fictional and archival found footage to examine divergent attitudes about the Vietnam War. Davis even uses some of the fictional found footage for comedic effect, ironically critiquing particular views about the role of the United States in world affairs.

The stylistic diversity in *The Fog of War* helps to develop the varied narratives and themes in the film. Even though McNamara is the only interview subject, Morris illustrates and interrogates his memories about political events, personal history, and his complex theories about politics and human nature.

Structure

The Fog of War employs a narrative structure, similar to *Mr. Death* and many other political documentaries. The film uses McNamara's life as the spine of the narrative structure, while also pausing to examine how McNamara both understood and influenced important political events. *The Fog of War* addresses a wide variety of time periods and events, including McNamara's childhood, his involvement in the Cuban Missile Crisis and the Second World War, his tenure as the president of Ford Motor Company, and later as secretary of defense under John F. Kennedy and Lyndon B. Johnson.

The narrative structure in *The Fog of War* is largely, although not strictly, chronological. For instance, the film begins with McNamara's time as secretary of defense and, in particular, his account of the Cuban Missile Crisis in 1962. The film then shifts back to 1918 and McNamara's earliest memory of a "city exploding with joy" at the end of the First World War. *The Fog of War* uses devices such as intertitles and cues in the interview testimony to clearly mark these shifts in time.

The Fog of War chronicles McNamara's life but also investigates his stories and explanations about the Second World War, the Cuban Missile Crisis, the Ford Motor Company, and most significantly, the Vietnam War. While *Mr. Death* uses another interview subject, scholar Robert Jan van Pelt, as the catalyst for the film's investigation, McNamara is the only interview subject in *The Fog of War*. Morris and McNamara share the same goal to reflect on and understand his past, however, and *The Fog of War* uses McNamara's own testimony to explore and scrutinize his life. At the beginning of the film, McNamara asserts that every military commander has made mistakes in the application of military power, and it is important to learn from past mistakes and not repeat these errors. McNamara then says, "In my life, I've been part of wars. Three years in the U.S. Army during World War II, seven years as secretary of defense during the Vietnam War, thirteen years at the World Bank across the world. At my age, eighty-five, I'm at an age where I can look back and derive some conclusions about my actions. My rule has been [to] try to learn, try to understand what happened. Develop the lessons and pass them on."[10]

McNamara is the primary catalyst for, and subsequently has some control over, this investigation into his life. For instance, after McNamara finishes discussing the Second World War, Morris transitions into the Vietnam War by using an audio conversation between McNamara and Lyndon B. Johnson about the "Vietnam Picture." Johnson says that he wants "somebody who can lay up some plans to trap these guys and whup the hell out of them. Kill some of them, that's what I want to do." McNamara replies, "I'll try and bring something back that will meet that objective." Morris then asks McNamara about how best to set up the subject of Vietnam, to which McNamara replies, "Yeah, well, that's a hard question. I think we have to approach it in the context of the Cold War. But first, I'll have to talk about Ford. I'll have to go back to the end of the war." We then see an intertitle indicating "1945," followed by McNamara's discussion of his tenure as the president of Ford Motor Company. The sequence follows McNamara's suggestion that, before he addresses the Vietnam War, he must discuss his time at Ford.

McNamara's influence on the film's structure does not diminish Morris's ability to conduct an independent investigation into McNamara's life. For instance, the above discussion between McNamara and Johnson complicates McNamara's claim at the end of the film about who is ultimately accountable for the Vietnam War, in which McNamara declares, "It's the president's responsibility." McNamara does express doubt about the direction of the war, but his obedience to "whup the hell" out of the enemy certainly places some responsibility on McNamara for the escalation of the war. In this context, McNamara's suggestion that he first discuss Ford is not merely an exertion of control over the project but also an indication of hesitancy about the matter.

Morris does not have the option of cutting to other interview subjects to contextualize McNamara's testimony, making the stylistic and structural decisions in *The Fog of War* more consequential in investigating McNamara's testimony. In the above sequence, Morris challenges the audience to connect McNamara's testimony about "the president's responsibility" with his desire to discuss Ford before Vietnam much earlier in the film. The viewer must also consider how these different pieces of testimony relate to McNamara's responsibility for the Vietnam War and his own struggle to come to terms with this involvement.

The Fog of War ends with a final evasion by McNamara, similar to Leuchter's concluding testimony in *Mr. Death*. Morris asks McNamara, "Do you feel in any way responsible for the war? Do you feel guilty?" McNamara responds, "I don't want to go any further with this discussion. It just opens up more controversy. I don't want to add anything to Vietnam. It is so complex that anything I say will require additions and qualifications." Morris then asks a final follow-up question: "Is it the feeling that you're damned if you do, and if you don't, no matter what?" to which McNamara says, "Yeah, that's right. And I'd rather be damned if I don't."

Morris's investigation throughout *The Fog of War* provides some answers to questions about responsibility, guilt, and truth, despite McNamara's evasions. For instance, McNamara is, to some extent, responsible for the consequences of the Vietnam War. McNamara's avoidance of these questions does not cast doubt on the film's conclusions but rather gives us insight into how McNamara understands and struggles with the past. This coming together of history and subjectivity is a central concern for Morris as he brings us the role of voice in *The Fog of War*.

■ Voice and Subjectivity

There are elements of a formal voice in *The Fog of War*, as with all of Morris's documentaries. McNamara's testimony reliably explains some facts about his past and personal feelings. Morris does not question or complicate some of these explanations, and viewers rely on them to make informative inferences throughout the films. We have no reason to doubt, for instance, McNamara's testimony about his time as president of Ford Motor Company.

The principal voice in *The Fog of War* is again an open voice, however. The combination of the film's visuals, testimony, and structure openly explore, rather than rigidly explain, the ways in which McNamara understands his own past. McNamara does not represent a reliable authority on his own subjective engagement with the world, and Morris uses the structure and film style in *The Fog of War* to provide context and criticisms of McNamara's testimony.

Morris's exclusive use of one individual's testimony together with an open voice is unique, especially for political films about war. Political documentaries traditionally employ voice-over narration to communicate information about the subject, as is evident in narration-heavy films such as *Memphis Belle* (1944), *The Battle of San Pietro* (1945), and *Night and Fog* (1955). Beginning in the 1950s and continuing up to the present, political documentaries became increasingly reliant on interview testimony, sometimes mixing it with voice-over narration as in *The Sorrow and the Pity*, or exclusively using interviews as in *The War at Home*.

These more recent documentaries often emphasize the personal testimony of the victims involved in the historical events. For instance, *Shoah* foregrounds the victims of the Holocaust, and *The War at Home* primarily focuses on the dutiful yet uninformed U.S. soldiers of the Vietnam War. Even though *Genocide* uses voice-over narration by celebrities Elizabeth Taylor and Orson Welles, Taylor provides dramatic readings of letters from those who suffered during the Holocaust.

In the vast majority of these political documentaries, the formal voice is generated by a broad consensus among the interview subjects. In *The War at Home*, Glenn Silber interviews a variety of Madison, Wisconsin, residents, including students, activists, and professors involved in the antiwar movement. Most of the individual testimony is consistent with the other testimony in the film, constructing a coherent picture of an increasingly politically aware city fighting against an unjust war. Silber does include some conflicting accounts, such as an archival interview with a police officer who characterizes the activists as violent and dangerous. These incompatible interviews are often quickly and clearly undermined. For instance, Silber includes footage of police officers beating activists with clubs, challenging the police officer's account of the conflict.

Political documentaries occasionally focus on one particular individual. For example, Eugene Jarecki's *Trials of Henry Kissinger* (2002) scrutinizes Henry Kissinger's rise to power and his role in the Vietnam War. Jarecki does not interview Kissinger, however, and uses a relatively small number of archival interviews with the former secretary of state. Jarecki instead interviews a variety of people who generally criticize Kissinger's political decisions and motivations, establishing a formal voice through this consensus.

As noted above, *The Fog of War* is not only organized around an individual but also exclusively focuses on his testimony. Morris's decision to give one interview subject such weight in the film provides McNamara a certain authority. Morris's dependence on and challenges to the veracity of McNamara's testimony establishes some formal-voice elements in the film.

The Fog of War is not an advocacy film, however. Morris is not primarily interested in using McNamara's testimony to argue that the United States was wrong to enter the Vietnam War. The political events in the film are instead opportunities for Morris to explore the ways in which McNamara grapples with events that, in many ways, were beyond his capacity to control and fully understand.

Morris explores these subjective elements in part by exposing potential complications, ironies, and mistakes in McNamara's testimony. For example, Morris investigates McNamara's involvement in the Second World War and, in particular, the firebombing of Japan. McNamara remembers how he analyzed bombing operations in order to make them more efficient. Based on his recommendations, Curtis LeMay ordered the B-29 firebombings that killed one hundred thousand Japanese civilians in a single night. McNamara says during the sequence, "I don't want to suggest that it was I who put in LeMay's mind that his operations were totally inefficient and [had] to be drastically changed. But, anyhow, that's what he did."

Instead of illustrating McNamara's inference about the impact of his reports on LeMay's decision to firebomb Japan, Morris cuts to a quick montage of McNamara's signatures on documents (see figure 7.2). McNamara's signatures do not conclusively undermine McNamara's testimony but instead function in a more open manner. The signatures suggest that McNamara

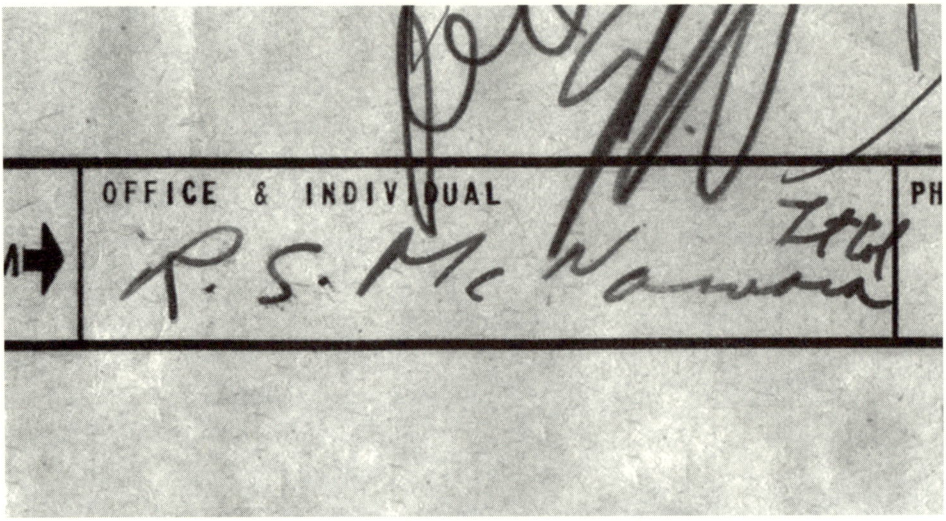

FIGURE 7.2. □ *The Fog of War: Eleven Lessons from the Life of Robert S. McNamara*

was more influential than he proposes, but the images do not establish that McNamara was ultimately responsible for the firebombing. This sequence, in part, raises the question of how McNamara's proficiency in quantification, efficiency, and control relates to his responsibility for the real-world effects of this expertise.

This question is expanded later in the film when McNamara explains how, during the Second World War, he was promoted to assistant professor at the Harvard Business School. The U.S. government had awarded Harvard a contract to establish an officer candidate program for the air force's "Statistical Control School." McNamara describes how the Business School used IBM sorting machines to select potential candidates. These machines quantified personal traits and achievements, and Morris illustrates the testimony with a variety of sorting machine cutaways (see figure 7.3).

"Statistical control" develops into a central attribute of McNamara's way of understanding the world. McNamara frequently analyzes problems by referencing proportions, percentages, and statistics. For instance, McNamara discusses the U.S. bombings of Japanese cities in terms of the percentage of the cities destroyed. After installing new safety equipment in Ford automobiles, McNamara "estimated that if there would be 100 percent use of the seatbelts, we could save twenty odd thousand of lives a year."

FIGURE 7.3. ◻ *The Fog of War: Eleven Lessons from the Life of Robert S. McNamara*

Morris highlights the role of "statistical data" throughout *The Fog of War*. For example, Morris connects the idea to a number of the McNamara "lesson" intertitles, such as "Lesson #5: Proportionality should be a guideline to war" and "Lesson #6: 'Get the Data.'" Morris also uses cutaway images to punctuate the connection between McNamara's worldview and statistical analysis. For instance, McNamara discusses how he increased the efficiency of bombing operations in Japan, and Morris cuts to the point of view of a bomber. Instead of bombs falling out of the hatch, however, numbers descend on a city below (see figure 7.4). The repeated references to statistical analysis and control, proportionality, percentages, and quantification, which are highlighted by formal elements such as highly stylized cutaway images, establish associational connections between different time periods in McNamara's life.

Morris uses the visual motif of falling dominos to further foreground McNamara's subjective desire to understand the world around him. More specifically, Morris repeats images of dominos falling across a map of Southeast Asia throughout *The Fog of War*. These dominos first act as a transition between the end of the Second World War and the beginning of the Vietnam War. McNamara reflects on LeMay's view that, if the United States had lost the war to Japan, he and other government officials would have been

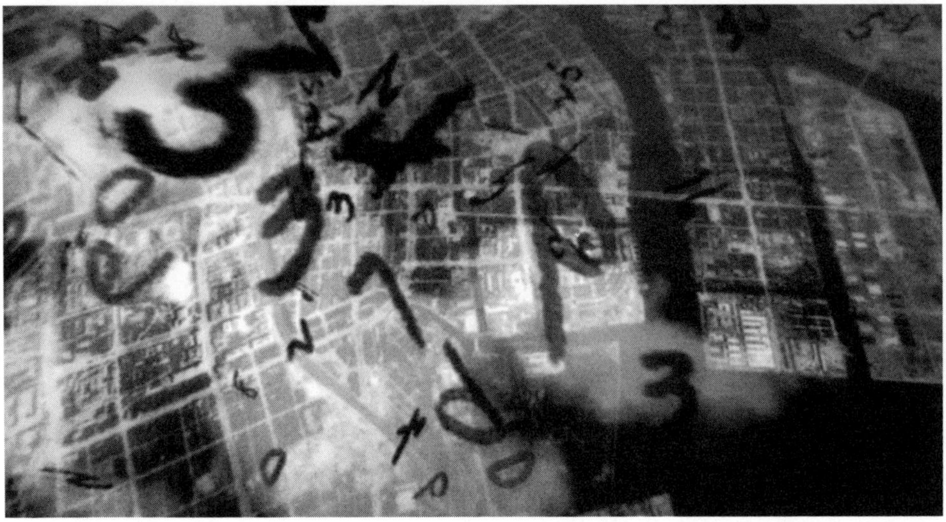

FIGURE 7.4. ◻ *The Fog of War: Eleven Lessons from the Life of Robert S. McNamara*

prosecuted as war criminals because of the devastating bombings across the country: "LeMay recognized that what he was doing would be thought immoral if his side had lost. But what makes it immoral if you lose and not immoral if you win?" We then see a sequence of dominos falling across the map, with Morris's characteristic use of close-ups, slow motion, and shallow depth of field (see figure 7.5). After a "1964" intertitle, Morris plays an archival audio conversation between Johnson and McNamara about the "Vietnam picture." This first occurrence of the domino visuals in *The Fog of War* serves a more illustrative function, relating to the "domino theory" foreign policy advocated by the U.S. government in its fight against communism. The idea was that if communism gained a foothold in a number of Asian countries, it would continue to spread, like a falling row of dominos, to neighboring countries.

Morris develops the connotations connected to the domino visuals as he repeats them throughout *The Fog of War*. A little over an hour into the film, McNamara discusses the misunderstandings surrounding the Gulf of Tonkin torpedo attacks against U.S. warships. We see a sequence of dominos carefully placed across a map of Asia as McNamara says that President Johnson authorized attacks on North Vietnam because of "a conscious decision on the part of the North Vietnamese political and military leaders to es-

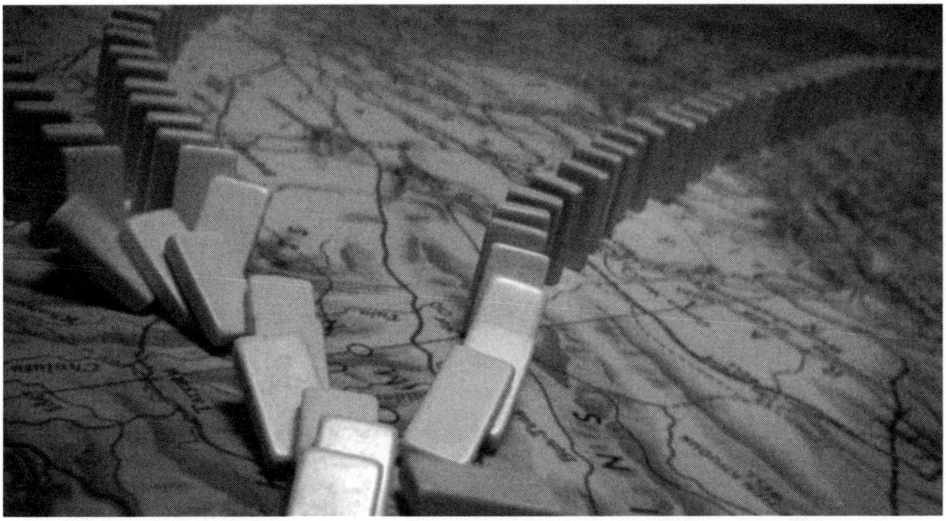

FIGURE 7.5. □ *The Fog of War: Eleven Lessons from the Life of Robert S. McNamara*

calate the conflict and an indication they would not stop short of winning." The dominos then begin to fall as McNamara reflects, "We were wrong, but we had in our minds a mindset that led to that action. And it carried such heavy costs. We see incorrectly or we see only half of the story at times" (see figure 7.6).

This sequence expands the domino visuals beyond the "domino theory" foreign policy, as McNamara is not explicitly talking about communism spreading across Asia. Morris creates an associative connection between the dominos and what McNamara calls the Johnson administration's "mindset" that led to the United States escalating the war, while also establishing a causal connection between the mindset of the administration with the intensification of the conflict.

This connection between the dominos falling across Asia and a subjective "mindset" is reinforced at the end of the film. McNamara reflects on the process of evaluating his past actions: "What I'm doing is thinking through with hindsight, but you don't have hindsight available at the time. I'm very proud of my accomplishments, and I'm very sorry in the process of accomplishing things, I've made errors." During this testimony, Morris plays the domino sequence in reverse as a long line of fallen dominos stand erect over a map of Asia. Again, the dominos are not representing the possibility of

FIGURE 7.6. ◻ *The Fog of War: Eleven Lessons from the Life of Robert S. McNamara*

spreading communism, but instead Morris connects the reverse-motion dominos to McNamara's own mental activity of looking back at his life.

These associational connections between the "domino theory," the United States' entry into and escalation of the Vietnam War, and McNamara's personal engagement with the war not only accumulate as the film progresses but also retroactively inform earlier appearances of the domino sequence. For instance, Morris places the domino sequence before the first transition to Vietnam, where McNamara discusses LeMay's recognition that his actions in World War II would be viewed as immoral if the United States was not victorious. McNamara asks, "But what makes it immoral if you lose and not immoral if you win?" This relationship between victory and morality links to the later sequences discussed above. The association helps contextualize the view that the United States needed to forcefully respond to North Vietnam's aggressive behavior, for example, especially if winning has some connection to morality.

These associations extend beyond the appearance of the domino motif. McNamara's moral query connects back to his earlier discussion of his philosophy studies at the University of California–Berkeley. McNamara describes how his classes in logic and ethics placed "stress on values and something beyond one's self, and a responsibility to society." The cutaways

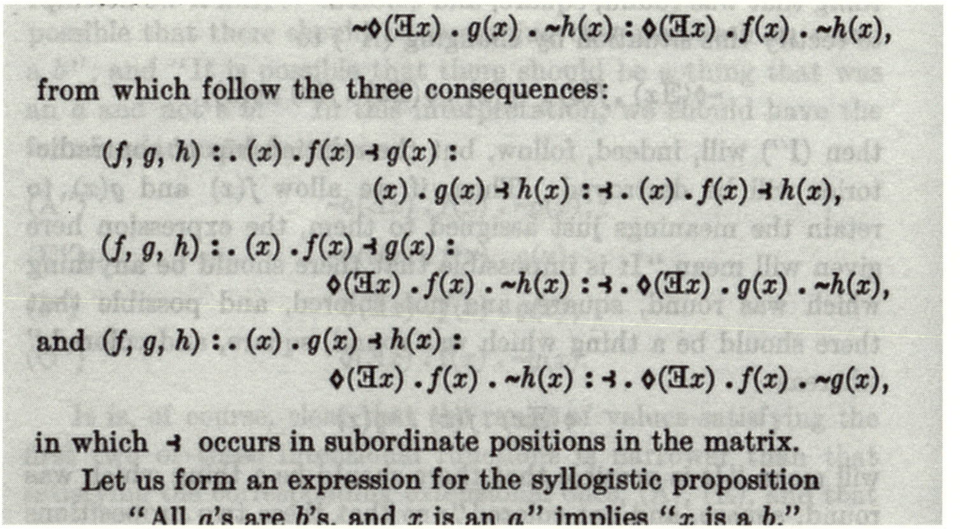

$$\sim\Diamond(\exists x) \,.\, g(x) \,.\, \sim h(x) : \Diamond(\exists x) \,.\, f(x) \,.\, \sim h(x),$$

from which follow the three consequences:

$$(f, g, h) :. (x) \,.\, f(x) \prec g(x) : (x) \,.\, g(x) \prec h(x) :\prec. (x) \,.\, f(x) \prec h(x),$$

$$(f, g, h) :. (x) \,.\, f(x) \prec g(x) : \Diamond(\exists x) \,.\, f(x) \,.\, \sim h(x) :\prec. \Diamond(\exists x) \,.\, g(x) \,.\, \sim h(x),$$

and $(f, g, h) :. (x) \,.\, g(x) \prec h(x) : \Diamond(\exists x) \,.\, f(x) \,.\, \sim h(x) :\prec. \Diamond(\exists x) \,.\, f(x) \,.\, \sim g(x),$

in which $\prec$ occurs in subordinate positions in the matrix.

Let us form an expression for the syllogistic proposition

“All *a*'s are *b*'s, and *x* is an *a*” implies “*x* is a *b*.”

FIGURE 7.7. ◻ *The Fog of War: Eleven Lessons from the Life of Robert S. McNamara*

during this sequence, which include formal logic equations (see figure 7.7), have a visual counterpart in the abstract graphs and figures that Morris uses during a discussion of the casualties in Vietnam (see figure 7.8). These connections in the visuals further prompt the viewer to apply these ethical questions to McNamara's beliefs, assertions, and actions.

Morris underlines a central thematic link throughout all of his documentary films when we reach McNamara's seventh lesson: “Belief and seeing are both often wrong.” In *The Fog of War*, Morris takes the viewer on an examination of philosophical concepts such as belief, knowledge, certainty, error, and deception. One of the challenges of Morris's films is that the audience cannot blindly trust the interview testimony, partly because of this problem with “belief and seeing.” The viewer instead must recognize the subtle and complex associations in the film's visual design, testimony, and structure without the reliable guidance of a narrator or interview subject.

The stakes for questioning “belief and seeing” are high in *The Fog of War*. As in *Mr. Death*, *The Fog of War* addresses highly charged political events for which McNamara bears some responsibility. There is an expectation, by nature of the subject matter, that Morris adequately hold McNamara accountable for his actions. Morris's decision to employ an open voice in *The Fog of*

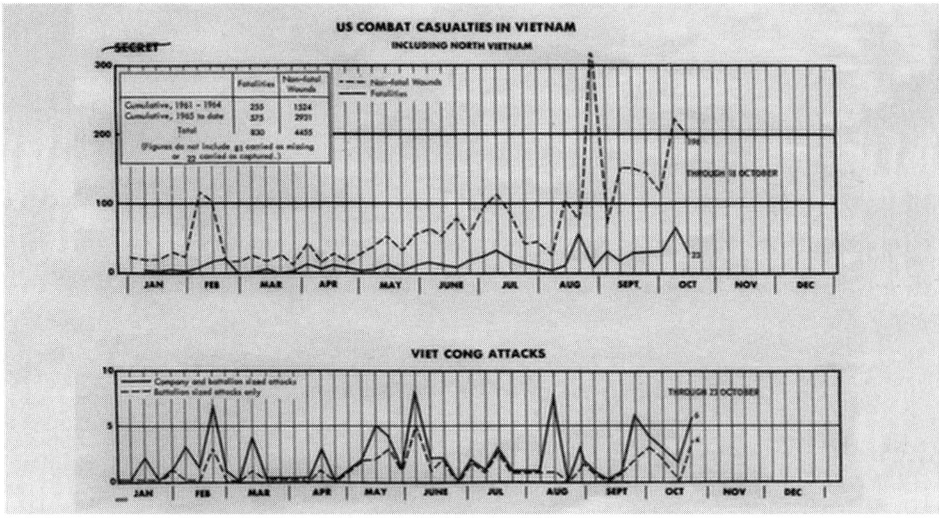

FIGURE 7.8. □ *The Fog of War: Eleven Lessons from the Life of Robert S. McNamara*

War raised the intensity of the ethical concerns about his approach to the documentary.

■ Reception and Ethics

In her book *The Art of Documentary*, Megan Cunningham asks Morris what makes his approach to the documentary innovative, to which Morris provides the following anecdote: "I think of my most recent film, *The Fog of War*. I was at a press conference at the New York Film Festival and a journalist asked, 'Are you aware you only interviewed one person?' And I said, 'Yes I am.' It was a stylistic choice! Of course, one could easily imagine a film about Robert McNamara that took on a completely different character than *The Fog of War*. A documentary where you would have had an array of experts, or people who had been connected with McNamara in one way or another all commenting on the man . . . as well as hearing from McNamara himself. And, of course, I did none of that. I specifically *chose* to do none of that. I mean, there's a reason for it, but the minute you decide to do something that is different you put yourself in peril."[11] We can understand the "peril" that Morris mentions in a number of ways. In one sense, interviewing only one person makes the process of storytelling more difficult, especially when the director must provide some historical context in the film. Jarecki's *Trials of Henry Kissinger* exemplifies a more traditional approach to this kind of profile documentary. Jarecki interviewed over a dozen subjects to provide this historical context, including different perspectives on Kissinger's life and role in American foreign policy.

Morris used sources such as archival photographs and audio recordings to help contextualize McNamara's life, but his exclusive use of McNamara's testimony in *The Fog of War* provoked some of the harshest criticisms in his career. A number of critics complained that Morris did not properly interrogate McNamara's close involvement in unjust and cruel wars. Paul Arthur argues, "Morris clearly allows this elder statesman to call the shots. . . . Misstatements of fact (regarding the size of the 1967 demonstration at the Pentagon) and highly contentious assertions (that the carpet bombing, then nuking of Japanese cities saved hundreds of thousands of Allied lives) slide by unchallenged."[12] Whereas Morris was once praised for complicating the presumed connection between documentary representation and reality, he was now being accused of irresponsibly neglecting this relationship.

This criticism came to a head in a series of articles written in *The Nation*. In his December 15, 2003, review of *The Fog of War*, Eric Alterman offers objections similar to Arthur's: "[Morris] too frequently lets McNamara elide and abuse the truth. . . . Morris is a brilliant filmmaker, but he is not a historian."[13] Morris published a response in *The Nation* about a month later, claiming the Alterman piece was "devoid of historical scholarship (despite his claim of having worked on his PhD for eleven years)."[14] Morris explains the film's contributions: "It is not my intention to exonerate McNamara for his involvement in the planning of the Vietnam War. What I do intend is to help correct a common misconception that President Johnson was bullied into a war that he had no intention of fighting."[15] Alexander Cockburn published two subsequent articles criticizing *The Fog of War* in *The Nation*, arguing that Morris "didn't do enough homework."[16]

Morris does complicate and question some of McNamara's claims throughout *The Fog of War*. But Morris's approach did not meet many reviewers' expectations of how a documentary should treat McNamara's contentious past. In the context of other documentary films, Morris does not provide the kind of immediate and stinging refutation of McNamara as we see in *Hearts and Minds*, where Peter Davis explicitly belittles General

Westmoreland's claims about how the "Oriental" places little value on human life.

The choice to exclusively use McNamara's testimony allowed Morris to foreground the role of human subjectivity in the film: "I restricted the point of view to one person. I wanted to know how someone like McNamara sees himself, how he interprets the events he helped to shape, how he came to make his decisions."[17] As Morris experienced with his initial cut of *Mr. Death*, this restricted point of view brings along with it expectations about providing, as Gary Indiana argued, "The factual glue necessary to place McNamara's role in either administration into any legible context."[18]

The particular arguments about the "factual glue" in *The Fog of War* aside, this debate raises a number of important questions about the responsibilities of a filmmaker making a political documentary: Must a documentary that intersects with topics such as the Holocaust or the Vietnam War have a primary interest in establishing the victims and those responsible? To what extent can the audience identify with someone on the "wrong side" of a political issue? Are the Holocaust and the Vietnam War proper subjects to explore issues related to human subjectivity?

Morris's films do not intend to answer these questions. They rather raise questions about the obligations and perhaps limits of his unique approach to the documentary form. Morris encounters many of these same questions and problems in his 2008 film *Standard Operating Procedure.* Morris takes up another political issue as he interviews participants in the Abu Ghraib torture scandal that occurred after the 2003 invasion of Iraq.

8 Standard Operating Procedure

ERROL MORRIS BECAME INCREASINGLY ENGAGED in political issues after the 2003 release of *The Fog of War*. In addition to directing commercials spots for the 2004 John Kerry and the 2008 Barack Obama presidential campaigns, Morris also developed an interest in the 2004 Abu Ghraib prison abuse scandal. The U.S.-led coalition took over the prison after the 2003 invasion of Iraq and used it as a detention center for suspected and convicted criminals. The prison gained international attention when accounts of physical and psychological abuse were made public. Early media coverage by *60 Minutes II* and the *New Yorker* explored the details of the abuse, including photographs of U.S. military personnel participating in acts of torture, sexual abuse, and homicide. Morris began researching the Abu Ghraib story in 2004 and later interviewed those involved in the scandal, which eventually developed into his 2008 documentary *Standard Operating Procedure*.[1]

The political nature of *Standard Operating Procedure* overlaps with *Mr. Death* and *The Fog of War*, but the specifics and context of the Abu Ghraib scandal mark a departure from his earlier films. In a 2008 interview with GQ magazine, Morris explains, "I usually like stories that have no fingerprints on them . . . and this story is covered in fingerprints. They're some of the most widely seen photographs in history."[2]

The Abu Ghraib scandal was a headline story for months after it broke, and the photographs became the subject of two documentaries that were released a year before *Standard Operating Procedure*: Rory Kennedy's *Ghosts of Abu Ghraib* (2007) and Alex Gibney's Academy Award–winning *No End in Sight* (2007). These Abu Ghraib documentaries existed within a broader category of Iraq War documentaries at the time, with more than two dozen released between the start of the Iraq War in 2003 and the April 2008 release of *Standard Operating Procedure*.[3]

Investigating the Abu Ghraib scandal brings with it certain expectations about properly representing history and condemning those responsible for unethical behavior. One of the distinguishing aspects of Morris's documentaries is that they are not primarily concerned with critiquing power structures and identifying ultimate responsibility for injustice. *The Thin Blue Line* does not attack the systemic problems in the criminal justice system; *Mr. Death* focuses on a marginal figure in the Neo-Nazi movement; and *The Fog of War* is not designed to condemn Robert McNamara for his involvement in the Vietnam War. Morris's films approach these issues by probing the details of a particular situation and exploring what they reveal about human subjectivity and more abstract, philosophical questions such as the nature and limits of human knowledge.

Standard Operating Procedure continues this practice of taking particular facts of past events and exploring their larger significance. Morris focuses on the photographs of the Abu Ghraib abuse and, in particular, details such as who took the photographs, when they were taken, and what is and is not included in the pictures. Morris then prompts the viewer to reflect on what these details reveal about the events at Abu Ghraib.

The photograph is a particularly useful analogy for Morris in his continuing exploration of human subjectivity. Photographs are, by nature, partial and incomplete records of the world, as they are taken from a particular viewpoint and they exclude everything that is outside the frame. Morris uses these limitations of the photograph to examine the limitations of knowledge and perspective in *Standard Operating Procedure.*

Morris mines the details of the Abu Ghraib photographs and the interview testimony to form a collective picture of a prison filled with confusion, absurdity, and incompetence. The prison abuses are not the result of an inherently evil person or power structure but rather intimately connected to the peculiarities of the human experience. Many reviews of the film criticized Morris's resistance to providing a pointed critique of the chain of command at Abu Ghraib, which we will examine at the end of the chapter.

Background

As with many of Morris's documentaries, the idea for *Standard Operating Procedure* had its origins in a newspaper article. Morris read a 2004 *New York Times* article by Susan Sontag about Abu Ghraib entitled, "Regarding the Torture of Others: Notes on What Has Been Done—and Why—to Prisoners by Americans."[4] Sontag examines the meaning and implications of the Abu Ghraib torture photographs and the relationship between photography, memory, power, and reality. Sontag also analyzes the Bush administration's use and avoidance of language such as "torture," "abuse," and "humiliation" to frame the discourse surrounding the photographs. Morris was intrigued by the issue and felt that he could contribute to this discussion about the photographs: "Everybody was theorizing about why the pictures were taken, but no one had talked to the people involved and asked why they took them and what they thought they showed."[5]

Morris originally planned to investigate the Abu Ghraib photographs within a broader study of war photography and in 2005 was aggressively researching a famous pair of mid-nineteenth-century photographs taken during the Crimean War.[6] Morris realized, "I can't just do the Crimean War photographs—because, you know, who is going to go to the multiplex?" so he decided to focus solely on the Abu Ghraib photographs. Morris and cinematographer Robert Chappell both saw a December 29, 2005, C-SPAN interview with Janis Kapinski, a former brigadier general in charge of Abu Ghraib during the detainee abuse. Morris decided to fly her to Cambridge, Massachusetts, for an interview and, over two days, accumulated fifteen hours of footage.

Morris would have a more difficult time interviewing the soldiers who were involved in the Abu Ghraib scandal. Specialist Charles Graner and Staff Sergeant Ivan Frederick II were both incarcerated for the prisoner abuses, and many of the others accused of wrongdoing were not enthusiastic about participating. Morris eventually convinced a number of these soldiers to be interviewed, including Sergeant Sabrina Harman, Private Lynndie England, Sergeant Javal Davis, Specialist Megan Ambuhl Graner, and Specialist Jeremy Sivits.

Morris received funding from Participant Productions and Sony Pictures Classics, and also invested his own money in the film. The budget ballooned to about five million dollars, by far the largest of Morris's career.[7] Morris's expansive research into the Abu Ghraib scandal was a contributing factor to this large budget, as he accumulated hundreds of hours of interview footage and thousands of documents. In addition, after initially considering shooting the cutaway footage in Iraq, Morris decided to build a piece of Abu Ghraib on a Los Angeles set for the reenactments.[8]

Standard Operating Procedure premiered on February 12, 2008, at the Berlin Film Festival, where it was the first documentary ever to screen in competition and won the Silver Bear.[9] Despite the award, the film was largely a critical and financial disappointment. Sony Pictures Classics released *Standard Operating Procedure* in the United States on April 25, and the film made under $230,000, Morris's lowest box office gross for any of his theatrically released documentaries.[10] *Standard Operating Procedure* did not win any other major festival or critical award, and the reviews of the film were mixed.

Standard Operating Procedure was also involved in a controversy concerning Morris's financial compensations to his interview subjects. The online blog *And the Winner Is* (now *ScottFeinberg.com*) first reported that, at a Tribeca Film Festival screening, Morris admitted to giving money to some of the film's interviewees. The *New York Times* picked up the story in an article entitled "Can a Paid Witness Remain Untainted?" that came out the week of the film's U.S. release.[11] The article acknowledges that it is not unusual for documentary filmmakers to pay their subjects, and other Abu Ghraib documentaries, including *Ghosts of Abu Ghraib* (2007), also provided financial compensation to the same interviewees that appear in *Standard Operating Procedure*. Morris was nonetheless asked about this issue frequently in interviews, and critics often noted the controversy in their reviews of the film. Morris responded that he paid the interview subjects in *Standard Operating Procedure* because "they asked to be paid, and they would not have been interviewed otherwise."[12]

In addition to *Standard Operating Procedure*, Morris also wrote extensively about the Abu Ghraib scandal. He collaborated with Philip Gourevitch on a book entitled *The Ballad of Abu Ghraib*, in which Gourevitch uses Morris's interviews and collected documents to investigate the abuses at the prison. Morris also examined the topic in a number of essays published in his *New York Times* blog and his 2011 collection of essays entitled *Believing Is Seeing (Observations on the Mysteries of Photography)*. In the preface to the book, Morris writes, "With each photograph we are thrown into an investigation. Who are these people? Why was their photograph taken? What were they thinking? What can they tell us about ourselves? What can we learn about the photographer and his motivations?"[13] These questions are central to Morris's examination of the Abu Ghraib photographs in *Standard Operating Procedure*, as Morris investigates how photographs can both reveal and obscure the truth about the past.

Style

Morris again uses his Interrotron interviewing machine in *Standard Operating Procedure*, and the interview visuals bear a strong resemblance to his earlier Interrotron films *Fast, Cheap and Out of Control*, *Mr. Death*, and *The Fog of War*. All of the interview subjects maintain eye contact with the camera lens, and Morris continues to use close framings of his subjects, often cutting to close-ups of their faces during the interviews.

Morris shot *Standard Operating Procedure* on high-definition video and, for the first time, shot in CinemaScope. The 2.39:1 aspect ratio provided ample space in which Morris could position the subject's head and body. Instead of the roaming camera that Morris used in *The Fog of War*, Morris uses this wide frame to digitally reposition the subject's body in the frame.[14]

Morris chose Danny Elfman to score *Standard Operating Procedure*. Elfman is a well-established film composer who had worked on fictional films such as *Pee-Wee's Big Adventure* (1985), *Dick Tracy* (1990), and *Mission: Impossible* (1996). Elfman's music for *Standard Operating Procedure* in some ways resembles Morris's previous minimalist scores by Philip Glass and Caleb Sampson. For instance, Elfman often organizes the music around the repetition of musical phrases, a steady rhythm, and musical consonance.

As mentioned in previous chapters, the music for *Mr. Death* and *The Fog of War* was considerably more expressive than the scores for Morris's earlier films. Elfman's music in *Standard Operating Procedure* continues this amplification of expressive elements, as the wide dynamic range and crescendos and diminuendos match the drama and emotion in the film. For instance, about a half hour into the film, Ken Davis describes how soldiers at the prison punished an accused rapist by stripping him naked and making him low-crawl on the concrete floor. Morris cuts from the interview to a reenactment, and the music erupts with loud timpani strikes and a cymbal crash. The music continues with a repeated musical phrase, similar to something we might hear in *The Thin Blue Line*, but over this repetition Elfman adds layers of musical growls and echo effects that match the disturbing imagery.

Morris also includes a wide variety of cutaway material in *Standard Operating Procedure*, including found footage, documents, photographs, computer-generated sequences, and staged reenactments. One distinguishing feature from previous films is Morris's use of computer-generated graphics to orga-

FIGURE 8.1. □ *Standard Operating Procedure*

nize and foreground particular elements in the cutaway footage. As Morris investigates the context surrounding the Abu Ghraib photographs, he includes a digitally constructed time line to retrace the chronology of the pictures. The Abu Ghraib photographs and Sabrina Harman's letters are often cluttered and difficult to read, and Morris uses computer-generated graphics to identify participants in the photographs and clarify certain phrases in these documents (see figure 8.1).

Morris's treatment of the reenactment footage constitutes the most significant departure from other documentaries at the time and from Morris's earlier films. Morris again worked with cinematographers Robert Chappell and Robert Richardson and shot the reenactment footage using a combination of digital video and 35 mm and 16 mm film stock. Part of what makes the reenactments unique is Morris's use of a very high frame rate to drastically slow the motion in the images. Slow motion has been an important device in Morris's reenactment sequences since *The Thin Blue Line*. At the time Morris was shooting *The Thin Blue Line*, the fastest available camera ran at about 120 frames per second, which is five times the normal speed. In *Standard Operating Procedure*, Morris used a Phantom v9 camera that can shoot up to twelve hundred frames per second. This high frame rate slows the movement in the images to the point where even the subtlest changes in figure position are greatly amplified. For example, Morris examines the use of dogs to intimidate the detainees at Abu Ghraib and, in particular, one instance when a dog attacked and severely injured one of these men. Morris uses the Phantom camera to slow reenactment footage of a dog barking and snapping to the point where the saliva launched from the animal's mouth becomes one of the most dynamic elements in the shot. Together with the close framing, expressive lighting, and shallow depth of field, the slow motion also abstracts the image into a striking and even beautiful play of light, shadow, and movement.

This coming together of highly stylized imagery and the horrors depicted in the images prompted criticism against *Standard Operating Procedure*. Rick Groen writes in his *Globe and Mail* review, "The film risks aestheticizing what it condemns, of moving too lyrically—slow-motion shots of water dripping from a crude showerhead—inside it's own cinematic frame."[15]

It is important to note that other documentaries at the time also employ stylized reenactments for violent and traumatic sequences. For example, *Taxi to the Dark Side* (2007) also uses expressive images to re-create the scenes of attack-dog intimidation in Abu Ghraib. In one sequence, Alex Gibney cuts to black-and-white still images of the dogs showing their teeth against a black backdrop. Gibney has clearly altered the images, but the film was not criticized for these kinds of stylized sequences. Gibney's presentation of the dog is more straightforward, as the animal is centrally framed and the black background directs the viewer's attention to the dog's head and teeth. Morris's shallow depth field also foregrounds the dog's teeth, but the slow motion, high-contrast lighting, and cropped framing all aestheticize and make beautiful a violent sequence in which a man was seriously wounded (see figure 8.2).

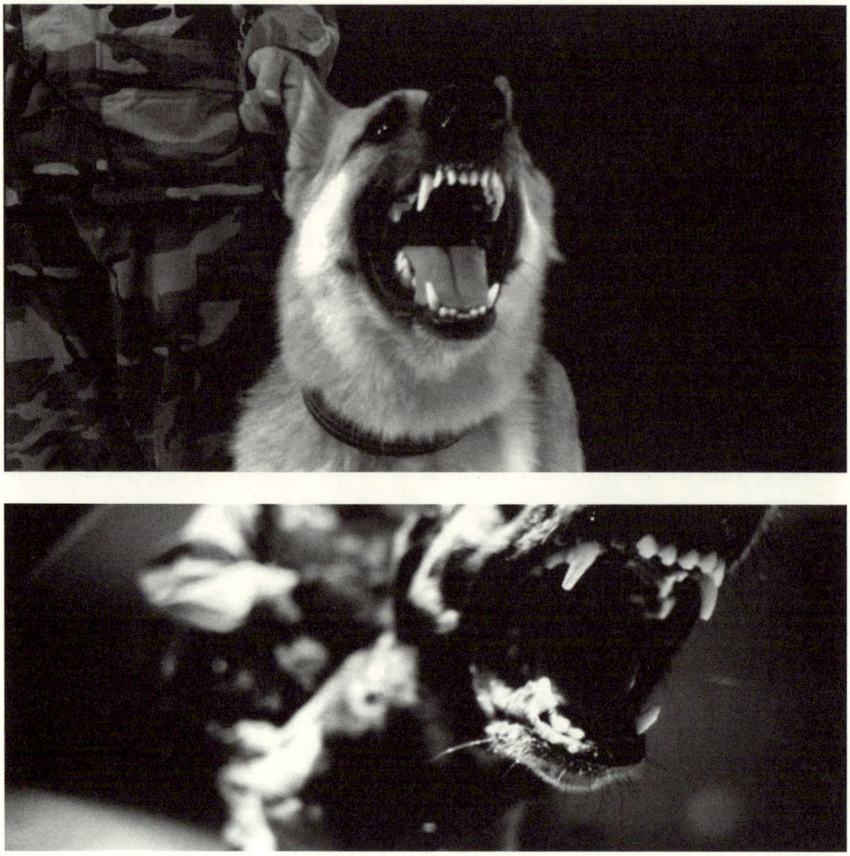

FIGURE 8.2. □ *Taxi to the Dark Side* and *Standard Operating Procedure*

■ Structure

One of Morris's challenges in *Standard Operating Procedure* was to provide a novel understanding of the iconic Abu Ghraib photographs that had dominated the headlines for months after their 2004 release. Morris addressed well-known topics in *A Brief History of Time* and *The Fog of War*, but he had not dealt with an issue that was as contemporary and controversial as the Abu Ghraib scandal. Morris was also contending with two other Abu Ghraib documentaries, Rory Kennedy's *Ghosts of Abu Ghraib* and Alex Gibney's *Taxi to the Dark Side*, both of which were released a year before *Standard Operating Procedure*.

Ghosts of Abu Ghraib and *Taxi to the Dark Side* both examine the Abu Ghraib scandal in the context of the United States' "War on Terror" and ask who is ultimately to blame for the torture. There are some differences between the films. For instance, *Taxi to the Dark Side* uses voice-over narration, stylized reenactments, and a rhetorical structure, whereas *Ghosts of Abu Ghraib* has a more conventional mix of found footage and interviews and relies on a narrative structure. But both films make a similar argument that is reiterated again and again: the torture was the product of a new system of detention and interrogation that was devised and implemented from the top of the chain of command, including President George W. Bush, Vice President Dick Cheney, Secretary of Defense Donald Rumsfeld, and legal counsel John Yoo.

Morris's *Standard Operating Procedure* is not centrally concerned with tracing responsibility up through the ranks of the military and U.S. government. Morris instead closely examines details such as the time and who was present when the pictures were taken. These specifics reveal information about the context and motivations at Abu Ghraib, which Morris then uses to explore how the soldiers understood the incidents at the prison and their own involvement in the scandal.

In comparison to Morris's previous documentaries, *Standard Operating Procedure*'s subject matter and overall structure are most closely related to *The Thin Blue Line*. Both films use a chronological narrative structure to investigate the events related to a horrific crime. Similar to the murder sequence in *The Thin Blue Line*, Morris returns again and again to the Abu Ghraib torture scenes in an attempt to determine what happened and why it happened.

And as in *The Thin Blue Line*, the beginning of *Standard Operating Procedure* helps establish the narrative structure of the investigation as well as important thematic elements in the film. Morris begins with the state of affairs in post-invasion Iraq and the soldiers' initial reactions to Abu Ghraib. The first line of the film by civilian interrogator Tim Dugan sums up this context succinctly: "Charlie Foxtrot, without a doubt" ("Charlie Foxtrot" is a military phrase that stands for "cluster fuck").[16]

After the title sequence, Morris introduces a number of interview subjects who establish the significance of the Iraq War photographs. Janis Karpinski, for instance, discusses Secretary of Defense Rumsfeld's visit to Abu Ghraib to monitor the progress of the prison. After touring the torture chambers and the hanging facility, Rumsfeld cut short his visit, saying. "Let some

FIGURE 8.3. □ *Standard Operating Procedure*

soldiers come over here, and we'll take some pictures. I don't need to see any more of the prison." Morris provides an image of Rumsfeld posing with U.S. soldiers (see figure 8.3).

In the context of Karpinski's testimony, we understand that the Rumsfeld photograph does not tell the whole story, as the photo-op conceals the fact that Rumsfeld was not properly monitoring the situation on the ground. Instead of employing what has become known as the Ken Burns Effect, where panning and zooming effects explore the details of the photograph, Morris places a thick black border around the image, suggesting there is something beyond the picture's frame.

Morris then establishes a chronological framework for the film. Javal Davis, Lynndie England, and Sabrina Harman discuss their first encounters with the Abu Ghraib prison, depicting it as in a state of disrepair and smelling of urine and body rot. They also describe their first encounters with prisoner mistreatment, including U.S. soldiers putting women's underwear on the detainee's heads, placing them in stretch positions, and depriving them of light and sleep. Davis reflects, "Something is not right here," and England says that the abuse seemed "weird and wrong, but when we first got there, the example was already set. That's what we saw. I mean, it was okay." This sequence helps establish the narrative framework for the film, as it introduces the space and initial problems with the prison.

Morris uses Harman's letters to her wife Kelly to pull together the soldier's initial disgust with the prison, their acceptance of the detainee abuse, and as introduced earlier by Karpinski, the importance of photography. Harman explains why she is taking pictures of the abuses at Abu Ghraib: "Not many people know this goes on. Want to get the pictures to prove the U.S. is not what people think." Harman then reflects: "I don't know, it's just—it's kind of hard to believe if I come up to you and I'm like, 'Hey, this is going on,' you probably wouldn't believe me unless I had something to show you. So if I say, 'Hey, this is going on. Look, I have proof,' you can't deny it, I guess."

The latter part of Harman's testimony becomes the thematic center for *Standard Operating Procedure* and introduces the primary questions that Morris interrogates throughout the rest of the documentary. At the heart of the film, Morris investigates what the pictures from Abu Ghraib reveal about the conditions there, what they conceal about the context in which they were taken, and the ways in which they deceive us into thinking something that may not in fact be true. The Abu Ghraib pictures are proof of something, and the narrative in the film is structured around investigating what that "something" is.

Morris uses Army Special Agent Brent Pack as a catalyst for this investigation. After the release of the torture photos, Pack was put in charge of examining the events at Abu Ghraib. Similar to Robert Jan van Pelt's investigation into Fred Leuchter's conclusions in *Mr. Death*, Pack's investigation helps structure the film as a whole. Pack describes his mission about fifteen minutes into the film: "They gave me twelve CDs and said there's thousands of pictures from Abu Ghraib. . . . The pictures spoke a thousand words, but unless you know what day and time they were taken, you wouldn't know what the story was." Brent Pack then presents the questions both he and the film aim to answer: When did the incidents begin? When did they end? How much time elapsed in between these photographs? How much effort was put into the detainee abuses? Who else was there in the room at the time? How could all of this go on without anybody noticing?

Morris investigates these questions by focusing on individual events that occurred at the prison. For instance, about forty minutes into the film, Harman introduces the pictures of a detainee named "Gilligan," hooded, standing on a box with his arms outstretched and wires dangling from his fingers. These photographs were among the most iconic and widely distributed images associated with the prison abuses, and one even appeared on the cover of a May 8, 2006, issue of the *Economist*.

Harman's testimony provides context for the photographs, including the reason Gilligan had wires on his fingers. Gilligan was accused of killing two criminal-investigation agents, and as a way to keep him awake and standing in the stress position, he was told that if he stepped off the box the wires would electrocute him. Harman also testifies that Gilligan was never physically harmed, and the wires were removed after the photos were taken. Morris cuts to both actual photos of the detainee as well as reenactment images that illustrate Harman's testimony. Harman and Megan Ambuhl also describe what happened to Gilligan later in his time at the prison: he began working for the soldiers, and they gave him extra meals for "helping out." Morris cuts to a more familiar image of Gilligan one last time at the end of the sequence, allowing the audience to see the picture in this new context (see figure 8.4).

The interview testimony and the visuals provide a context for the iconic Gilligan pictures. The photographs themselves demonstrate the inhumane treatment of the detainee, but they do not show why Gilligan was at the prison, and more importantly, they obscure Gilligan's subsequent relationship with the soldiers at Abu Ghraib. *Standard Operating Procedure* adopts this task of illuminating the context outside the frame of the Abu Ghraib images.

As Morris answers certain questions in the film, such as the backstory for Gilligan, other questions remain open. For instance, who specifically was involved in these incidents of abuse? Is this kind of treatment "standard operating procedure," or is it merely a one-off instance of malicious behavior?

We return to Brent Pack intermittently as he continues his investigation into the Abu Ghraib photographs in an attempt to sort out these larger questions. For example, after the Gilligan sequence, Pack describes how the metadata in each picture file helped him determine when the pictures were taken and who else was taking pictures at the same time. Pack's discussions about his methodology may at first seem digressive to the primary questions of the investigation, but it is the manner in which he rearranges and analyzes the photographs that helps answer many of these questions about Abu Ghraib. Returning to the photographs of Gilligan, Pack discovers that there were three different cameras taking pictures of Gilligan at the same time.

FIGURE 8.4. ◻ *Standard Operating Procedure*

This finding helps us understand who was present during the interrogation as well as what was outside the frame in each picture.

Pack eventually reaches a conclusion about one of the primary questions in *Standard Operating Procedure*: which photographs constitute criminal acts, and which show "standard operating procedure"? Pack testifies the pictures of physical injury, sexual abuse, and humiliation depict criminal acts, and the images of men stripped naked, handcuffed in stress positions, and wearing women's underwear show practices designed to acquire information and are thus "standard operating procedure." Morris dramatizes Pack's judgments using a red rubber stamp on the images, and many of the "S.O.P." stamps are placed on some of the most disturbing images throughout the film, such as that of Gilligan standing on the box with wires hanging from his fingers.

Pack's judgment that this treatment constitutes "standard operating procedure" is in part based on the idea that the images suggest harsher treatment than actually took place in the prison. At the same time, Pack's judgment lifts some, although not all, of the responsibility for the offenses off the soldiers and onto those who make the policies. The absurdity that these practices are considered standard operating procedure is an implicit condemnation of those who determine what is acceptable. This criticism is not as explicit as in *Ghosts of Abu Ghraib* and *Taxi to the Dark Side*, but Morris does make a point of including the following title at the end of the film: "No one above the rank of Staff Sergeant has served time in prison for the abuses at Abu Ghraib."

At its core, *Standard Operating Procedure* is not designed merely to work out the details of who participated in the abuses at Abu Ghraib, what the images reveal about these abuses, and whether these actions were encouraged by U.S. policy. As with all of Morris's films, *Standard Operating Procedure* is interested in exploring the ways in which people understand themselves and the world around them. Morris provides an investigation into the soldiers' subjective engagement with the conditions at Abu Ghraib that runs parallel to Pack's investigation.

■ Voice and Subjectivity

Standard Operating Procedure's explanation of what the photographs reveal and conceal about the detainee abuse would seem to indicate a formal voice in the film. Compared to Morris's previous films, *Standard Operating Procedure* does closely connect to the formal voice, as Morris gives Pack and the other interview subjects a great deal of authority to describe the conditions and events in Abu Ghraib. Morris handles other questions with an open voice, however, in particular those that deal with decision making at the prison.

The combination of a formal voice explaining the events at Abu Ghraib and an open voice exploring motivation and personal psychology is best illustrated in Morris's treatment of another iconic image in the Abu Ghraib scandal: Lynndie England holding a leash attached to a detainee known as "Gus" as he lies naked on the ground. Megan Ambuhl, Ken Davis, and England describe how Gus was brought to Abu Ghraib because he was involved in a drunken altercation. While at Abu Ghraib, Gus had stopped eating and was subsequently given intravenous therapy throughout the day. Ambuhl, Davis, and England also testify that Gus crawled out of his cell by himself, although the picture may indicate that England dragged him out. Charles Graner then placed the tie-down strap around Gus's neck and told England to hold the strap while he took photographs. They then removed the strap from Gus's neck, and he stood up by himself. Morris presents this information about the Gus photograph as accurate and multiple compatible testimonies strengthen the authority of this account.

Throughout the *Standard Operating Procedure*, Morris gives the interview subjects, many of whom participated in detestable behavior, the authority to present an unquestioned account of the events at Abu Ghraib. Davis explains how a detainee was shot after smuggling a pistol into the prison, England describes falling in love with Graner, and Jeremy Sivits testifies about Staff Sergeant Ivan Frederick's physical abuse of prisoners. Morris presents these accounts as reliable and harmonious with the other testimony in the film. Morris also employs a variety of images, including photographs, documentary footage, and staged sequences, to help illustrate and reinforce the testimony about the prison.

Standard Operating Procedure does not merely establish what happened at the time the photographs were taken. Morris is also interested in *why* these actions took place, introducing the role of human psychology along with the open voice in the film. Returning to the "Gus" images at Abu Ghraib, the issue of human subjectivity emerges at the end of the sequence. England entertains reasons for Graner asking her to hold the strap while he took photographs: "He would have never had me standing next to Gus if the camera wasn't there. A ninety-pound to a hundred-pound female, short female at that, holding a strap that's attached to his neck. I'm dominating him. Maybe that's what Graner was going for. Maybe it was for documentation, maybe it was for his own amusement. I don't know what was going through his head, but he took it."

Standard Operating Procedure explores this question of what was "going through the soldiers' heads" during their time at Abu Ghraib. Unlike many of the clear, unchallenged accounts of what occurred at Abu Ghraib, the question of *why* these events occurred is more complex and opaque. About ninety minutes into the film, Brent Pack reflects on the role the photographs will play in our future understanding of the Iraq War and suggests that the soldiers were not properly trained and under a great deal of stress at Abu Ghraib. Pack also says that "at the time, they were in a warzone where the

FIGURE 8.5. □ *Standard Operating Procedure*

rules get fuzzy sometimes." And it is in this confused, fuzzy space that Morris places not only the rules of war but also the role of the subjective at Abu Ghraib.

Morris then returns to the Gus photographs. England describes the difference between the actual photographs of her and Gus and the image released to the media, in which Graner had cropped Ambuhl out of the picture (see figure 8.5). England suggests one reason Graner would remove Ambuhl from the photograph: "Maybe it was to secretly protect her, because now that I know that they were closer than what I thought, at the time. Maybe he was trying to protect her." England then explains that she was carrying Graner's child, and when she told Graner the news, he responded by rejecting England and his child.

These reasons and justifications for the conduct at Abu Ghraib do not carry the same authority as the explanations about what happened at the prison, in part because there are many explanations given and no one reason adequately accounts for the events. For instance, Graner's romantic involvement with Ambuhl is a possible option for what was "going through his head" at Abu Ghraib, but it was one of many possible reasons for his behavior. While it helps explain why he cropped Ambuhl out of the picture, or maybe even why he decided to put England in the picture, it does not help explain why he and the others engaged in many of the other sadistic acts at Abu Ghraib. Throughout the film, the interview subjects propose a wide variety of explanations and motivations for their behavior, including frustration with daily mortar attacks, the demand to follow orders, and in the case of cropping the picture of England and Gus, trying to protect a romantic interest.

These explanations also generate contradictions and ironies in the film. For instance, Sivits explains that he agreed to take pictures of soldiers mishandling and abusing the prisoners because "I'm a nice guy. . . . I try not to have anybody mad at me. That's the way I've always been, but I guess being a nice guy doesn't always pay off." There is a clear irony in using the desire to be "a nice guy" as a reason for participating in the horrific treatment of others. There is another, more subtle irony here, as Sivits's pictures helped bring to light the detainee abuse at Abu Ghraib. This was not a positive event for the soldiers accused of wrongdoing, but it did expose a truth about the handling of the war in Iraq.

The disconnect between Sivits's understanding of the photographs and the viewer's engagement with his explanations strips some authority from Sivits's testimony. More than questioning his account of *what* happened at Abu Ghraib, Morris prompts viewers to probe his explanations of *why* it happened and the effects of the incidents more broadly. In this way, Morris is conducting an exploration, as opposed to an explanation, of how these soldiers understand their own actions. The film suggests reasons for the soldiers' behavior, including inexperience, frustration, and self-preservation.

Human subjectivity is always a complex, befuddling element in Morris's films, and the answers to why people think or behave certain ways ultimately remain open. Pack reinforces this position at the end of *Standard Operating Procedure*: "The photographs are what they are. You can interpret them differently, but what the photograph depicts is what it is. You can put any kind of meaning to it, but you are seeing what happened at that snapshot in time.

You can read emotion on their face and feelings in their eyes, but it's nothing that can be entered into fact. All you can do is report what's in the picture."

Pack's analysis of the Abu Ghraib photographs points to the interplay of the formal and open voice in *Standard Operating Procedure*. The pictures are a record of something that happened in Abu Ghraib, but they do not tell the whole story. If we look closer at both the photographs and the people who participated in them, we can come to a better understanding of what happened and why it happened. But there is also something more enigmatic and elusive about the situation that Pack describes as the "emotion" and "feeling" of the detainees, which Morris expands to the soldiers at Abu Ghraib.

Morris again uses stylized reenactments to foreground these subjective elements in *Standard Operating Procedure*. The beginning of the film establishes this connection between the reenactment and subjectivity as Sabrina Harman describes her first day at the prison in a letter to her wife: "We drove in and two helicopters were landing, taking prisoners off. I am scared of helicopters because of the dream." Harman then describes a dream of an exploding helicopter, and Morris illustrates this with a slow-motion shot of a helicopter bursting into flames and falling toward the camera.

Harman's helicopter dream links the stylized reenactment with a subjective experience, which Morris repeats and refines throughout *Standard Operating Procedure*. About thirty minutes into the film, Morris introduces Tim Dugan, a contract interrogator at Abu Ghraib. Accompanying Dugan's testimony, we see a reenactment of a hooded detainee kneeling in a prison hallway with fans spinning overhead. On the audio track, a sound effect reminiscent of a helicopter links back to Harman's dream of the helicopter exploding. Dugan's first line reinforces the connection between the reenactment and the dreamlike: "The big word that always comes up for me is surreal."

We find a similar image-sound connection near the end of the film, as Javal Davis discusses the amnesty period during which much of the evidence concerning the abuse of prisoners was destroyed. Morris again cuts to the prison hallway image with the helicopter sound effect, but instead of the detainee in the foreground, scraps of paper fall to the ground (see figure 8.6). Davis then acknowledges that he will be a scapegoat for the prison abuses: "Sacrifice the little guys. That's how they cover it up. I'm a twenty-eight-year-old, young, American, a volunteer soldier, and I'm going to get everything

FIGURE 8.6. ◻ *Standard Operating Procedure*

blamed on me." The visual and aural similarities between the scenes prompt the audience to connect Harman's dream, Dugan's surreal experience at the prison, and Davis's distressing recognition about his future. Abu Ghraib was a confusing, bizarre nightmare for many of the soldiers, and through the course of the film, Morris tracks their experiences in the prison from a dreamlike world to a horrible reality.

The reality of Abu Ghraib involves questions about responsibility for the events at the prison, and the reenactments help foreground these issues. For example, about an hour into the film, Morris addresses the murder of one of the Abu Ghraib detainees. Sergeant Anthony Diaz describes being asked to secure a detainee during an interrogation. He realized the detainee was dead after removing his hood: "I even got some blood on my uniform, because he was dripping. It kind of felt bad because, you know, I know I'm not part of this, but it kind of makes you feel like you are 'cause you are there with the guy." Morris cuts to a reenactment of blood dripping in slow motion from a man's nose, framed in close-up and backlit, and falling on a piece of fabric. Diaz connects the blood on his uniform with a sense of responsibility, and Morris's extended visual exploration of the blood cues the audience to further reflect on the issue of who is to blame for the events at Abu Ghraib.

So, is Diaz in any way responsible for the death of the detainee at Abu Ghraib? Diaz was not involved in the actual beating and murder of the man, but is Diaz absolved of any fault just because the prisoner was already dead? How much did Diaz know about the abuse before he encountered the murdered detainee? Does Diaz's decision not to report the murder make him to some degree responsible for the events at Abu Ghraib? Morris's handling of these questions about responsibility, knowledge, and guilt are not as straightforward as those in *The Ghosts of Abu Ghraib* and *Taxi to the Dark Side*, which are primarily concerned about clearly identifying those who facilitated the prison abuse. Throughout *Standard Operating Procedure*, Morris raises and explores, rather than clearly answers, these questions.

■ Reception and Ethics

The style and structure in *Standard Operating Procedure* provide a framework through which the viewer understands the events at Abu Ghraib, makes connections between individuals, and engages theoretical questions about human nature. Morris's framework shapes but does not determine the audience's responses, and this reluctance to provide clear answers angered many critics. In addition, the film's flamboyant visual style led to the accusation that Morris is more interested in aesthetic flourishes than engaging reality and truth. Although Morris has received similar criticisms throughout his career, these complaints occurred more frequently and with more force in *Standard Operating Procedure* than in any of his previous films.

Many reviewers objected to the ways in which Morris aestheticized the horrors of Abu Ghraib. Jim Slotek explains in the *Toronto Sun*, "The people who hate this movie seem to hate it [because it] is like an episode of CSI, with digital science, flashy graphics, floating text, artful black-screen interludes [and] dramatizations."[17] Clarence Tsui from the *South China Morning Post* writes, "What undermines *Standard Operating Procedure* . . . is the excessive artifice in some of these scenes" and, in particular, "the re-enactments of the

FIGURE 8.7. ▫ *Taxi to the Dark Side*

violence, filmed in extreme close-ups and slow-motion."[18] Ron Steinman's review in *Digital Filmmaker* echoes this complaint, noting the connection to Morris's career in television advertising: "[The visuals] are far too slick, looking as if they are from an expensive TV commercial."[19]

So why does Morris's stylized aesthetic constitute a problem for the film? Many critics note the uncomfortable mixture of *Standard Operating Procedure*'s subject matter and Morris's particularly handling of the visuals. Stephen Hunter writes in the *Washington Post*: "[Morris's] stylizations are well known, and perhaps, given the seriousness of the subject matter, this might have been an ideal time to abandon them," and Peter Bradshaw suggests that "something closer to the austerity of Claude Lanzmann's *Shoah* would have been more in order."[20]

Morris has employed similar stylized reenactments in previous films with serious topics, including the murder of a police officer in *The Thin Blue Line*, the Holocaust in *Mr. Death*, and the Vietnam War in *The Fog of War*. In addition, some of the other Abu Ghraib documentaries such as Alex Gibney's *Taxi to the Dark Side* also use stylized reenactments but did not receive similar criticisms. This leads us to Morris's particular stylistic treatment of the subject matter and, more specifically, his depiction of violence. Morris has previously explored violence in reenactments; for instance, we repeatedly see the

FIGURE 8.8. □ *Standard Operating Procedure*

murder scene of Officer Robert Wood in *The Thin Blue Line*. Morris's handling of this violence is fragmented and implied, however, as we see the smoking gun, the twisting of the officer's body, and its impact on the ground, but we never see the bullet entering the body.

The reenactments in *Taxi to the Dark Side* are similar to those in *The Thin Blue Line*. For instance, interview subjects describe knee strikes against Afghan prisoner Dilawar the night before he died. During the testimony, Gibney cuts to fragmented images of the reenacted beating, including a high-angle shot of a prison guard abusing the prisoner (see figure 8.7). The violence is obscured by both a fence in the foreground of the image as well as the torture being thrown out of focus. Much like the shooting in *The Thin Blue Line*, the torture is not made visually explicit.

Morris's approach to the reenactments in *Standard Operating Procedure* is considerably different. Morris sometimes fragments and abstracts the sequences, but he also graphically explores other scenes of torture. For instance, as Javal Davis describes how interrogators waterboarded prisoners, Morris cuts to a vivid close-up of water pouring over the detainee's hooded face (see figure 8.8). These images not only clearly depict the abuses but also are beautifully composed and lit, as in figure 8.8, where the slow motion combined with the overexposure on the prisoner's face creates a striking interplay of motion, light, and shadow. Perhaps one problem for critics is not merely that a film should not so clearly depict or reenact torture but also that it should not be a source of beauty or pleasure.

While some critics complained that Morris was too explicit in his approach to the visuals, other critics argued that Morris was not explicit enough about who was to blame for the abuses at Abu Ghraib. Manohla Dargis writes in her *New York Times* review: "A group of young soldiers committed crimes at the behest of their superiors. [Seymour] Hersh, among others, has voiced his opinions on who deserves the blame, but beyond a throwaway image of President Bush, Mr. Morris himself remains basically silent on this crucial point."[21] This critique is similar to those raised against *The Fog of War*, where critics argued that Morris did not properly investigate and criticize McNamara's beliefs and actions. The view is that the people in power are the ones that are ultimately responsible and should bear the brunt of the criticism, as they do in Iraq War documentaries such as *The Ghosts of Abu Ghraib* and Vietnam War documentaries like *Hearts and Minds*.

One of Morris's challenges in the *Standard Operating Procedure* project was to provide a unique perspective on an issue that had been frequently examined in the news and previously released documentaries. Morris's interest in exploring human subjectivity and the relationship between photograph and the real world provides an original contribution to the discussion about the Abu Ghraib scandal. At the same time, many critics felt that, in addressing this subject, Morris has certain obligations to identify and criticize those who are responsible that take precedence over his peculiar interest in these more abstract philosophical issues.

9 Tabloid

BY 2008, ERROL MORRIS HAD DIRECTED eight documentaries, two seasons of his *First Person* television series, one fiction film, and numerous television commercials. There were many more projects that were never funded, including an examination of spontaneous human combustion entitled *Ablaze!* (or *Fire from Heaven*), a film called *Weirdo* about the breeding of a giant chicken, and the story of one man who attempted to build an interstate highway across Minnesota.[1] Morris's interest in these sensational, tabloid stories is evident in his early films, such as the relocation of dead pets in *Gates of Heaven* and growing sand in a jar in *Vernon, Florida*. Morris himself even characterizes *Gates of Heaven* as "a tabloid story from *The San Francisco Chronicle*."[2]

This whimsical fascination with the strange that characterized much of Morris's early work appeared to shift as he began making films that dealt with the Holocaust, the Vietnam War, and the abuses at Abu Ghraib. While there are strange, absurd, funny moments in all of Morris's films, the subject matter in these later films are distinctively more somber. J. Hoberman refers to *Mr. Death*, *The Fog of War*, and *Standard Operating Procedure* as Morris's "atrocity trilogy."[3]

Morris's 2010 *Tabloid* tells an outlandish story involving crime, sex, and canine cloning. Joyce McKinney is a former Miss Wyoming who, in the 1970s, fell in love with Mormon missionary Kirk Anderson. When Anderson left the United States for England, McKinney believed he had been brainwashed and abducted by the Mormon Church. McKinney traveled to England with a team of male associates and abducted Anderson, taking him to a cottage in Devon. Typical of a Morris documentary, accounts of what happened next begin to conflict. McKinney claims that she then had a weekend of loving, consensual sex with Anderson. According to a police report later submitted by Anderson, McKinney shackled him to a bed and forced him to have sex with her against his will.

The incident became a headline story in British tabloid papers in the late 1970s. The *Daily Mirror* and the *Daily Express* both pursued the story and frequently published breaking developments, making McKinney a national celebrity. McKinney returned to the United States, and with the exception of an incident where she stalked Anderson in the mid-1980s, she maintained a private life for three decades. News articles began to emerge in 2008 about a woman named Bernann McKinney who paid a South Korean firm seventy-five thousand pounds to clone her deceased pit bull terrier.[4] Newspaper reports later identified Bernann as Joyce McKinney.[5]

Tabloid is a meditation on storytelling, examining the various, conflicting accounts of McKinney's life and the "Manacled Mormon" tabloid story. *Tabloid*'s narrative structure and graphic-heavy visual design foregrounds the components and motivations for each particular story. *Tabloid* is not a critique of the news industry or a reflexive commentary on documentary film's inability to capture reality. Morris's analysis rather takes us into the human peculiarities and errors in the storytelling and retelling process, revealing the ways in which we construct and maintain our particular views of the world.

■ Background

Morris read a 2008 *Boston Globe* article about McKinney's dog cloning and was intrigued by the connections between her past and her pet replication.[6] Morris was interested in filming another *First Person* television series at the time and contacted McKinney to film an episode about her life, but she declined. The following year, Morris was planning another television series on Showtime called *Tabloid*, and he again contacted McKinney. She agreed, and Morris conducted a six-hour interview for the series pilot. After the interview, Morris changed his mind: "I . . . thought this is not a half hour for television. This is something more interesting. At least for me. And so we convinced Showtime it wasn't a series, it was a movie."[7]

Morris spent three days shooting a total of six interviews, including conversations with Peter Tory of the *Daily Express*, Kent Gavin of the *Daily Mirror*, and cloning scientist Dr. Jin Han Hong. Morris edited the film for three months and *Tabloid* premiered at the 2010 Telluride Film Festival.[8] After screenings at festivals including Telluride, the Toronto International Film Festival, and DOC NYC, Sundance Selects acquired the North American distribution rights to *Tabloid* in January 2011.[9] The film continued to play at festivals before the theatrical release in the summer of 2011. *Tabloid* grossed just under seven hundred thousand dollars over eleven weeks in theaters, playing at its peak in thirty-seven theaters across the country.[10] *Tabloid* is Morris's fifth-highest grossing documentary, positioned between *Fast, Cheap and Out of Control* and *Mr. Death.*

Tabloid underperformed at the box office but received generally positive reviews from film critics. The *New York Times* praised Morris for exposing, "once again, an impossible and perfect embodiment of just how curious our species can be."[11] *Tabloid* won the San Francisco Film Critics Circle award for Best Documentary and appeared on numerous "best of" lists at the end of 2011. The film was not nominated for an Academy Award, although Morris suggested that "if there was an Academy Award for best performance in a documentary, [Joyce McKinney would] win."[12]

McKinney was not as happy with her role in the film. She described the film as a "celluloid catastrophe," complaining that the film made her look "like an S&M hooker."[13] McKinney made her feelings known at many of the early screenings of the film, including in Austin, San Francisco, Seattle, and New York City. McKinney heckled the film during the screenings, even yelling "liar" at the screen. At a Museum of Modern Art screening, McKinney arrived in disguise and, at the end of the film, announced "I'm Joyce McKinney!"[14] McKinney would also join Morris for the question-and-answer sessions after the screenings, complaining about the inaccuracies in the film and the audience's responses. At a New York University screening, McKinney scolded the room: "It hurt me when you guys laughed."[15]

McKinney took her fight against the film to the Internet as well. Adopting names such as "truthteller" and "2Tell_it_like_it_is2," McKinney issued "intent to sue" notices against the publishers and other commenters for libel and defamation.[16] McKinney frequently described the details of the production and called the film "perverted," "pornographic," and "trashy."[17] She also claimed that there is a Mormon conspiracy to silence her and make her look crazy.

It does not appear as if McKinney has sued any journalist or Internet commenter, but she did file suit against Morris, producer Mark Lipson, and distributors Sundance Selects and IFC Films. In the suit filed in the Los Angeles County Superior Court on November 2, 2011, McKinney claimed that she was tricked into the *Tabloid* interview because she was told it was for a Showtime television series and she would be able to clear her name. McKinney argued that the subsequent film portrayed her as "crazy, a sex offender, an S&M prostitute, and/or a rapist." She also accused Morris's "cronies" of stealing valuable personal photographs and memorabilia, and said she only signed the permission under duress. McKinney claimed that, in March 2010, Lipson threatened to kill her service dog if she did not sign the permission: "At one point, [the] plaintiff clenched her hand tightly to avoid taking the pen that Lipson thrust at her and Lipson stabbed her hand with the pen, causing her hand to bleed, and screamed 'sign it, sign, it, or the dog will die!'"[18]

In response to the lawsuit, Morris and the other defendants filed an anti-SLAPP (strategic lawsuit against public participation) motion, claiming that McKinney's lawsuit stifled free speech. Morris argued that McKinney was a public figure and her story was a matter of public interest. McKinney's "public" status was due to the widely published stories about her abduction of Anderson and her dog cloning. Los Angeles County Superior Court judge James Steele sided with Morris on the lawsuit, agreeing that McKinney was a "limited-purpose" public figure and that she voluntarily agreed to participate in the film. Steele also ruled that the film contained "a substantial portion . . . of [the] Plaintiff's version of the Anderson event."[19]

Ironically, McKinney's lawsuits have the same kind of tabloid appeal as her adventures in Mormon kidnapping and dog cloning. The lawsuits also return us to fundamental questions about Morris's approach to the documentary. While McKinney maintains that the film distorts and belittles her, others claim that Morris is too kind to McKinney in the film. For instance, J. Hoberman from the *Village Voice* writes, "When it comes to interrogating her . . . Morris is no tougher than he was with Robert McNamara. . . . McKinney's schizoid, weirdly impish pronouncements are lovingly transcribed and allowed to stand unchallenged by her interviewer."[20]

We have noted these divergent reactions to Morris's films throughout his career. They point us to Morris's handling of documentary style and structure, as well the subtle interplay of factual claims and human subjectivity in his film. Morris again introduces new formal elements in *Tabloid*, including a unique visual style that leaves behind one element that is perhaps most frequently associated with his films: the reenactment.

■ Style

Morris and longtime cinematographer Robert Chappell used the Interrotron interview device connected to a Red One digital camera for the interviews in *Tabloid*. As discussed in earlier chapters, Morris's Interrotron places some limitations on filming the interviews. For instance, the interview subject needs to be seated relatively close to the Interrotron. Chappell notes, "You can't back up much more than five to eight feet from the subject because they need a clear picture of Errol on the teleprompter."[21] This distance restriction had a number of consequences for the interview visuals. Morris is limited in how wide he can frame his subject and consequently how much information he can put in the interview background. Using a CinemaScope aspect ratio, Morris frames all of his subjects in *Tabloid* in a medium close-up and, as in all of his films after *A Brief History of Time*, has a spare background.

Morris's use of digital technology allowed him to experiment with the interview footage. Similar to *Standard Operating Procedure*, Morris digitally repositions the interview subjects in the frame, easing the impression of jump cuts in a single interview. Morris also uses digital repositioning for narrative and expressive purposes. For instance, McKinney describes Kirk Anderson's mysterious disappearance while they were dating: "I don't mean he left me, I don't mean he abandoned me, I don't mean he left me for another woman; I mean he evaporated into thin air. He wasn't the kind of person to just run off like that. His things were still at my place and, you know, it was just weird."[22] At the end of each phrase, Morris repositions McKinney in the frame. McKinney's physical shifting is expressive of her confusion about Anderson's sudden absence and adds a rhythmic pulse to the interview.

Morris's voice is also more present than in any of his previous films. We hear Morris asking questions at the end of *The Thin Blue Line* and briefly interacting with Robert McNamara in *The Fog of War*, but Morris's interactions in *Tabloid* more clearly direct the testimony. For example, McKinney describes the romantic night she was having with an aroused Anderson at the Devon cottage. Anderson suddenly resists her advances and begins praying. Morris plays into the tabloid interest of the moment by asking, "Does he still have the erection while he is chanting?" Morris's question here and elsewhere amplify the lurid nature of McKinney's story. It is hard to know how frequently Morris does this in his unedited interviews, but he chose to include these moments in *Tabloid* more than in any other film.

Morris once again incorporates a diverse range of visual elements in *Tabloid*, including interview footage, newspaper headlines and clippings, photographs, and animated maps. Morris also integrates found footage from a variety of sources including television news, McKinney's home movies, and fictional footage from *Brief Encounter* (1945), *Caged* (1950), *Brother Sun, Sister Moon* (1972), *The Godmakers!* (1982), and a 1957 *Leave It to Beaver* episode.

For the first time since *Vernon, Florida*, Morris does not include reenactments in one of his films. There is a staged quality to some of the found footage Morris uses in the film, however. Morris bookends *Tabloid* with scripted footage from the early 1980s that filmmaker Trent Harris shot of McKinney reading from a book she was writing at the time.

Morris introduces new stylistic elements in *Tabloid*, including push transitions between interviews. A push transition is when the second clip in a transition pushes the first out of the frame. These push cuts make the transitions between interviews more apparent to the audience and add dynamism to the visuals.

The most notable new visual element in *Tabloid* is Morris's playful use of superimposed graphics. Morris had increasingly used titles for identifying people, dates, and places in more recent films after rejecting them in his first four films. *Tabloid* uses titles to identify the interview subject, although Morris frequently layers them with different descriptions. For example, when we are first introduced to McKinney, we have a series of identifying titles that quickly layer on top of each other in the following sequence: "Joyce McKinney Ex-Beauty Queen," "Joyce McKinney Sex Hostess," "Joyce McKinney Little Miss Perfect," and then back to "Joyce McKinney Ex-Beauty Queen" as the others fade away (see figure 9.1).

Morris also uses title graphics to fill in narrative gaps in the film. For instance, McKinney discusses her cloned puppies from South Korea and their resemblance to the original dog, Booger. McKinney says that one of the puppies opened the door to the minibar refrigerator the same way that Booger used to, but she has trouble remembering the name for the appliance: "You know how they have those little refrigerators with little wooden doors, like a cabinet in the hotels?" Morris then superimposes "minibar" over the interview image to assist McKinney and for comic effect (see figure 9.2).

FIGURE 9.1. ◻ *Tabloid*

FIGURE 9.2. ◻ *Tabloid*

John Kusiak composed the music for *Tabloid*. Kusiak had scored many of Morris's *First Person* episodes and had contributed to *Fast, Cheap and Out of Control*, *Mr. Death*, and *The Fog of War*. The music in *Tabloid* most resembles *Fast, Cheap*, with lively melodic repetitions and prominent mallet and string instruments. Kusiak explains Morris's unusual approach to film music: "What's interesting about Errol's style is that he likes to have music early on in the process and he likes to actually edit the film to the music rather than the traditional Hollywood approach in which the film is edited completely using temp music and then given to the composer after it is complete and the composer writes music for it."[23]

The sound effects in *Tabloid* are particularly expressive and playful. We

FIGURE 9.3. □ *Tabloid*

frequently hear the clicks of cameras, whips, and bells as Morris assembles graphic elements on screen. These sound effects often emphasize and exaggerate the testimony. For instance, McKinney describes the moment when Kirk Anderson enters her car in England before she drives him to the Devon cottage. McKinney describes Anderson as robotic: "It was like he had a personality alteration. Kirk number one and Kirk number two. Kirk number one was the man I fell in love with." Morris includes bird sound effects that match flowers over the Anderson's picture. McKinney continues, "Kirk number two was Cult Kirk," and Morris places spirals over his eyes accompanied by laser sound effects (see figure 9.3).

Tabloid's frenetic, exaggerated style ties to its interest in the embellishments and errors in the different stories of the interview subjects. The visual and aural style works together with the film's structure to raise and answer questions about McKinney's life and explore the peculiarities of human subjectivity. *Tabloid* also directs our attention to the storytelling process, both in the tabloid press and in the ways in which we construct stories about our own lives.

■ Structure

Tabloid is a predominantly chronological account of McKinney's life. McKinney briefly describes her "Leave It to Beaver" childhood at the beginning of the film, which quickly transitions into her first meeting with Anderson.

McKinney and a variety of interview subjects then discuss McKinney's trip to England, her disputed kidnapping of Anderson, and its aftermath. The last half hour of *Tabloid* follows McKinney's largely isolated life in North Carolina, followed by her return to newspaper headlines when she clones her deceased dog Booger.

Tabloid employs a narrative structure that begins by introducing questions and thematic elements that are explored throughout the rest the film. Similar to *The Thin Blue Line*, *Mr. Death*, and to some extent, *Standard Operating Procedure*, *Tabloid* presents competing accounts of historical events. Morris provides reasons to doubt, but not dismiss, much of the testimony in *Tabloid*, and the viewer must test the reliability of the claims.

The film begins with found footage of McKinney reading from her book *A Very Special Love Story*: "Once upon a time there was a little princess, the most beautiful little princess in all of the land. . . . But the little princess was unhappy, for she was lonely. Someday, she would find her kind, handsome prince, and he would sweep her up on a big white horse, and he would take her away and marry her, and they would live happily ever after." Parts of McKinney's story overlap with the events in the film. She was a pretty young woman, and she did find the love of her life. Anderson never did take her away, however, and there was a great deal of unhappiness as a result of that relationship. There are also unresolved connections between her fairytale and her real life. It is unclear the extent to which Anderson swept her off her feet and ultimately how much he loved her.

McKinney's life serves as the narrative spine for *Tabloid*, although the film is also centrally interested in how tabloid presses reported her life. Peter Tory, a reporter for the *Daily Express*, and Kent Gavin, a photographer for the *Daily Mirror*, provide the perspective of the press. McKinney describes her story as "nice" and "tender," whereas Tory and Gavin highlight the salacious nature of McKinney's life. Tory and Gavin's stories also occasionally conflict as each is trying to out-scoop the other.

As we follow the events in McKinney's life, the testimony from all of the interview subjects diverges, converges, and then diverges again. For instance, everyone in the film agrees that McKinney flies to England with Jackson Shaw, a pilot, and Keith May to meet with Anderson. This unified account of events begins to fracture as the interview subjects describe the rescue or abduction of Anderson. There is continued agreement between Shaw and Tory as Shaw describes arriving outside a building and seeing Anderson, who was clearly not being held captive. McKinney then reveals that she has chloroform and a fake gun that she planned to use to abduct Anderson, and Shaw decides to drop out of the mission.

Tory picks up the story where Shaw leaves off and describes how McKinney and May continued with their plan: "So she arrives with Keith May, lurks around, waits around outside the Temple of, whatever it was, Latter-Day Saints of something or other, waiting for this huge shuffling figure to come out with his short Mormon haircut and pointed the gun at him and said 'get into the car.'" Shaw reinforces the agreement in the testimony by saying that May used the gun to get Anderson out to the car. There is continuity between Shaw's and Tory's testimony, and Morris does not give us reason to doubt that part of the story.

McKinney then provides her version of the story that conflicts with Shaw's and Tory's versions. She says that she waited in the car while May went in to meet Anderson. May tells Anderson that McKinney is in the car, and Anderson willingly leaves his Mormon companion to meet McKinney. McKinney's version supports her larger claim that her relationship with Anderson in England was consensual, although it does not conform to Shaw, Tory, and eventually Anderson's account of the events. Morris does not clearly resolve this conflict, although he does flash the title graphic "kidnapped" over McKinney's image as she laughs about Anderson leaving the Mormon companion.

The structure of *Tabloid* foregrounds these nodes of disagreement in the interview testimony. The film pauses at these moments to explore the nature and extent of the dissent. This discrepancy between the interview subjects rises to a climax about an hour into the film. Tory describes how McKinney contacted him about selling her story to *Daily Express*. McKinney provides the story, which Tory now calls a "sanitized" version of the truth, that depicts her as an innocent, sweet-natured woman who was a victim of circumstance. Morris then moves to the *Daily Mirror*'s Gavin, whose investigation produces a different story about McKinney. Gavin uncovers McKinney's classified ads in the *Hollywood Free Press* for erotic services as well as countless photographs that Gavin describes as "unpublishable" because of their explicit nature.

The *Daily Mirror* publishes their story entitled "The Real McKinney" accompanied by a nude picture of McKinney, and the *Daily Express* publishes her story with the title "My Undying Love" and a picture of McKinney as a nun. Tory describes both stories and concludes, "somewhere in between maybe is the truth."

The Thin Blue Line and *Tabloid* both investigate conflicting accounts of the same series of events, but *Tabloid* does not provide the same kind resolution to these disputes. For instance, the film indicates that, as Tory suggests, the truth is somewhere between the *Daily Mirror* and *Daily Express* articles, but there are a great deal of options in that space. The film raises doubt about the reliability of the interview subjects, a topic that we will further examine in the next section on the film's voice.

The film ends with McKinney discussing her post-scandal life, including the cloning of her dog Booger. The dog cloning gained international attention, and the press eventually discovered that the dog owner was the same McKinney as in the "Manacled Mormon" case. McKinney was confused by the press's interest in that fact: "I don't see any connection at all between cloned puppies and a thirty-two-year-old sex-in-chains story."

Morris illuminates this connection through a dog motif that recurs throughout *Tabloid*. Dogs are first introduced in the title sequence with McKinney posing next to a dog, accompanied by the title "A Very Special Love Story." The connection between dogs and love/intimacy is later repeated as Gavin describes how McKinney would bring her dog to her sexual encounters. The final thirty minutes of *Tabloid* is devoted to McKinney's love of dogs.

McKinney's lifelong search for love, through her connection with dogs and Anderson, becomes the catalyst for much of her actions in her life. The underlying theme of McKinney's quest for love is restated at the end of the film, when we return to Trent Harris's footage of McKinney reading from her book: "After her miraculous escape to America, Joyce retreats to seclusion to write a book about her love story. She vows never to marry knowing fully that she could never love another man other than Kirk. For she will grow old alone. A love that once spanned an entire continent and ocean still exists. Time changes, but the scene is still the same. Joyce is now a lonely old woman. Like Narcissus, she is pining to death, dying of a broken heart. That's the conclusion of my book. But the book of love has never ended."

The end of the film reiterates the importance of love in McKinney's life as well as the narrative structure in the film. We have followed McKinney's life in a relatively chronological fashion, pausing at moments when the interview subjects disagree about what happened. These disputes create narrative questions; generate dramatic, suspenseful, and comedic moments; and underline what is a central thematic concern in the film: the act of storytelling.

■ Voice

The end of *Tabloid* restates McKinney's lifelong interest in finding love. McKinney's retelling and forecasting the story of her life underscores Morris's underlying interest in how stories are created and retold. Morris does not investigate storytelling in order to inject a formal voice that determines the "true" story about McKinney's affair with Anderson or her life as a prostitute. Morris instead employs an open voice to explore the ways in which these stories reveal the peculiarities of human subjectivity.

The information in *Tabloid* is, perhaps inevitably, filtered through the self-interests of the interview subjects. The film uses a number of devices to prompt the viewer to go beyond merely understanding the testimony and reflect on the process by which that testimony was constructed. *Tabloid* is structured around disagreements between interview subjects that are often not clearly resolved. As with many of Morris's films, these unsettled disputes deny authority to any particular interview subject and facilitate the film's interest in the potential mistakes and unintended meanings in the testimony.

All of Morris's films use stylistic devices to foreground themes related to human subjectivity. Reenactments have been particularly important, in part because Morris can carefully control stylistic elements within the reenactment to direct the viewer's attention. The milkshake in *The Thin Blue Line*, the concrete chiseling in *Mr. Death*, and the dominos in *The Fog of War* all highlight important details through framing, composition, lighting, and their repetition throughout the film.

Morris does not use reenactments in *Tabloid* but employs other stylistic devices to emphasize this interest in stories and what they reveal about the storyteller. For instance, *Tabloid* develops a collage aesthetic with the still images, animating a combination of different newspaper headlines and pictures that dance in the frame. In addition, the camera often pans over pictures and headlines that are visibly taped to a white background. These stylistic decisions highlight the constructed nature of the visual material. Similar to Morris's handling of the Abu Ghraib photographs in *Standard*

Operating Procedure, *Tabloid* presents cutaway material as deliberately created in part to prompt the audience to reflect on the nature and purpose of their creation.

Morris further develops the newspaper clipping and font motif to highlight the storytelling components in *Tabloid*, including the embellishments, distortions, and evasions in the interview testimony. Title graphics are conventionally used in documentaries to provide reliable information about interview subjects and other relevant information. For instance, a title over an interview will provide an expert's name and profession, or an intertitle identifies the time and place of subsequent archival footage. These titles are conventionally among the most reliable pieces of information provided in a documentary.

Morris uses title graphics but cues the viewers to question the reliability of these graphics, thereby encouraging them to also question the dependability of the interview testimony. One method Morris uses to complicate the title graphics is to provide different, sometimes contradictory titles for the same subject. For example, Morris reiterates the title of McKinney's book with a newspaper clipping, which is then overlaid with "Love in Chains," "Little Miss Perfect," "The Manacled Mormon," and then the film title "Tabloid" (see figure 9.4). The inconsistent nature of these titles introduces what is later revealed as differing accounts of McKinney's life and her character. The sequence also establishes a newspaper font aesthetic that Morris repeats throughout the film.

Morris also uses these unstable titles when identifying the interview subjects in *Tabloid*. McKinney's first interview is accompanied first by the title "Joyce McKinney Ex-Beauty Queen." The following titles are then superimposed on the first: "Joyce McKinney Sex Hostess," "Joyce McKinney Little Miss Perfect," and then back to "Joyce McKinney Ex-Beauty Queen." The "Little Miss Perfect" title is indicative of McKinney's self-description, whereas "Sex Hostess" is closer to Peter Tory and Kent Gavin's account of McKinney. Morris returns to a less evaluative title, but the shifting titles foreground the different ways in which McKinney is judged.

Everyone in the film is subject to this shifting-title introduction. Even people who are never interviewed, such as Kirk Anderson who refused the interview and Keith May who died in 2004, are titled in the same way. These title sequences diminish some authority from interview subjects such as Tory,

FIGURE 9.4. □ *Tabloid*

whose first title "Journalist" shifts to "Gossip Columnist Daily Express." Tory's profession in part motivates his testimony, which often highlights the scandalous, sensational elements of McKinney's life. The juxtaposition of "journalist" with "gossip columnist" prompts the viewer to ask about the relationship between the two. This does not completely undermine Tory's testimony, but it does provide potential motivations for his testimony.

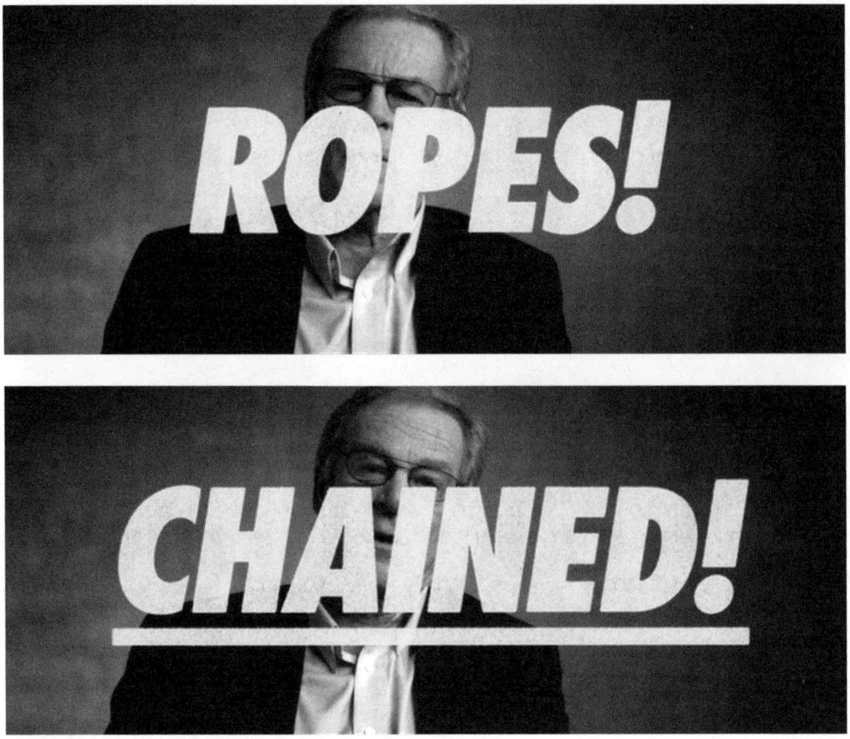

FIGURE 9.5. □ *Tabloid*

Tabloid also uses these superimposed titles to highlight words and phrases in the testimony. Morris often chooses language that foregrounds the ways in which the stories have been changed or exaggerated that, in turn, provides some insight into the ways in which the subjects view the world. For example, Tory first describes Anderson and how McKinney not only fell in love with him but also became obsessed with him. Morris flashes "obsessed" on the screen, matching the testimony. Tory correctly identifies McKinney's obsession with Anderson, an obsession that continues throughout her life.

Morris continues to use these superimposed titles during Tory's testimony. Tory later describes how McKinney drove Anderson to Devon after kidnapping him: "He was taken in and chained to, Joyce claims it was ropes [title: ropes] not chains, but chains sounds better. Anyway, he was allegedly chained [title: chained!] to the bed" (see figure 9.5). Tory first acknowledges that he is only using the term "chained" because it sounds better, which is connected to his profession as a writer for a tabloid newspaper. Tory then describes Anderson as having been "allegedly" chained, but Tory appears to be the only one alleging this. The superimposed titles emphasize this shift in language and help reveal how Tory's personal motivations shape the story he is telling.

Tory's storytelling is not merely tied to his professional interests. After explaining how Anderson's "chain" was just long enough for him to reach the toilet, Tory describes how McKinney and May tied Anderson to the bed: "Subsequently, with the help of Keith May, [he] was spread-eagled." Morris then repeats the same clip of Tory saying "spread-eagled." Tory continues, "Which is this wonderful bondage word, was spread-eagled (title: spread-eagled) to the bed and Keith May discreetly left the room."

Tory later repeats the phrase "spread-eagled" a number of times. For example, he again uses "chains" to describe Anderson's imprisonment: "It had kinky sex, it had religion, it had a beauty queen, kidnap at gunpoint, chains, being spread-eagled, it had Mormon missionaries; there was something in that story for everyone. It was a perfect tabloid story." Morris highlights the different elements in the list through sound effects. For instance, a whip sound accompanies "kinky sex," and ringing bells follow "religion."

Tory's reiteration of "spread-eagled" and Morris's repetition and titling of the phrase signal that Tory's interest in Anderson's rape position goes beyond a profession interest. Much like his description of McKinney being obsessed with Anderson, Tory seems to have a personal obsession with the sordid details of the McKinney case. Tory's fixation changes the way he tells the McKinney story, and Morris uses structural and stylistic elements to foreground that transformation.

Tory is not alone. All of the interview subjects in the film have their own self-interests and obsessions that, at the very least, flavor the testimony. McKinney clearly wants to present herself as innocent and naive. Jackson Shaw is physically attracted to McKinney, an attraction that began with their first meeting when McKinney wore a see-through blouse (see figure 9.6).

Morris does not exempt himself or the film from this world of self-interest. We frequently hear Morris playing up the scandalous elements in the film. For instance, McKinney describes getting rid of Anderson's Mormon undergarments during their first night together in Devon: "I said [to Anderson], 'How am I supposed to give you a backrub with this Mormon

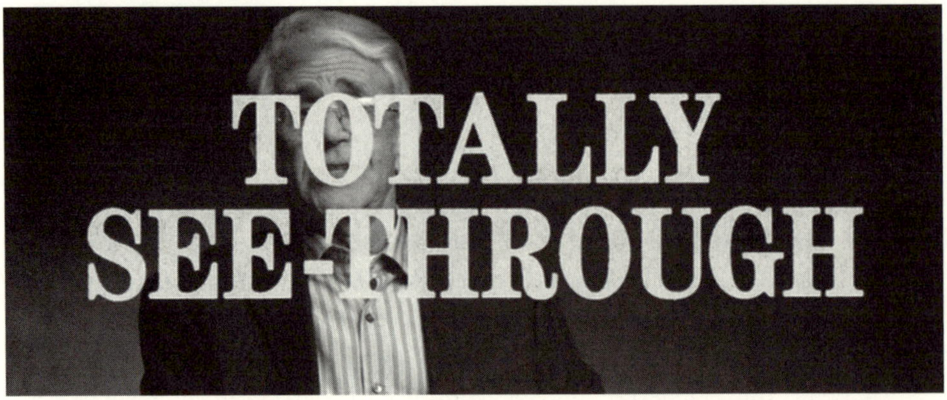

FIGURE 9.6. ▫ *Tabloid*

thing on?' And I ripped the ugly things off because they smelled, you know, and they had those occultic symbols. And I didn't want anything ugly there in our beautiful moment, you know. It was like a honeymoon cottage. And we burned them." Morris then exclaims, "You ripped off his magic underwear and burned them?" McKinney's testimony is attempting to emphasize the romantic nature of their first night, but Morris's question emphasizes the violence ("ripped" and "burned") and comedy ("magic underwear") in the testimony. Morris repeats this kind of participation throughout *Tabloid*, often constructing questions and feedback that function as tabloid-like headlines in the film. Morris's film is a self-aware tabloid film, and Morris uses his own participation as a way to prompt the audience to reflect on the constructed nature of the different stories in the film.

About thirty minutes into the film, McKinney describes Anderson's deception during her trial in England. McKinney reflects, "You can tell a lie long enough 'til you believe it." McKinney's insight applies to not only Anderson but also everyone in the film. *Tabloid* is less interested in the "lie," however, and more in the "believe." That is, Morris is less interested in investigating the truth of whether Anderson left willingly with McKinney, whether McKinney "spread-eagled" Anderson in Devon, or whether McKinney was stalking Anderson at the airport in 1984. Morris is more interested in how we all engage in the activity of story construction and what that reveals about the way we understand our relationship to the world.

■ Reception and Ethics

McKinney angrily describes the news coverage of Booger's cloning near the end of *Tabloid*: "You should have seen the way Associated Press . . . slandered me so bad. In fact, if there is an attorney listening to this and wants a good libel suit, I've got one." McKinney's offer is indicative of her litigious nature, as she not only sued Morris and his associates but also threatened dozens of critics and commenters who were not sympathetic to her story.

Lawsuits against documentary filmmakers are not particularly rare, and there have been a multitude of allegations in these lawsuits. Some plaintiffs argue that the filmmaker commercially benefitted from their life story, such as Georges Lopez in Nicolas Philibert's *To Be and To Have* (2002) and Randall Dale Adams in *The Thin Blue Line*. Defamation lawsuits against filmmakers are perhaps the most common. Rapper Lil' Wayne sued Adam Bhala Lough because of his unfavorable representation in *The Carter* (2008), as did real estate mogul David Siegal against filmmaker Lauren Greenfield and her film *The Queen of Versailles* (2012).

McKinney's lawsuit may be able to tell us something about Morris's interests and approach as a filmmaker. Part of McKinney's complaint was that *Tabloid* depicted her as "crazy, a sex offender, an S&M prostitute, and/or a rapist."[24] Again, *Tabloid* is not primarily organized around condemning any of its interview subjects. The film does highlight inconsistencies, errors, and self-interest in the testimony, but this is also one of the most generous public depictions of McKinney's story.

Is there a way to better understand McKinney's objection about her representation in the film? As with many of Morris's films, part of the hostility is connected to Morris's stylistic approach. McKinney's lawsuit against Morris addresses Morris's playful use of titles and graphics and his occasional quickly cut sequences. Philip Wong, an associate professor of psychology at Long Island University, provided a statement on behalf of McKinney stating that the quick flashes of visual material in *Tabloid* can have a subconscious effect on the viewers. Wong warns, "In the film *Tabloid*, manipulation of attention and perception leads to material being presented at the fringes of a viewer's awareness, which can facilitate the development of rogue beliefs."[25]

Amy Taubin's analysis in *Film Comment* does not address the claim that *Tabloid* facilitates "rogue beliefs," but it does connect Morris's stylistic decisions to the manipulation of the viewer: "The problem has been that increasingly in [Morris's] theatrical features since *The Thin Blue Line* ([19]88), he has piled on film tropes calculated to manipulate the sensations of the viewer (ominous music, dramatic lighting, grandiose close-ups) at the expense of analysis."[26] One common denominator appears to be the issue of control and manipulation. This is not an unusual objection against a Morris film. Although his approach to the documentary form has changed quite a bit since the late 1970s, he has been consistently criticized for heavy-handedly manipulating both the subject and the viewer.

This chapter and previous chapters have made the case that Morris does manipulate the viewer. Morris wants to direct the audience's attention in order to tell a story and highlight particular thematic interests. He in part relies on a carefully controlled visual and aural style because he does not include voice-over narration or completely reliable interview subjects, which are conventionally used to guide the viewer.

The critical responses to Morris's films often depend on the seriousness or the political implications of Morris's chosen topic. Taubin's review of *Tabloid* in is again particularly instructive here. In the middle of her review, she scolds Morris for his previous political films: "It . . . cannot be said too often that the almost complete absence of a political framework and a moral position in both *The Fog of War* ([20]03) and *Standard Operating Procedure* ([20]08) is deplorable as is the obsequiousness with which Morris treats Robert McNamara in the former and his contempt in the latter for the dehumanized grunts of Abu Ghraib."[27]

Tabloid could be politically or ideologically consequential. At the same time that *Tabloid* was released in theaters, the News International phone-hacking scandal was breaking in England. A number of British newspapers, including the tabloid *News of the World*, had illegally hacked into phone conversations, including those of politicians, celebrities, and victims of crimes and war. Armond White notes the connection, writing, "The recent scandal that closed Britain's *News of the World* because of phone hacking . . . helps to ambush *Tabloid*; it will encourage viewers to hold Morris' account to a higher standard."[28] Many reviewers characterize the film as "light" in subject matter and tone, however, which tempers their criticism of the film. Taubin continues, "*Tabloid* is intimate in scale and its politics or rather ideology is that of romantic love and its representations."[29]

So why is *Tabloid*'s modest, light-hearted subject more appropriate for Morris's approach? Morris provides a key to this distinction that reinforces part of my argument in this book: "To me, there are two kinds of mysteries. There's the mystery of what really happened, say, the shooting of the Dallas police officer, who pulled the trigger? Who committed the crime? There's an even deeper mystery, the mystery of what's inside people's heads. You look at Joyce McKinney and you wonder, who is this person? Why did Joyce do all of these things? What was the idea behind it? What motivated her? What was she hoping to achieve?"[30]

Morris's films often address the "what really happened" mysteries. *The Thin Blue Line* firmly establishes David Harris as the triggerman, and *Mr. Death* clearly disproves Fred Leuchter's theories about the gas chambers at Auschwitz. Morris's stylistic and structural decisions are ultimately more invested in the "deeper" mystery. Morris has, throughout his career, explored the peculiarities and the limitations of the way that we all understand the world. And this primary interest can frustrate viewers who want traditional advocacy documentaries.

Morris's distinction is only part of the answer, however. Morris's documentaries are difficult, complex, and enigmatic. They evade simple equations such as, stylized visuals equals manipulation, reflexive, and postmodern. They require close analysis and careful contemplation, as they are often doing many things at once. *Tabloid* is using testimony to establish what happened in the past at the same time as it is digging into the subjective implications of that testimony. *Tabloid* is telling an engrossing story at the same time as it is engaging difficult epistemological questions.

Conclusion

AS WE CONCLUDE OUR EXAMINATION of Errol Morris's films and filmmaking career, let us again reflect on a central feature of Morris's approach to his documentaries: the reenactment. The practice of integrating reenactments in a documentary has a number of implications and potential problems. A reenactment seems to rely on some conception of an originating event in reality that is then reenacted for the purposes of the film. The resulting tension between the real event and the staged scene raises a number of questions about the nature and function of the reenactment: To what extent does the reenactment replicate or distort the real world? Does the filmmaker have an ethical responsibility to communicate the extent to which the reenactment is reliable? Is the reenactment just as removed from reality as any other stylistic or structural element in the documentary? Does the presence of a reenactment constitute a fundamental break with the documentary tradition?

Scholars and critics developed a view of Morris's documentaries around the complex nature of the documentary reenactment. They argued that Morris's films function primary to raise these kinds of questions about documentary representation, and the presence of staged sequences helps cue the viewer to recognize the inherent problems with the documentary form. In addition, Morris's highly stylized treatment of these reenactments, which are in stark contrast to standards of documentary realism, further highlight their constructed nature.

The reflexive elements in Morris's work are not merely located in his use of reenactments. For instance, Morris strips authority from interview subjects by foregrounding the inconsistencies and contradictions within individual testimony and between different interview subjects. As a result, Morris's films do not have the kind of consensus that we find in other interview films, which raises questions about the reliability of the documentary interview as a practice.

Ultimately, the standard view of Morris's work not only claims that his films raise these questions about documentary representation but also offers an answer as well: nonfiction films are fundamentally incapable of providing access to reality and truth. The documentary tradition has maintained a naive belief that it can give viewers access to the world, when in fact these films are as constructed, artificial, and fictional as are Morris's reenactment sequences. Morris's films do reveal a truth, but it is a truth about the documentary tradition rather than a truth about the real world beyond it.

The Cinema of Errol Morris presents an alternative to this view of Morris's work. Instead of positioning Morris outside of the nonfiction tradition, we have examined his films within the context of contemporaneous documentaries, documentaries with similar subject matter, and the documentary tradition as a whole. We can understand Morris's films in these different contexts as rejecting, borrowing, and transforming a wide variety of documentary conventions, including the staged reenactment, which has been an important feature in the nonfiction tradition for more than one hundred years. Through a close analysis of the style, structure, and voice in each film, we have noted that Morris's films are primarily designed to engage the real world and human subjectivity. Morris's films are narratives that raise and answer questions, elicit emotions, and foreground thematic issues such as the nature and limits of human knowledge.

There are a number of advantages to this approach. First, it provides a more nuanced understanding of Morris's films, taking into account the interplay of stylistic and organizational elements in the films. Instead of having a single conceptual function, Morris's films are highly complex and challenging, as they make claims about the real world, explore human subjectivity, address difficult philosophical questions, and experiment with documentary aesthetics.

Morris's engagement with reality is particularly important in understanding how his films function. Although Morris sometimes employs an open voice that does not determine the audience's responses, Morris's films also offer historical clarity. Morris believes in the possibility of knowledge about reality, and his films lead the viewer to concrete conclusions about the world. The formal analyses of Morris's films in this book examine the dynamic between the open voice and Morris's investment in reality.

By placing Morris's films in the context of other documentaries, we can also see how this complexity and experimentation is not merely an anomaly in Morris's films. Nonfiction filmmaking is different from traditional characterizations as a formally conservative tradition that is constrained by naive ideas about realism, advocacy, and reality. The history of documentary is instead populated with stylistically adventurous, structurally innovative films that have a complex relationship with reality and truth. The documentary form is one that allows for these kinds of diverse and demanding films, and Morris's work is an informative example of that flexibility.

One aspect of Morris's career that we have not yet addressed is his influence on other documentary films and filmmakers. Morris was not the first nonfiction filmmaker to include elements such as reenactments or artificial lighting in his films. There are, however, innovative features in his approach to documentary style, structure, and theme that have influenced other filmmakers. Although it is difficult to precisely track and quantify one film's impact on subsequent work, we can note some general connections and similarities.

Arguably the most influential aspect of Morris's documentaries is his unique approach to the visuals, in particular his highly stylized reenactments. Morris's systematic use of devices such as shallow depth of field, slow motion, and fragmented framings throughout each film as well as over the course of his career helped to establish a visual brand for Morris that other filmmakers adopted and transformed.

This approach to the visuals is not easy to replicate, as it is expensive to shoot on 35 mm stock and acquire the equipment and personnel to shoot these carefully controlled reenactments. In addition, because these sequences are so stylized, the filmmaker may feel the need to make the reenactments a significant element of the film's aesthetic. Otherwise, it may seem unusual to drop in a Morris-like sequence while the rest of the film does not match that distinctive style. Despite the difficulties, many filmmakers were inspired by and imitated Morris's approach to the reenactment. We can see the influence of Morris's highly stylized reenactments, especially the use of close framings, high-contrast lighting, and slow-motion photography, in Kevin Macdonald's 1999 documentary *One Day in September.*

Morris's influence is not isolated to his visual style, as some filmmakers also used Morris's approach to structure as inspiration for their films. For instance, the concept and organization of Jessica Yu's 2007 documentary *Protagonist* bears a close resemblance to *Fast, Cheap and Out of Control*. As with

Morris's documentary, *Protagonist* focuses on four seemingly unrelated men and weaves together their interviews to locate subtle connections between their lives, interests, and subjective views of the world. Many reviewers of the film also noted this connection between the two films, in part because it is such a peculiar format for a documentary.

There are also examples of filmmakers making a more wholesale incorporation of Morris's approach to the documentary. Many reviewers noted how the combination of a bizarre subject and reenactment-heavy cutaways in Robinson Devor's *Zoo* (2007), about a man who dies after engaging in sexual intercourse with a horse, were similar to Morris's documentaries. Recently, political documentaries have integrated numerous elements from Morris's *Mr. Death*, *The Fog of War*, and *Standard Operating Procedure*. Chris Smith's 2009 *Collapse*, about the obsessions of author Michael Rupport, exhibits a number of very strong connections to *Mr. Death* and *The Fog of War*. For instance, the film profiles an individual, employs a stylized approach to the interview footage, uses a frenetic mix of visual material including stylized reenactments, and even adds a Philip Glass–like score. Several reviewers identified Judith Ehrlich's and Rick Goldsmith's *Most Dangerous Man in America* (2009) as a companion piece to *The Fog of War* because it shared so many topical and stylistic features.

Beyond comparing Morris's films with individual films or filmmakers, Morris's broader, more lasting contribution is in his experimentation with the conventions and the possibilities of the documentary. Much like Dziga Vertov, Robert Drew, and Werner Herzog, Morris helped to further expand the options of what documentary filmmakers can do with the form. Morris often tests different aesthetic approaches and narrative functions for traditional documentary elements such as staged sequences and the open voice.

Morris's most significant contribution is his exploration of human subjectivity. Morris's documentaries have a vested interest in establishing facts and conditions in the real world, in part because his films are often investigations into what really happened or went wrong in reality. Reality also provides a background against which Morris explores the complexities, the peculiarities, the contradictions, and the absurdities of the ways we view the world.

There are clear continuities in Morris's treatment of subjectivity. First, Morris presents his interview subjects as generally honest in their testimony.

In his investigations, Morris does not structure his films to catch people in lies or identify them as dishonest in nature. There are also no true heroes or villains in Morris's films, and "good" and "bad" are not defining or distinguishing traits for Morris's interviewees. All of Morris's subjects instead struggle to understand and come to terms with the world around them. Some of these subjects, such as Stephen Hawking in *A Brief History of Time* and Rodney Brooks in *Fast, Cheap and Out of Control*, are not flawless but have made genuine contributions to our understanding of the world. Others, such as Emily Miller in *The Thin Blue Line* and Fred Leuchter in *Mr. Death*, completely miss the mark, and their mistakes and self-deceptions have a grave effect on those around them. All of the interview subjects, however, are on a similar mission and are struggling with a similar issue: to try to understand themselves and the world.

This treatment of his interview subjects is one of the most unique features in Morris's films, and it sets him apart from most other documentary filmmakers. Morris gives his subjects the space to express their thoughts and recount their personal histories but is also willing to critique these subjective elements. This practice is in sharp contrast to the vast majority of interview-based documentary films, which examine the thoughts and beliefs of the admirable and sympathetic, and quickly expose and judge those who are deceitful and malicious. Instead of making sweeping judgments on his subjects and their testimony, Morris often locates a complex of truth, misjudgment, fantasy, and absurdity all in a single subject or even in a particular piece of testimony.

A primary goal of this book is to reveal and explore these complexities in Morris's filmmaking. Morris's films draw upon documentary conventions while also experimenting with the possibilities of nonfiction style and structure. His documentaries examine subjectivity but are also heavily invested in the real world and truth. Morris offers judgment and perspective in his films while leaving some questions open for the viewer. Morris's films challenge our expectations about how documentaries engage their subject matter and prompt the viewer to ask questions about the ethics of his approach to the form.

Morris is able to construct challenging, complex films that are also some of the most commercial successful documentaries in the history of the form. His success at the box office is a testament to one of the most overlooked aspects of his abilities as a filmmaker: his talent as a storyteller. Morris is able to take these complexities at every level of his films and construct them in an emotionally and intellectually engaging way that has considerable market appeal. Morris's films are not mere conceptual exercises designed to comment on documentary practice but rather movies that explain, explore, experiment, and entertain.

NOTES

Introduction

1. P. J. O'Connell, *Robert Drew and the Development of Cinema Verite in America* (Carbondale: Southern Illinois University Press, 1992), 35.

2. Noël Carroll provides a helpful discussion of this reaction against Direct Cinema in his article "From Real to Reel: Entangled in Nonfiction Film," in *Theorizing the Moving Image*, 224–52 (Cambridge: Cambridge University Press, 1996). Also, in "Moving Pictures and the Rhetoric of Nonfiction Film: Two Approaches," Carl Plantinga notes how skepticism toward such notions as documentary truth, reality, and objectivity is representative of broader postmodernist theoretical trends (in *Post-Theory: Reconstructing Film Studies*, ed. David Bordwell and Noël Carroll, 307–24 [Madison: University of Wisconsin Press, 2012]).

3. Bill Nichols, *Introduction to Documentary* (Bloomington: Indiana University Press, 2001), 125.

4. Jay Ruby, "The Image Mirrored: Reflexivity and the Documentary Film," *Journal of the University Film Association* 29, no. 4 (Fall 1977): 3.

5. Renee R. Curry, "Errol Morris's Construction of Innocence in 'The Thin Blue Line,'" *Rocky Mountain Review of Language and Literature* 49, no. 2 (1995): 157. Richard K. Sherwin makes a similar argument in "Framed," in *Legal Reelism: Movies as Legal Texts*, ed. John Denvir, 70–94 (Urbana: University of Illinois Press, 1996).

6. For this reason, Bill Nichols uses *The Thin Blue Line* as a model of the reflexive mode of representation. Nichols identifies four different modes of representation in his book *Representing Reality*: expository, observational, interactive, and reflexive. (*Representing Reality: Issues and Concepts in Documentary* [Bloomington: Indiana University Press, 1991], 32–75). He adds the performative and poetic modes in subsequent writings on documentary modes of representation.

7. Nichols, *Representing Reality*, 58.

8. Brian Winston, *Claiming the Real: The Documentary Film Revisited* (London: British Film Institute, 1995), 254.

9. In addition to Winston and Brian McIlroy, Dagmar Barnouw also explicitly presents this argument in his article "Seeing and Believing: The Thin Blue Line of Documentary Objectivity," *Common Knowledge* 4, no. 1 (1995): 129–43.

10. Ibid., 136–37.

11. Sherwin, "Framed," 77.

12. John D. Dorst, "'Sidebar Excursions to Nowhere': The Vernacular Storytelling of Errol Morris and Spalding Gray," in *Folklore, Literature and Cultural Theory: Collected Essays*, ed. Cathy Lynn Preston, 119–35 (New York: Garland, 1995), 127–28.

13. Shawn Rosenheim, "Interrotroning History: Errol Morris and the Documentary of the Future, in *The Persistence of History: Cinema, Television and the Modern Event*, ed. Vivian Sobchack, 219–34 (New York: Routledge, 1996), 229.

14. Winston, *Claiming the Real*, 254.

15. Michael Covino, "Gates of Heaven," *Film Quarterly* 33, no. 3 (1980): 47–50; Ira Jaffe, "Errol Morris's Forms of Control," *Film International* 14, no. 2 (2005): 4–19.

16. In our examination, the terms "postmodern" and "reflexive" are used just as the critical literature on Morris has used them. There are many possible connections between Morris's documentaries and these critical concepts, some of which remain unexplored by documentary scholars. My response to the reflexive and postmodern readings of Morris's films is not a definitive argument against any possible reflexive or postmodern reading of these documentaries.

17. Linda Williams attempts to reconcile the postmodern position and *The Thin Blue Line*'s link to the real world. She introduces the notion of a documentary as "a set of strategies designed to choose from among a horizon of relative and contingent truths." Although Williams provides a more nuanced view of the role of truth in *The Thin Blue Line*, it is not clear how David Harris's guilt or Randall Dale Adams's innocence is either relative or contingent. By the end of the film, Morris establishes both as unconditional truths. Linda Williams, "Mirrors without Memories: Truth, History, and the New Documentary," *Film Quarterly* 46, no. 3 (spring 1993): 14.

18. In his essay entitled "The Philosophy of Errol Morris: Ten Lessons," Carl Plantinga articulates some of these positions about Morris's investment in truth and interest in human subjectivity. Plantinga provides ten "lessons" concerning Morris's approach to documentary film, including "Objective Truth Exists; Truth Can Be Known; Truth Is Difficult to Know" and "Humans Construct Frameworks of Belief—Fables or Dreamscapes—to Make Sense of Their Lives and Their World." Plantinga's views on Morris's work help inform this examination of the ways in which Morris's films function at a more local level to express these theoretical positions. Plantinga, "Philosophy of Errol Morris: Ten Lessons," in *Three Documentary Filmmakers: Errol Morris, Ross McElwee, Jean Rouch*, ed. William Rothman, 43–60 (Albany: State University of New York Press, 2009).

19. In this section, we will rely on Plantinga's distinction between the formal narrative structure and the open or associational structure to help explain how Morris organizes his films. Carl Plantinga, *Rhetoric and Representation in Nonfiction Film* (Cambridge: Cambridge University Press, 1997), 120–46.

20. Ibid., 101–19.

21. Ibid., 107.

22. Noël Carroll, "The Power of Movies," *Daedelus* 114, no. 4 (Fall 1985): 98.

23. Plantinga, *Rhetoric and Representation*, 108.

24. Ibid.

25. In addition to the critical reviews of Morris's films, we will also consider the literature on ethnographic filmmaking in my discussion of ethics. Ethnographic film scholars often consider the ethical implications of filmmakers inserting themselves in a community and representing their way of life. Morris's films frequently focus on or actively construct such a community of participants, and his willingness to critique these people taps into many of the primary concerns in ethnographic scholarship.

Chapter 1. *Gates of Heaven* and *Vernon, Florida*

1. Errol Morris, "It Could All Be Wrong: An Unfinished Interview with Errol Morris," by Paul Cronin, *The Sticking Place*, 2003–2007, accessed December 8, 2009, http://www.thestickingplace.com.

2. Tom Luddy, interview, in *A Brief History of Errol Morris*, dir. Kevin MacDonald (New York: Independent Film Channel, 2000).

3. Errol Morris, interview, in *A Brief History of Errol Morris*.

4. Errol Morris, "The Ashtray: The Ultimatum (Part 1)," *Opinionator* (blog), *New York Times*, March 6, 2011, http://opinionator.blogs.nytimes.com/2011/03/06/the-ashtray-the-ultimatum-part-1.

5. Ibid.

6. Ibid.

7. Mark Singer, "Profiles: Predilections," *New Yorker*, February 6, 1989, 43.

8. Ibid., 43.

9. Ibid., 46–47.

10. Ibid., 47.

11. Richard K. Ferncase, *Outsider Features: American Independent Films of the 1980s* (Westport, CT: Greenwood Press, 1996), 108.

12. Singer, "Profiles," 50.

13. Ibid., 58–59.

14. This characterization of observational films is not universal, as many observational films do not share all of these features. For instance, Robert Drew's *Primary* (1960) contains some voice-over narration.

15. Stephen Mamber, *Cinema Verite in America: Studies in Uncontrolled Documentary* (Cambridge, MA: MIT Press, 1974), 2.

16. David Bordwell, *Figures Traced in Light: On Cinematic Staging* (Berkeley: University of California Press, 2005), 167.

17. Covino, "Gates of Heaven," 47.

18. Ibid., 48.

19. Errol Morris, "Eye Contact: Interrotron," interview by *FLM Magazine*, *Errol Morris's Globe Department Store*, winter 2004, accessed March 8, 2008, http://errolmorris.com/content/eyecontact/interrotron.html.

20. Rosenheim, "Interrotroning History," 223.

21. Alan Rosenthal, *Writing, Directing, and Producing Documentary Films and Videos* (Carbondale: Southern Illinois University Press, 1990), 180.

22. David Bordwell, *On the History of Film Style* (Cambridge, MA: Harvard University Press, 1997), 262.

23. W. Hugh Baddeley, *The Technique of Documentary Film Production* (New York: Hastings House, 1975), 273.

24. Singer, "Profiles," 39.

25. The only use of nondiegetic music occurs at the beginning of *Vernon, Florida*.

26. Errol Morris, "Interview: The Museum of Modern Art with Ron Rosenbaum," *Errol Morris's Globe Department Store*, fall 1999, accessed January 20, 2010, http://www.errolmorris.com/content/interview/moma1999.html.

27. Errol Morris, "Interview: Errol Morris," by Noel Murray, *The Onion: AV Club*, September 14, 2005, accessed December 11, 2009, http://www.avclub.com.

28. David Bordwell and Kristin Thompson, *Film Art: An Introduction* (New York: McGraw-Hill, 1997), 129.

29. Bordwell and Thompson provide a useful analysis of how the associational structure works in Wiseman's *High School* (1968) in *Film Art*, 409–15.

30. Plantinga, *Rhetoric and Representation*, 126–27.

31. *Gates of Heaven*, directed by Errol Morris (1978; Santa Monica, CA: MGM Home Entertainment, 2005), DVD. This source is used for all *Gates of Heaven* quotations in this chapter.

32. *Vernon, Florida*, directed by Errol Morris (1981; Santa Monica, CA: MGM Home Entertainment, 2005), DVD. This source is used for all *Vernon, Florida* quotations in this chapter.

33. We will use Carl Plantinga's distinction between the formal and open voice, which he articulates in *Rhetoric and Representation*, 101–19.

34. Bill Nichols, "The Voice of Documentary," in *Movies and Methods*, ed. Bill Nichols, 258–73, vol. 2 (Berkeley: University of California Press, 1985), 266. The apparent omniscience of these interview voices is similar to how we engage with traditional third-person voice-over narration.

35. While the thought of sand growing might at first seem absurd, Morris later learned that the Martins might have been correct in their observations: "I was giving a lecture at Brandeis University. I was in the middle of my spiel. Sand doesn't grow, but they think it does. Someone in the audience—a professor of geology or something like that—said that sand from the White Sands Proving Grounds is not beach-sand. It's gypsum, and gypsum absorbs moisture. When the Martins took the sand from New Mexico to Florida, they took the sand from an extremely arid climate to a climate with high humidity. Maybe the sand was growing" (Morris, "Eye Contact: Interrotron").

36. Mamber, *Cinema Verite*, 4.

37. Morris, "Interview: The Museum of Modern Art."

38. Nichols, *Representing Reality*, 53.

39. Plantinga, *Rhetoric and Representation*, 111.

40. Ibid.

41. Ibid., 126.

42. Ibid., 131.

43. Nichols, *Representing Reality*, 54.

44. *The War at Home*, directed by Barry Alexander Brown and Glenn Silber (1979; New York: First Run Features, 2003), DVD.

45. Rosenthal, *Writing, Directing*, 177.

46. Ibid.

47. "Gates of Heaven," *Variety*, October 4, 1978, 19.

48. Harry Haun, "Nothing to Write Home About at N.Y. Film Festival," *Los Angeles Times*, October 15, 1978, M36.

49. Janet Maslin, "The Screen: 'Vernon, Florida' Looks at Town's Eccentrics," *New York Times*, October 8, 1981, C14; "Vernon, Florida," *Variety*, October 21, 1981, 30.

50. Covino, "Gates of Heaven," 48.

51. *Hearts and Minds*, directed by Peter Davis (1974; New York: Criterion Collection, 2002), DVD.

52. David MacDougall, "Prospects of the Ethnographic Film," *Film Quarterly* 23, no. 2 (1969–1970): 25.

53. Covino, "Gates of Heaven," 47.

54. Gene Siskel, "Ten Shining Films Penetrate Today's Gloomy Picture," *Chicago Tribune*, January 3, 1982, G4.

55. Roger Ebert, *The Great Movies* (New York: Broadway Books, 2002), 186.

56. Singer, "Profiles," 50.

57. Plantinga, *Rhetoric and Representation*, 118.

58. Covino, "Gates of Heaven," 48.

Chapter 2. *The Thin Blue Line*

1. Singer, "Profiles," 59–60.

2. Alvin Klein, "Film Dissects Murder and Justice," *New York Times*, October 23, 1988, 12LI.

3. "Law: They Call Him Dr. Death," *Time*, June 1, 1981, accessed April 16, 2008, http://www.time.com.

4. Singer, "Profiles," 61–62.

5. Ibid., 61.

6. Douglas Martin, "Randall Adams, 61, Dies; Freed with Help of Film," *New York Times*, June 25, 2011, accessed February 20, 2014, http://www.nytimes.com.

7. Singer, "Profiles," 61.

8. Randall Dale Adams, William Hoffer, and Marilyn Mona Hoffer, *Adams v. Texas* (New York: St. Martin's Press, 1991), 234, 307–8.

9. Ibid., 242, 253.

10. Singer, "Profiles," 64.

11. Adams, Hoffer, and Hoffer, *Adams v. Texas*, 281.

12. Lawrence Cohn, "Truth-Tellers Start to Tell Tales," *Variety*, May 11, 1992, 22, 54.

13. Such criticism ultimately led to a change in the nomination procedures for the Academy of Motion Picture Arts and Sciences in 1995. The new rules required a second panel of judges to share the workload and would help introduce new viewpoints in the process. William Grimes, "Oscar Rules Change for Documentaries," *New York Times*, July 13, 1995, C13, C16.

14. Raymond Fielding, *The American Newsreel, 1911–1967* (Norman: University of Oklahoma Press, 1972), 37.

15. *The Thin Blue Line*, directed by Errol Morris (1988; Santa Monica, CA: MGM Home

Entertainment, 2005), DVD. This source is used for all *Thin Blue Line* quotations in this chapter.

16. Plantinga, *Rhetoric and Representation*, 126.

17. To further support this connection, the Mystery Writers of America awarded *The Thin Blue Line* the Edgar Award for Best Movie.

18. David Bordwell, *Narration in the Fiction Film* (Madison: University of Wisconsin Press, 1985), 64. In Bordwell's description, *syuzhet* can be loosely defined as "plot" and *fabula* as "story."

19. Adams, Hoffer, and Hoffer, *Adams v. Texas*, 30.

20. Bordwell, *Narration in the Fiction Film*, 65.

21. In his online blog, Errol Morris provides several pieces of evidence to support this fact, including Officer Turko's 1976 affidavit as well as photos showing the Burger King just around the corner from the scene of the murder. Errol Morris, "Cartesian Blogging, Part Two," *Errol Morris* (blog), *New York Times*, June 9, 2008, accessed August 1, 2008, http://morris.blogs.nytimes.com/2008/06/09/cartesian-blogging-part-two.

22. Morris also notes that there were not any Whataburger signs in Brooklyn where they were shooting the reenactments (Morris, "Cartesian Blogging").

23. In an interview with Bill Moyers, Morris acknowledged that telling a good story in *The Thin Blue Line* was his highest priority. Bill Nichols, *Representing Reality*, 45.

24. Errol Morris, "Interview with *The Believer*," *Errol Morris's Globe Department Store* April 2004, accessed May 7, 2008, http://www.errolmorris.com/content/interview/believer0404.html.

25. Plantinga, *Rhetoric and Representation*, 115.

26. Errol Morris, "A Conversation with Errol Morris by WPR's Brian Bull," WPR, July 2, 2004, accessed August 14, 2008, http://www.wpr.org.

27. Morris uses a similar-looking map to illustrate both Vidor, Texas, and the "Lady in Red's" native Romania.

28. The editor of *Heaven*, Paul Barnes, was also the editor of *The Thin Blue Line*.

29. Morris, "Interview with *The Believer*."

30. Michael Renov, "New Subjectivities: Documentary and Self-Representation in the Post-Verité Age," *Documentary Box*, July 31, 1995, accessed July 16, 2008, http://www.yidff.jp.

31. Morris, "Interview with *The Believer*."

32. Dave Kehr, "Documentary 'The Thin Blue Line' Turns on a Morbid Edge" *Chicago Tribune*, September 16, 1988, L6.

Chapter 3. *A Brief History of Time*

1. David Beers, "Errol Morris, Film's Best Known Bottom Feeder, Travels through Time with Skywalker Stephen Hawking," *Mother Jones* 12, no. 3 (May/June 1992): 46.

2. Philip Gourevitch, "Interviewing the Universe," *New York Times*, August 9, 1992, 44.

3. "Creativity," *Advertising Age*, October 2, 1989, 4.

4. Lawrence Van Gelder, "'Time' on Film," *New York Times*, June 1, 1990, C12.

5. Timothy Ferris, "When Science Is the Star," *New York Times*, August 16, 1992, 7.

6. "Documentary Movies at the Box Office," *Box Office Mojo*, December 9, 2009, http://www.boxofficemojo.com.

7. Stephen Hawking, *A Brief History of Time: From the Big Bang to Black Holes* (New York: Bantam Books, 1988), vi.

8. Robert Pollack, "All Those Words and So Little Time to Read Them," *Wall Street Journal*, August 10, 2001, W5.

9. Hawking, *Brief History of Time: From the Big Bang*, 159.

10. Hawking, *Brief History of Time: A Reader's Companion* (New York: Bantam Books, 1992), viii.

11. Ibid.

12. Gourevitch, "Interviewing the Universe," 44.

13. Ibid.

14. Glyn Jones, "Talking Heads and Hawking's Life," *New Scientist*, May 2, 1992, 46.

15. Ferris, "When Science," 7.

16. Todd McCarthy, "A Brief History of Time," *Variety*, January 20, 1992, 143.

17. *Box Office Mojo*, "Documentary Movies."

18. "Triton Spans 'History of Time,'" *Hollywood Reporter*, April 10, 1992, 25.

19. Sybil DelGaudio, "If Truth Be Told, Can 'Toons Tell It? Documentary and Animation," *Film History* 9, no. 2 (1997): 193.

20. Although there is some overlap, we will not include nature documentaries, such as *Winged Migration* (2001) or *March of the Penguins* (2005), in my examination of science documentaries. The primary reason for this is that these films do not often engage with the more theoretical aspects of the natural world and thus have different challenges in representing their subject matter. If a film engages the natural world on a more conceptual level, we will include it in this discussion of science documentaries. For instance, Jean-François Brunet and Peter Friedman's *Life and Times of Life and Times* (1996) reflects on the nature of and seeming contradictions in Darwin's theory of evolution. Nature films can certainly be considered science documentaries, and there are exceptions and gray areas between these groupings. It is useful in our examination of *A Brief History of Time*, however, to separate out the nature documentary as a distinct nonfiction tradition.

21. Van Gelder, "'Time' on Film," C12.

22. Anthony Vagnoni, "Reality Check: Acclaimed Documentarist Errol Morris, Director of 'The Thin Blue Line' and the Up-coming 'A Brief History of Time,' Brings an Unusual Spin on Realism to Commercials," *Advertising Age*, June 1, 1992, 24C.

23. Twenty six percent of the interview images are framed in medium close-ups, and 74 percent are framed in medium shots.

24. Hawking, *Brief History of Time: A Reader's Companion*, viii.

25. Ibid.

26. *A Brief History of Time*, directed by Errol Morris (1991; New York: Criterion Collection, 2014), DVD. This source is used for all *Brief History of Time* film quotations in this chapter.

27. Beers, "Errol Morris," 46.

28. Henry Sheehan, "A Brief History of Time," *Hollywood Reporter*, August 18, 1992, 32; Kenneth Turan, "A Brief History of Time," *Los Angeles Times*, August 21, 1992, Calendar 1.

29. Jones, "Talking Heads," 46.

30. *Huey Long*, directed by Ken Burns (1985; Hollywood, CA: PBS Paramount, 2004), DVD.

31. Gary Panetta, "'Brief History of Time,'" B3; McCarthy, "Brief History," 143.

32. Daniel Neman, "'Time': Hawking for the Non-theoretical Physicist," *Richmond Times-Dispatch*, November 13, 1992, C5; Michael MacCambridge, "Film Struggles with Tough Subject / Book Isn't Very Film-Friendly," *Austin American-Statesman*, October 30, 1992, 7.

33. Bruce Westbrook, "'Brief History' Investigates the Nature of Truth," *Houston Chronicle*, June 11, 1993, 3.

34. Richard Schickel, "The Thrust of His Thought," *Time*, August 31, 1992, 66; Vincent Canby, "If You Fumbled the Book, You'll Love the Movie," *New York Times*, August 21, 1992, C3.

Chapter 4. Television Commercials and *Errol Morris' First Person*

1. Megan Cunningham, "Errol Morris: Revealing Unexpected Realities," in *The Art of the Documentary: Ten Conversations with Leading Directors, Cinematographers, Editors, and Producers*, ed. Megan Cunningham, 46–73 (Berkeley, CA: New Riders, 2005), 48.

2. Jennifer Pendleton, "Hollywood Buys the Concept," *Advertising Age*, November 9, 1988, 158.

3. Tricia Laine, "Hollywood Ads Up," *Entertainment Weekly*, April 3, 1998, 12.

4. Henry Goldblatt, "Art Imitates Advertising," *Fortune*, May 25, 1998, 40.

5. The following account of the television commercial industry is based on Larry Elin and Alan Lapides's detailed account in their *Designing and Producing the Television Commercial* (New York: Pearson Education, 2004), 19–22, 109–24.

6. Vagnoni, "Reality Check," 24C.

7. Reginald Oberlag, "Errol Morris to Join @radical.media for Spots," *Shoot*, December 19, 1997, 7.

8. Ibid.

9. Elin and Lapides, *Designing and Producing*, 116.

10. Erin Galliher, "Talent Show: Hollywood Directors Bring Talent to the Small Screen," *Forbes*, June 5, 2009, accessed August 20, 2009, http://www.forbes.com.

11. Morris, "It Could All Be Wrong."

12. Vagnoni, "Reality Check," 24C.

13. Robert Fernandez, interview by author, October 5, 2009.

14. Cunningham, "Errol Morris," 72.

15. Nick Paumgargen, "Oscar Night: A Movie for Everyone," *New Yorker*, April 1, 2002, accessed July 11, 2010, http://www.newyorker.com. We will examine the specifics of Morris's Interrotron machine in the next chapter.

16. Morris first used the Interrotron interview for Fred Leuchter, whom Morris would

later feature in *Mr. Death: The Rise and Fall of Fred A. Leuchter, Jr.*, the day before he started filming the interviews for *Fast, Cheap and Out of Control*. *Fast, Cheap and Out of Control* marked the first film that featured the Interrotron, as it was released before *Mr. Death*. Morris was unable to get approval on a patent for the Interrotron because photographer Nubar Alexander took a photograph of George Mendonça next to the device for the *New York Times Sunday Magazine* during this shoot for *Fast, Cheap* and the caption mentioned the Interrotron. Morris was unaware that a patent application must be filed within a year of the first public mention of the device and subsequently lost the right to do so. Errol Morris, e-mail message to author, January 22, 2009.

17. It is important to note that Morris was not the first to use a pure white background in advertising. For instance, the 1960s print advertisements for the Volkswagon Beetle often set the car against a pure white backdrop. Some television ads also used this setting before Morris. For instance, the 1992 "Cranebird" ad for Sony Boxes uses a white background against which a crane responds to animal sounds coming from a Box speaker (Sony, Ad Agency PMSvW/Y&R, Netherlands). Or, a year later, a campaign for milk used a pure white background for a tap-dancing competition between a professional dancer and a cow (Ad Agency Advico Young & Rubicam, Switzerland, 1993). This use of a white backdrop can also be connected to artists outside of the advertising world, as with the work of photographers Richard Avedon and August Sander.

18. Robert Goldrich, "DGA Spot Nominees: Acord, Fincher, Morris, Murro, Pytka," *Shoot*, January 16, 2004, 18.

19. Philip Gourevitch, "Swingtime: Former Bush Voters Advertise Their Disaffection," *New Yorker*, August 23, 2004, 34.

20. Sandy Hunter, "Greasing the Ad Engines: Errol Morris," *Boards*, August 1, 2000, accessed August 24, 2009, http://www.boardsmag.com.

21. Robert Goldrich, "Primetime Commercial Emmy Judges See Double," *Shoot*, July 20, 2001, 1.

22. Goldrich, "DGA Spot Nominees," 18.

23. Morris, "It Could All Be Wrong."

24. Cunningham, "Errol Morris," 73.

25. Sandy Hunter, "Greasing the Ad Engines."

26. Morris, "It Could All Be Wrong."

27. Fernandez, interview.

28. Jed Alger, interview by author, August 30, 2009.

29. Alison Sloane Gaylin, "Errol Morris," *Shoot*, March 23, 2001, 48.

30. The above features of Morris's commercial career are also common for many feature-film directors. For instance, most of the other well-established feature-film directors in the commercial industry, including Wes Anderson, Spike Lee, Terry Gilliam, and Spike Jonze, produce brand commercials. In addition, many of these directors' commercials have the same intimate, reciprocal relationship with their feature films. For example, Morris is not the only director using his commercial shoots to help produce his films. When Tarsem Singh was making *The Fall* (2006), he shot a significant amount of the film while shooting commercials in Europe, Asia, and Africa (Patrick Goldstein, "A

'Fall' No One Wants to Take," *Big Picture* [blog], *Los Angeles Times*, June 26, 2007, accessed August 18, 2014, http://articles.latimes.com/2007/jun/26/entertainment/et-goldstein26). These feature directors also use their commercials as opportunities to experiment with new technologies and visual techniques. David Fincher used his Nike "Fate" commercial, which follows the lives of Troy Polamalu and LaDainian Tomlinson from childhood to NFL stardom, as a testing ground for a number of the visual techniques in *The Curious Case of Benjamin Button* (2008).

31. Errol Morris, "An Hour with Errol," interview by Dave Avdoian, *New England Film*, June 1, 2001, accessed November 10, 2009, http://newenglandfilm.com.

32. Rosenheim, "Interrotroning History," 223–24.

33. Ibid., 221.

34. Christopher Noxon, "People Just Strange Enough to Be Real," *New York Times*, March 19, 2000, 59.

35. Dana Harris, "Morris, IFC 'First' With Docu," *Daily Variety Gotham*, January 25, 2001, 5.

36. "Best Television 2000," *Time*, December 10, 2000, accessed December 4, 2009, http://www.time.com.

37. Rosenheim, "Interrotroning History," 223–24.

38. Ibid., 224.

39. Doug Abel, interview by author, November 27, 2009. Although there is a great deal of emphasis on the planned, staged, and controlled in Morris's work, this is an interesting example of how Morris does integrate a degree of chance into his documentaries.

40. Morris, "It Could All Be Wrong."

41. Morris, "It Could All Be Wrong."

42. "Mr. Debt," *Errol Morris' First Person—Complete Series*, directed by Errol Morris (2000; Santa Monica, CA: MGM Home Entertainment, 2005), DVD.

43. "The Killer Inside Me," *Errol Morris' First Person—Complete Series*, directed by Errol Morris (2000; Santa Monica, CA: MGM Home Entertainment, 2005), DVD.

Chapter 5. *Fast, Cheap and Out of Control*

1. Cunningham, "Errol Morris," 69.

2. Errol Morris, "Interview with Errol Morris," *Sony Pictures Classics: Fast, Cheap and Out of Control*, 1997, accessed December 8, 2009, http://www.sonypictures.com.

3. Cunningham, "Errol Morris," 64–65.

4. Rodney A. Brooks and Anita M. Flynn, "Fast, Cheap and Out of Control: A Robot Invasion of the Solar System," *Journal of the British Interplanetary Society* 42 (1989): 478–85.

5. Cunningham, "Errol Morris," 66.

6. Morris, "It Could All Be Wrong."

7. Cunningham, "Errol Morris," 65.

8. Nancy Lutkehaus, "Fast, Cheap and Out of Control: Errol Morris (and Others) at Sundance 1997," *Visual Anthropology Review* 13, no. 1 (1997): 77.

9. *Box Office Mojo*, "Documentary Movies."

10. Morris, "It Could All Be Wrong."

11. Cunningham, "Errol Morris," 49.

12. Morris, "It Could All Be Wrong."

13. Morris, "Interview with Errol Morris."

14. Cunningham, "Errol Morris," 66.

15. Errol Morris, "Director: Errol Morris," interview by D. W. Leitner, *Millimeter*, October 1, 1998, accessed December 8, 2009, http://digitalcontentproducer.com.

16. Cunningham, "Errol Morris," 66.

17. Stephen Hunter, "'Fast, Cheap': Kook's Tour of Some Very Odd Jobs," *Washington Post*, November 7, 1997, G07.

18. Jaffe, "Errol Morris's Forms," 6–7. The first few chapters argue that the documentary tradition is not as tied down to the constraints of "clarity, causality, and continuity" as many documentary scholars, including Jaffe, suggest. The nonfiction tradition is instead quite varied, flexible, and filled with innovation and experimentation. Morris's interest in stylistic and structural experimentation is not a rejection of the documentary form but rather an important participant in this nonfiction tradition.

19. *Fast, Cheap and Out of Control*, directed by Errol Morris (1997; Culver City, CA: Sony Pictures Home Entertainment, 2002), DVD. This source is used for all *Fast, Cheap and Out of Control* quotations in this chapter.

20. Owen Gleiberman, "The Week: Fast, Cheap and Out of Control," *Entertainment Weekly*, October 24, 1997, 46.

21. Larry Worth, "Fast, Cheap and Out of Control," *New York Post*, October 3, 1997, 54.

22. Errol Morris, "Errol Morris: Phone Interview," by Peter Chattaway, November 12, 1997, accessed December 8, 2009, http://peter.chattaway.com/articles/errol.htm.

23. Morris, "Director."

24. David Ansen, "The Wrong End of the Telescope," *Newsweek*, February 11, 1980, 82.

25. Morris, "Errol Morris: Phone Interview."

Chapter 6. *Mr. Death: The Rise and Fall of Fred A. Leuchter, Jr.*

1. Barry Gewen, "Holocaust Documentaries: Too Much of a Bad Thing?" *New York Times*, June 15, 2003, AR1, AR7.

2. Annette Insdorf, *Indelible Shadows: Film and the Holocaust* (Cambridge: Cambridge University Press, 2003).

3. Michael deCourcy Hinds, "Making Execution Humane (Or Can It Be?)," *New York Times*, October 13, 1990, 1, 8.

4. Ibid., 8.

5. Morris, "Interview: The Museum of Modern Art."

6. Mark Singer, "The Friendly Executioner," *New Yorker*, February 1, 1999, 36.

7. Morris, "It Could All Be Wrong."

8. Singer, "Friendly Executioner," 36–37.

9. "Mr. Death (1999)," *Box Office Mojo*, January 31, 2010, http://www.boxofficemojo.com.

10. Nichols, *Representing Reality*, 4.

11. *Mr. Death: The Rise and Fall of Fred A. Leuchter, Jr.*, directed by Errol Morris (1999; Santa Monica, CA: Lions Gate Entertainment, 2003), DVD. This source is used for all *Mr. Death* quotations in this chapter.

12. Morris, "It Could All Be Wrong."

13. Morris, "Interview: The Museum of Modern Art."

14. Morris, "It Could All Be Wrong."

15. Stephen Holden, "A Sly Study in Delusion and the Myth of Objectivity," *New York Times*, December 29, 1999, E1.

Chapter 7. *The Fog of War: Eleven Lessons from the Life of Robert S. McNamara*

1. Morris, "It Could All Be Wrong."

2. Ibid.

3. Bob Davis, "Great Orchestrations and Historic Machinations: A Troubled Legacy," *American Cinematographer*, March 2004, 28.

4. Livia Bloom, "Clearing the Fog: Errol Morris Answers for His Film," *Independent Film and Video Monthly*, April 2004, 47–48.

5. "The Fog of War (2003), *Box Office Mojo*, January 31, 2010, http://www.boxofficemojo.com.

6. Errol Morris, "Ounce of Preventive War, Pound of Destruction," *Los Angeles Times*, December 19, 2003, accessed January 30, 2010, http://articles.latimes.com.

7. Errol Morris, "Where's the Rest of Him?" *New York Times*, January 18, 2005, 21.

8. Errol Morris, "Not Every Picture Tells a Story," *New York Times*, November 20, 2004, 19; Errol Morris, "Photography as a Weapon," *Opinionator* (blog), *New York Times*, August 11, 2008, accessed January 30, 2010, http://opinionator.blogs.nytimes.com/2008/08/11/photography-as-a-weapon.

9. Davis, "Great Orchestrations," 28.

10. *The Fog of War: Eleven Lessons from the Life of Robert S. McNamara*, directed by Errol Morris (2003; Culver City, CA: Sony Pictures Home Entertainment, 2004), DVD. This source is used for all *Fog of War* quotations in this chapter.

11. Cunningham, "Errol Morris," 59.

12. Paul Arthur, "The Fog of War," *Film Comment* 39, no. 6 (2003): 73.

13. Eric Alterman, "The Century of the 'Son of a Bitch,'" *Nation*, December 15, 2003, 10.

14. Errol Morris, "'Fog of War' vs. 'Stop the Presses,'" *Nation*, January 26, 2004, 2.

15. Ibid.

16. Alexander Cockburn, "The Fog of Cop-Out," *Nation*, February 9, 2004, 9; Alexander Cockburn, "McNamara: The Sequel," *Nation*, February 23, 2004, 8.

17. Errol Morris, "Picture Clearing: 'Fog's' Morris Plans Doc Series," interview by John Dempsey, *Daily Variety Gotham*, June 14, 2004, 22.

18. Gary Indiana, "Sorry, Charlie," *Artforum*, January 2004, 31.

Chapter 8. *Standard Operating Procedure*

1. Morris also published a book with Philip Gourevitch entitled *The Ballad of Abu Ghraib* that provides an account of life in the Abu Ghraib prison (New York: Penguin, 2008). Much of the book is based on interviews Morris conducted for *Standard Operating Procedure*.

2. Errol Morris, "The Great Interrogator," interview by Chris Heath, *GQ*, May 2008, accessed May 9, 2010, http://www.gq.com.

3. These Iraq War documentaries include *About Bagdad* (2003), *Soldier's Pay* (2004), *Control Room* (2004), *Last Letters Home* (2004), *Voices of Iraq* (2004), *Uncovered: The War on Iraq* (2004), *Off to War* (2005), *Why We Fight* (2005), *Gunner Palace* (2005), *Alpha Company: Iraq Diary* (2005), *The Dreams of Sparrows* (2005), *In the Shadows of the Palms* (2005), *Iraq in Fragments* (2006), *Bagdad ER* (2006), *The War Tapes* (2006), *Iraq for Sale* (2006), *The Ground Truth* (2006), *My Country, My Country* (2006), *When I Came Home* (2006), *Alive Day Memories* (2007), *Body of War* (2007), *Ghosts of Abu Ghraib* (2007), *Taxi to the Dark Side* (2007), *I Am an American Soldier* (2007), *No End in Sight* (2007), *Year at Danger* (2007), and *Fighting for Life* (2008).

4. Susan Sontag, "Regarding the Torture of Others: Notes on What Has Been Done—and Why—to Prisoners, by Americans," *New York Times*, May 23, 2004, 24–29, 42.

5. Errol Morris, quoted in Wendy Ide, "On the Other Side of Evil," *Times* (London), July 10, 2008, 18.

6. The following account of Morris's interest and entry into making *Standard Operating Procedure* is based largely on Chris Heath's interview with Errol Morris in *GQ* magazine (Morris, "The Great Interrogator").

7. Michael Cieply and Ben Sisario, "Can a Paid Witness Remain Untainted?" *New York Times*, April 26, 2008, B7.

8. Errol Morris, "Doc Week: Errol Morris on *Standard Operating Procedure*," *Comingsoon.net*, April 18, 2008, accessed May 9, 2010, http://www.comingsoon.net.

9. Scott Roxborough, "'Elite' Wins Golden Bear at 58th Berlinale," *Hollywood Reporter*, February 17, 2008, accessed May 10, 2010, http://www.hollywoodreporter.com.

10. "Standard Operating Procedure (2008)," *Box Office Mojo*, May 10, 2010, http://www.boxofficemojo.com.

11. Scott Feinberg, "Not Your Standard Doc," *And the Winner Is* (blog), April 22, 2008, accessed May 10, 2010, http://andthewinneris.blog.com/2008/04/22/not-your-standard-doc; Cieply and Sisario, "Can a Paid Witness," B7.

12. Cieply and Sisario, "Can a Paid Witness," B7.

13. Errol Morris, *Believing Is Seeing (Observations on the Mysteries of Photography)* (New York: Penguin, 2011), xxii.

14. Nicolas Rapold, "Errol Morris Interview Uncut," *Film Comment* (July/August 2011), accessed August 10, 2013, http://www.filmcomment.com.

15. Rick Groen, "Outside the Frame, a Terrible Subject Comes into Focus," *Globe and Mail*, May 2, 2008, R18.

16. *Standard Operating Procedure*, directed by Errol Morris (2008; Culver City, CA: Sony

Pictures Home Entertainment, 2008), DVD. This source is used for all *Standard Operation Procedure* quotations in this chapter.

17. Jim Slotek, "Standard Operating Procedure Is Anything But," *Toronto Sun*, May 2, 2008, E8.

18. Clarence Tsui, "Standard Operating Procedure," *South China Morning Post*, October 19, 2008, 2.

19. Ron Steinman, "Standard Operating Procedure: A Critique," *Digital Filmmaker*, June 2008, accessed May 5, 2010, http://digitalfilmmaker.net.

20. Stephen Hunter, "A Question of Standards," *Washington Post*, May 23, 2008, WE25; Peter Bradshaw, "Iraqi Horror Picture Show: Errol Morris' Documentary Takes On the Full Bone-Chilling Barbarity of Abu Ghraib," *Guardian*, July 18, 2008, 11.

21. Manohla Dargis, "We, the People behind the Abuse," *New York Times*, April 25, 2008, E1.

Chapter 9. *Tabloid*

1. Singer, "Profiles," 38.

2. Billy Baker, "59 Minutes with Errol Morris: The Documentary Filmmaker and Amateur Tabloid Archivist Goes Dumpster-Diving in His Own Basement," *New York*, July 11, 2011, accessed May 28, 2013, http://www.proquest.com.

3. J. Hoberman, "Scandal and Subjective Reality in Errol Morris's *Tabloid*," *Village Voice*, July 13, 2011, http://www.villagevoice.com.

4. Fiona Macrae, "Dead Dog's Owner Creates FIVE Cloned Puppies of Her Beloved Pet," *Daily Mail*, August 5, 2008, http://www.dailymail.co.uk.

5. Richard Pendlebury and Richard Shears, "A Cloned Dog, a Mormon in Mink-Lined Handcuffs and a Tantalizing Mystery," *Daily Mail*, August 7, 2008, http://www.dailymail.co.uk.

6. "Dog Redux," *Boston Globe*, August 11, 2008, A13.

7. Leah Carroll, "Errol Morris on 'Tabloid': 'It's a Nutso Story,'" *Atlantic*, July 15, 2011, http://www.theatlantic.com.

8. Sally Griffith, "Interview with Errol Morris (Director of *Tabloid*)," *Grow Sunday*, November 2011, http://www.growsunday.com.

9. Dana Harris, "Errol Morris' 'Tabloid' Goes to Sundance Selects," *Indiewire*, January 18, 2011, http://www.indiewire.com.

10. "Tabloid," *Box Office Mojo*, accessed August 11, 2014, http://www.boxofficemojo.com.

11. A. O. Scott, "Was It Love? The 'Manacled Mormon' and His Kinky Weekend," *New York Times*, July 14, 2011, http://movies.nytimes.com.

12. Dave Itzkoff, "Subject of Errol Morris Documentary 'Tabloid' Files Suit against Filmmakers," *ArtsBeat* (blog), *New York Times*, November 7, 2011, http://artsbeat.blogs.nytimes.com/2011/11/07/subject-of-errol-morris-documentary-tabloid-files-suit-against-filmmakers.

13. John Anderson, "Weather a Scandal and Now a Movie," *New York Times*, July 8, 2011, http://www.nytimes.com.

14. Ibid.

15. "Documentary Film: Errol Morris on 'Tabloid,'" *Prospero* (blog), *Economist*, November 23, 2010, http://www.economist.com/blogs/prospero/2010/11/documentary_film.

16. J. R. Jones, "Movie Review: *Tabloid*," *Chicago Reader*, July 14, 2011, http://www.chicagoreader.com.

17. Scott Tobias, "Interview: Errol Morris," *A.V. Club*, July 14, 2011, http://www.avclub.com.

18. Matt Reynolds, "'Tabloid' Subject Say Movie Maker Errol Morris Defamed Her," *Courthouse News Service*, November 7, 2011, http://www.courthousenews.com.

19. Eriq Gardner, "Lawsuit against Filmmaker Errol Morris Raises Interesting, Bizarre Questions," *Hollywood Reporter*, August 27, 2012, http://www.hollywoodreporter.com.

20. Hoberman, "Scandal and Subjective Reality."

21. Jon Silberg, "True Confessions: Errol Morris Is Back Behind the Interrotron for Tabloid," *Videography*, August 2011, http://www.creativeplanetnetwork.com.

22. *Tabloid*, directed by Errol Morris (2010; Orland Park, IL: MPI Home Video, 2011), DVD. This source is used for all *Tabloid* quotations in this chapter.

23. John Kusiak, interview by PRX, *Public Radio Exchange*, August 14, 2011, http://www.prx.org.

24. Reynolds, "'Tabloid' Subject."

25. Gardner, "Lawsuit against Filmmaker."

26. Amy Taubin, "Magnificent Obsessions!" *Film Comment* 47, no. 4 (July/August 2011): 48.

27. Ibid.

28. Armond White, "Yellow Journalism," *New York Press*, July 13, 2011, http://nypress.com.

29. Taubin, "Magnificent Obsessions!" 48.

30. Julia Smith, "Errol Morris, Director of 'Tabloid': Interview on the Sound of Young America," *Maximum Fun*, July 18, 2011, http://www.maximumfun.org.

BIBLIOGRAPHY

Adams, Randall Dale, William Hoffer, and Marilyn Mona Hoffer. *Adams v. Texas*. New York: St. Martin's Press, 1991.

Advertising Age. "Creativity." October 2, 1989, 4.

Alterman, Eric. "The Century of the 'Son of a Bitch.'" *Nation*, December 15, 2003, 10.

Anderson, Carolyn, and Thomas W. Benson. *Reality Fictions: The Films of Frederick Wiseman*. Carbondale: Southern Illinois University Press, 1989.

Anderson, John. "Weather a Scandal and Now a Movie." *New York Times*, July 8, 2011. http://www.nytimes.com.

Ansen, David. "The Wrong End of the Telescope." *Newsweek*, February 11, 1980, 82.

Arthur, Paul. "The Fog of War." *Film Comment* 39, no. 6 (2003): 73.

Baddeley, W. Hugh. *The Technique of Documentary Film Production*. New York: Hastings House, 1975.

Baker, Billy. "59 Minutes with Errol Morris: The Documentary Filmmaker and Amateur Tabloid Archivist Goes Dumpster-Diving in His Own Basement." *New York*, July 11, 2011. Accessed May 28, 2013. http://www.proquest.com.

Barnouw, Dagmar. "Seeing and Believing: The Thin Blue Line of Documentary Objectivity." *Common Knowledge* 4, no. 1 (1995): 129–43.

Beers, David. "Errol Morris, Film's Best Known Bottom Feeder, Travels through Time with Skywalker Stephen Hawking." *Mother Jones* 12, no. 3 (May/June 1992): 46.

Bloom, Livia. "Clearing the Fog: Errol Morris Answers for His Film." *Independent Film and Video Monthly*, April 2004, 46–48.

Bordwell, David. *Figures Traced in Light: On Cinematic Staging*. Berkeley: University of California Press, 2005.

———. *Narration in the Fiction Film*. Madison: University of Wisconsin Press, 1985.

———. *On the History of Film Style*. Cambridge, MA: Harvard University Press, 1997.

Bordwell, David, and Kristin Thompson. *Film Art: An Introduction*. New York: McGraw-Hill, 1997.

Boston Globe. "Dog Redux." August 11, 2008, A13.

Box Office Mojo. "Documentary Movies at the Box Office." December 9, 2009. http://www.boxofficemojo.com.

———. "The Fog of War (2003)." January 31, 2010. http://www.boxofficemojo.com.

———. "Mr. Death (1999)." January 31, 2010. http://www.boxofficemojo.com.

———. "Standard Operating Procedure (2008)." May 10, 2010. http://www.boxofficemojo.com.

———. "Tabloid." Accessed August 11, 2014. http://www.boxofficemojo.com.

Bradshaw, Peter. "Iraqi Horror Picture Show: Errol Morris' Documentary Takes On the Full Bone-Chilling Barbarity of Abu Ghraib." *Guardian*, July 18, 2008, 11.

A Brief History of Errol Morris. Directed by Kevin MacDonald. New York: Independent Film Channel, 2000.

A Brief History of Time. Directed by Errol Morris. 1991. New York: Criterion Collection, 2014. DVD.

Brooks, Rodney A., and Anita M. Flynn. "Fast, Cheap and Out of Control: A Robot Invasion of the Solar System." *Journal of the British Interplanetary Society* 42 (1989): 478–85.

Canby, Vincent. "If You Fumbled the Book, You'll Love the Movie." *New York Times*, August 21, 1992, C3.

Carroll, Leah. "Errol Morris on 'Tabloid': 'It's a Nusto Story.'" *Atlantic*, July 15, 2011. http://www.theatlantic.com.

Carroll, Noël. "From Real to Reel: Entangled in Nonfiction Film." In *Theorizing the Moving Image*, 224–52. Cambridge: Cambridge University Press, 1996.

———. "The Power of Movies." *Daedelus* 114, no. 4 (Fall 1985): 79–104.

Cieply, Michael, and Ben Sisario. "Can a Paid Witness Remain Untainted?" *New York Times*, April 26, 2008, B7.

Cockburn, Alexander. "The Fog of Cop-Out." *Nation*, February 9, 2004, 9.

———. "McNamara: The Sequel." *Nation*, February 23, 2004, 8.

Cohn, Lawrence. "Truth-Tellers Start to Tell Tales." *Variety*, May 11, 1992, 22, 54.

Covino, Michael. "Gates of Heaven." *Film Quarterly* 33, no. 3 (1980): 47–50.

Cunningham, Megan. "Errol Morris: Revealing Unexpected Realities." In *The Art of the Documentary: Ten Conversations with Leading Directors, Cinematographers, Editors, and Producers*, edited by Megan Cunningham, 46–73. Berkeley, CA: New Riders, 2005.

Curry, Renee R. "Errol Morris's Construction of Innocence in 'The Thin Blue Line.'" *Rocky Mountain Review of Language and Literature* 49, no. 2 (1995): 153–67.

Dargis, Manohla. "We, the People behind the Abuse." *New York Times*, April 25, 2008, E1.

Davis, Bob. "Great Orchestrations and Historic Machinations: A Troubled Legacy." *American Cinematographer*, March 2004, 28, 30–32.

DelGaudio, Sybil. "If Truth Be Told, Can 'Toons Tell It? Documentary and Animation." *Film History* 9, no. 2 (1997): 189–99.

Dorst, John D. "'Sidebar Excursions to Nowhere': The Vernacular Storytelling of Errol Morris and Spalding Gray." In *Folklore, Literature and Cultural Theory: Collected Essays*, edited by Cathy Lynn Preston, 119–35. New York: Garland, 1995.

Ebert, Roger. *The Great Movies*. New York: Broadway Books, 2002.

Economist. "Documentary Film: Errol Morris on 'Tabloid.'" *Prospero* (blog), November 23, 2010. http://www.economist.com/blogs/prospero/2010/11/documentary_film.

Elin, Larry, and Alan Lapides. *Designing and Producing the Television Commercial*. New York: Pearson Education, 2004.

Errol Morris' First Person—The Complete Series. Directed by Errol Morris. 2000. Santa Monica, CA: MGM Home Entertainment, 2005. DVD.

Fast, Cheap and Out of Control. Directed by Errol Morris. 1997. Culver City, CA: Sony Pictures Home Entertainment, 2002. DVD.

Feinberg, Scott. "Not Your Standard Doc." *And the Winner Is* (blog), April 22, 2008. Accessed May 10, 2010. http://andthewinneris.blog.com/2008/04/22/not-your-standard-doc.

Ferncase, Richard K. *Outsider Features: American Independent Films of the 1980s*. Westport, CT: Greenwood Press, 1996.

Ferris, Timothy. "When Science Is the Star." *New York Times*, August 16, 1992, 7.

Fielding, Raymond. *The American Newsreel, 1911–1967*. Norman: University of Oklahoma Press, 1972.

The Fog of War: Eleven Lessons from the Life of Robert S. McNamara. Directed by Errol Morris. 2003. Culver City, CA: Sony Pictures Home Entertainment, 2004. DVD.

Galliher, Erin. "Talent Show: Hollywood Directors Bring Talent to the Small Screen." *Forbes*, June 5, 2009. Accessed August 20, 2009. http://www.forbes.com.

Gardner, Eriq. "Lawsuit against Filmmaker Errol Morris Raises Interesting, Bizarre Questions." *Hollywood Reporter*, August 27, 2012. http://www.hollywoodreporter.com.

Gates of Heaven. Directed by Errol Morris. 1978. Santa Monica, CA: MGM Home Entertainment, 2005. DVD.

Gaylin, Alison Sloane. "Errol Morris." *Shoot*, March 23, 2001, 48.

Gewen, Barry. "Holocaust Documentaries: Too Much of a Bad Thing?" *New York Times*, June 15, 2003, AR1, AR7.

Gleiberman, Owen. "The Week: Fast, Cheap and Out of Control." *Entertainment Weekly*, October 24, 1997, 46.

Goldblatt, Henry. "Art Imitates Advertising." *Fortune*, May 25, 1998, 40.

Goldrich, Robert. "DGA Spot Nominees: Acord, Fincher, Morris, Murro, Pytka." *Shoot*, January 16, 2004, 18.

———. "Primetime Commercial Emmy Judges See Double." *Shoot*, July 20, 2001, 1.

Goldstein, Patrick. "A 'Fall' No One Wants to Take." *Big Picture* (blog), *Los Angeles Times*, June 26, 2007. Accessed August 18, 2014. http://articles.latimes.com/2007/jun/26/entertainment/et-goldstein26.

———. "How Many Great Movies Got Their Start as a TV Commercial?" *Big Picture* (blog), *Los Angeles Times*, March 17, 2009. Accessed October 5, 2009. http://latimesblogs.latimes.com/the_big_picture/2009/03/do-all-great-mo.html.

Gourevitch, Philip. "Interviewing the Universe." *New York Times*, August 9, 1992, 18–53.

———. "Swingtime: Former Bush Voters Advertise Their Disaffection." *New Yorker*, August 23, 2004, 34.

Gourevitch, Philip, and Errol Morris. *The Ballad of Abu Ghraib*. New York: Penguin, 2008.

Grierson, John. *Grierson on Documentary*. Edited by Forsyth Hardy. New York: Praeger, 1971.

Griffith, Sally. "Interview with Errol Morris (Director of *Tabloid*)." *Grow Sunday*, November 2011. http://www.growsunday.com.

Grimes, William. "Oscar Rules Change for Documentaries." *New York Times*, July 13, 1995, C13, C16.

Groen, Rick. "Outside the Frame, a Terrible Subject Comes into Focus." *Globe and Mail*, May 2, 2008, R18.

Harris, Dana. "Errol Morris' 'Tabloid' Goes to Sundance Selects." *Indiewire*, January 18, 2011. http://www.indiewire.com.

———. "Morris, IFC 'First' with Docu." *Daily Variety Gotham*, January 25, 2001, 5.

Haun, Harry. "Nothing to Write Home About at N.Y. Film Festival." *Los Angeles Times*, October 15, 1978, M36.

Hawking, Stephen. *A Brief History of Time: A Reader's Companion*. New York: Bantam Books, 1992.

———. *A Brief History of Time: From the Big Bang to Black Holes*. New York: Bantam Books, 1988.

Hearts and Minds. Directed by Peter Davis. 1974. New York: Criterion Collection, 2002. DVD.

Hinds, Michael deCourcy. "Making Execution Humane (Or Can It Be?)." *New York Times*, October 13, 1990, 1, 8.

Hoberman, J. "Scandal and Subjective Reality in Errol Morris's *Tabloid*." *Village Voice*, July 13, 2011. http://www.villagevoice.com.

Holden, Stephen. "A Sly Study in Delusion and the Myth of Objectivity." *New York Times*, December 29, 1999, E1.

Hollywood Reporter. "Triton Spans 'History of Time.'" April 10, 1992, 25.

Huey Long. Directed by Ken Burns. 1985. Hollywood, CA: PBS Paramount, 2004. DVD.

Hunter, Sandy. "Greasing the Ad Engines: Errol Morris." *Boards*, August 1, 2000. Accessed August 24, 2009. http://www.boardsmag.com.

Hunter, Stephen. "A Question of Standards." *Washington Post*, May 23, 2008, WE25.

———. "'Fast, Cheap': Kook's Tour of Some Very Odd Jobs." *Washington Post*, November 7, 1997, G07.

Ide, Wendy. "On the Other Side of Evil." *Times* (London), July 10, 2008, 18.

Indiana, Gary. "Sorry, Charlie." *Artforum*, January 2004, 31.

Insdorf, Annette. *Indelible Shadows: Film and the Holocaust*. Cambridge: Cambridge University Press, 2003.

Itzkoff, Dave. "Subject of Errol Morris Documentary 'Tabloid' Files Suit against Filmmakers." *ArtsBeat* (blog), *New York Times*, November 7, 2011. http://artsbeat.blogs.nytimes.com/2011/11/07/subject-of-errol-morris-documentary-tabloid-files-suit-against-filmmakers.

Jaffe, Ira. "Errol Morris's Forms of Control." *Film International* 14, no. 2 (2005): 4–19.

Jones, Glyn. "Talking Heads and Hawking's Life." *New Scientist*, May 2, 1992, 46.

Jones, J. R. "Movie Review: *Tabloid*." *Chicago Reader*, July 14, 2011. http://www.chicagoreader.com.

Kehr, Dave. "Documentary 'The Thin Blue Line' Turns on a Morbid Edge." *Chicago Tribune*, September 16, 1988, L6.

Klein, Alvin. "Film Dissects Murder and Justice." *New York Times*, October 23, 1988, 12LI.

Kusiak, John. Interview by PRX. *Public Radio Exchange*, August 14, 2011. http://www.prx.org.

Laine, Tricia. "Hollywood Ads Up." *Entertainment Weekly*, April 3, 1998, 12.

Lutkehaus, Nancy. "Fast, Cheap and Out of Control: Errol Morris (and Others) at Sundance 1997." *Visual Anthropology Review* 13, no. 1 (1997): 77–86.

MacCambridge, Michael. "Film Struggles with Tough Subject/Book Isn't Very Film-Friendly." *Austin American-Statesman*, October 30, 1992, 7.

MacDougall, David. "Prospects of the Ethnographic Film." *Film Quarterly* 23, no. 2 (1969–1970): 16–30.

Macrae, Fiona. "Dead Dog's Owner Creates FIVE Cloned Puppies of Her Beloved Pet." *Daily Mail*, August 5, 2008. http://www.dailymail.co.uk.

Mamber, Stephen. *Cinema Verite in America: Studies in Uncontrolled Documentary*. Cambridge, MA: MIT Press, 1974.

Martin, Douglas. "Randall Adams, 61, Dies; Freed with Help of Film." *New York Times*, June 25, 2011. Accessed February 20, 2014. http://www.nytimes.com.

Maslin, Janet. "The Screen: 'Vernon, Florida' Looks at Town's Eccentrics." *New York Times*, October 8, 1981, C14.

McCarthy, Todd. "A Brief History of Time." *Variety*, January 20, 1992, 143.

McIlroy, Brian. "Observing and Walking the Thinnest of Lines: Phenomenology, Documentary Film and Errol Morris." *Recherches Semiotiques/Semiotic Inquiry* 13, nos. 1–2 (1993): 285–99.

Morris, Errol. "The Ashtray: The Ultimatum (Part 1)." *Opinionator* (blog), *New York Times*, March 6, 2011. http://opinionator.blogs.nytimes.com/2011/03/06/the-ashtray-the-ultimatum-part-1.

———. *Believing Is Seeing (Observations on the Mysteries of Photography)*. New York: Penguin, 2011.

———. "Cartesian Blogging, Part Two." *Errol Morris* (blog), *New York Times*, June 9, 2008. Accessed August 1, 2008. http://morris.blogs.nytimes.com/2008/06/09/cartesian-blogging-part-two.

———. "A Conversation with Errol Morris by WPR's Brian Bull." WPR, July 2, 2004. Accessed August 14, 2008. http://www.wpr.org.

———. "Director: Errol Morris." Interview by D. W. Leitner. *Millimeter*, October 1, 1998. Accessed December 8, 2009. http://digitalcontentproducer.com.

———. "Doc Week: Errol Morris on *Standard Operating Procedure*." *ComingSoon.net*, April 18, 2008. Accessed May 9, 2010. http://www.comingsoon.net.

———. "Errol Morris: Phone Interview." By Peter Chattaway. November 12, 1997. Accessed December 8, 2009. http://peter.chattaway.com/articles/errol.htm.

———. "Eye Contact: Interrotron." Interview by *FLM Magazine*. *Errol Morris's Globe Department Store*, winter 2004. Accessed March 8, 2008. http://errolmorris.com/content/eyecontact/interrotron.html.

———. "'Fog of War' vs. 'Stop the Presses.'" *Nation*, January 26, 2004, 2.

———. "The Great Interrogator." Interview by Chris Heath. *GQ*, May 2008. Accessed May 9, 2010. http://www.gq.com.

———. "An Hour with Errol." Interview by Dave Avdoian. *New England Film*, June 1, 2001. Accessed November 10, 2009. http://newenglandfilm.com.

———. "Interview: Errol Morris." By Noel Murray. *The Onion: AV Club*, September 14, 2005. Accessed December 11, 2009. http://www.avclub.com.

———. "Interview: The Museum of Modern Art with Ron Rosenbaum." *Errol Morris's Globe Department Store*. Fall 1999. Accessed January 20, 2010. http://www.errolmorris.com/content/interview/moma1999.html.

———. "Interview with Errol Morris." *Sony Pictures Classics: Fast, Cheap and Out of Control*, 1997. Accessed December 8, 2009. http://www.sonypictures.com.

———. "Interview with *The Believer*." *Errol Morris's Globe Department Store*. April 2004. Accessed May 7, 2008. http://www.errolmorris.com/content/interview/believer0404.html.

———. "It Could All Be Wrong: An Unfinished Interview with Errol Morris." By Paul Cronin. *The Sticking Place*. 2003–2007. Accessed December 8, 2009. http://www.thestickingplace.com.

———. "The Most Curious Thing." *Opinionator* (blog), *New York Times*, May 19, 2008. Accessed May 10, 2010. http://opinionator.blogs.nytimes.com/2008/05/19/the-most-curious-thing.

———. "Not Every Picture Tells a Story." *New York Times*, November 20, 2004, 19.

———. "On the Other Side of Evil." Interview by Wendy Ide. *Times* (London), July 10, 2008, 18.

———. "Ounce of Preventive War, Pound of Destruction." *Los Angeles Times*, December 19, 2003. Accessed January 30, 2010. http://articles.latimes.com.

———. "People in the Middle." *Opinionator* (blog), *New York Times*, October 28, 2008. Accessed January 31, 2010. http://opinionator.blogs.nytimes.com/2008/10/28/people-in-the-middle.

———. "Photography as a Weapon." *Opinionator* (blog), *New York Times*, August 11, 2008. Accessed January 30, 2010. http://opinionator.blogs.nytimes.com/2008/08/11/photography-as-a-weapon.

———. "Picture Clearing: 'Fog's' Morris Plans Doc Series." Interview by John Dempsey. *Daily Variety Gotham*, June 14, 2004, 5, 22.

———. "There Is Such a Thing as Truth." In *This I Believe: The Personal Philosophies of Remarkable Men and Women*, edited by Jay Allison and Dan Gediman, 162–64. New York: Henry Holt, 2006.

———. "Where's the Rest of Him?" *New York Times*, January 18, 2005, 21.

Morris, Errol, and Philip Gourevitch. *The Ballad of Abu Ghraib*. New York: Penguin, 2008.

Mr. Death: The Rise and Fall of Fred A. Leuchter, Jr. Directed by Errol Morris. 1999. Santa Monica, CA: Lions Gate Entertainment, 2003. DVD.

Musser, Charles. "Film Truth, Documentary, and the Law: Justice at the Margins." *University of San Francisco Law Review* 30, no. 4 (1996): 963–84.

Neman, Daniel. "'Time': Hawking for the Non-theoretical Physicist." *Richmond Times-Dispatch*, November 13, 1992, C5.

Nichols, Bill. *Blurred Boundaries: Questions of Meaning in Contemporary Culture*. Bloomington: Indiana University Press, 1994.

———. *Introduction to Documentary*. Bloomington: Indiana University Press, 2001.

———. *Representing Reality: Issues and Concepts in Documentary*. Bloomington: Indiana University Press, 1991.

———. "The Voice of Documentary." In *Movies and Methods*, edited by Bill Nichols, 258–73. Vol. 2. Berkeley: University of California Press, 1985.

Noxon, Christopher. "People Just Strange Enough to Be Real." *New York Times*, March 19, 2000, 59.

Oberlag, Reginald. "Errol Morris to Join @radical.media for Spots." *Shoot*, December 19, 1997, 7.

O'Connell, P. J. *Robert Drew and the Development of Cinema Verite in America*. Carbondale: Southern Illinois University Press, 1992.

Panetta, Gary. "'Brief History of Time' Build on Paradoxes, Puzzles." *Peoria Star Journal*, November 29, 1992, B3.

Pardi, Robert J. "The Thin Blue Line." *Films in Review* 39, no. 12 (1988): 614–15.

Paumgargen, Nick. "Oscar Night: A Movie for Everyone." *New Yorker*, April 1, 2002. Accessed July 11, 2010. http://www.newyorker.com.

Pendlebury, Richard, and Richard Shears. "A Cloned Dog, a Mormon in Mink-Lined Handcuffs and a Tantalizing Mystery." *Daily Mail*, August 7, 2008. http://www.dailymail.co.uk.

Pendleton, Jennifer. "Hollywood Buys the Concept." *Advertising Age*, November 9, 1988, 158.

Plantinga, Carl. "American Documentary in the 1980s." In *A New Pot of Gold: Hollywood Under the Electronic Rainbow, 1980–1989*, by Stephen Prince, 370–89. New York: Scribners, 1999.

———. "Moving Pictures and the Rhetoric of Nonfiction Film: Two Approaches." In *Post-Theory: Reconstructing Film Studies*, edited by David Bordwell and Noël Carroll, 307–24. Madison: University of Wisconsin Press, 2012.

———. "The Philosophy of Errol Morris: Ten Lessons." In *Three Documentary Filmmakers: Errol Morris, Ross McElwee, Jean Rouch*, edited by William Rothman, 43–60. Albany: State University of New York Press, 2009.

———. *Rhetoric and Representation in Nonfiction Film*. Cambridge: Cambridge University Press, 1997.

Pollack, Robert. "All Those Words and So Little Time to Read Them." *Wall Street Journal*, August 10, 2001, W5.

Rapold, Nicolas. "Errol Morris Interview Uncut." *Film Comment* 47, no. 4 (July/August 2011). Accessed August 10, 2013. http://www.filmcomment.com.

Renov, Michael. "New Subjectivities: Documentary and Self-Representation in the Post-Verité Age." *Documentary Box*, July 31, 1995. Accessed July 16, 2008. http://www.yidff.jp.

Reynolds, Matt. "'Tabloid' Subject Say Movie Maker Errol Morris Defamed Her." *Courthouse News Service*, November 7, 2011. http://www.courthousenews.com.

Rosenheim, Shawn. "Interrotroning History: Errol Morris and the Documentary of the Future." In *The Persistence of History: Cinema, Television and the Modern Event*, edited by Vivian Sobchack, 219–34. New York: Routledge, 1996.

Rosenthal, Alan. *Writing, Directing, and Producing Documentary Films and Videos*. Carbondale: Southern Illinois University Press, 1990.

Roxborough, Scott. "'Elite' Wins Golden Bear at 58th Berlinale." *Hollywood Reporter*, February 17, 2008. Accessed May 10, 2010. http://www.hollywoodreporter.com.

Ruby, Jay. "The Image Mirrored: Reflexivity and the Documentary Film." *Journal of the University Film Association* 29, no. 4 (Fall 1977): 3–11.

Schickel, Richard. "The Thrust of His Thought." *Time*, August 31, 1992, 66.

Scott, A. O. "Was It Love? The 'Manacled Mormon' and His Kinky Weekend." *New York Times*, July 14, 2011. http://movies.nytimes.com.

Sheehan, Henry. "A Brief History of Time." *Hollywood Reporter*, August 18, 1992, 32.

Sherwin, Richard K. "Framed." In *Legal Reelism: Movies as Legal Texts*, edited by John Denvir, 70–94. Urbana: University of Illinois Press, 1996.

Silberg, Jon. "True Confessions: Errol Morris Is Back Behind the Interrotron for Tabloid." *Videography*, August 2011. http://www.creativeplanetnetwork.com.

Singer, Mark. "The Friendly Executioner." *New Yorker*, February 1, 1999, 33–39.

———. "Profiles: Predilections." *New Yorker*, February 6, 1989, 38–72.

Siskel, Gene. "Ten Shining Films Penetrate Today's Gloomy Picture." *Chicago Tribune*, January 3, 1982, G4.

Slotek, Jim. "Standard Operating Procedure Is Anything But." *Toronto Sun*, May 2, 2008, E8.

Smith, Julia. "Errol Morris, Director of 'Tabloid': Interview on the Sound of Young America." *Maximum Fun*, July 18, 2011. http://www.maximumfun.org.

Sontag, Susan. "Regarding the Torture of Others: Notes on What Has Been Done—and Why—to Prisoners, by Americans." *New York Times*, May 23, 2004, 24–29, 42.

Spigel, Lynn. TV by Design: Modern Art and the Rise of Network Television. Chicago: University of Chicago Press, 2008.

Standard Operating Procedure. Directed by Errol Morris. 2008. Culver City, CA: Sony Pictures Home Entertainment, 2008. DVD.

Steinman, Ron. "Standard Operating Procedure: A Critique." *Digital Filmmaker*, June 2008. Accessed May 5, 2010. http://digitalfilmmaker.net.

Tabloid. Directed by Errol Morris. 2010. Orland Park, IL: MPI Home Video, 2011. DVD.

Taubin, Amy. "Magnificent Obsessions!" *Film Comment* 47, no. 4 (July/August 2011): 45–48.

The Thin Blue Line. Directed by Errol Morris. 1988. Santa Monica, CA: MGM Home Entertainment, 2005. DVD.

Time. "Best Television 2000." December 10, 2000. Accessed December 4, 2009. http://www.time.com.

———. "Law: They Call Him Dr. Death." June 1, 1981. Accessed April 16, 2008.http://www.time.com.

Tobias, Scott. "Interview: Errol Morris." *A.V. Club*, July 14, 2011. http://www.avclub.com.

Torrance, Kelly Jane. "'Standard' Questions, No Answers: Abu Ghraib Film Recounts Horrors but Provides Few Insights." *Washington Times*, May 23, 2008, D08.

Tsui, Clarence. "Standard Operating Procedure." *South China Morning Post*, October 19, 2008, 2.

Turan, Kenneth. "A Brief History of Time." *Los Angeles Times*, August 21, 1992, Calendar 1.

Vagnoni, Anthony. "Reality Check: Acclaimed Documentarist Errol Morris, Director of

'The Thin Blue Line' and the Up-coming 'A Brief History of Time,' Brings an Unusual Spin on Realism to Commercials." *Advertising Age*, June 1, 1992, 24C.

Van Gelder, Lawrence. "'Time' on Film." *New York Times*, June 1, 1990, C12.

Van Wert, William. "Last Words: Observations on a New Language." In *Between Mirage and History: The Films of Werner Herzog*, edited by Timothy Corrigan, 51–72. New York: Methuen, 1986.

Variety. "Gates of Heaven." October 4, 1978, 19.

———. "Vernon, Florida." October 21, 1981, 30.

Vernon, Florida. Directed by Errol Morris. 1981. Santa Monica, CA: MGM Home Entertainment, 2005. DVD.

The War at Home. Directed by Barry Alexander Brown and Glenn Silber. 1979. New York: First Run Features, 2003. DVD.

Westbrook, Bruce. "'Brief History' Investigates the Nature of Truth." *Houston Chronicle*, June 11, 1993, 3.

White, Armond. "Yellow Journalism." *New York Press*, July 13, 2011. http://nypress.com.

Williams, Linda. "Mirrors without Memories: Truth, History, and the New Documentary." *Film Quarterly* 46, no. 3 (spring 1993): 9–21.

Winston, Brian. *Claiming the Real: The Documentary Film Revisited*. London: British Film Institute, 1995.

Worth, Larry. "Fast, Cheap and Out of Control." *New York Post*, October 3, 1997, 54.

INDEX

WESLEYAN FILM

A series from Wesleyan University Press
Edited by Lisa Dombrowski and Scott Higgins
Originating editor: Jeanine Basinger

Anthony Mann
by Jeanine Basinger

It's the Pictures That Got Small
Hollywood Film Stars on 1950s Television
by Christine Becker

The South Korean Film Renaissance
Local Hitmakers, Global Provocateurs
by Jinhee Choi

The Art of Comedy
The Films of Frank Tashlin
by Ethan de Seife

The Films of Samuel Fuller
If You Die, I'll Kill You!
by Lisa Dombrowski

Kazan Revisited
edited by Lisa Dombrowski

The Lives of Robert Ryan
by J. R. Jones

Physical Evidence
Selected Film Criticism
by Kent Jones

The New Entrepreneurs
An Institutional History of Television Anthology Writers
by Jon Kraszewski

Action Speaks Louder
Violence, Spectacle, and the American Action Movie
by Eric Lichtenfeld

Hollywood Ambitions
Celebrity in the Movie Age
by Marsha Orgeron

Brutal Intimacy
Analyzing Contemporary French Cinema
by Tim Palmer

The Cinema of Errol Morris
by David Resha

Soul Searching
Black-Themed Cinema from the March on Washington to the Rise of Blaxploitation
by Christopher Sieving

Paul on Mazursky
by Sam Wasson

A Splurch in the Kisser
The Movies of Blake Edwards
by Sam Wasson

ABOUT THE AUTHOR

DAVID RESHA is an assistant professor of media and film studies at Birmingham–Southern College in Birmingham, Alabama. He also serves on the board of directors for the Alabama Moving Image Association.